JULIA O'FAOLAIN

was born in London in 1932, the daughter of Eileen and Sean O'Faolain. She was brought up in Dublin and educated at the National University of Ireland, Rome University and the Sorbonne. She has worked as a teacher of languages and interpreting, and as a translator.

A distinguished writer of fiction, Julia O'Faolain is the author of *Godded and Codded* (1970); *Women in the Wall* (1975); *No Country for Young Men* (1980); *The Obedient Wife* (1982); and *The Irish Signorina* (1984). She has also published three collections of short stories, *We Might See Sights* (1968); *Man in the Cellar* (1974); and *Daughters of Passion* (1982). Together with her husband, the American historian Lauro Martines, she edited *Not In God's Image* (1973). A documentary history of women in the West, it has also been published by Virago.

Julia O'Faolain and her husband lived for many years in Italy and the USA. They now commute between London and Los Angeles with their son.

VIRAGO
MODERN
CLASSIC

NUMBER

170

W·O·M·E·N
I·N T·H·E
W·A·L·L

·

JULIA O'FAOLAIN

·

Virago

Published by VIRAGO PRESS Limited 1985
41 William IV Street, London WC2N 4DB

First published in Great Britain by Faber & Faber 1975

British Library Cataloguing in Publication Data
O'Faolain, Julia
  Women in the wall.
  I. Title
  823′.914 [F]   PR605.F3

  ISBN   0-86068-442-3

Printed in Finland by Werner Söderström Oy,
a member of Finnprint

FOR LAURO

GENEALOGY OF FRANKISH KINGS RULING IN GAUL DURING PERIOD COVERED BY NOVEL

Clovis (died A.D. 511)

Thierry (d. 534)

Clodomer (d. 524)

Childebert I (d. 558)

Clotair I (died A.D. 561)
married 1. Guntheuca
2. Chunsina
3. Ingunda
4. Aregunda
5. Radegunda
6. a concubine
7. Vuldetrada

2 Chramn (d. 560)

3 Gunthar

3 Childeric

3 Charibert I (d. 567/8) — Chrodechilde

3 Guntram (d. 592) of Burgundy

3 Sigibert (d. 575) of Austrasia married Brunhilde, sister of Galswinthe

Childebert II (d. 595)

3 Clotsinda

4 Chilperic (d. 584) of Neustria
married 1. Audovera
2. Galswinthe
3. Fredegunda

6 Gundovald (not recognized by Clotair)

1 Theudebert

1 Merovech

1 Clovis

1 Basina

3 Riguntha

3 Clodobert

3 Samson

3 Dagobert

3 Theodoric

3 Clotair II (died 629)

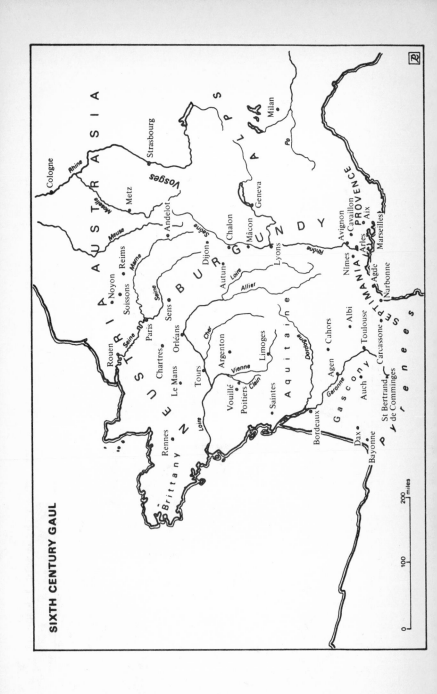

SIXTH CENTURY GAUL

AUSTRASIA

Cologne
Rhine
Moselle
Strasbourg
Metz
Meuse
Andelot
Noyon
Reims
Marne
Soissons
Seine
Rouen
Paris
Chartres
Sens
Orléans

NEUSTRIA

Rennes
Brittany
Le Mans
Tours
Loire
Vouillé
Poitiers
Clain
Saintes
Vienne
Argenton
Cher
Limoges

BURGUNDY
Vosges
Aube
Dijon
Autun
Loire
Allier
Chalon
Mâcon
Lyons
Rhône
Geneva
ALPS
Po
Milan

Aquitaine
Dordogne
Agen
Garonne
Cahors
Albi
Toulouse
Carcassonne
St Bertrand de Comminges
Gascony
Bordeaux
Dax
Bayonne
Pyrenees

SEPTIMANIA
Nîmes
Avignon
Cavaillon
PROVENCE
Arles
Aix
Marseilles
Agde
Narbonne

0   100   200 miles

R

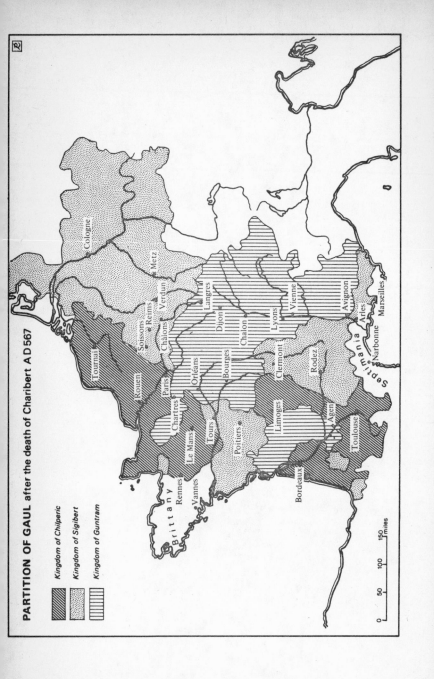

PARTITION OF GAUL after the death of Charibert AD567

Kingdom of Chilperic

Kingdom of Sigibert

Kingdom of Guntram

Cologne

Metz

Tournai

Rouen   Soissons Reims
         Verdun

Paris   Châlons   Langres

Chartres Orléans   Dijon

Le Mans Bourges   Chalon   Lyons
Tours   Vienne

Rennes   Poitiers   Limoges   Clermont   Avignon
Vannes   Arles
Brittany   Agen   Rodez   Septimania
         Bordeaux   Toulouse   Narbonne   Marseilles

0   50   100   150 miles

Introductory Note

Almost all the characters in this story lived in Gaul thirteen centuries ago and left behind odd, slivered images of themselves. I have tried to put these together as one might, taking a few surviving sherds, try for the shape of a lost and curious pot. I have bent known facts hardly at all. I did fill in gaps. Two characters are invented—Ingunda and Fridovigia—another, Agnes, is made to remain as abbess for longer than she did and to end more unhappily. The political plot is an invention but its background and component elements come from chronicles of the time. I have chosen to suppose that Agnes and Fortunatus had a love affair. It has usually been held that his playful and passionate letters to her expressed a purely chaste feeling. Perhaps. Perhaps not. Recent evidence tends to show that flesh subdued by monastic vows can and does requicken. Celibacy of the clergy, as it is being questioned now, was only partially and reluctantly accepted then. The behaviour of the renegade nuns is far more outrageous in the chronicles than in my account. Radegunda's visions are described by her contemporary biographer, Sister Baudonivia.

My setting is the Wild West of an age often called 'Dark'. It was a world as fissile and fragmented as our own and its end was often thought to be in sight. Unlike ourselves, thinking people then did not embrace the fragmentary quality of experience but reacted by trying to contain bolting certitudes under grids of inflexible belief. They longed for coherence. In retelling this story, I too have tried for it. But it is, I repeat, a story. For fancy—however empathic—to coincide with one of history's secrets would be a miracle as odd as any in which the Merovingians believed.

The action of this novel spans the two decades between 568 and 587. There are some flashbacks to earlier events remembered by Radegunda and Agnes. Every change in time is indicated by a date in the margin. The monologue of the anchoress, although presented at various points throughout the novel, takes place entirely in the last two years, 586 and 587.

Chapter One

The mad cannot sin.   A.D.

Darkness chews at my brain. Chinks multiply. It 586
seeps in.

Don't let it! It is a duty to struggle against the Princes,
Powers and Dominations of the World of Darkness and
against the evil spirits who inhabit the air.

A losers' battle?

No.

We are all at war: the Church Militant.

I see—I choose to—the late evening view from the
convent garden: field and vineyard strips angled like a
backgammon board with shadows, forests, a prickle of
light: the river Clain. Our buildings straddle the city
walls so that turrets built for defence are now part of our
cloister and so, by God's grace, still used for defence.
Our chaplain used to say that. Father Fortunatus. There
is only one door. The abbess keeps the key. It is iron and
drags at her waist. The knobs in her backbone show
through her woollen robe when she bends. It is the only key.
All rooms remain unlocked. By Rule. There are many.
I can recite their names and uses: a memory test. Refectory,
spinning-, weaving-, drying-rooms, book-room and so
forth. It is too easy. I listed them yesterday with everything
they contain: woad, madder, soap, grease, shears, everything. The words flow fluently as water and prove nothing.
Memory survives judgment. I must think and talk to
myself clearly and sequentially. *Every day*. It is important
that I do, for that is what will help keep me sane.

In reality I have not seen the convent for a long time.
I do not know how long. For a while I kept count of the
days. I can see cracks of light. I know when it is day and

when night. Also, I can hear the bells ring for lauds, prime, terce, sext, nones and for the nocturnal offices. I kept count for seven months and thirteen days. Then I fainted. It was light in the cracks when I lost consciousness. It was dark when I came to. Hours later? Days? I could not tell. I could have asked the sister who brings me food. But a recluse does not speak. It was a sign. I understood that. Counting the days was wrong. It showed attachment to the world and I had sworn that I would renounce the world. Therefore I had done wrong to hold on to time. Time is of the world. So: I gave up counting the days. That must have been a long time ago. For a while I thought maybe I should not watch the cracks of light either. I used to close my eyes or turn my back on the cracks. But I understood that that, too, was wrong. I had sworn of my own free will to live as a recluse. So now I must live. Dying would be a sin against the Holy Spirit and against the Will of God. I must not deny the Light. Daylight figures the Light. The world lives in my memory and I do not blot it out for I am not to die but to live meagerly. All my strength must go into staying alive, into staying sane so that whatever I do or suffer remains deliberate. Therefore I allow myself to watch the cracks of light and to notice when they pale and when they turn yellow as they do when the sun is shining on the world outside. I even hold up my hand and drinking-flask to the light and look at them. The flask is of bluish glass full of tiny air bubbles and my hand is pink and lumpy and covered with old scars.

When I was a child, news came to the convent of a boy who had been walled up by his own wish eight years before. He had been twelve years old then and for eight years lived as I do now in a narrow space between two walls, fed, as I am fed, through a crooked slit which let in only cracks of light. For eight years he lived in sanctity. Then demons took hold of him and he began to shout that he was being burned and scorched and that the saints of God were thrusting burning needles through his body.

His torment was so great that he succeeded in removing one of the great stones from his prison. Flinging down the wall, he came forth, howling that he was in the grip of atrocious pains and yelling that the saints were the cause of his torment. Raving! He was brought to many shrines but his madness could not be cured. I heard it said then that the demons had gained power over him through his pride. He had aimed too high, starving himself beyond reason, denying himself water and trying perhaps to empty his mind of all but heavenly thoughts. "We are not angels," our chaplain told us then. "Heaven is not our sphere. If we try to be angelic we will be punished. We will be flung back into our own bestial animality." Our abbess had the same opinion of violent penances. "Beware," she used to say, "lest in scouring off the rust, you break the vessel itself."

Radegunda's most scorching memory was not private.

Half Gaul shared it with her for it was in every harpist's repertory. It was not only her worst memory, it was also her first for it had burned out everything that had been in her mind before. Some earlier images did survive but could not be deciphered and only glowed with a dark, tantalizing phosphorescence, as old ink-marks might on a fire-blackened page.

The combustive memory was itself suspect. It was too ample, too vivid. Radegunda had been eleven when her family was massacred and had, of course, understood what was happening. The trouble was that she had heard the event described scores of times since, complete with accounts of incidents which she, as a girl, could not possibly have witnessed. These became as real to her as those she had. As time passed, the harpists added more violent detail. The smells of blood and smoke, the burning bones and the wrench of falling rafters were like acid in Radegunda's nose. Once she fainted at a banquet during a particularly graphic retelling of it all.

"Poor lady!"

"Didn't that fool of a harpist know who she was?"

"How could he? He's new here."

"All the same ..."

The incident gave the story a new lease of popularity and she had to listen to it even more often. Mournfully, if the passing minstrel knew she was in his audience, with a relish of war-cries and reckless strummings if he did not, her murdered relatives' names were chanted at banquets and the fall of her house celebrated to honour its conqueror, Clotair, who had taken her captive on the night of the massacre and become her husband in her eighteenth year.

Sitting among Clotair's drink-sodden warriors at a table littered with knives and remnants of broken meats, she would sometimes occupy her mind with an effort to unravel the bloody tapestry of her history and disentangle what she had seen from what she hadn't. She did this stoically, for her feelings were few and focused and she had learned to steer them forward rather than back. Still, they had their roots in that night in Thuringia when the Franks had swept in and burnt her uncle's palace. The shock had curdled her sensibility as rennet curdles milk. She knew that. She thanked God for it. It had been his way of turning her against the world, the flesh and the devil.

Devils were the first element to be discounted in the harpists' version of Thuringia's defeat. Monsters, magic, a spontaneous yawning of the unhallowed German fens which had threatened to devour the Christian cavalry—these were clearly a biased story-teller's rendering of the fact that her uncle had had trenches dug in the hope that the Frankish horses might fall into them. Unhappily for him and her, only a few had. But could she have known even this at the time? Probably her only authentic memories would be indoor ones, for the attack had taken place in winter, a season which the hardy Franks found congenial for fighting. So what indoor memories could she recover? She groped, closing her eyes to remember better and

16

smelled the resinous wood of her uncle's palace walls.

In one room all the women sat around a fire—that was A.D.
sinister in itself for in normal times slaves and mistresses 531
should have been rushing to get their chores done before the
short winter daylight ended. The fire had been neglected.
Accumulations of ash sifted up through the logs and
choked the flames. Damp filtered the light, swaddling the
wooden palace in a mist as clammy and, at times, translucent as the nacred track of a snail. Late in the afternoon,
a few shafts of brightness percolated through. It was
about then, Radegunda was sure, that a burst of shrieks
roused the women and drew one of them to the back room
where she and her cousins were playing with a stolen
scramasax.

"What's the matter?" the woman scolded. She was one
of Radegunda's younger aunts. "Where did you get that
sword?" she shrieked. "Give it here."

She grabbed it, aimed a blow at several dodging children,
missed and did not bother to try again. "What kind of
foolery is this? At a time like this?" Her voice jumped.
She seemed to be only half thinking of what she was
saying. Alert for sounds from outside, she paused.
"Listen . . ." Nothing. Taking a deep breath, she began
to shout once more. "I . . ." But she was like a marauding
vixen in a poultry yard: ears half tuned to the fowl, half
to the watchdog. Her eyes flicked. Sensing something in
the doorway at her back, she turned. The sword was still
in her hand.

At this point, Radegunda might recoil, quailing before
her own memory. But the images were compelling. This
was something she had seen with her own eyes and the
action had to be played through.

The armed stranger standing behind the children's
aunt must have been startled by her sudden movement
and by the pointing sword. Almost before the children
were aware of his presence, he had jerked the weapon
from the woman's hand and rammed his own into her

17

belly. She fell forward: skewered. He shoved her off with his knee, releasing his weapon with the same movement. She crumpled as softly as a bale of falling cloth.

The children's screams stayed jammed in their throats. The man did not move either. He stood, staring at his bloodied sword. Then several other men crowded in behind and past him, grunting and exclaiming in excitement. All had drawn weapons. One pushed across the room, making for the large coffer on which Radegunda was sitting. Too stunned to flinch, she waited as he loomed towards her: a great, greasy, intent, uncaring man. He swept her off the coffer with a movement which was neither vindictive nor angry, but indifferent, as though he had been removing an inanimate object, then broke the lock with a light, thrifty blow and raised the lid.

In a moment all the men were bent over the chest. Radegunda, still lying where she had fallen, saw her cousin, Hamalafred, crawl across the floor behind the men's legs. He was making for the fallen short sword. Hamalafred was thirteen years old. Radegunda was sure of this for there had been talk of his joining the Thuringian warriors when they left to fight the Franks and he had been bitterly disappointed when the decision went against him. It was his bad luck to be short for his age although everyone admitted that he was quick tongued and clever as a bag of cats. His fingers were clenching on the sword-handle when one of the men turned, saw him and stepped heavily on his wrist. Hamalafred's face reddened and swelled. Laughing, the man lifted his foot and gently rolled rather than kicked the boy into the corner where Radegunda already lay. With the same lazy movement, the man bent, took her arm and drew her into the light.

"Well!" Gargling small chuckles of amusement around his throat. "What have we here? Young! A bit young maybe, but nice! A nice filly!" He spun her round. "Nice!" he repeated and picked up her skirt. "Pretty little ankle! War's got its points! Hey!" He called to the men who were still examining the contents of the coffer. "Look at this!" He lifted the skirt a little higher. "Nice knee too! Hey, Count Leudast, what fine do you impose in your court on a free Frank who uncovers a free-born virgin's knee? In peacetime I mean?"

"Six *solidi*," shouted one of the men at the coffer without looking up.

"Aha!" said the first soldier with satisfaction. "Six *solidi* for this, eh? And what"—he raised the skirt higher—"for uncovering a thigh? A nice, firm female thigh like this?"

"More than you could afford, you old lecher!"

"And for uncovering the backside? How much? Tell me. I'd like to know!"

Radegunda jerked out of his grasp and dived for the door. Her foot slipped in something and she stumbled but managed not to fall. She rushed out, then spun, clutching the door-jamb. Again she whirled. There were men all over the place. Lighted tapers pierced the twilight; glints flew from cutting edges; shadows multiplied silhouettes. One approached, throwing light on her foot, which was wet where she had stepped in her dead aunt's blood. Her sandal was coated with it. Her glance ran along the track left by her feet to where the light showed her aunt lying on her back. A stain had spread over the dead woman's middle. Her eyes were wide but nerveless. Radegunda turned abruptly away.

The man who had lifted her skirt stood beside her. "Nowhere to run," he remarked. "May as well stay with me. I'm as good as the next, little pagan!"

"I'm not a pagan," she shouted in a breathy explosion. "I am Princess Radegunda and a Christian. I want to see your king."

"Clotair? He's probably poking your mother this minute."

"My mother is dead. She was killed the—last time this happened. This has all happened before!" Radegunda's composure cracked. "And now," she shrieked, "again, I . . ." She began to cry but, after a few first uneven wails, got the sound curiously under control so that it must have seemed premature at such a time and more like the cry of a professional mourner than of a child. "All over again," she wailed, "and again! I don't want it! No! Not again and always happening and happening. I can't—where is your king?"

"Stop that! Stop it!" The Frank was annoyed. He pushed her around the dead body and across the room to a bench where several small children were packed together. Radegunda let herself be pressed in between them. Shoulders against the wall behind, as though gathering her last dregs of strength, she stared into the eyes of the man who had just removed his hand from her shoulder. Smells of sweat, garlic, urine, rasped metal and—yes— blood and the rancid smell from the butter-dressing in his hair bore down on her. His face came so close to hers that his beard was brushing her skin and the black tunnels of his nostrils blew hot breath on her mouth. She did not scream now. The face hovered. She saw growths of nasal hair puff and ebb like seaweed in a tide. Then the whole thing withdrew.

"You stay there!" said the Frank. "The kings will be coming in here to check the loot. Thierry and Clotair." He nodded at the coffers whose contents had by now been piled on the floor. "It has to be brought back to Gaul to be split up fair and square. If you *are* a princess, one of them may want you. Maybe they both will. Maybe they'll split *you* up, poor little shrew! Split you up the middle with their kingly cocks! You might have been better off with me. Our kings are not what you'd call gentle!" Giving her a kind of soft punch on the shoulder, the Frank left.

The other men followed him shortly after, locking the door behind them on the loot and on the children who were also loot. All night and part of the next day the room stayed locked while the Franks celebrated their victory and slept off their celebration. Shouts, quarrels, even the strains of a harp reached the children who clung together,

20

bunched in the corner furthest from their aunt's corpse. Radegunda had her small brother, Chlodecharius, on her lap.

"Try to sleep," she told the other children when she felt this might be possible. "The worst is over. Tomorrow they'll be sober. There'll be no more killing."

"What happened Aunt Amalaberg? Basina?"

"Where's my mother?"

"Don't think of it. It's over now."

"Over?"

"Over."

"Nothing's over!" The words broke out in a dry crackle. Hamalafred was trying not to cry. The sound of a spit followed and the other children could imagine the pale arc between the clap of his lips and the wet smack on the middle of the dark floor. Nothing was over, he repeated. Nothing ever would be, did they hear, did they? Never until the blood-price was paid in full. His wavery boy's voice fought in his throat with tears, fury and every weakness assailing it. It would be paid, he promised. It would. As soon as he was big enough to exact it. And not in gold either. No wergeld would satisfy him. "Blood," he whispered, trying to stem the tears he did not want to shed. Blood was what he wanted to shed. Only blood could avenge the lives lost this night. Frankish blood. Brown blood, purple, black. A hunter's son, he'd seen every kind before now. He had helped disembowel grouse, boar, elk and aurochs. It had all been an apprenticeship. He had tasted blood in blood sausage when the stuff jelled and grew stringy with softly melting strings which you pulled through your teeth. He'd chewed it and was hungry to chew human—Frankish—organs; no composition would do. He'd stick their Frankish gold solidi up their Frankish arses. No matter how long he had to wait, the day would come. He would hang Frankish captives from trees by the sinews of their thighs and catch the drips in a basin. He would roll wooden wains over their massed bodies, would . . .

"Hamalafred, shut your mouth! Stop it, Hamalafred." The girl screamed then checked herself. There was a pause and when she spoke again it was through a throat clenched like a restraining fist. "Can't you see", she asked reasonably, "that this is the worst thing of all? That you're doing the worst thing? Can't you?"

He couldn't.

"You're frightening the little ones," she tried.

He had an answer to that which he gave more calmly, however, his voice reaching with taut emphasis across the darkness. "They've got to see it the way I do," he said. "We owe revenge to our dead, Radegunda. We owe it to the living. Blood has to be paid for. That's the law," he explained patiently and responsibly, being thirteen years old and, for all he knew to the contrary, already the head of his house. "If people weren't afraid of being made to pay the price", he told her, "they'd kill each other the way they do crows and rats—the way the Franks kill, who think we're too weak to make them pay." At this point Hamalafred's voice changed. It began to creak and wheeze as though struggling through a closure narrow as the neck of a miser's pouch. A moment later he was sobbing and Radegunda fancied she could smell his tears. "They'll find out different," he wept and sounded suddenly like a small boy again. "I'll make them ... pay ... one day ..." It was an incantation, vivifying and medicinal: a counter reality more real to him for the moment than the cold room, his weakness and the captivity ahead.

But Radegunda felt then and later that he had summoned evil forces to pour their poison inside his and her very veins. "Blood-price," he said, as though that would be the end of it. Radegunda bit her tongue and, tasting it, spat into the darkness. She had her own reasons for placing scant hope in blood feuds.

When Hamalafred and Radegunda were infants, Thuringia had been ruled jointly by their two fathers who were brothers and lived in peace with each other. Then one day Hamalafred's mother Amalaberg, who was a woman of ambition, did something which was to affect all their lives. She laid the table for her husband's dinner in such a way that the cloth only covered one half of it and left the rest bare. "A man", she told him, "who is content with half a kingdom must be content with half a table." The meaning was clear and the insult galling. Her husband had had no rest from that day until he had allied himself with the Franks, murdered his brother and seized his lands. Along with the lands he took his brother's children and brought them up as his own. Radegunda had therefore learned to call him "father" and Amalaberg "mother" before learning from some household slaves the true story of her parentage.

"That law of yours, Hamalafred," she broke harshly into his croonings, "isn't much good to me! If it were such a good law, it would have some guidance for me, wouldn't it? It would tell me whether I should love your parents as my own or have a blood feud with them. But it doesn't, does it?"

Hamalafred had no time for doubts on a night like this. "You're a female, Radegunda!" He sniffed noisily as though gathering himself together after his weakness. "Anyway, I'm your cousin. You're my family now. I'll avenge your parents and my own together. I'll ..." He talked on like this. All night. His voice was charged with the same excitement as his enemies' outside the room whose hunting-fever was high, whose emanations seeped through the wooden walls to infect the young male with their own zest. "I'll kill," he sobbed and swore. "I will!" And from the hall came back the war-songs: "*We* killed," the Franks were exulting. "*I'll* kill," groaned Hamalafred antiphonally, "I will, I will, I will ..."

To Radegunda this dialogue sounded like the calls of rabid beasts. She covered her ears but this did not prevent her hearing the little boy on her lap, her four-year-old brother, Chlodecharius, take up the chant: "Kill," he crowed in his little boy's voice, "kill, kill, kill." Radegunda wept.

"It was my Gethsemane", she said of that night years later when she was describing it to Fortunatus, a friend and poet who had offered to write a lament for the destruction of her people, "and my Damascus."

Radegunda had by then become a pedant. Pedantry was a rampart against barbarism. She had become a nun. Religion was a rampart against violence. Before reaching the shelter of these ramparts, however, she had had to spend fourteen years as wife to King Clotair.

"Wasn't it horrifying for you," Fortunatus wondered, "to be betrothed to your people's ..." he hesitated over the choice of word, "conqueror?"

"His Majesty", remarked the nun with circumspection, "was, as you know, generous with me in the end. This convent," she spread her hands in a benedictory gesture— the left indicated the convent itself, the right blessed the fields and gardens trembling in the blazing noon of summer in the Loire country—"this was his gift, or rather it was paid for by my morning-gift which he let me keep when I left him for a greater Spouse."

Fortunatus bowed his head. "At the beginning, though?" he prompted.

"The beginning?" The nun reached back. "That night was my beginning. That night I began to long for a reverse-world, a world where things would be the opposite of the way they are. That's the easiest way to imagine, you know: you just reverse, turn things upside down. There would be no blood-price, no war, maybe even," an apologetic hand alighted briefly on the poet's sleeve, "no men. In a way, this", again she uptilted her hands, managing with a single move to point to the convent and compare it to heaven, "is such a world. Apart from you, Fortunatus, a man so exceptional as to be part angel, we have no men here, no blood-price, no war, no anger even." She smiled. "We live the way we ourselves want."

"I have heard", the poet teased her, "of monasteries in the East whose monks so distrust the principle of femininity that they refuse to have cows or nanny-goats on their farms—to the detriment of their diet."

The nun nodded. "*They* think the greatest sin is the sin of Eve, but the sin which has always chilled my blood is the sin of Cain. Perhaps all that means is that the sexes *are* happiest apart."

"You were going to tell me about your marriage to King Clotair."

"He used to say"—the nun laughed a surprisingly conjugal laugh, the knowing little laugh women keep for talking about husbands—"that I was more like a nun than a queen. He said it before I ever thought of becoming a nun myself. It would have seemed impossible, you know. At first ..."

"He was an affectionate husband then? Tolerant?"

"All he demanded was the body. My body can be forced to do anything."

"But he did wait to marry you for—was it six years?"

"Until I was seventeen. Yes. He had me educated: a caprice. Like having a wild horse trained perhaps? One of our silver-coated Thuringian mares. He captured herds of them and—as with me—broke them in. I suppose it amused him to take the princess of a pagan people—it's true: my people were largely unbaptized and less Romanized than the Franks—to take *me* and bring me up like the daughter of a senatorial family."

She looked at the poet. Unblinking eyes. Very large, transparent, apparently unfocused. They disturbed him. After fishing for a useful image all he had come up with was the fact that they reminded him of a goat's. Idiotic comparison. A goat's eyes, for God's sake—he'd checked—were yellow and not beautiful at all. Whereas Radegunda's ... Still, the comparison had something. It was the transparency perhaps, the diffuseness. Empty of memory. Clotair had left little trace. But then Radegunda was a German and Germans were like that: curiously free of memory's murk. A German could tell you his grandfather's name perhaps. Never more. Or didn't choose to? They had come from Asia not so long ago but could tell nothing

25

of their origins. Nothing of those decades of journeying on wooden waggons across Oriental lands. A peculiar freedom that gave them, he supposed, reflecting that his own racial past tugged at his thoughts like water-weeds at the keel of a boat.

"Tell me," he asked, remembering something he had read, "do German women still bring weapons to their husbands as a dowry?"

"I was brought up", she reminded him, "a Romanized Frank. I'm grateful to Clotair for that. It was while I was being educated in his villa at Aties on the Somme that I found my reverse-world: Christianity. I had been baptized in Thuringia, of course, but ..."

"He didn't live at Aties? Clotair?"

"No. But he was not alone while waiting for me. Clotair in all had seven wives or, to be finical, six and one official concubine. The distinction is subtle. As for unofficial concubines ..." The nun threw up her hands, laughing.

"A man of passion!" The poet stared into the heart of a nasturtium trumpet. "*Abundantia gallica* ... Gaul abounds in life. The Franks do. The royal sons of Clovis perhaps more than the rest and Clotair was the most immoderate of *them*, wasn't he? Anyway, *he*'s dead so safer to talk about!" Fortunatus mimed comic alarm. "You know," he confided, "he—they all—fascinate me, terrify me too, which is excellent for my verse. When I'm at court I walk a tightrope, my head is dizzy, my senses keen as blades, my mouth dry. I am like a rabbit staring at a hound. I adore that hound: he is the anti-me. I would like to write a panegyric to his immoderacy, to his appetites, guts, kidneys and bowels which are all of so much better quality than my own. To his teeth. Instead, what *do* I do? I write panegyrics to Clotair's son and very worthy successor, Chilperic, whom Gregory calls 'the Nero and Herod of our time' and praise him for what? For his moderation! Why do I do It? It's a game, a game whose pleasures I only half understand myself. There's the obvious one of trying it on, seeing just how much flattery the monster

26

will take. Then there's my penchant for the horrible which I castigate by denying it—Radegunda, you are annoyed! I've said the wrong thing! Forgive me. You know how I let words carry me away. They mean nothing."

The nun did not pretend to smile. "Forgive me, Fortunatus, if I say that there is something disgusting about innocence. You are pure and impurity fascinates you! You do not know evil and so you make the word 'evil' your toy."

"Should I be tried in the furnace of reality?"

"Maybe you should! No, nobody should. You should believe in reality, though. Believe it's real. Respect it. It is because things are remote from you, filtered through books and hearsay, that you feel you have to dress them up, make metaphors. You are inquisitive, Fortunatus! You have renounced the flesh, but you do not renounce the *thought* of the flesh and, since you are a man of words, you enjoy it more avidly at second hand." She looked him in the eye. "You want me to tell you about my married life with Clotair."

"I have offended you. I'm sorry. I thought we were friends. I had come to identify with many of your feelings. It's not all that hard for me. We had several invasions during my time in northern Italy: the Ostrogoths, the Byzantines. *They* came as allies but invading allies, you know . . ." He shrugged. "The Lombards are there now. My family may have been wiped out for all I know—but I shan't appeal to your sentiment. As for my 'inquisitiveness' as you call it—you holy people are harsh—the reason for it is a bit, a significant bit, to the side of where you put it. A poet needs an extra dimension around his poem, one of unspoken knowledge, things I feel and recognize about you but which I will not say . . ."

The nun stood up. She was tall, almost a hand's span taller than the poet. She fell to her knees. "Forgive me," she said. "I have been lacking in charity."

The poet jumped. "Radegunda, *please*! Oh dear. . ." He crouched opposite her so that now they looked like

27

lovers taking a vow. "Please get up!"

"Not until you forgive me. I failed in human understanding. I often fail."

"I forgive you. I forgive you. Please get up!"

She let him help her up.

"I hate it when you do things like that. *Your* kneeling to *me* is so ... disproportionate ... almost mocking somehow."

"I knelt to my offended fellow creature."

"Yes." Fortunatus felt around him on the stone seat for his nasturtium-trumpet. It was torn. He spread it flat and held it to his eye, staring through its flaming membrane at the sun. "It is true," he admitted, "you have lived closer to action than I. Yet, I like to believe my writing is a form of action too. I explain my position on this in one of my poems. Perhaps you remember? The one praising Launebodus for building a church to St. Saturninus? No? Oh, well, the gist is that to record the acts of the virtuous spurs others on to imitate them. As you know, I am taking notes for the story of your life. This makes my curiosity a little holy, don't you think?"

Fortunatus closed his dazzled eyes and put the bruised nasturtium on his tongue, hoping to revive it with his saliva.

"By the same token," said Radegunda, "if you wrote down the bloody doings of Queen Fredegunda you might deter your readers from indulging in vice. Have you ever, when at court, asked her to satisfy your holy curiosity?"

The poet swallowed the flower. He coughed, hawked it up and spat it out: a red glob. "Sorry!" He wiped his mouth. "I write about martyrs. I don't aspire to join them. Each to his trade. Forgive me, but that sort of talk makes me nervous. Even here you never know who ... Besides, there is something distasteful about the queen: fleshy." The poet made a prim mouth. "I prefer to lie about her, to present her as she ought to be."

Radegunda stood up.

"I was fleshy", she said, "in my youth. Carnal. But

28

wanton kittens make sober cats. Don't despair of Frede-gunda." She smiled without embarrassment. "I have to go," she said.

He had been bracing himself for a withdrawal but was disappointed.

"Compline," she explained with careful courtesy. Convent offices provided endless pretexts for retreat. "God be with you."

"And with you," said Fortunatus. "You will", he could not resist begging, "tell me later about what went before: your marriage with Clotair, how he came to let you go . . . and anything else", he begged, "you'd care to tell me. See what you can remember."

Chapter Two

Radegunda remembers.

A.D.
552

She remembers lying beside Clotair, her lord. Outside the wooden dwelling which is called a 'palace' but is really no more than a hunting-lodge, she hears the wind. It whips like black wire. This lodge is one of many, for Clotair loves to hunt. On horseback he is as skilful as a Hun and when walking looks incomplete. His legs arch, straddling an absent mount. When he rides down a boar or stag, Clotair becomes that beast. He feels with it, relishing the clash between its cunning and his own. He knows its tricks, sees the snap of twigs and saplings with the creature's own surprise, feels a vegetable exhilaration as he hurtles through the bush and, in the loamy giddiness of a green-tunnelled track, would swear the beast shares his eagerness for its death. When he has it cornered, its antlers, if it is a stag, enmeshed perhaps in a branch, it is with a hard, unwavering exuberance that he plunges his weapon in its flesh.

With the same authority he plunges in and out of Radegunda's memory. Even here, she cannot control him. The innocence in the midst of his foulness—the scope of his crimes is biblical—makes him hard to reject, impossible to quite condemn. He slithers from definition, radiant in retrospect like some dampish satyr gambolling in the light. She tries to skimp and dim his image, but the merest touch of Clotair is like ginger in a stew. Its pungency swamps the rest.

Radegunda has galloped after her lord at the hunt and sat with him at table. Now she lies beside him on the feather mattress of their gold-balustered bed. He is kneeling up, his thighs bandy in their triumphant arch,

30

his arms under her belly as he pulls her, backside foremost, towards him so that her buttocks rear into the space between his thighs. She can feel his hairy parts delicately brushing her skin as Clotair plays with her body. He plays gently, frolicsomely, nuzzling and teasing as a soft-mouthed hound will play with a frail young puppy. His touch is light. His fingers ripple along her spine with the movement of lake-waves on a beach. Face in the linen sheet, she imagines her own long white vulnerable back and wonders does it remind him of the back of the deer he killed at the hunt. She clenches her teeth and forbids her flesh to respond to his. She grinds her face into a goose-down pillow, bites her hand until she can taste blood and prays to the Christian God to deliver her from pleasure. Clotair rams his member into the recesses of her body and she screams. "Oh God!" she screams, "No," she screams, "No, God, No!"

Clotair is laughing.

"*I* am your god," he whispers. "You were on your knees praying to *me*! You couldn't help it, Radegunda! You are as proud as the boar in the forest but you can't resist me any better than it can! I can feel your pleasure," he says with lordly confidence. "I feel it as surely as my own."

"I do my conjugal duty."

"No, my pet, you do much more! Much, much more!" He caresses her and she lies rigid in the dark, hating her own response to his caress.

Hating it still in memory, she is glad to remember what happened next.

When he was asleep, she sat up very, very quietly, edged to the side of the bed and was stealing out of the room when he called:

"Radegunda!"

"My lord?"

"What is it? Where are you going?"

"I have to go outside a moment."

"Even the saints piss!" He laughed. "Even my nun-like wife! Ha!"

A moment later he was snoring.

The man lying across their door was asleep. Radegunda stepped over him and walked downstairs and out through the hall where more men and serving-girls were lying about, many of them in each other's arms. She opened the outer door and the black wind struck her body like the blow of a club. She stepped outside, pulling the door behind her with difficulty. She removed her heavy fur coat under which she wore nothing. Then she rolled naked in the snow, moving quickly lest the skin freeze to the hard, frozen ground underneath and be torn from her body. When she could stand it no longer, she put on her fur coat and crept back into the palace and through the hall. She was stiff with pain and her body was shaking violently. She did not return to where Clotair was sleeping but let herself into a small room containing a wooden kneeler and a chest. Opening the chest, she took out a folded garment, shook it out and, again removing her fur cloak, put it on. It was made of haircloth. She knelt on the kneeler.

But she was not alone for long. Her prayer was interrupted by a knock and a whisper from beyond the door.

"Radegunda, it's Chlodecharius."

"Come in."

A young man wearing woollen breeches and a fur tunic slipped quietly in, kissed her, then sat on the chest.

"I saw you just now", he whispered, "trying to freeze the memory of his touch from your skin. You still hate him."

"He is my husband. I owe him obedience."

"You owe him a short sword between the ribs. Or a poisoned stirrup-cup. Who chose him for your husband? Not you. Not your family." The young man's face was pale. His eyes were flecked like a trout's belly. His hands twitched as he talked and there was a tic in his cheek. "The bloody murderer," he whispered. Trembling and trying not to, he gripped the edges of the chest and his knuckles went white as ivory dice.

"God will judge his murders," whispered Radegunda. She shivered.

"You'll get a fever from these nightly outings of yours! That'll be another murder God will have to judge."

"He treats me well."

"Well! I've seen the marks of a whip on your back. It was striped like a slave's just now when you were out there! My sister's! And I ..." The young man trembled furiously.

"I whipped myself."

"You must think I'm a moron if you think I'll believe ..."

Radegunda took a discipline from behind the kneeler and lashed herself with it on the back. Peeling down the haircloth dress, she showed the mark. The young man groaned.

"Why?"

"To subdue my flesh."

Chlodecharius laughed without amusement. "A nun! They all say it! Washing beggars' feet. Distributing alms, praying all night—and now this! Ha!" His sour laugh swelled cautiously. He didn't want to be overheard. He whispered in a voice gasping with emotion, coughed, tried to stifle his cough and was shaken by dry, soundless, probably painful convulsions. It was clear that his own weakness maddened him. "You," he managed at last, "you commit ad-adultery with Ch-Christ! You deceive your earthly husband with a heavenly one. The king with God! Nice, I suppose, the perfect slap to his pride—but, well, that's no solution for me!"

"You?"

"He is going to have me killed." Chlodecharius slipped off the coffer and began to walk silently about. His breath came in nervous gasps. "On the sly. An accident? A brawl? A highwayman? Poison? What do I know? I've been tipped off. I talk too much, it seems. My anger irks him. My silence too. I lurk. I look morose. My humiliation gives him no pleasure but some anxiety and Clotair doesn't suffer any irk at all for long. I suppose he suffered as he did because *you* please him. He likes to violate your

33

white, unwilling flesh. It must be a novel enough sensation to sleep with a would-be nun: cuckolding the creator as it were. It's kept you in favour and me alive for fourteen years. Perhaps it's losing its novelty? Anyway I've been tipped the wink. The thing is: where do I go? To Constantinople to join Hamalafred? It's a longish journey in mid winter with the roads under ells of mud. But the danger is urgent. Also, there's another matter ..."

"Chlodecharius! You wouldn't leave me?"

"It may be a matter of method, sister: whether I go feet first or with them firmly under me. From what I've been told I'd be unwise to delay. We both know Clotair. Not just a killer in war but—well, though there's no need to go back so far, remember how he butchered his infant nephews!"

"Take refuge in a church or with his brother. There's no love between them."

"Radegunda, help me kill him."

Radegunda made the sign of the cross. "Chlodecharius, you're a Christian!"

"So's Clotair. It's never stopped him, has it? It won't stop him killing me! Radegunda, you're the last of my family. You're my only ally here. Give me your fur cloak. With it on—we look enough alike—I can slip into his bedroom and avenge our family! Put an end to your martyrdom. Even," he was leaning over her, gripping her shoulder, hissing with excitement, "even if they kill us both afterwards, Radegunda, we will die with honour!"

"Honour!"

"Listen, we needn't die at all." His breath was beery on her face. His eyes flickered like fish. Suddenly rigid, he listened for a sound at the door. Nothing there? "Radegunda!" tightening his grip on her shoulder-bone, "we can saddle horses and escape to the court of Metz or Paris or Brittany. The three of us."

"Three?"

"Agnes ..."

"Agnes?" Radegunda's voice rose imprudently. "Little

34

Agnes—you've been ..."

"No! I'm in—I want to marry her. She wants it too."

"She's only ... Agnes is only eleven! How could you? A *child*!"

"Almost twelve: the canonical age for matrimony. We could get married now. An understanding priest ..." The flickering eye. He was irresolute. She daren't trust him. Soft lower lip and besides ... No.

Radegunda stood, gripping the arm-rest of the kneeler with fingers fierce as claws. "You'd take Agnes from me! You'd sully her flesh. Make her ... into a ... female! Chlodecharius, Agnes is my pupil. I was teaching her noble things. How to live alone! I spend hours with her every day, I trusted her and all the time you were insinuating yourself, worming in. How come she never spoke to me of you? Why was she ashamed?"

Chlodecharius let go her shoulder, stepped away. "There's nothing wrong with loving, Radegunda. Or being shy about it. You chose Agnes because you were lonely, because she is innocent, gay ... We are brother and sister. Is it so odd we should have the same tastes?"

"Taste!" Radegunda spat the word with contempt and a spray of spittle as though cleaning her mouth after it.

"In friendship ..."

"*Friendship*, Chlodecharius! Do you truly mean 'friendship'? 'Amicitia'? How come then that she is ashamed of yours and hides it from me. You've aroused her senses, haven't you? You've made her ashamed? How far have you gone? Tell me."

The young man's face was lean and pointed: a hound's face. Now its pallor was unevenly suffused with pink. He stared angrily at his sister: "Radegunda, are you making a jealousy scene?"

"Jealousy?"

"What else?" He walked to the window, pulled back a shutter and peered out. "Dawn. I told you my life is in danger. There's something going on in Thuringia. I've been waiting for news. But the roads are impassable.

35

Maybe next spring—unless Clotair has intercepted a message? Listen, the matter of Agnes is unimportant. I wish to God I'd never mentioned ... look, she's just a *child* I'm fond of." Chlodecharius spun round and hissed bitterly in his sister's ear, "Don't you suppose I get lonely in this court? I am kept under surveillance, spied on, expected to be in sight. Absence is interpreted to mean plotting, silence to mean bitterness. I must be seen to enjoy myself, to laugh, hunt, chase women ..."

"So you choose my pupil, a girl whose spirit I have been trying to protect ..."

"You are ungenerous, Radegunda! Maybe that was why I liked her. After all you brought me up too, remember? You infused a little of your sadness into us both. We console it in each other. You don't ask what I meant about Thuringia. Now that something's finally moving, after all these years, don't you care? There may be a war!" Snapping his fingers in front of her eyes. "Radegunda! Are you listening?"

"Listening! Your mind stinks, Chlodecharius. I may have brought you up but you have escaped me! It stinks of sex and death: the double curse God inflicted on man when he threw him out of Eden. Fallen Man is subject to death and so must reproduce himself by sexual means. That is the meaning of the serpent that grows out of man's loins and plunges itself into women: rot, Chlodecharius, puncturing, blood, pain! Our family is sensual, Chlodecharius! We must restrain our nature!" She licked the lathering anger on her lips.

Chlodecharius shrugged. "Is it life or death you hate? Are you reproaching me with wanting to kill Clotair or marry Agnes? Which?"

She turned away, sank back to the kneeler, let her face fall into her hands. "Both," she whispered. "I want Agnes to be pure as I can never be again. Ever."

Chlodecharius's voice came from behind her back, cold now and very steady: "What about me, Radegunda?"

She raised and turned her head. He was trembling and

his mouth was set in a mean, sour line. Hating her. Poor Chlodecharius! Twenty-four years old and nothing to be proud of. Weak in a place where weakness was shame. She loved him but her love was like lava inside a volcano. It did not easily emerge. "You must", she said, "be patient. Listen, I will intercede with Clotair for you. If I ask him a direct favour he will never deny me. I will do this when he wakes tomorrow!"

Her brother walked back to the shutter. "It's tomorrow now," he said. "No use arguing then: *you* ask the favour on your knees and *I* get a reprieve—for the moment. His humour changes with the wind and we are at its mercy. We are like leaves stripped from a tree. We have no root, no place, no nourishing sap. Exiles. Is there any difference between us and slaves? I will talk to you of this again. Meanwhile be thinking. Think what it would mean if we could get away and reach Constantinople. To Hamalafred and Amalaberg!"

Radegunda walked over to him. She ran a finger down the hollow of his cheek. It was as much of a gesture of affection as she could manage. "We would be exiles still, Chlodecharius!"

"How can you say that?" The young man was congested. "Hamalafred", he urged, "has made himself a position there. He has received titles from the Emperor. We would have a family there! Blood-ties, affection, security! My God, Radegunda, what else makes life worth living? Land, Radegunda, is not what makes a home! It's kin, kin to defend you and back you up! Kin, Radegunda, kin! Blood-kin. If someone maims me or kills me to whom is compensation due? To my next-of-kin. And if I have none to demand it, am I not the most vulnerable man alive? Am I not weaker than a slave since a slave's master will defend him? In his own interests! That's what exile means, Radegunda. We're dependent on Clotair's whim! But in Constantinople . . ." His pale, mackerel-flecked eyes were sensuous with longing. "Constantinople," he whispered urgently, "Radegunda . . . *think*!"

She shook her head. "Life *is* a place of exile."

Suffocating with his need to convince, with his need for his own herd, his frustration at her stubbornness, he shook her: "Life", he whispered, for caution was bred into his very passions, "is life and to deny it the refuge of slaves and frightened women! Can you be sure that this", he plucked at the haircloth shift she was wearing, "and that", kicking at the wooden kneeler, knocking the discipline to the floor, "are not covering up a weakening of the bowels? Cowardice?"

"I hope I would not fear to die for my faith. Many have!"

He sighed, dropped his hands. "You'd die all right—but would you live? Your faith is not in life. You have closed it off! You have closed me off!"

"Chlodecharius, I pray for you every day!"

He shrugged. "That I may have a Christian death, I suppose? You grudge me Agnes. You say my mind stinks. Oh you have Christian, dutiful feelings for me—I suppose they're worth the ones you have for Clotair!"

Radegunda's teeth were chattering. Fever or perhaps cold had seized her body. "I know when someone is trying to manipulate me, brother. I am not your toy or tool. As you said: dawn is here. Let us say good-night. I shall do what I promised." She kissed the young man on the cheek, gripped his arm and said: "Sleep well. Try to pray for the gift of peace."

Removing the hair-cloth shift, she pulled on her fur coat, left the room, crossed the hall and again slid into Clotair's bed. In his sleep, the king reached for her, groaned as his hand came in contact with icy skin, then, dreaming perhaps that he had come to the bed of an ice-maiden or one of those accursed princesses forced to wear scaly fish-tails, rolled his hot, confident, hairy body on top of hers. Radegunda, remembering that she had a favour to ask of him in the morning, allowed him to probe for the magma inside her frozen flesh. Again her cries were muffled in the bed-furs which were made from the skins of red

38

foxes whose relatives were probably hunting at this moment in the snowy landscape outside.

Afterwards they slept or rather Clotair did while Radegunda woke and dreamed in an ebb and flow so coherent that she could not tell which bits were dreams and which not. She dreamed she was embracing Chlodecharius, hotly kissing him, weeping, begging his forgiveness for her harshness of a while before. Again she held him in her arms as the four-year-old baby she had held on her lap in the wooden wain which brought them, swaying and jolting over the old Roman roads, into Gaul. It was so easy to talk to a child. She marvelled at her ease and at his crows of pleasure. She was telling him the story of the little princess in the swan's-down coat who flew away over the frozen marshes which the wain was crossing, back across silver lakes and sighing reeds to Thuringia. Then she was telling Agnes the same story, little Agnes, a Gallo-Roman girl whose father had died in Clotair's service and whom Clotair had given her to bring up. Wind shook the bones of the place. Branches skittered against its planks. Clotair moved towards her again and she awoke and pushed him from her, dozed and found herself caught in the middle of a hot embrace between Chlodecharius now grown distastefully to manhood and the childish Agnes. She pushed them violently apart; her hand landed in something clammy. Then she was really awake and Agnes was beside and then on top of her, shaking her and shrieking: "He is dead, Radegunda, they killed him! Wake up! He crawled into my bed to die, to die, Radegunda! Oh God, oh God! I put my arms around him like this, Radegunda, like this and I felt ... Jesus, Mary, help me! I shall die ..."

Agnes's arms were around Radegunda's neck. She was lying on her and there was a thick clamminess between their breasts. The child's weight pinned the fur cover down across the queen's thighs. Agnes wailed. Clotair leaped from sleep, reared in the bed and yelled a war-cry. Henchmen rushed in the door and all was pandemonium.

When the screams had subsided and a shutter had been thrown open to let in the daylight, Agnes was found to be soaking in blood. At first they thought she was wounded and it was only when a wail raised in another part of the palace told them that Chlodecharius had been found in Agnes's bed with a knife in his back that they understood what had happened. A bloody track led from Agnes's bed to the little room where Radegunda's kneeler and coffer were kept.

"How did it happen?"

"Who?"

"Why?"

Radegunda did not join in the panic. She held Agnes, letting the child pant out a story which she recognized almost before it was told.

"I woke up, Radegunda, and there he was stumbling towards my bed. Chlodecharius! He had never come before but still I wasn't surprised, because ... He let out a sort of sigh. And fell down beside me. 'Agnes!' he said. Like that. I thought it was a game. I put my arms around him and felt the ... the knife-handle. And the blood. Radegunda! I didn't understand. Even then, I didn't. I tried to shake him. To get him to say what was the matter. And why he wouldn't say anything. I tried to tease him, to *tickle* him even, oh Radegunda, I ..."

The child fell silent. Her stomach pumped in and out and small pants were strangled in her throat. The henchmen's exclamations were checked. Eyes slid quick glances at Clotair. Radegunda stared straight at him. He frowned. His eye dodged hers and he began to shout that this should be looked into, punished, given immediate attention, priority. The culprit would be caught. His glance winged around the room, dipping to avoid Radegunda's. He gave orders for the moat to be examined and the palisade. Signs of strangers' passage were to be reported. At once. His own men must be made to account for how they had spent the night. Nobody was exempt. Nobody. Let the knife be brought to him. Someone might recognize it. The clatter of his talk was like the sounds boys make with clappers to scare crows from crops. His glance sliced air like a slanty knife.

Radegunda waited for him to finish. She gripped the baluster of the marriage bed.

"My Lord," she said, "I shall lay out my brother's body with my own hands."

Clotair nodded without looking at her. As she wished. Whatever she thought fit.

"Then, my Lord, I crave your permission to leave this court. After the funeral I want to go to Medardus, the Bishop of Noyon, and beg him to consecrate me as a deaconess. I am unfit for matrimony. It will be better if I consecrate my life to God and leave your majesty to take a fitter wife. We have been married fourteen years. God has not blessed our union with children. It would be impious to fly against heaven's clear dictate. Chlodecharius was my child as well as my brother. Now he is dead I beg your majesty's permission to give my life to God."

The henchmen's silence thickened. It was congested, palpable. Like gruel in their throats, like ice before their eyeballs. They wrapped themselves in it, insulated their nerves and waited. Some must have been remembering other occasions when Clotair's will was thwarted or his pride assailed. Savage acts ... There were many to choose from. Expecting another, they were braced, for Clotair's rage could whirl off-target, bolt like a freshly branded beast and flatten whatever lay along its unpredictable passage.

Clotair frowned. Head bent, he squinted at the daylight glittering on the gold balusters of his bed and on the tufty flames of its fox-fur cover. His own beard and hair flared with the same red, foxy vigour. His spirit too was foxy, like that of all his race, known for their nerve and perfidy in the tremulous chronicles of their time. A shudder threw his body into a rampant posture.

"So, Radegunda!" he roared. "You want to leave me. Is that it?"

41

"For God, my Lord!"

"For God! For God!" The tawny head was thrown back. "Well! What do you say to that?" he challenged his men. "Ha? What kind of a king do you think reigns up there," with an upward jerk and flounce of his mane, "what sort must he be if he's not afraid to steal the wife of a king as great as me?"

No answer. This was a tricky one. The henchmen's eyes stayed lowered. Only Radegunda stared straight at Clotair awaiting his reply. For a moment they locked glances. Clotair broke the lock. Shaking his spine like a wet dog, he said irritably, "Go then, woman! Go lay out your brother and go to God when you choose. Go! Go!"

He turned and walked out of the bedroom.

Chapter Three

Hilarious and worn, Fortunatus was back from another trip. He had stayed in villas porous with inner courtyards where peacocks and turtle-doves were kept for table and display. He had lived high, suffered discomfort on the roads back and returned with a baggage of fresh anecdote. He had seen a merchant from the East with a coat made from phoenix-breasts joined so cunningly as to show no join.

"Like the seamless robe of Christ," he told Agnes, for it was time to sound a pious note after betraying what was perhaps too frank a delight in the crass richness of villa life. "Moreover the phoenix, since it rises after death, signifies Christ. The peacock too . . ."

Its colours moved in the prism of his eye.

"We shall seem dull to you now."

"Oh, if you only knew how glad I am to be back!"

They told each other this in a number of ways, drawing on formulae from Ambrose, Cicero, Jerome and anyone else who came to mind; it was polite to do this and prolonged conversations which might otherwise have died. They had, they assured each other, been parted in body but not in spirit. Honourable love, fragrant as honey, bound them so to each other and to Radegunda and to God that neither of them was ever alone. Yet they rejoiced to see each other again with the body's eye. Each to the other was as a spring to a thirsty man. In all sisterliness. And brother-lines. And *caritas*. And so forth. Agnes broke into all this with a practical suggestion:

"You must be exhausted! And starving! I shall send over a meal from the convent kitchen."

She did. A very good one: beef braised with leeks and

43

coriander, fleabane, parsley, basil, chervil, fennel and vinegar and served with a sauce made from honey and must. With this came several kinds of vegetable, gravy and, finally, a milk pudding swimming in heavy cream.

Fortunatus ate with enthusiasm and afterwards, since he was simmering still with the excitement of his journey but had no one to talk to as visiting hours at the convent were now over, decided to write her a thank-you poem. He had already begun tapping out the meters before he had finished the meal. Strong trochees. One meter-beating finger dived into the dessert and found it finger-furrowed already. Agnes must have shaped the concoction with her own hands. Fortunatus licked his creamy digit with an odd shudder of happiness.

POEM TO THE HOLY ABBESS AGNES TO THANK HER
FOR A MILK PUDDING

> Moulded in cream I found your fingers' trace
> Where, skimming it, they'd left their track.
> Say, who could sculpt with such exquisite grace?
> Was it from Daedalus you learned the knack?
> Rare love whose image skimmed my way
> Though the fair form itself had gone!
> Sadly, this melting imprint will not stay,
> My share in you blurs and grows wan.

A.D. 586 A recluse does not easily forget her animal nature. I am sure I am more aware of my body than any whore of Babylon or meretrix. I am all body. More than a lizard toasting its long belly in the sun, more than a woman in labour or the libidinous Queen Fredegunda, I live in my flesh, think flesh, *am* flesh. My flesh cannot be ignored; it smells as the queen's is unlikely to do since she can take baths and walk away from her excrement. My feet slip in mine. My shoes are caked with it. My skin itches all over. My mind too is like an itchy place. My thoughts are scratching nails. Over and over old itches they scrape and scratch. Where would I get new matter for them?

44

I have long ceased to pray. My life, my smelly, itching, mindless life must be my prayer. I offer my filth so that I may be cleansed. I offer the lives I never lived. I offer the baseness of the life I do live. I offer its narrowness, the shrivelling of my mind and my efforts to keep it from shrivelling. I offer my awareness and my forgetfulness, my mistakes and my shame. I have to compensate. I am a child of sin. I am illicit flesh.

Scream! I shall! *Scream*! Not yet. Yes. I must. Now. I need this relief if I am to keep sane and I must stay sane if I am to pay again and again, day after day. Scream: that licence I must allow myself or I shall go mad as my mind itches, itches, scratches over the old itch, bleeds, scratches, itches...

I have screamed. The nuns hear. "The woman in the wall is screaming again," they say. They are used to it. Their recluse is no saint.

Agnes's memories were less precise than Radegunda's. A.D. Fortunatus questioned her inquisitively. Coming to the 568 kitchen-garden when it was her turn to do the garden chores, he interrupted her as she was staking bean-vines.

"Let me help. Then we can talk."

"I should do it myself," said Agnes scrupulously. "The Rule says we should let no one wait on us."

"The Rule means servants," said Fortunatus, "not charitable friends." He picked up a ball of string and began to tie the young plants to the stakes Agnes had driven in. "Nonsense," he said. "No protests." Then he began to ask her when she first knew she had a vocation. Had she known right from the time Radegunda decided to leave court that she too was called to the religious life? How had she felt the call? When? He was handling the delicate bean tendrils roughly, twisting them so that she was afraid they might break and tying the string so tautly it was in danger of cutting through the stems.

"Please," she begged, "let me do it." Taking the string from his hands.

"Tell", he went to sit down in a rose bower, "about the call."

Agnes released the plant he had twisted and ran her fingers along it, feeling the resilience of stem and root. "I don't think I ever had a call," she said carefully.

"But you made a choice! You chose the religious life."

"Did I?"

Fortunatus sighed.

The nun turned to him. Green light from the bower fell on her face shadowing her dark Gallic eyes. They were wide and long and disconcerted the poet who was reminded that this woman was not yet thirty and had been loved while still a child by the dead Chlodecharius. Although she wore the same heavy unbleached habit of rough wool, her shape was quite different to that of Radegunda. Both of these rigorous women had been brushed by passion. The thought excited him.

"The two of you went straight to Radegunda's estate at Saix when you left the court?"

"No. We went to the Bishop of Noyon. Radegunda wanted him to make her a deaconess. We needed to become part of the Church's family. We needed its protection." A smile. "And as you see we have had it since." She laughed. Her voice was a young girl's.

And why not, thought Fortunatus. She had not lived. Under those unbleached layers of wool her body was like an apple kept in storage. Apples in the convent granary stayed fresh until the next season came around. Thinking of their pale pith, he found, with amusement, that his teeth were itching to bite one. He would ask her for a basket of them when he left. Gull-greedy, his liking for food was a joke between the two nuns and himself. They, whose Rule forbade them to eat meat themselves, enjoyed cooking it for him and the poem he had just sent Agnes in gratitude for her milk pudding was one of a series on his appetites and their skill. Trivial concerns for a poet but, as Symmachus had written—and if true then how much more so now—"What else is there for us but to exchange

46

old courtesies?" Watching the nun who had returned to her work, Fortunatus remembered that here was a subject neither trivial nor recognized by Symmachus: the sacrifice of Christians who gave up this world for a better one. Agnes, her pale flesh hidden beneath her pale habit, was making that sacrifice with every moment of her life. Only Christian martyrs ranked higher than a dedicated virgin. He could—would write about that. She was storing up grace on which others could draw: a bank for the world-lings—himself included—who, spiritual grasshoppers flayed by their own passions, must come at the end of their singing summer to beg the careful ant for a little of the extra she had so generously been saving for them. Spiritual wealth was impossible to hoard; it was at the service of the community. Yes, he could make a worthy poem, perhaps several on the theme. Flesh was the poet's clay and he would make use of paradox: he would describe purity in terms of Agnes's union with her Mystic Spouse. He would describe the Judge of the world coming to her nuptial chamber and plunging into the immaculate purity of her bodily cavities. Fortunatus shuddered. He was a most verbal man. Words inflamed him as no reality un-filtered by them could do. His own flesh had begun to leap and heat. Better go.

"Sister," he called to the nun when he had put the garden wall safely between them, so that she could only see his head floating disembodied above its mossy coping, "pray for me."

She smiled with an openness which astounded him until he recalled that she, after all, knew nothing of his lust. She was separated from him now not only by the wall but by wreaths of vegetable fibre which criss-crossed between his eye and her creamy, sunlit habit, weaving her into the garden foliage, withdrawing her from his private speculation as a nymph or dryad might be with-drawn and dissolved into the pagan forests which spawned them. Aroused a second time by this memory of old verse about which he, like so many Christian poets, felt ambiguous—it represented civilization and pagan immorality—Fortunatus had the flashing certitude that he would never feel the same again about this woman.

"My homage and greetings to Mother Radegunda," he called.

"I'll tell her."

As he left, she was still smiling, still standing among the greenery, looking appealing, vulnerable, dangerously soft.

A.D. 552   "Soft! that child is soft all through!" complained Agnes's wet-nurse. "I worry about her," she told the other women in the work-rooms of the women's quarters. "She's my responsibility. Who else will look after her? The queen?" She made a sign to ward off the evil eye. "Look at her crying now!" she nodded at Agnes, "crying her eyes out for that boy who, when all's said and done, was only a German. Let the Germans kill each other I say!" The nurse lowered her voice. "And the Franks too," she whispered. "Let their blood manure the earth of Gaul. It's thirsty for it. Not for our tears. It's had too many of them! Come along now, Agnes." The woman walked over to where the little girl was sitting in the winter sunlight which fell like coins through the pitted marble window-panes. "Keep those eyes fresh for live young men. Let's go and have a bath in the stream since there are no heated baths in this place. We'd better go while the sun's high or we'll be chilled to the bone."

Agnes said she wanted to stay in the palace.

"Palace!" said the nurse with contempt. In the old days the slaves on Agnes's father's estate were better lodged, she could tell her that. All show here and no comfort! "What could you expect", again she lowered her voice, "of Franks?" Constantly moving from one ramshackle "palace" to the next! Why couldn't they stay put in one properly appointed villa? But no: they were like wild oxen! They ate the harvest on one royal estate then moved on to the next. Nomads! "Where's the German queen?" she wanted to know.

48

"Washing his body. Preparing it," said Agnes. She was playing with a piece of string, making knots and nets with her fingers and would not look up.

"People are whispering about her!" the nurse said. "She won't be in favour long. It's dangerous to be friendly with her now. Mark my words!"

Agnes plucked loops off the fingers of her left hand with those of her right, twisted, then plucked them back, making a kind of hammock. "She's leaving," she said. "She is going away to be a deaconess. She wants me to come with her."

"*What's that?*" The nurse grasped the child to her, anxiously putting a hand over her mouth. "Speak quietly. Your voice is ... So she's running away then? It's worse than I thought?"

Agnes continued weaving and reweaving her cat's cradle. It was a protection. A kind of screen against the alarm her nurse was so eager to pass on to her.

"Revenge", the nurse was saying in a misty whisper, "is a meal that's as tasty cold as hot. Tastier cold sometimes. And no man, especially a king, likes to be rejected. Clotair's arm is long. He can bide his time. You remember that, Agnes. When lightning strikes a tree the cattle that shelter under it get killed. Keep away from the queen. She's whetting a knife for her own throat. She's contemptuous of happiness," said the nurse, "and you, my pretty, are made for it!"

"That's what Chlodecharius said."

"He did?"

"Yes."

"Well, he knew more than I gave him credit for."

Agnes began to cry.

"No more of that now!"

The nurse was angry. Crying, she reminded, never mended broken pots. What was needed now was to get Agnes married. She had no kin to protect her. The sooner she found some the better. Mummolus, the king's major domus, a Gallo-Roman distantly connected with Agnes's dead father, would help. Once married, Agnes would be all right. Meanwhile she must wear her amber necklace because amber had magic properties and ... Agnes stopped listening. Yes, that would probably all happen. She would be married. She supposed. But her mind could not latch on to the idea. It remained dangerously empty and while it did in came the very image she had wanted to keep out: the pale, taut face of Chlodecharius. Very earnest, talking in nervous spurts, not laughing ever but touching her as cautiously as he had the dragon-fly he had caught one day as it hung, foolishly poised above a pond.

"Like a courtier," he had said. "It sees the dazzle, not the danger. I should talk! I should have left Clotair's court long ago!"

"Would you leave your sister?"

"If she won't come with me."

"She *is* married to the king."

"Do you know how many wives he's thrown out? What's sauce for the goose is sauce for the gander. I keep telling her. Sooner or later she'll fall out of favour and then ..." Chlodecharius stroked Agnes's hand.

"I wonder what will become of you, little Agnes? Will you marry one of Clotair's leudes? Some great strapping Frank with hair bursting out of his nose like a prawn's feelers?"

"No I won't," Agnes laughed and shivered.

"Ah, but my sister said 'no' too. Only when she ran away, Clotair came after her and got her back. It only made him madder for her. What does my sister teach you, Agnes?"

"Prayers. Latin."

"She's trying to turn you into a copy of herself. But you're not like her. She torments herself. Do you know why? Because she can't live as she wants to so she chooses to live worse. That way the choice at least is hers. It's pride. She's proud as the devil."

"What am I like?"

"Nothing yet. You're still at the tadpole stage. You might become a frog—or a butterfly. If you're nicely treated and petted and looked after then you'll be a very lovely butterfly. I wish I could take you with me to Constantinople and see it happen."

"Can't you?"

"No."

But on other days he had said he could and would and had described the city as full of gold and spices and strange, domed, majestic palaces. While he spoke he held her hand and Agnes had the feeling he was saying a long, slow goodbye. She was not sure she really liked being with Chlodecharius who was so gloomy and a little dull. She might have had more fun with someone jollier but then, there was no jollier person around. Besides, she was really a little young for courting so it was flattering to be kissed and told in his sad, renunciatory way, that she, unlike himself, was made for happiness. He sounded sure. "You're like water," he told her, "you'll flow where the stream-bed carries you. Radegunda and I are stubborn. Weapons jangled at our birth. Our stock is bloody. Did you know that her name means 'Council in Combat'? Clotair's means 'Famed in Battle'. Well-matched, you see."

There was always a vague apprehensiveness about him, a halo of blackness such as clings to things after one has been staring at the sun, but Agnes wasn't sure he hadn't manufactured it himself by his own wild glaring at doom. He puzzled her and she always left him with a feeling of relief, giddiness and a sense of something left unfinished. The way back to her own apartment led past the courtyard where boys from the palace school took their recreation and sometimes she paused there to chat and cast slanting glances around her. Experimenting. If Chlodecharius enjoyed her company, why didn't they? Usually, they laughed and told her she was too young for such games and that she should run back to her nurse. Once though— just a few days ago—one of them said:

"Well, let's see then, little flirt. Let's see just what you've

51

got there!" He drew her into a corner where he began to do things which made her kick and scream until he put his mouth over hers—his tasted horribly of stale wine—and held her thighs and arms. As this kept both his hands busy, he was unable to go on doing what he had been doing before, but Agnes's terror only increased as his body bore down on her with its menacing, uneven shape. She managed to bite his tongue, then his lip, tasted his blood and, as he wrenched away from her, screamed for Chlodecharius. Suddenly she was released. Chlodecharius was there and the two young men were fighting while the rest of the palace students stood around shouting and laying bets. The one Agnes had bitten was younger than Chlodecharius but bigger and much tougher. Chlode-charius took a bad beating. At the end of the fight he had to be taken to Fridovigia who applied poultices and gave him a specific against headaches consisting of wine in which she had dissolved eleven grains of pepper and several crushed worms.

"No need to bleed him. He's done that himself."

It was two nights later that he came to Agnes's bed. Although it was dark she recognized his step and was neither surprised by his coming nor by the lurching hesitancy of his gait. If Chlodecharius came at all it would be hesitantly. She whispered his name to encourage him and show that she was neither asleep nor afraid.

"Ag ... nes!"

"Yes? .. What is it?"

He stood swaying by the edge of her bed then lowered his weight heavily on to it and rolled bumpily towards her.

"Are you all right, Chlodecharius?"

He was heavy. Hoping to shift some of his weight, she got her arms around him. Clasping him, she felt one of her palms filled by a hard smooth protrusion. It took her several moments to realize what it was.

"Listen!" Agnes's nurse was shaking her. "You're contaminated too! The king doesn't like to be blamed. You're the one who went rushing about shouting the news

52

so the death couldn't be passed off as natural."

"A knife," said Agnes glassily, "it was a knife!"

People had said—even to her face—that she had now been 'marked for life' as a bad day is marked by a black stone. She didn't feel marked, not connected at all really to the dead man. People thought he had been her lover but he hadn't been.

"How could he?" Fridovigia had shouted, raging against the gossips, shooing them away. "She's a child. Leave her alone. She's not eleven yet," Fridovigia had lied, making her sign against the evil eye. "She's eight years old, young, young, just grown quickly, that's all."

"And don't you cry", she said to Agnes now, "too much at his funeral. Don't cry at all." She would have shooed his memory out of Agnes's head.

In songs sung by the royal harpist, girls' hearts stopped at the same moment as their lovers' even when those lovers died in distant battles. Death found a quick and parallel path in each love-twinned body. But Fridovigia's grasp on reality was clearly superior to the harpist's. Agnes felt nothing at all. Like a drawing on sand rubbed out by the tide, like writing on a scraped tablet, Chlodecharius's memory was already almost gone. Agnes, faced by the insignificance of any—and so of her own—life, again began to cry.

Her nurse could have slapped her.

"Now why?" she asked furiously. "Why?"

"Because I *didn't* love him. Nobody did."

"What rubbish! What do you know? His sister did, didn't she? If she's capable of love. That sort turn their eyes to heaven and their thoughts to themselves. You'd do well to do the same. I might as well save my breath to cool my porridge. Do you want to join him in the grave?"

"No."

"Well then?"

They'd be digging it now. Sliding the spade in. Cutting sods. Tug of roots yielding as tiny connecting filaments snapped first serially, then all at once. Smell of pollen

53

and rank greenery when she and Chlodecharius met in hideouts in the woods. The undergrowth was so thick that once Clotair's hunt had ridden by without seeing them and another time a boar sow with her litter of striped cream-and-brown cubs passed so close that they could have put out a hand and caught one.

"Why doesn't she smell us?"

"We smell of the forest," he told her. "Earthy."

Would his wraith haunt her now, returning in reproach with earthy smells, mouth clenched on the coin which must be placed in it before burial to pay his passage over death's river? But why her? Was it her fault? She shrugged, intrigued yet impatient at her life's thread having thickened so interestingly before she was twelve.

"Listen," said her nurse.

Agnes put her fists over her eyeballs and rubbed them in a child's gesture. "Oh, nurse," she complained in a high babyish voice, "I'm so tired, you can't imagine. So ti-ired. I want to sleep."

It had been dark by the early afternoon and now, hours later, the terracotta oil lamps disposed around Radegunda's bedroom had begun to smell and smoke. A servant came in offering to pinch off the burnt ends of the papyrus wicks, but the queen sent him away. Smoke wreaths snaked through the air and the light solidified their outline, hardening them into ropes and chains. The room was choked with coffers, for Radegunda's possessions had been moved in from the marriage chamber where Clotair now slept alone.

"Not", said his queen harshly, "that I expect that to last more than a night or so."

Most of the coffers were open and the gleam of gilt embroidery and jewels cut like knife-tips through the smoke. The bed had been piled with tunics, mantles, sleeves, head-veils, silk bonnets and a variety of other garments. Coloured motifs—losanges, crosses—caught the light, floating like bright geometric fish on a dark

54

underlying sea of fabric. Stools and benches bore translucent scent-bottles of glass and alabaster.

"I shall take everything," said Radegunda. "Why should I go naked to my new Spouse? It will be my dowry and I shall give it to the Church."

She walked briskly about the room, selecting and rejecting garments, talking excitedly. Occasionally, she shook out a long rippling length of silk or linen which hung like a memory in the firelight, then was folded away. A pearl-studded belt was uncoiled then rolled tightly up again with a clap.

Agnes sat on the small stool used for climbing on to the bed—it was the only one unencumbered—stared at the jewels, blinked in the smoke and listened. The queen had been talking since their return from the funeral. Occasionally she came over to Agnes, bent towards her and stared hard into her eyes. Her own were blue and bright like the paste inlay in her *cloisonné* jewel-box:

"I hope", said she, "you are making a true sacrifice. I would not want you to come with me because you were afraid to stay at court. You must come because you want to make a gift of your life to God."

Agnes did not reply.

"You may feel regrets", Radegunda told her, "now and later. They do not matter. What concerns me is the purity of your intention."

"My nurse, Fridovigia, says ..."

"Take no notice of what she says. She's a worldly woman."

"She will come," Agnes said, "if I do."

"If?"

Agnes scraped her sandal against the side of her stool. She leaned backwards and felt her shoulders sink into the feather tick behind. She wriggled back into its embrace, feeling it press forward around her like a nest. She would have liked to stay there forever.

"You *are* coming?" harried the queen.

Agnes said something about Chlodecharius but Radegunda was not deviated.

"He is with God," she said. "We must be concerned now for ourselves. Death is the rule of this world. His was not exceptional. If you stay here you must expect to see murders. The manner of this one makes me believe God has special plans for you. He sent you a dying lover to point the way the flesh must go. The flesh, Agnes, is future carrion. If you stay, you will begin to crave its enjoyment with another man. You will marry. Your nurse is probably planning a marriage already."

"Yes."

"Ah! And is that what you want?"

"No."

Radegunda looked pleased. "I had feared you might hope for a family. Are you sure you don't? A family . . ."

Could not, Agnes decided, be counted on. People left you. Radegunda was leaving. Chlodecharius had and, before that, her parents dead so long ago that she could remember neither them nor the villa they had lived in except through Fridovigia's opulent recollections: glimpses of malachite and porphyry glimmering and darkening like weed in the wall of a wave. Drowned vistas, they dissolved under scrutiny like reflections on water.

"It's over," Agnes had finally shouted at her that morning. "Can't you see! They're dead!"

Fridovigia wanted it all to begin again: ceremonies, painted rooms, a husband for Agnes who would provide babies and a household of solid figures. In Agnes's eyeview the figures danced impishly away. The only one to be truly counted on was Fridovigia herself. And, because she could be counted on, there was no need to give in to her. Radegunda was far less reliable.

"Please don't go away, Radegunda," Agnes begged. "Don't you leave me too. I love you, Radegunda!"

"That mustn't be your motive. I am casting off all human affections. If you come with me as my sister in God I will love you accordingly. Will you?"

Love? Yes. "But", said Agnes, "is it forever?"

"Would you play the harlot with God. Give him the gift of yourself then take it back?"

The queen was excited, looked for an excitement to match her own in the little girl. But Agnes resisted. When she was with Radegunda she saw her, some of the time, with Fridovigia's sardonic eye. When away from her she missed her tenseness, the yearnings which burned in her—and decided she could not let her go. Instinctively, she bargained, held back.

"Must I decide now?"

"Yes. I leave tomorrow. We will need the night to pack. You may think", persuaded Radegunda, "that your regret for the world means you should not make this leap. But without regret there would be no sacrifice. It is the nerve and core of it. I feel none and so my home-coming will be less pleasing to God than your sacrifice. Come over here, Agnes and sit with me." Radegunda swept a row of gold ornaments off a bench. "You are nervous," she smoothed Agnes's hair which the girl had been biting and twisting through her fingers. "Listen, I know you are weak. It's because I know it that I want to spare you the disappointments you'd meet if you stayed in the world. It is because I know them that I want you to escape them. Can't you let me save you, Agnes?" The queen's tone was tender, coaxing. She ran her splayed fingers gravely down the girl's face and neck, then past her chest, waist, knees, right down to her sandals which were muddy. In embarrassment Agnes caught the hand. "Now," said Radegunda, "while you are young and almost unhurt, fresh, now is the time to give yourself to God. Once you've taken the decision you'll never have to think again. You'll find peace."

Agnes listened. The voice was mesmeric and very convinced. It talked of love, a haven, gentleness and how Agnes needed to feel secure. The words were comforting, persuasive. "God," said Radegunda and the word, Agnes could tell, meant something violent and personal and satisfying to Radegunda. At the same time it was very

57

vague, a chameleon word which sometimes meant 'me'—
as in "give yourself to God, love God"—and sometimes
very elusive matters indeed.

"You are beautiful, Radegunda!"

"Yes!" Radegunda touched her own body quickly,
fingers light and splayed, skimming it in the same gesture
which she had used on Agnes's. "I am astonished to find
my flesh still fresh. When I am not looking at it I imagine
it rotting off my bones like the flesh of game which has
been hung too long in kitchens. It has been too long in
human embraces. When I come from the bath I am
tempted to go to the stables and roll my body in the dung.
Its cleanness is so illusory."

"Radegunda, don't be unhappy! I'll do whatever you
want."

Radegunda touched her cheek to Agnes's. "My doe,
my frail plant! All I want", she whispered, "is to protect
you. Can you trust me?"

"Oh, yes." Caught up now in a thrilling fellowship.

The queen stood up. Other women must be invited into
it, she declared. "Think how many are sacrificed to the
brutish lusts of men! You", she promised, "will be our
first abbess when we found the convent I am planning.
It may not be for some years, so you will be older but
still pure. You, my dove, will have made the whole sacrifice.
You will have come unsullied to Christ's love so it is
only fair that on earth as in heaven your place should be
above my own!"

Agnes jerked her hand from the queen's. "I don't
want to, Radegunda. I spoke too quickly. I'm sorry."

The queen chuckled. She lifted her face to the ceiling,
flinging up her chin so that all Agnes could see from below
was the white trumpet of her neck rising in the lamplight
like the corolla of a St. Joseph's lily. "You are afraid,"
cried the queen. "You are beset by regrets and doubts!"

"Yes, yes I am."

"Don't you see?" Radegunda fixed Agnes with an
ecstatic eye, "don't you see that that proves you have

58

chosen the noblest and bravest course? Your doubts come from the prince of this world," said Radegunda, "the devil, Agnes. It is when he is nearest defeat that he makes his strongest assault on God's chosen ones! You *will* have regrets, but you must *not* look behind you. What lies behind? Nature. Natural love and that, I don't have to remind you, is cursed by the curse God put on our first parents. Sexual love is linked with death. The dying creature leaves the product of its sexual couplings to take its place and so the race is continued—but why should it be, Agnes?"

"There is . . . happiness, Radegunda. People are happy sometimes!"

Agnes felt the weakness of her response, feeling the words which the queen had released into the air hanging still just beyond earshot. Their energy reverberated. Their conviction. They had come at her like swarms of palpable things, like insects perhaps, projectiles or small, fierce birds. She had paid only vague attention to their meaning—familiar, heard before—but an animal pulse in her quickened to the feeling behind them registering it as sustained and hard to resist. She could sense it building up in the small room, accumulating and surging in a wave destined to carry her off. The queen was flushed. She held her body tautly as though seeking to stretch and dip into herself to find stored inner powers. Agnes felt she was being treated to a display worthy of a larger audience, as though the queen had been trying out a new persona and Agnes had happened to be there and to see. But no: it was not as deliberate as that. Radegunda was driven, illumined by forces which Agnes could only know through her and at second hand. Maybe God spoke through her?

Radegunda was speaking again but more gently now. "Let us pray for guidance, child." She drew the girl towards a jewelled reliquary in a corner of the room.

Standing in front of it, their hands stretched forward in the old Roman way, they prayed.

59

Chapter Four

Help!
Daniel whom the Lord saved from lions, save me!
Hilary and Martin make haste to succour me. May the
Cherubim, Seraphim, Thrones ... No, no it's all right.
I'm awake! Intact. I think? Yes. Thank God, Hilary,
etcetera.

I wasn't sure. For moments there it seemed so real!
Someone was shoving me into a pit of adders. I could feel
the pain and when I woke up there *was* a hiss! It's the
damp wood smouldering in my fire! Cold! God, and I've
got an ague! It's these Gaulish winters. It was cold in
my dream and it still is! The window of course. Pitted
panes are so impractical in this climate. I'll shove a cloth
over it.

Dreams are omens. One should take notice. Who was
shoving me into that pit? A patron? Yes, some patronly
figure: impressive, faceless, long-haired. A king then?
Or a woman? Who? Oh, rubbish. It was just a hodgepodge
of memories turned turtle. After all, when I first came to
Gaul I was often cold. I was so poor I had, as the saying
goes, to put one hand in front and one behind to hide my
shame. A draughty costume! Patrons clothed me then.
The mind is like the water-mill the monks at St. Mary's
Outside the Walls have set up to grind their corn. It
churns things about. I was probably thinking of patronage
before I dropped off. Why not? I live on it—and *that*
bread has choked many. To look no further, think of poor
Boethius executed on his patron's whim! I, born six
years later in the same province, was brought up on the
tale. Our grandchildren will be. It gives off a shock. If
that could happen to a man of consular rank, what security

is there for the rest of us? Hmm? Maybe there is an omen there after all? *My* patrons are less civilized than King Theodoric and wit's a tricky commodity when patrons are barbarians. Fear the Franks, Fortunatus, even when they bear gifts. Oh, I do. I do. Ours is the age of suspicion which is probably no bad thing. Our ancestors, we are told, did not fear enough. Pleasure they lived for: sweet juice clotting on the burst plum. They even took a sick pleasure in their own end. What can all that have been like? I can't enjoy pleasure at first hand at all. Only through books. Except for food of course—but that's an elementary pleasure: the ABC of the flesh. A major assault on flesh's citadel frightens me. I don't think I'm unique. Fear nowadays lodges in the seat of pagan immortality: between the legs. I mean it does in men like myself, men with a sense of the past. Not in Franks who couple like aurochs, mindlessly. Do I envy them? "The rose", says Ausonius, "lives on in the ages of her seed." A sad, cyclic sort of immortality. As you spill your seed you spill some of yourself. You embrace death, burying yourself. "The roses at their birth consent." To die. A freezing thought. But what Frank thinks like that or thinks at all? He just spills, tanks up, respills—and the future will indeed belong to his seed. To the seed of the worst Franks too since the best go into monasteries. God I wish I could sleep at night. There's another animal function denied to me. Magpie mind, be quiet. It won't. I did make love once and wish I hadn't. Do I feel remorse or just regret? Hard to tell. I was punished so fast. God sent me a sign that this was not the path he had picked for me. Fortunatus was not meant to go gathering rosebuds while the flower and his youth were fresh. Ausonius again. He's a bad influence. Hardly a Christian at all. If I could locate the poison he has injected into my mind, I would have it sucked out by leeches. I would have a Syrian surgeon remove it. If thine eye offend thee cut it out. Mine inner eye offends me. I am half a pagan. It comes from education which is insidious as St. Jerome knew. He loved the old books and feared them.

Sooner or later I suppose I shall take orders and be safe. Is compromise so very despicable?

I almost took them when I was twenty. Because of the girl, I didn't. I suppose it was because of her? Or was it? I'll have to face that memory or it will go on tormenting me all night, buzzing like a fly on the edge of my mind. All right then: I was younger than twenty, actually, eighteen and backward in worldly matters, a student at Ravenna school. Most of us were vaguely intending to be priests. It *is* the obvious career. More or less what the civil service used to be. Celibacy was just beginning to be strictly imposed on clerics and the old practice of keeping one's wife on as housekeeper had been banned. The change-over was not smooth. A few old priests tried to cheat. There were scandals and endless talk, especially among students. Some of my comrades said it was meaningless to give up something without knowing what it was. One fellow called Clement, a lively, irreverent boy from Milan, said that no one had the right to dedicate an imperfect instrument to the service of God and better test its worthiness first. The implication was that, for all our talk, we were terrified of women. We were.

"Shall we organize a trial?" Clement proposed one evening. "I think in all honesty you owe it to God and yourselves to find out more about yourselves. The priesthood is for men sound of wind and limb—so what about that limb? The most important of all. I can promise you that trying it on a woman is not at all the same thing as auto-stimulation!" No castrate, he reminded us, could be a cleric.

This dig was offensive to those of us who came from genuinely religious homes and were struggling with the uncertain leanings of our flesh. Someone asked him did he receive money for drumming up business for local pimps. He wasn't in the least upset.

"What's it to you?" he asked. "Were you thinking of offering your sister?"

62

There was a fight. I moved away but Clement's suggestion kept echoing in my head. I am a man whose impulses get filtered through the mind and can there develop a dangerous strain. I fantasize, I debate. In the moral maze which I construct over weeks of dither, my original appetite battens like the Minotaur, takes on quirks and intensity until finally it threatens to burst out with the urgency of a primeval need. In this case it did. I went to a brothel.

I knew where the brothels were. Everyone does. They are tolerated, even approved by the Church since, like sewers, they concentrate the filth and make it easier to keep the rest of the city clean. If there were no sewers our streets would be smeared with excrement. If there were no brothels, decent women would be in constant danger of being assaulted by sex-starved soldiers and other riffraff.

So in I went. I asked for a girl and she took me past a curtain to a cubicle almost entirely occupied by a bed. She was wearing some loose garment which she simply pulled open. I fancied she was looking at me with the same expression that Clement had: mocking me. Even her nipples looked like pursed mouths and mocked me. My senses were in a turmoil. I could hardly see. My ears were drumming and the humours were storming through my body. I grabbed her to me—and realized that for almost the first time in days I was not erect. She coaxed me back to the required state by various loathsome arts. I didn't loathe them then but their images return to shame me. I coupled with her. I slaked my lust. I—yes, I was so enthralled by her, so in *thrall*, that I was talking to her, promising to come again and ask for her by name, I was even—was I?—yes, I was actually quoting a poem to her by Sidonius or someone when the screaming began. It was horrifying. It reminded me of the screams of a butchered pig and seemed to come from the next cubicle. Actually, it was three rooms off. The girl jumped up.

"Oh God," she said. What did *she* know of God? I

63

was offended at her using his name. "Oh God, she's dying. It's Celia." She pulled on her garment as fast as she had whipped it off. "Wait," she told me and left.

I had no intention of waiting. Nausea was already rising in me. *Post coitum*, etc. and, besides, that screaming reminded one harrowingly of the human condition and the fact that we are all dust. I had been embracing dust, lavishing sentiment on it. I wanted to get home and wash.

I had just managed to find my clothes—the girl had undressed me, throwing them in various directions—and was on the point of leaving when she came back, pushing the curtain aside and caught me by the arm.

"She's dying. Do you know anything of medicine? You're a student, you must! Come."

"I'm a ..." I wanted to say "a student of theology", but the ridiculousness, the blasphemy of such an avowal in such a place restrained me. "I know nothing about medicine. Let me go."

But she took no notice. "Well, someone has to help," she said. "The midwife's drunk. Out cold and the physician won't come. Oh holy angels, help her! She's having an abortion but it's gone wrong!"

I slapped the girl's mouth. "Blasphemy!" I shouted.

The girl touched her mouth in surprise. It was bruised. She was, I noticed now, only about fourteen: a child.

"You're asking the holy angels", I explained, for she clearly didn't understand, "to help you commit a sin."

But as well tell that to a calf or a puppy dog. The girl crouched and began to embrace my knees. She was whimpering. I pulled her up. "Please," she was begging hysterically, "*please* help my sister." She had managed to pull me down a corridor and now pointed to a curtain like the one in front of her own cubicle. The screams were coming from behind it. I pulled it aside and was faced by the open mouth of a woman's matrix. For a moment I had the delusion that *it* was screaming at me. Then I saw the rest of the body and its head. The face was pale, straining and wet with sweat. The mouth was gagged but the gag had

64

come loose and the screams were coming past it with the regularity of a baby's. A pot of herbs were placed on a brazier and the steam from it had filled the room and begun to condense and rain down in drops from the ceiling. The smell of mallows and fenugreek was over-powering. The girl's ankles had been strapped to her thighs and a stout cloth passed across her chest and under her arms to bind her firmly to the bed. Bundles of faggots had been placed under the bedposts.

The first girl—I had not actually learned her name—said "The abortion's gone wrong. There's an impediment. It won't come. Help me shake her. Take hold of the foot of the bed and I'll take the top."

She bent down and actually managed to raise the bed on which her sister was strapped. She was strong. Probably when she wasn't working as a whore she had to do heavy jobs. Most of those girls are slaves. I stared at her.

"Help me!"

"Are you sure this is the thing to do?"

"Yes. They gave her sneezing powders and that didn't work. Then they tried fomentations. Then they shook the bed. Now we must try again."

Mechanically—my mind was stunned—I did what she said. We raised the bed several times and brought it down sharply. The faggots broke its fall. We did this about eight or ten times. Suddenly the sick girl gave a nerve-shattering shriek and fell silent. Her sister ran round the bed. I didn't look at what she was doing. She was in my line of vision and anyway I was suffering from nausea. I was suffering too from shame for, after all, what I had been doing not ten minutes before might well, in a few months' time, produce just such another scene as this one. I began to imagine I had been responsible for what was happening to Celia. The two girls fused in my mind and when the girl—my girl—stepped away from the bed holding a basin full of blood I fainted.

When I recovered I was in another room. A man was holding some sort of acid to my nose. He turned out to be the brothel-keeper, a Greek and very anxious that I should not report what I had seen. It was not, he assured me, illegal—a lie—but would not be good for business either. I could have my money back and was welcome to come again any time I liked. He apologized for the incident. But why mention it to anyone? People came here for a bit of fun, after all, not for ...

"What happened to the girl?" I asked.

"Oh, she's all right. They're both all right. They'll be dancing tomorrow. We can't allow them to have babies, naturally. We're quite used to this sort of thing. She's had the best of care. The midwife had just stepped out for a minute but she's back now. Everything is all right. Really. Would you like a glass of honeyed wine?"

I refused with courtesy. Curtly, however, and left. *He* was being coherent. For what had I come to his place if not in search of women and wine? How could I blame him? That God blamed *me* was clear from what I had found there, and from the memories which haunt me and won't be conjured away. They have kept me from sleeping again with women, contaminating their beauty for me with an awareness of what lies beneath the thin white veil of their skin.

A week later I picked a fight with Clement and gave him a knocking about. He must have wondered why. It was unworthy and ineffective. A persistent disquiet has stayed with me since and I cannot diagnose it. Almost as though I could not accept the human condition—which is in itself an act of blasphemy. We are fallen and imperfect. That's dogma. Our society, it follows, must be imperfect too. God's kingdom is not of this world.

And Ausonius's roses? Did he know what the birth and death he so blithely invoked smell like? That smell of blood, mallows and fenugreek is in my nostrils now. Well, perhaps I lack liver.

Cold again. Poke up the fire. If only I were at Gogo's villa now or at Duke Lupus's where the heat is diffuse, unlike my fire which burns my knees while my backside freezes. Those Gallo-Romans know how to live! I couldn't believe it when I came on my first Gallo-Roman villa. Even now something weeps in me when I see one of those porticoed façades. How long can they last? Yet the owners go on playing chess and backgammon and laying out lawns and pruning vines. Just as though this were still the Roman diocese of Gaul. I suppose there is something a touch deliberate, theatrical even about Lupus's ease. He gives me too many presents for one thing. His grandfather would not have extended such a welcome to poets. There were more around.

Am I the last?

What a responsibility? Should I flame? Grow incandescent? Overblow like a ripe rose reddening the earth? Die—when I do—in a spasm of passion or smoulder wetly like this wet-peat age?

If Radegunda heard me! "Pagan posturings!" she would say.

I should work on my acrostic: nothing pagan about that. It's the subtlest I've devised and will consist of four holy proverbs—which should please her—placed two aslant, one vertically and one athwart to form two superimposed crosses so cunningly concealed in a poem that they might pass unperceived if not picked out in coloured inks. That'll impress the patrons! "An astounding piece of work, Fortunatus! Unique. The ancients themselves never ..." "Oh spare my blushes, my lord bishop," (or duke? Why not send it to Lupus? Or the kings?) "it is a trifle, merely a token of my profound and heartfelt etcetera. The cross, they say, is the ladder to heaven and so I have sent your lordship (or majesty) two. Not that your lordship needs ..." Flourish and reflourish. Meanwhile my fingers are frozen. Skin sticking to the pen. Rub. Shake. Swing. Pull. Have a drink of mulled wine. Oh these lonely, lonely nights! To think I was once gregarious! *In taberna quando sumus*. I had, have, a nice voice. But who would sing alone? Alone, all alone and with enough lamp-oil to see the night through. Few men around here can afford that—but then

67

few suffer from insomnia. Does that make me Fortunatus or infortunatus? Old question. Radegunda too is probably awake but praying—and so not alone. I perhaps should pray but am always afraid of boring God. "Arrogance," says Radegunda. "Humility," say I but acknowledge that the boundary-line is thin. "Words don't matter," she says and I disagree. For me words matter more than anything. I cannot cope with what cannot be put into words. Like her experiences. Her trances which she describes as "beyond words". But can anything human be "beyond words"? "Yes," she says and to some extent I believe her. I believe she does come in contact with a life source, the godhead perhaps, anyway a level of reality unreached by the rest of us and which she can't describe. What I cannot accept is that *I*, with her help, may not manage eventually to grasp and describe it. I harry her, pressing for precision about these forays, these edgings into the un-definable. I wait. I am like a cartographer questioning some sun-stunned mariner who has been lost off the map, trying to chart the contents of a raving mind, appalled but stimulated by the news that there are wastes about which *nothing is known* — in cartographer's terms — and that *I* may be the one to draw the first map. She needs me to write her life. I shall ensure that when it is finished she will be more revered than any saint who has not had the benefit of my promotion. Careless of the world's opinion, she won't appreciate this. Others will: my patrons and perhaps even God.

I knew within an hour of meeting her that I was meant to stay and be her biographer. That was two years ago. There were practical reasons too but they were merely clues to a destiny I had already somehow divined. I told her and she offered me this house. "Destiny" was the word to sway her. Not my sort of word at all. As though it had been put into my mouth. Everything did seem to happen without my taking much initiative. It wasn't even my own idea to come here. It was King Chilperic's, her stepson. Odd go-between!

He's a truly nasty piece of goods, a memorable monster: epic, ruthless and, when I first saw him, visibly bloody. His finger-nails were packed with it. A smear was drying on his beard. He'd been hunting and his appearance startled me into a Virgilian quotation about black and flowing gore—not the most tactful greeting to a multiple murderer. As soon as I'd said the words I wished I'd swallowed them. But he was pleased and the quote—a well-worn one from a *florilegium* of pagan writings for Christian readers—struck the court as betokening astonishing learning on my part.

"We Franks", he told me, "are heirs to the whole Gallo-Roman system and that includes poetry. I'm a bit of a poet myself but I don't delude myself as to my talents. Latin isn't my first language. Now you are a godsend. Ravenna's loss will be Soisson's gain. Write me an ode."

He gave me a purse of gold *solidi* and I wrote an ode in praise of all the qualities it might have been appropriate for him to possess. He was flattered but possibly bored by such a list of—even fictional—virtues.

"I think you should meet my stepmother," he told me. "An extraordinary woman. Very holy. You'll have to go to Poitiers. I'll give you an escort. Our roads, unfortunately, are unsafe. One can't see to everything at once. We are plagued by civil wars. My brothers are most rapacious. I sometimes wish my father had strangled them at birth. He killed his nephews so as to prevent civil war in his own time but had no thought for mine. Unforesighted. But, as you know, Rome had a lot of civil war so we needn't feel ashamed."

I accepted the escort. I was coming as far as Tours anyhow where I had vowed to visit St. Martin's shrine to thank the saint for curing a bad case of ophthalmia which at one point had looked like costing me my eye. Poitiers was close. The escort would be useful. Under the protection of the kingdom's chief murderer, I would be safe from the knives of lesser ones. I was learning how Gaul is governed. Even disorder has its order—the only one future generations may know. Mine is perhaps uniquely cursed in that it retains a memory of true, institutional order, without any hope of its revival. Like the Garden of Eden, order was and was taken away: a sour and godly trick. All gone now. Illiteracy obliterates memory. The last image of the Roman experience survives in the language— Latin—and even that is crumbling like a weedy aqueduct, gnawed at by epidemics of prepositions which subvert its syntax as termites do timber. *I* root them out of any text I can, just as I would destroy the termites.

Another glass of wine. It's sweet, warm and dulls the devils of the mind. Odd: warmth and sweetness, the most scarce of all sensations in a Gaulish winter are the very ones God chooses for reaching Radegunda. When she has fasted for days she tastes honey on her tongue and when she has been kneeling on cold flags gets a feeling of heat about the heart. Or are these lazy metaphors? I'd like to lick her tongue with mine. Find out what she means by "a taste of honey". In the gospels God is the Word but comes to her as a sensation. Another sign that language is collapsing. I dedicate my middle age to shoring it up. My letters to our half-literate bishops are lessons. I send them flattery in careful prose, hoping that when they've sucked out its sweetness, some sense of its form may stick in their skulls. "Gaul", I wrote to Bishop Felix of Nantes, "need never envy the Orient the rays of the rising sun since she is illumined by the rays of your glory..." Extravagant? Yes, but his schemes for irrigation and land-reclamation *are* impressive. "Pray make of my unworthy limbs a footstool", I begged Bishop Martin with rather less cause, "and lean your weight on my chest." He sent me some excellent wine and papyrus in exchange. Several patrons are better than one, which is another reason why I didn't stay with Chilperic but came all the way across Gaul to here, rattling my bones on a wooden waggon. A ghastly journey: I saw ditches rank with filth, carcasses of animals in various stages of decomposition, abandoned infants, beggars dead from exposure, pagan

70

shrines surrounded by every sort of idolatrous rubbish including some stinking horses' heads set on poles and picked at by daws. Water was suspect, food inedible and I was obliged to wear three different relics to keep off disease. At the inns we heard stories of ritual cannibalism. The economy seemed to have broken down. Murrain was widespread—hence the dead cows—and cured by rubbing oil stolen from church lamps on the cattle's heads. For poverty there was no cure. Life seemed an increasingly poor gift.

At one point while clip-clopping down that knobbly spinal column which is the Roman road from Orléans, I began to hallucinate from fatigue and the flow of tree trunks dazzled and confused my eye like the riffled pages of a book. The sun dissolved in a brownish mist pierced by rays which seemed to assemble with the trees in shapes of giant weaponry, flying ships, Babylonian towers innumerable storeys high. I had a sensation of speed, light, a scission of sensibility and—most horrifyingly—of impermanence. It was a vision of hell, I decided, as the shapes changed, reshaped and changed again. Change and impermanence are, after all, the very properties of the devil.

For the last two days of my journey I was raving with fever. I arrived—I've been told since—pale as a parsnip and gaunt as a cormorant at Radegunda's door. Certainly I was in a receptive state. She fed me and flattered me, telling me how she had always preferred poets to all other guests when she was still King Clotair's wife.

"Not that any who came were of *your* stature!"

Chilperic's letter—out of vanity?—had promoted me.

She confessed she wrote verse herself. A mania, I decided. First Chilperic, now his stepmother. Well, maybe it was their way of seeking order. But when she showed me the convent, I saw she had managed to create order in practice. Its perfection actually pained me. It was so calm, so pleasantly predictable, the sort of haven in which I would have dreamed, if my dreams had been good ones, of living. The nuns wear white robes and clogs, eat sparingly so as to keep down the passions of the flesh, drink watered wine and perry. Everyone helps with the housework. She herself, she told me, worked in the kitchen garden. She was not the abbess. Agnes was, her spiritual daughter. A pretty young nun came in: Agnes, asked about my journey and my comfort, then left. A drift of some fragrant herb stayed behind. I was still faintly feverish with images of that foul rattle-bone journey still humped in my inner eye: a mental stew of bad memories. One: vomiting bad food from some inn into a ditch whose porridgy waters suddenly confronted me with an eye, a single one only a hand's span away from my vomiting face. I had to finish then, seized by convulsions, hold on to a bush to keep from falling in. When I stood up it was still there, nakedly unlidded, staring at me. Too big to be human. A horse's, perhaps, which someone had gouged out for some whim or pagan practice? Wiping my mouth with a dockleaf, I stumbled back to my waggon. I suppose there was nothing to it really. A horse's eye? But it kept returning, suspended in front of my own, enlarged, staring at me: the anthropomorphic eye of Savage Gaul. Pagans, I remembered hearing, had been buried with their horses. King Clovis's father had. Why? I asked my escort but they shrugged. Said *they* were Christians, didn't know, spat, mumbled. Their Latin was primitive. One said something in German dialect and the rest laughed.

Suddenly—from the refuge of the convent—going back with those men was horrible to me. I didn't want to spend another night in their company or on those mangling roads.

"This," Radegunda was saying, "is our *hortus,* our kitchen-garden. We have laid it out on the model of a Roman villa's. I think we have every plant here that you would find there. This is where *I* work so you must allow me to be a little vain."

She showed me myrtle, wallflower, lupins, tansy, fennel, dill, burdock, mint, chervil, spurge and a hundred other plants. The paths were straight and weeded, the stone benches clean. A nun brought honey-cakes and perry. Through a window I could hear a psalm. When it stopped I could sense feminine presences moving somewhere out of sight in silent conformity to some unchanging time-table.

"This", I told the nun, "is a poem you have created here. It scans beautifully."

She had been joking with me before, playing the hostess as she likes to do. She can often be silly. It is a release, I think, a relief after the concentration of prayer. Now she gave me a sober look from those odd German eyes of hers which are often unfocused as though the focus were somewhere beyond reach. I already knew she saw visions. I had heard stories about her at court and along the way in unreliable inns where they talk with equal credulity about *strygae* whose powers can only be destroyed if one eats their hearts and about miraculous cures effected by saints. I must say I had been repelled and had not really been looking forward to meeting Radegunda. But there is nothing of the village freak in her. She has a German intensity but is as cultivated as a Roman matron. Only that curious blue of her eyes, reflected in the hollows of her cheeks and brimming in the shadows thrown by her veil, distinguished her from one. I was reminded of those heretics who believed that light was gathered in the bodies of saintly people whose virtue managed slowly to eliminate all the darkness within them until, ultimately, they rejoined a realm of pure primeval felicity and light. There is a transparency about Radegunda. Bluish veins show through her skin and one could see, looking at her, how the heresy might persuade.

"This is an image of heaven," I told her.

"How do you imagine heaven?"

"As ordered, unchanging. Like your convent."

"Do you think it wrong to withdraw and seek one's own salvation?"

I said I didn't see how it could be, she that she had

73

often worried about this. Before founding the convent she had run an alms-house and a hospital.

"But I gave up. I decided the good we could do was hopelessly limited. How could it be just to cure one sick person and refuse hundreds? Yet that was what we had constantly to do. It made us angry. It made us unable to pray. Then, too, I decided that since men's bodies live only a short time and their souls forever, I would do better to pray for their souls than to bring their bodies a wretched and partial help. Sometimes I think this world is hell. I would believe it but have been told it is a heresy."

There was a coherence about her which made me aware of how hesitant and diffuse my own life was. She began to talk about the impermanence of matter—hardly a discovery but this fact was so physically real to her that it became so to me. Radegunda is the most physically compelling person I have met. When she picks a flower as she did next—some blue flower, a large luscious thing with a golden centre—and says "This flower will fade," it begins to wilt. Suggestion? Hypnotism? Miracle? I don't know. I *saw* the great soft, almost animal thing— it had furry purple protuberances like a hound's dewlaps— shrivel and dry.

"Look," she said. "I could hate beauty. It is a mockery, a comforting lie told to a sick man since it will wither in his hands. It is like the grain we mix with poison to kill slugs. I would truly hate it if I did not see it as as an image of permanent beauty. If I didn't see this flower as a reflection of a heavenly flower, I would crush it."

Her voice was cold, almost bitter. The shadows in her face were the colour of the flower. Her own beauty was at that most poignant stage: almost gone, returning at brief moments to flood and replump her face. Like an after-image. A turn of her head and it had disappeared. It was surely growing rarer in its returns. I looked at the flower. Had she been vain? Her intensity had worn out her body before its time.

"Have you", I risked, "no appetites?"

74

"They are my torments. I stifle them. I delight in tormenting them as they would me. They come from the devil." She laughed. She could have been describing a sport.

"Don't you enjoy life at all?"

"Oh, indeed. This life is a trial. One must face one's trial with gallantry. Here we live our life gaily but without becoming attached to it. The balance is delicate."

She gave me a great foaming splash of smile, spontaneous and humourless. I looked at her suspiciously.

"Gaily? Is the convent gay?"

"Very. Stay with us and you'll see. My nuns are my plants. I delight in their growth. When our community expands, I am almost sorry since it means we know each other less well. But it is a sign of our success. And we can't refuse women who need to come here. You know what dangers women face in Gaul today! I don't mean sin!" A shrewd narrowing of the lips. "One can commit that in a convent. I mean quite brutal dangers."

I forget the rest. She has made this speech so often since, I may even be remembering things she said some other time to a new batch of novices or to some visitor. Radegunda is a balanced person. Her life is neatly divided into the mundane and the transcendent. Mine is not. Listening to her I found her rejections of the body had the effect of conjuring it up for me in its quintessential fleshiness. As if I had been reading Ausonius's lament for his roses, my limbs tingled for some speedy mortal embrace. Curiously, she had, without meaning to, performed the same trick as he. By reminding me of the death-laden canker common to all human flesh, she had set my own exhilaratingly on fire. The herbal fragrances around me, relief after my journey, the young women I could sense behind the cloister wall, Radegunda's own renunciatory passion, all combined had set my head boiling in a red curdle of excitement not at all free of religious emotion. I was aware that I had lost the balance she had recommended. I had fallen off the thin line between a stoically gay acceptance of life and wanton revelling in it: fallen neither to one side nor the other but, like a novice walker of tight-ropes, had slipped astraddle so that the thin sharp line had me by the balls.

"Let me stay here," I begged Radegunda. "I am a light and frivolous man, undirected but eager. I feel that here with you I might achieve unity of thrust."

She agreed and my last memory of that occasion is holding her cold, dry, disciplined hand and staring at a sky which was pale grey, tinged with salmon like old Gaulish ceramics, while I came as near as I ever do to mental prayer and assured God that it was up to him now to save me from the contradictions he has put into me.

Chapter Five

News of the queen's coming had preceded her.

Bishop Medardus was in his vestibule wearing his robes and accompanied by the two deacons without whom a bishop might not receive a woman's visit.

"I hope", Radegunda greeted him, "that one day, with Christ's help, the dung of my soul may be cleared by the mystic rake of your prayers."

He began to talk about her reputation for virtue. "Happy the husband," said he, "who . . ."

"I have left him," said Radegunda. "I am renouncing my worldly family to enter the family of the Church. I am counting on you, my lord bishop, to consecrate me as a deaconness."

"Your Highness", the bishop's voice had changed pitch, "is surely speaking in metaphor."

"No. I have left Clotair. I must beg your grace to spare me the sound of a title I have renounced. I am your grace's most devoted daughter in Christ, Radegunda."

The bishop shot a glance at his deacons. "Oh God," he shouted, "You have sent me a trial."

Radegunda smiled.

"Did you", he asked, "mean what you said just now? You have left the king?"

"I have."

"Then it *is* a trial! Madame—you must allow me to call you that. Anything less would be . . . Does the king know you are here?"

"Yes."

"Yes?" The bishop clasped his hands and unclasped them again. "You have quarelled." He nodded. "Is he following you?"

"No. He gave me permission to come and money and attendants for the journey. They are resting in your kitchens."

The bishop sighed. "May we sit down? Is there anything I may do for your bodily comfort before we discuss this matter further?"

She said there was not.

"Very well," said the bishop in a brisker tone. "You have, naturally, considered the vow you took on entering the holy state of matrimony, its indissoluble nature and the Church's maternal concern for weaker souls who might be scandalized and led into sin by the sight of a royal lady running away from her husband? I am," he raised a repressive hand, "for the sake of saving time, prepared to believe the circumstances are exceptional. Has the king established a concubine under the conjugal roof?"

"No, my lord."

"Threatened your life?"

"No."

"It is, forgive me, *you* who are leaving *him*?"

"It is."

"I can do nothing for you." The bishop looked anxious. "I'm sorry."

"My brother", said Radegunda slowly, "died with a knife in his back scarcely an hour after warning me that Clotair was planning to kill him. He was my last surviving blood relation. That was not ten days ago."

"Allow me to extend condolences, heartfelt condolences. I understand your grief. And I know the rest of your family too were ... Yes ..." The bishop inhaled a deep breath then expelled it. He did not look at his deacons but his body seemed to have sharpened into an organ sensitive to their least blink or tremor. He held this perceptive pose for moments, then: "Unfortunately, Madame, assassination, *even if proven*," he began to gabble, expelling the words speedily and as though with distaste, "cannot provide, *is not recognized* by the Church as providing grounds for ..."

"Grounds," Radegunda exploded, "grounds are not hard to find. Clotair has never lacked for grounds. Or cared for them. He does somersaults on them. Dances all over them! I am his fifth wife. He kept two of my predecessors concurrently and *they* were sisters. The impediment of consanguinity was overlooked then, my lord bishop. You know that I myself was dragged by force to the altar. The impediment of constraint was overlooked." She spoke sharply but without heat and as though the case she was stating had not been her own.

"I see", said the bishop, "your reputation for learning is well grounded. Your reputation for charity—readiness to forgive—may be less so."

"The king gave me a free permission to leave."

"He may change his mind."

"If your lordship consecrates me as a deaconess I shall belong to the Church. He will be unable to claim me back."

"That is precisely what would create . . . complications," said the bishop. "The Church is not a home for runaway wives."

Radegunda bowed her head. "It was not my intention", she said, "to blacken my husband. If you had welcomed me as a sheep hungry for the comfort of the fold I would have shown a gentler side of my nature." She lifted her head and looked at him. "Of a nature which I long to suppress, Oh, my lord, if you know how I yearn to lose myself in God!"

The bishop looked away. "In God . . . yes," he said. "You are tired of yourself and of your marriage and looking for a new fold to belong to. A new start. And *I* am to be the Good Shepherd and welcome you in. I know. I know."

He looked at his deacons. This involved him in turning his head and looking over first one shoulder, then the other. Abruptly, as though annoyed by this, he beckoned them forward. He then turned his stare towards Radegunda for several minutes: an astute, hard stare. "You", he said at last, "are trying to use the Church as a convenience."

79

"My lord ..."

He raised a hand. "You are a grown woman," he challenged, "not young, the wife of a king, you cannot be as naïve as you pretend nor can you expect *me* to pretend to be."

"You are afraid of Clotair?"

The bishop brushed the notion off as though chasing a fly. "No. I believe what you told me. Am I right to do so?"

She nodded. "Yes."

"So the immediate impediment is removed. We are left with the principle." Again he stared at her, his frown forbidding her to speak. A little wearily he proceeded. He was not a young man and had probably said all this before—or perhaps disliked having to say it at all? He was a strong-faced man—all bone, jaw and cheek-bone with a jagged crag of nose—and compromises may not have agreed with him. But then he was a prince of the Church, whose function was neither quite spiritual nor quite temporal and he must have known what it was to dance from one foot to the other. He told Radegunda about this at some length, gabbling at times, rushing along, occasionally lifting a shoulder or twitching his fingers as his river of reasoning balked then frothed past some repellent obstacle. They were, he said, sitting in a vestibule and the world too was a vestibule leading to eternity. Agreed? Agreed. But while one was in a vestibule one *was in it,* was one not? The bishop sighed angrily and the deacons jumped nervously. Radegunda wiped travelling dust from her face with a cloth.

"Yes," she said soothingly. "Yes, my lord!"

"So we have to cope with the given and the given is human nature. Laws will not be perfect, governments can only be as just as fallen human nature can make them. To expect more would be to deny the fallen nature of Man. Yet we must have government; we must have rules or that fallen nature will break into anarchy. So, there will be hard cases, contradictions ... it is our Christian duty to accept them. To refuse them and go off looking for perfection is to fly in the face of God. The Church has given thought to cases like yours. Two centuries ago, the Council of Gangres ... Criadus," the bishop shouted at one of his deacons, "what did the Council decree? About married women ... Wake up, boy. The Council of Gangres—or was it some other Council? About them leaving their husbands—Criadus!"

The deacon began to recite in a singsong scholar's lilt: "Canon Fourteen, your grace, of the Council of Gangres rules that 'If a woman abandon her husband and spurn the nuptial state in which she hath lived with honour on the plea that she who hath been joined in wedlock shall have no part of the glory of the celestial Kingdom, let her'", the boy hesitated, got a nod from Medardus and finished quickly, "'be accursed'."

"Thank you, Criadus. We must, you see, preserve the family. Extraordinary conduct is disruptive. Obviously, people cannot be encouraged to leave their station in life on the pretext of a call from God. Coopers must make barrels, cobblers shoes or the farmer would have nowhere to put his wine and we should all go barefoot. Women were created to bear children and care for their husbands. Those whom their parents dedicate at an early age can pray for the rest. Widows too. Everyone to their place. What would happen to humanity if serfs deserted the land and wives their husbands? We are all equally bound, my lady, priests and bishops, kings and counts. The foot supports the body and the brain thinks for all. This is elementary but you oblige me to spell it out."

The bishop's voice had grown mild and speedy as though he were, in the old saying, saving his breath to cool his porridge. It was his duty and interest to get all this said. His eye however was wary. Radegunda was waiting. Her mouth was set, her stare stark and she was clearly not one to be swayed by common sense however cogently presented. She *was* extraordinary and would disrupt. The deacons watched her and wondered why.

She knew they were wondering. No matter what she said, they would be puzzled and others would too, for people were not convinced by words. Only by acts. Acts were as real as stone walls. You could get round or over them. You could knock them down but you did not question their veracity.

"I can see", the bishop had reached the stage for conceding, "that your case is hard but I cannot advise you to go against Church law and what may well turn out to be against the royal will, because Clotair... my best advice is for you to return to him. Can you not make the sufferings of your conjugal life into an offering which will certainly be more pleasing to God than a broken marriage-vow?"

Radegunda stood up. So did the bishop.

"Bishop Medardus," she said, "I came to you for holy counsel and you gave me human advice. My mind was turned towards God's kingdom, yours to Clotair's. You quote a recent Council but I could quote the gospels' advice that we should leave all for the kingdom of heaven's sake. You know the texts. I will not bore you with them. Instead I shall remind you of something Clotair's henchmen say: 'You cannot run with the hare and hunt with the hounds. The peasants have an even clearer way of putting this: 'You cannot,' they say, 'side with the cow and the clover'. I, my lord, am the clover. Will you let me be devoured? You hesitate. Very well. I shall leave. Not for Clotair's court. I cannot return there. However the Church may view it, we have dissolved our bond. By refusing me protection, you condemn me to a lone and dangerous existence."

She walked towards the door. The bishop moved quickly to cut her off.

"You know I cannot let you go."

"I will stay on one condition."

"It is unrealistic," the bishop told her. "Deaconesses are not being consecrated any more. Church policy in the West is against it. Several Councils have pronounced on the matter. As early as twenty years ago the Council of

Orléans expressly forbade it. How can *I* defy the voice of a Church Council?"

"Other Councils allowed deaconesses?"

"Earlier ones. Yes."

"And God's truth is one and indivisible?"

The bishop's voice was gentle, almost seductive. "Lady, these sophistic questions are beneath us both. We are, I believe, two honest Christians devoted to our faith and submissive to God's will. It would be unworthy if we were to examine the day-to-day measures of those entrusted with Church government with an eye to discovering contradictions. These are matters not of faith or morals but of administration. The power of all governors comes from God. We must trust their acumen. It has proven inexpedient to allow women to receive even minor orders in the Church. Moreover, how minor an order was that of deaconess? In the East, from what I hear, they are turning into priests in petticoats. Women are distributing communion and hearing confessions. . . ."

"Is it better for men to hear women's confessions?"

Medardus shrugged. "I see no need to confess to a particular person at all. Public penance for a great and public sin, private penance for a private sin is the tried rule of the Church." He put his hand on the queen's arm. "Will you not take off your cloak and allow me to extend to you the hospitality of my poor house? This matter you have brought me cannot be settled like the sale of a horse."

"I shall show you, my lord, that I am neither rigid nor unsupple in my resolves."

She allowed him to lead her back through his tapestried atrium to an open terrace warmed at this hour of the afternoon both by a lemony winter light and several braziers. Plants hung in pots suspended from the arches supporting the terrace roof. The walls were frescoed. She was on the point of sitting down when a clash of voices broke out in the vestibule she had just left. The bishop's servants were trying to prevent someone entering.

Radegunda returned to the atrium in time to see a tall Frankish nobleman push past, stride forward then, on seeing her, pause. He was not a dozen ells away. A tufty, high-complexioned man, brightly dressed and hung with a clutter of appendages: dagger, sword, purse, keys, a necklace, bangles, a swastika-shaped belt-buckle and a shoulder-fibula in the form of a hound whose head was turned back towards its own tail. These, like the bristling or swelling by which certain beasts express alarm or aggression, gave the man a heightened presence. Radegunda knew him. He was the local count whom she had seen several times at court. A drinker, fighter and wencher. Vigour sprang from his flesh like drops from a wet dog or sparks from an anvil. Clotair's flesh had had the same property and, like Clotair's too, this man's muscles moved under his skin like bubbles under the scum of a pot of simmering soup. Radegunda could feel that the male in him was alert to her female awareness of this. She turned to the bishop.

"Your Grace, with your permission, I will go and pray in the basilica. I do not wish to meet Count Leudast."

The bishop accompanied her across the hall so that they passed within feet of the count. Radegunda gave him a chill nod, then walked quickly behind a tapestry which the bishop had drawn back to let her pass. From the corner of her eye, she saw the count suppress a movement towards her. Then the tapestry fell and hid him. The bishop told her the way to the basilica which adjoined the church house.

"I shall come for you there", he promised, "as soon as Leudast has left. You know, of course," a look of wavering complicity, "why he's here?"

"Yes."

"I", said the bishop bitterly, "am between two fires."

"One is the devil's," Radegunda told him. "But you are unsure which. You distrust my resolution! You think that what *I* take for God's call may be a female whim!"

There was a sound from the room they had just left.

84

The bishop made a silencing gesture, lifted the tapestry and withdrew.

Radegunda was now in a corridor one end of which led to the basilica, the other to the inner apartments of the palace. Behind the tapestry she could hear the count's voice raised in vehement, half-jocular reproach. Then her own name.

To the right was the way to the basilica. On the left, she caught sight of a small lamp burning before a reliquary: the bishop's private oratory. She went in, stood before it and tried to pray. But her limbs were trembling. Her temples hammered. Pulling a stool against the wall, she sat and leaned back. Had Clotair sent Leudast? Surely not? His remorse should be good for a few more weeks. Days anyway. No. News of her arrival had most probably leaked out of the bishop's kitchens where her attendants were undoubtedly eating and talking their heads off. It had reached Leudast who would feel it his duty to stop the queen running away from his lord and hers. A king with horns, even mystical ones, was a diminished king. Or was his coming here sheer coincidence? Radegunda's mind blackened. She was hungry, tired, uncomfortable and beset by an obscure distress. Whatever had brought him, Leudast's irruption in the place and at the moment when she was seeking sanctuary was surely a warning! His smell lingered in her nostrils. She had caught a whiff of it as she passed him and been reminded of Clotair's. King and count were the same sort of meaty man who eats and drinks heavily and whose hair, skin and mouth smell even when freshly rinsed. Knowingly or not, Leudast was Clotair's emissary, an emissary from the world and the flesh.

She stood up and walked back to the reliquary. It was gold *cloisonné* ornamented with geometrical motifs and could not be more than a few generations old. The pagan *lares* would once have stood here. She held out her hand to the casket and felt the power of the dead saints whose relics were inside move like a current up her arm.

She left the oratory. As she passed the tapestry covering the entrance to the atrium, the count's voice arrested her. He was shouting and must have been walking up and down, for the sound ebbed and returned. She heard her own name, then: "Come down from heaven, bishop, you and I know. . ." She could not catch his next words. Suddenly his voice boomed so close that she could feel her heart jump. ". . . especially while the king is bound for Germany . . . political consequences. The lords will agree with me. Every man Jack . . . His legitimate queen. Not a concubine. If you try anything on we'll surround the building and carry her off. What's more, we'll . . ." Leudast lowered his voice, whispered something, then finished with a roar of laughter.

Radegunda ran towards the basilica as fast and silently as she could. Her way led through the sacristy, a small room filled with coffers. She paused here and, drawing the entrance curtain carefully behind her, proceeded to turn the keys in the coffers one after the other and to lift their lids. The first was full of sacred vessels, gold chalices, ciboria and the like. She closed that and tried another. It was full of vestments. A third held rough, sackcloth habits of the sort worn by public penitents on Ash Wednesday. Radegunda quickly pulled off her outer garments and put on one of these then walked into the basilica. A small boy was lighting tapers before the high altar. Radegunda called him but he took no notice. She walked over, pulled his arm and showed him a ring which she had not thought to remove.

"It's gold. Would you like it?"

The boy gaped. Dressed in sacking, her face still dirty from the journey, she did not, she realized, look like someone capable of distributing such largesse. Besides, wouldn't possession of a gold ring be beyond such a boy's coveting? But she had nothing else.

"I'll give it to you," she said firmly, "if you take a message to Bishop Medardus and bring me back his reply."

"Who says the bishop will let me in?"

"Tell him Queen Radegunda sent you."

Again the stare: slow, suspicious, servile. The boy shifted his feet and gave her the passive glance which numbs fear and conceals—what? Nothing perhaps, a waiting, a calculated passivity which soaks inward from the look on the face so that appearance becomes reality. The boy was a church serf, an orphan or the son of serfs; he could not easily be moved to cause trouble or present himself at the bishop's house. Radegunda made up her mind quickly. She went back to the sacristy, dressed once again in her own clothes and returned. She arranged her face and displayed the jewellery which she had concealed from caution during her journey. She called to the boy:

"Now do you believe I am Queen Radegunda? All right then. Take this ring and show it to the bishop's doorkeeper. Tell him the queen sent you and tell him to say this to the bishop." Leaning so that her face was on a level with the boy's, she pronounced very slowly and clearly, "Tell him that if he does not make haste the bull will have eaten the clover."

Pressing the ring into the child's hand, she made him repeat the message.

Fortunatus has been questioning me. Again. I answer. Sometimes innocently. Sometimes with caution. Either way I see my past take shape in his mind, held fast there like the fish which froze last December in our pond. I tell him this and ask: what if the fish, under the pressure of the fall which feeds the pond, had been about to explode when the ice enclosed it? Your gloss is the ice. I don't recognize my life in your *Life*, Fortunatus. He brushes this off. He wants to write an edifying book and tailors my past for his purpose. He doesn't tell me the shape he intends to impose on it but his questions tell me what it is: sanctity. When I first understood this I was outraged.

Now—an exercise in humility—I have resolved to let him do it. After all, why should *my* truth matter to anyone but God? Maybe—a knife-thrust of despair—there have been no real saints? But people need to believe there have. Still, each time Fortunatus has been questioning me, I return to my memories like a housewife to possessions which have been disarranged.

He leaves out the play with costumes—too wily for a saint—when, like a circus actress, I played myself, the great and glittering queen, so as to cow the little serf into doing what I wanted, then changed promptly back into the haircloth habit in the hope of cowing the bishop. It smacks a little of comedy and Fortunatus doesn't like mixing genres. He has gone off now with the scene between me and Medardus neatly set out on his tablets: an encounter between two saints. He may be half right. Medardus was a holy man: shrewd and possessed of some fortitude although in his dealings with me it took some time to show itself. Since his death he has been credited with a number of miracles. Perhaps I saw him at his worst? He was afraid of Clotair and Leudast, devoted to order and knew little of marriage. I remember how long he kept me waiting in that basilica. I was by the high altar dressed in the habit and determined not to move until he came. I knew he must come sooner or later to celebrate benediction, but he did his best to tire me out. I could not be sure he had got my message but I knew he knew I was there and what I was up to, for small boys and old women and junior clerics of every description kept pressing their noses against the grille of the rood-screen then trotting off in the direction of his palace. It was considerably past the hour established for the ceremony when he turned up with Leudast and several ruffians pushing behind him. I was half frozen for the habit was loosely woven and draughts whistled through it. I was afraid to let go of the altar lest Leudast try to have me dragged from the sanctuary, yet it felt like ice. It was a great slab of cold marble and my bones were paining with the cold. I had by then no particular certitude that God wanted me there. I only knew I could not bear to return to Clotair and that only the Church could protect me if he chose to get me back. Earlier, I had been sure of God's approval, but there, in the cold, my certitudes began to run out. I began to think I was mad to try and goad a bishop into defying a king. Mad to believe any one woman's existence mattered. Mad above all to spend one more moment in that cold. If only I could be warm. My mind numbed. My God, I kept saying—and that was *all* I was saying to God—if only I were less cold! *Cold*: the word anaesthetized thought, anaesthetized fear and even the impulse to leave and get warm. I simply clung on there, my teeth clattering like shaken dice, my body rippling with shudders. I had been tired already by the journey from Soissons and by hunger, for I had refused to eat until Medardus would agree to consecrate me. I was saddle-sore, too, and my bladder was swollen. The cold held my flesh like iron pincers. It held me there— maybe it was sent by God? When Medardus turned up, it numbed my fear of Leudast who came up behind the bishop shouting to the people that the bishop was trying to steal their king's wife from him and shut her up in a mon- astery. A crowd edged up the nave. Weapons were drawn and, at one point, the count's men were trying to pull the bishop backwards while he clung to the rood-screen and tried to edge past it into the sanctuary of the presbyterium and the altar itself. He told me later that he was not doing this with any idea of consecrating me as deaconess. All he hoped for was to reach the altar so as to address the crowd from a position of relative safety. Of course the count's men had no intention of letting him do this. It was while this scuffling was waving back and forth that I remembered the words I had planned earlier and brought them out loud and pat as a prayer: "Oh bishop!" I shouted and all the people began to yell: "It's the queen! Let her talk! Silence for Queen Radegunda." I waited for their silence, numb still and stiff as the fish in its frozen pond. "Bishop," I recited, "if you hesitate to ordain me and show more fear of this violent man", I pointed at Leudast, "than you do of God, know, Shepherd, that you will be asked to render an account of the soul of your abandoned sheep!"

It was short and sharp: the sort of speech that sticks in people's heads. I knew that. After all, I had spent fourteen years as a king's wife. I knew how speeches are made. But I couldn't have altered it if I'd needed to. I was numb. I just drew it out like a refrain or lesson learned by rote. It would have to do. It did.

When I had said my say, my mind went black. I noticed no more until Medardus was laying on his hands and reciting the prayer for consecrating a deaconess: "Oh God, Creator of man and woman, who didst not disdain to let your only son be born of a woman . . ."

After that, power surged into me. I felt warm and strong and it was many months until it left me again. The people had saved me. They had turned on the count and he had had to give in to them. At once I called one of my servants and sent for a gold belt I had brought in my luggage and demanded that it be broken up there and then and the gold sold so that its price might be distributed among the poor. I laid several jewelled garments as an offering on the altar and, later, in the course of my journey to shrines which lay on the way to my villa at Saix, near Poitiers, I offered up the rest of my wardrobe.

Chapter Six

Leaving his roomful of refractory papyrus, Fortunatus
came on a cold morning after an insomniac night, to the
convent garden. A moon, thin as a tide-sucked shell,
was fading. So was the frost. Frills survived on cabbages
and on the polls of earth-clods. Their bared fronts recalled
the tonsure favoured by Celtic prelates who shaved their
foreheads. Romans preferred to wear a central bald patch
ringed with hair commemorative of the crown of thorns.
The frost was Celtic. Fortunatus remarked on this to
Agnes whom he met on her way from matins. Joking.
Childishly. If one was expected to amuse—which he was:
it was his function at the convent—and wished for once
to keep off piety and always—my God, since hers was
for God—sex, what was there left but childishness?

"Odd", said he, going on as he had begun, "that the
black night's track should be white. Look at that frosty
script. Messages? A code if we could only crack it?"

"You think", said she, "that there are acrostics in
nature like the ones you put in your poems?"

Tart! Disliked his whimsy.

"Why not?" Challenged. Surely a Ravenna scholar
could dazzle a provincial nun? "If this world", he urged
argumentatively, "is—as we believe—the shadow of a
more real one, mustn't its shifts and shapes be clues to
old, lost meanings? Felicities perhaps from the time
before it fell? Memories of Eden?"

Agnes did not take this up. She was anxious about ink
supplies for the copying room. "Mundane concerns!"
She gave him a grin whose irony struck him as uncertainly
directed. At herself? Him?

He wouldn't have this. Scribes, he reminded her, were

engaged in a ghostly warfare. Copying the word of God. "They preach with their fingers, speak with their hands. Their pens wound the devil with every stroke. Each word is a missile. You", he teased, "are a general! Ink is your artillery."

She laughed. The wind, with its multiple airy snouts, snatched at her heavy skirt, nuzzling the body underneath. He watched the bunching, recalcitrant cloth. Her hands beat at it until a gust threw a great wad of the stuff between her knees. She stumbled and he, with a laugh of pleasure, alive suddenly to the element's complicity, caught and set her back on her feet.

"It's like being at sea!"

Smell of hyacinths. A glassy sky had been scraped clear by this combing wind. Her habit, fluttering rakishly like ripped sails, swelled yet made her look unsteady.

"Agnes!" Her cheeks were bright with cold. Behind her, a willow's red, tensile limb cut the air. He flung a flourish of words at her, convinced that she was sharing his excitement.

"I'm cold!" She cut through it. Her hands were clasped tightly around her chest. "What are we doing here?" She shivered. Hadn't been listening. She looked, he saw as they moved towards shelter, as though she were calculating how much soap she should order from the serf women on the estate. She was probably doing just that. Soap, honey, wax for candles, shingles, wool . . . Her face had a crabbed look like a steward's memo tablet. Fortunatus felt absurd. Honey and candles were pressing concerns. Real. He wanted to touch the solid stuff of her sleeve. Once more. His fingers tingled. Perhaps he could pretend to brush something off it?

"You were saying", she reminded him politely, "about the Garden of Eden?" They had reached a doorway.

"Was I?" Was she remembering the kitchen-garden where he had lusted after her? Months ago. Of course not. She hadn't noticed. Had been thinking of beans. She would imagine the Garden of Eden, he thought savagely, as laid out in bean-rows. A stupid woman. Angrily, he clutched her wrist.

"A beetle!"

Full of scallions, garlic and mustard for our first parents to season their salad with! He squeezed her wrist roughly.

"Don't kill it!"

He removed his hand.

"They say", she said, "that when we can make sense of every mystery, it will be the end of the world."

"Who?"

She shrugged. "People. Some saint maybe? It could be a warning against being too clever. That was the first sin, wasn't it? Eating the apple of knowledge?"

"A metaphor!" said Fortunatus, hating metaphors and all deviousnesses which suddenly struck him as feminine. Oh for simplicity, solid things and the white tooth's passage through crunchy fruit. Why had he come to the garden this morning? He felt angry with Agnes.

"It's a warning," she was saying, "anyway. Maybe God does not want his obscurities unriddled. I mean, look at Radegunda. She's never had a clear revelation, has she? Yet she's in touch with God for days at a time."

"But the Christian meaning is for everyone."

"The part we grasp with our minds. But the soul is more private than the mind. More lonely. So is the body. You're a poet. Can you describe pain?"

"Hot. Tremulous. Shooting jagged rays through the flesh..."

She laughed. "If I'd never felt pain I wouldn't know what you meant! You're reminding me. That's all. It's like saying something tastes 'as sweet as honey'! But supposing someone had never tasted honey?"

"Pleasing, a shock to the taste buds."

"That could be pepper, cinnamon, any spice at all."

"It could be a kiss."

"Could it?"

"Yes."

"That's interesting. Well. I have to go and see the

steward. God be with you, Fortunatus."

"And with you."

He waited in the hope of seeing Radegunda but was told she was busy. Fridovigia brought him some oat-cakes and fermented pear-juice in a blue glass flask.

"Roman," she said, lifting it to the light. "Imported. Like yourself. The abbess's parents had stacks of these. They liked Roman imports of all sorts."

She grinned. Fortunatus was aware of a thought wending its way through her talk. She was sewing, waiting for him to finish so that she could take back the glass and flask. Servants had to be devious. Maybe someone like Fridovigia had invented metaphor? Fortunatus was amused by the fancy.

Suddenly she spat furiously. She had broken her needle. "Bone!" she exclaimed, crinkling up her eyes and aiming a moistened end of thread at a new one! "We have to use bone needles like peasant women!"

"Let me."

He handed her back the threaded needle.

"God bless your eyesight. You have a fine sense of direction. Follow your eyesight, young man!"

"I'm not so young: thirty-nine."

"Young enough. Who's younger around here?"

"You mean 'In the country of blind men the one-eyed are kings'?"

"Now you're putting words into my mouth!"

She grumbled about the needles Radegunda had issued. "Won't let us use metal ones. We must humble our pride, she says. Well, all I can say is it's inefficient. The same thing with food. I'm waiting to hear we're to give up wheat and live on maslin grain and turnip pottage. Maybe the only reason we don't is because *she*'s never heard of them! When the rich play at poverty it would make a cat laugh. There's more waste here and less to show for it than in the estates of the abbess's parents where I was brought up. The steward feathered his nest

94

and still ran things more thriftily than here where the nuns take turns at burning the bread and turning the milk. Like little girls playing house. 'It's the principle that counts,' says the foundress. Well, practice is worth a cartload of principle in my humble opinion! The joke is *she's* the worst cook of all. But insists on taking her turn. 'From humility' if you please! Stubbornness is another word for it. It would make your heart bleed to see the nuns eating the messes she cooks up. Now Agnes is a good cook as you well know. I taught her and I learned from a great cook on her father's estates. They had good raw materials of course. They had falconers and kept tame fowl: peacocks, pheasants, turtle-doves. Not that there's any eating on tame turtle-doves. They pine when they're kept in captivity. Pine away to skin and bone. I often think poor Agnes is like a captive turtle-dove. Not that she'd ever admit it. They always live in pairs, turtle-doves. If they don't they pine worse. And poor Agnes is lonely. Have you noticed how thin she is?"

"Are wild turtle-doves better?" Fortunatus asked.

"Well they're fatter. There's more meat on them. But the danger with them is you never know on what they've been feeding." Fridovigia's talk kept time with the impulsions of her thumb as it forced the blunt bone needle through the cloth then pulled it out, in again, then out. "I knew a man", she said, "ate one that had been feeding on hellebore. Now a little of that is a good cure for mental diseases but too much can kill you. Luckily, I was there and guessed what the matter was, so I got him to vomit up his meal. There are some", said Fridovigia, "who could do with a dose of that same hellebore. For their own mental health." Fridovigia's needle moved like a tooth. White and venomous, it rushed through the openwork on the edge of her cloth, weaving frothy designs, loops and little raised crosses. "And for other people's too," she finished and broke the thread on her teeth.

Stone. Grey with silver flecks, black spottings and A.D.

saffron stains. When I look long enough at my stone slit where the light falls I see every colour. There are lichenous infusions, pre-growths which, over years, may come up as moss. To a mite such moss might be a forest, so there are estates in my wall whose pores are caverns to the mites. My skin is porous too, multicoloured and grows forests of pale hair. This has paled and thickened while I have been here. The wall too is changing. Damp leaves pale pockings and dilapidates the edges. When the rays of late and early sunlight hit it, they make rainbows on its uneven surface. As my wall grows softer, I grow bonier. We are becoming more alike.

"Good God", we say. But is "good" good enough for God? If God is "good" and Radegunda is, are they the same?

Here in my wall, everything seems the same. The food they bring me tastes of stone. The water is stony and I too am half petrified, accepting, half dead already, like an animal in winter. I accept. I am choked with familiar thoughts, with sameness, filled up like a sewer or vault which, once filled, is level with the ground and inexistant. I want to exist. How? The bow accepts the arrow but fires it out. How? Movement of the mind is the last to stop. Stir it. How?

Live, Ingunda!

God then, let me say, is foul, unjust, evil, wrong, limited and unimaginative. There: I have denied him. Shall I be forgiven? Let repent? If he is just he will allow me to say he is unjust since in all justice the life I was loaded with was unjust. Agnes's life was unjust. Fortunatus—I have no feelings about him. I want to turn things round but in him there is little to turn. Weighted neither on top nor bottom, like certain chess pieces, you may turn him about and he looks no different.

But God is evil, the devil good. There: I have asserted and assaulted and could believe it too. Why am I not upset? Shaken? Has God—who is good if he is at all—withdrawn all interest from me? Have I rubbed out my own self? I would have stoked a fire to flame in like Radegunda who burned with holy heat. I want my blood to drum, even madly, even unholily and with shame. I want to live. To feel, suffer, be—and I don't. Why am I not upset, seared, terror-stricken, shamed, why? Is this my punishment? God has withdrawn himself. He denies me since I denied him. And I cannot repent or feel at all. God, let me feel, suffer as I did other times. Please, please, let me even desire strongly to do this. Oh, you are turning my mind and conscience too to stone. I shall be a stone and stonier no matter what I do. I am turning into this wall. Give me sorrow, pain. Anything.

God!

Devil!

Anyone! Someone! Interfere. Affect me. Answer. Send a sign. Anything. Send an ant or a woodlouse walking down my window-slit. Send the sound of rain. Wind. Do not leave me alone.

I am alone. A stone. Forgotten. A nothing. A vacancy. There is nothing out there.

Godevil! Devilgod! Strike. Answer! Is silence your answer?

No. It is my own silence.

Pale, pallid stone. Indifferent Ingunda. How long since I thought my last thought? Here I perch like a stuffed owl, unfit for visions even of mice. Was I wrong to choose this wall? But what is 'wrong'?

ShitGod! Foul maker of shitpies who made me! Why? Why? I am shit made of shit by ShitGod for shit from shit for shit everlasting since all ends in shit the source and end of all.

I *want to repent*! I want to believe. Feel. Live. Pray even?

My nose is my only live organ. Everything smells. I cannot eat or very little but all night and day I smell. Smells of hell. We know smells of shit and sulphur come from hell.

Base nose! I shall break it. Against this wall.

I would still smell. The hellsmell is in me.

Save me. Anyone.

If only I could wash. Or burn. Or die.

I'll bash my nose against the wall. Oh God. Oh God. Oh God. It hurts. It hurts. Hurts. Hurt.

But at least I *feel* again. At least that. Oh God, the hurt!

A.D.
569
Venantius Honorius Clementianus Fortunatus had formally begun his *Life of Radegunda* and was visiting the convent every day. As often as not, the foundress was unavailable but convent gossip was, if anything, a better source than she was. Sitting in the leafless rose-bower— it was spring—he wore a grey fur wrap, took notes and kept an eye on the nuns' comings and goings.

"Psst!" he called to a novice who was emerging from the tower where Radegunda was in retreat. "Anything new?"

The novice jumped. Startled. Outsiders were not allowed within the convent precincts. Fortunatus had a dispensation granted him by several bishops and by the two kings who had a claim on Poitiers. These two, Sigibert and Chilperic, who would willingly have murdered each other—and were to die murdered by persons unknown— were united in their regard for the poet. For them his verse incarnated the last glory of Roman culture: an elusive form of loot which they paid for in solid coin and sundry privileges.

"Well," he asked, "has she eaten today?"

"No." The novice, a girl from northern Gaul, stared at him with excitement. "Nor moved," she told him. "She's standing as stiff as an icicle in front of her relics. Like this!" The girl held up her hands, palms forward in a gesture Fortunatus remembered once seeing a caged mouse assume to signify its submission to a stronger one.

The girl bent towards Fortunatus. "I touched her", she confided, "and her flesh was cold as ice. She didn't budge!"

"I see. What about her eyes?"

"Fixed," said the girl. "Wide open and fixed. She never blinks."

Fortunatus fixed his own eyes sharply on the novice, "You're not just saying this, are you?"

The girl looked so shocked that he saw she was not.

"All right," he waved her away. "I mustn't keep you from your holy occupations, Sister."

It was disappointing to have to rely on the testimony of someone so simple. Radegunda was in rapture. In that tower, so close to where he sat that he could have thrown a stone inside, a woman was in union with God. The ecstasy she was experiencing, her love-transaction with the Great Lover, was the most thrilling mystery of all existence. Thinking of it excited the poet physically. He felt a compelling urge to participate in the power which must, he felt sure, be emanating from the nun at this moment. Grace: he saw it in terms of heat, energy, an enhancing and elevation of the spirit. Of the senses even. His fingers tingled as he wrote his notes: "As Danae received Zeus in a shower of sunlight, so Radegunda was receiving Christ." No. He ran his pen through that. Pagan imagery! Dangerous. Especially here in Gaul where paganism died hard and many, after hearing the Christian mass in the morning, crept off by twilight to worship at some old pagan shrine. Besides, the Christian was a more ethical experience. The enraptured saint's will was absorbed into the divine one. Radegunda became one with God.

The poet felt suddenly bereft.

If Radegunda's "I" became absorbed, then how could one reach her? The fire and ecstasy were exclusive and excluding. He felt a sensation of cold, shivered, sneezed and pulled his fur cloak about him. Letting his pen drop, he began, in some depression, to grapple with this paradox: what fascinated him in Radegunda was her rapture, but the rapture obliterated her individuality, the self with which a human could connect. Fortunatus had for some time enjoyed a strong, he would have said "spiritual" relationship with the nun, anyway a friendship, but, at this moment, the moment when he most wanted her,

99

she was beyond his reach.

Despondently, he picked up his pen and began to write about grace, the spiritual fund amassed by exceptional members of the Christian community, yet available to all. He threw down his pen. He didn't want the grace available to all. He wanted ... With revulsion, Fortunatus realized that his feeling for Radegunda at this moment was lust. The images before his inner eyes were unmistakable. He shook his head violently from side to side, denying those images, blurring, mixing and inducing an anaesthetizing, optical haze.

Radegunda, he remembered with distaste, was fifty, badly worn by a life of penance, not in the least attractive. Unseemliness aside, the idea was sacrilegious. . . . He shook his head faster and faster until thought was drowned in a wave of giddiness, nausea and incipient pain.

"I . . ." thought Agnes guiltily. "Ego . . ."

It was a forbidden vocable. Her "I" should long ago have been merged and lost in God. The brief character should have been erased by her monastic vow, leaving her as blank as a fresh page or her own white habit. There were no mirrors in the convent but the other sisters showed her how she looked: a five-foot, shapeless bundle of pale wool, waiting for God to put his character on her. Receptive. She hoped.

Meanwhile there were things to be done.

Radegunda was in retreat: Lent. She had been in her cell now for three weeks. Besides, she left decisions anyway to Agnes. Radegunda could not escape prestige. People came from distant provinces to touch objects previously touched by her. The gardeners did a roaring trade. Patients afflicted by nervous disorders waited around the convent walls until they caught a glimpse of her. Then frequently had fits. In the course of these they yelled that the saint's glance had exorcised and forced demons to depart from inside them. Invariably, the debouching spirits put on a last performance, uttering obscenities and contorting the host bodies in lascivious spasms. Local people enjoyed this and were hoping that their saint might yet compete with St. Martin whose body had been treacherously stolen from them by the men of Tours more than a century earlier. His tomb attracted gifts and pilgrims from all over Christendom and had contributed maddeningly to the prosperity of the rival city. St. Martin's prestige had even won the citizens of Tours a royal tax exemption.

All this and more was reported to Agnes by Fridovigia who had steadfastly refused to leave her and equally steadfastly refused to become a nun. She survived as a sort of convent hanger-on, a position which would have violated the Rule's prohibition of servants if Fridovigia had been even minimally efficient. As she was not, she could be regarded as a charity-case or Agnes's private gadfly sent by God to temper her as he no doubt sent the epileptics and hysterics to temper Radegunda.

"I can't listen now," said Agnes. "I have to see how the bath-house is coming along. I want the masons out of there by Easter. And the altar-cloths should be laundered carefully. That gilt embroidery is delicate. Then there's the blessed bread to be baked. Why don't you go and weigh the flour, Fridovigia? If there isn't enough someone will have to grind more."

Fridovigia paid no attention. Head on one side, she was staring ironically at Agnes. "You remind me of your mother," she said. "Just the same at your age, she was. Anxious. A bit fussy. Even to the way you fiddle with your key! *She* was a good manager. I daresay there was as much going on in your father's villa as there is in this convent! She knew how to enjoy herself too. The banquets they used to have ... She always presided. She wasn't a prude. Mind you she was a fine-looking woman in her day. If you wore a little make-up you might look like her. Oh, I know it's against your Rule, but it would tone down your cheeks. They're too bright. Many's the beauty came out of a pot of ceruse! And if you only wore something

better than this!" The nurse plucked contemptuously at
Agnes's lumpy skirt. "Your mother's clothes were made
of Byzantine stuffs. Well, they say you can dress a broom-
stick to look like a queen and *I* say the opposite's just as
true. But then, I suppose, why should you bother? Here!
But still when I think of all the gentlemen who used to
admire her ... All that liveliness, laughter, music,
parties..." Fridovigia's eyes glazed. The past she was
remembering might have been her own. Had become her
own. "Then to think of her leaving no son, no heir,
nothing..." She let her hands fall in despondency.
"I'd look for the bright side," she said, "only I'd be hard
put where to look."

"Will you remember my message about the flour?"

"There was a Roman gentleman", said the nurse
unheedingly, "who was mad about her when she was the
age you are now! He was some sort of a big noise, a high
official or something. From Rome. He used to play music
to her and send her poems. A black-eyed gentleman.
Always joking. A funny thing but do you know who
reminds me of him?"

"No," said Agnes. "I do not and I have work to do."
She walked off quickly towards the bath-house but
Fridovigia followed her, panting a little.

"Let me tell you something ..." she began.

"Please," said Agnes, unable to keep the annoyance
out of her voice, "don't keep on about my mother."

"I wasn't going to," Fridovigia said huffily. "I was
going to tell you of something I saw this morning on my
way here. In town. Can't you walk a bit more slowly,"
she complained. "Anyone would think you were running
from a bull!" Agnes slowed down. Fridovigia sighed.
"I'm not getting younger and neither are you. Do you
realize you'll soon be thirty? What was I saying? Oh yes:
a terrible thing. I passed the basilica on my way over this
morning and there were *three* babies on the steps. In this
weather! Can you imagine? The deacon was just opening
the church door and there they were. One was dead: blue

with cold! How do the women do it, I ask you? It must have been there for hours. Of course they abondon them while it's still dark for fear of being seen. With the hunger that's around, nobody's going to bring them up. Only the Church—but what kind of a future is that for a child? The Church ..."

Agnes began walking quickly again. The old woman got on her nerves. Her monologues all tended obscurely in the same direction. Obstinate, insinuating, rarely speaking directly enough to risk contradiction, Fridovigia gnawed at the thread of Agnes's life. Love and disapproval seeped from her. She was all self-abnegation in a bad cause: that of winning Agnes back from Radegunda's influence. Years of defeat had taught her nothing. Humbly she lurked, congratulating herself silently, and sometimes not so silently, on not speaking her mind, yet spoke it by her sheer presence. Her figure in a room or at the turn of a corridor was an interrogation mark, a lament, a bleak, beseeching shadow which suffered and challenged the usefulness of convents, proclaimed her disappointment in Agnes, her foster child, and in her own son, a bad hat, who hung round Poitiers getting into fights and disgracing her; proclaimed her dependency, her utter incapacity to live for herself, her claims on Agnes. She hovered now while Agnes spoke to the masons about finishing the bath-house, then followed her into the sacristy and back to the laundry-house.

"Let me carry those." She tried to take the piles of embroidered sacred cloths from Agnes's arms.

"No," said Agnes, not wanting Fridovigia to feel useful. Recognizing her own meanness, she stopped. "All right then, take the top ones." She tilted the pile of cloths towards the old woman whose reactions were too slow. A heavy gold altar-cloth fell to the ground and the nurse, in her nervousness, trod on it. "What a fool you are!" said Agnes irritably. "Why do you hang round me? You're not fit to be in a convent. Pick it up and put it back, then go away, will you. Go away."

The old woman obeyed in hurried silence and had pattered down the corridor and clicked the outer door behind her before Agnes's temper had abated enough to call her back. Anger and shame were still struggling in her when she reached the laundry-rooms where the sisters who should have been on duty were nowhere to be seen.

Dropping the pile of cloths into a coffer, she ran back after her old nurse, but when she reached the garden the woman had disappeared. Just as well maybe. Agnes might have wounded her again by her apologies. She was not yet controlled enough for gentleness. Her mind and temperament felt like one of the hair shirts which Radegunda wore constantly next her skin. Agnes seemed to have an internal one: all the parts of her sensibility rubbed abrasively against one another. "I am a bad nun, a bad abbess," she thought, "a bad Christian, I . . . There is too much 'I' in me." She found the nuns who should have been in the laundry, scolded them and sent them back there and set off for the kitchens which were in a separate building. "It's the spring," she thought. "It annoys me."

In the bakehouse she found two slatternly young novices mixing the dough for the blessed bread with great raw hands garnished with black-rimmed nails. By now her indignation was worn out and it was in the gentlest of voices that she told them to go off and wash. Left alone, she began to shape the dough. The mound of it was bigger than herself, for the convent alone would have two hundred communicants at Easter and the church of St. Mary Outside the Walls probably more. Calm, she told herself, calm, and gave herself up to the soothing mechanical task which might have been hers if she had not been abbess. So many "if"s. Her mind spiralled after them. Firmly, she brought it back to the immediacy of dough. Oh the relief of what was purely physical! She liked the elastic quality of the damp dough, enjoyed pummelling and slapping it down, feeling it yield then slowly swell back, arching into the palms of her hands and nuzzling upwards through the slits in her fingers. She scraped her hands clean with a wooden spatula, dipped them into the flour bin, then plunged them once more into the mixture. A minute later they had got a cramp from the effort and she had to rest them. Fluttering her fingers and pulling at her knuckles, she moved for a moment to the back window.

Fortunatus was outside and, thinking she had fluttered at him, waved back. Agnes made a sedate gesture. Could she, he mimed the question, come out? No. He mimed resignation and went back to his writing. He was sitting in an arbour. Roses. But they had not yet bloomed and the grey stringy vines sifted pale sunlight on to his head. The tufts of his eyebrows cast shadows around his eyes which gleamed occasionally like water deep in a well. Black eyes—who had been talking about black eyes?

The two young nuns came back with scrubbed hands and Agnes left them to finish working the dough. She went for a moment to the convent chapel to pray. Terce. Sun poured through stained-glass windows making coloured tesselations on the floor: red and blue. Pray for the blue-faced baby that died. What use? It had surely been unbaptized. Hell's limbic border for it: a neutral, unrealizing place. The Church would keep and bring up the live ones as Church serfs. They would be exempt from military service. But might die before experiencing that unique advantage. Have mercy on them, oh Lord. Preserve them from starvation and avoidable disasters: tumours, fevers and malignant growths, from yaws and leprosy, gangrene, rot, abscesses, plagues and slow material decay. Agnes had worked with Radegunda at her hospital at Aties and her alms-house at Saix: well-run places where fresh linen was given out twice a week, baths scheduled in rotation, wholesome food laid on trestle tables and dispensed by Radegunda herself who took joy in this, in washing the filthiest inmates and in kissing lepers' sores.

"Nobody", Fridovigia had remarked with healthy disgust, "will want to kiss lips that have kissed the like of *that*!"

"Oh," said Radegunda tartly, "I won't have much trouble resigning myself, Fridovigia, to getting no kisses from *you*!"

You couldn't shake Radegunda. She had visions and vision, being fortified by encouragement from on high. Agnes, who never said so, felt lepers and indeed most people would be better off dead and had no business procreating if they were going to leave the product on the basilica steps—or perhaps at all. She was not blaming them—how blame such unchoosing victims?—but just saw little point in helping them prolong lives spent in ditches, alms-houses and the edges of roads. Many, having had limbs amputated by frost or torture, could not work. She was pursued by memories of departing patients who stared at her through scales of mucus and thanked her foolishly for her cruel help. "Give up," she wanted to cry, but instead sent them off with bundles of clean clothes, bread and dried meat which might last at best a week. "God be with you," she said in disbelief. Maybe, if too much sin did not prove necessary for survival, they might one day manage to be with God? Agnes crossed herself and left the chapel. In a way it had been a relief to give up charity-work and withdraw into a convent. Prayer, at least, reached to the root of matters. But Radegunda was better at that too. Agnes's job was to keep the convent going so that others might pray efficiently.

She continued her round now, checking briefly on the wine cellar, the weaving and spinning rooms, the reading room where manuscripts were being copied and the granary. Her last call was back to the bakehouse where the two young novices, intent on what they were doing, did not notice her entry. They were eastern Franks and she could not understand their dialect, but knew from its pitch and tremor that they were engaged in something more exciting than baking bread. Their backs were turned to her and she had to rap firmly with her ring on the door before they turned. Their faces were red, she noticed, but perhaps that was the heat from the oven? Then she saw what was on the table. For a moment she thought it was a corpse: a man's. But it was only dough. They had moulded it into the shape of a life-sized—indeed somewhat outsized—naked man. With some skill. Even, Agnes noticed with quick dislike, the most intimate elements had been crudely though recognizably supplied. The girls looked up at her mildly. Her face, she saw from theirs, must be awry with shock. And their flush, she knew then, did come merely from the oven which was gaping red and ready for the body of bread.

"What," she managed to control her voice, "in God's name, is that?"

"The Easter Christ," said the elder novice in her thick dialect. "Don't you know? We always do it like that in our part of the country." The girl spoke with anxious kindness and Agnes realized that she must be astonishing the girls by her agitation. But even while a sane voice in her mind told her this, repugnance was bubbling through her.

"You know," explained the second girl, "'This is my body! People eat the body of Christ. Everyone gets a bit: the eyes, the toes. It depends—and you can tell what kind of a year you'll have by the part you get to eat . . .'"

By the part . . . Agnes's eye bounced off the generous penis and testicles of powdered white dough. Did eastern Franks really practise the custom quite so integrally or were these girls having some foul joke at her expense? There was a lot of paganism still in those areas, but all the same . . . Her eye skidded back then back again to the girls whose glance was surely too innocent? Were Frankish —or any men's—bodies really like that? How did these girls know? And did one also eat . . ?

"Eat?" she screamed in a voice which shocked herself as much as it did the two shattered novices—Agnes had a reputation for self-control—"How can you talk like that? You're pagan cannibals! You understand nothing of Christianity! This is sacrilege! Oh my God . . ." Agnes clenched the table and her teeth in a supreme effort to pull herself together. After all, she reminded herself, this was still only dough. Not consecrated yet. "Roll it up," she directed with enforced gentleness. "Make plain round loaves with a cross in the middle of each. Handle the dough as lightly as possible. It's been mauled too much already. And I'm sorry I shouted at you. I apologize. You had better talk to the chaplain. Get him to explain the mystery of transubstantiation. I will arrange for him to give you some of his time when he comes tomorrow. Meanwhile, remember", she said, "that we do not eat our God." She left, walked into the kitchen-garden and let herself fall on a stone bench where she lay trembling with her eyes hidden in her sleeve.

She lay there quietly until her body had relaxed. Sun motes were caught and splintered on the downy nap of her cuff. They made swirling spectra which survived, when she closed her eyes, then changed into insistant, unwelcome images. She berated herself for a bad nun, and abbess. The Frankish novices had been crude but surely innocent. Now she had disturbed that innocence, given scandal. What was religion, after all, but a channelling of dangerous passions into safe celebrations? "Eat me" said Christ, "and do not eat others. Love me so as not to love other men. Let your mind dwell on me and lust will leave you. . . ." Agnes's mind tried to cope with the recurring image of the pubic curls the Frankish girls had sketched on the doughy underbelly with the curved tip of a knife. Priapean. Why were such girls nuns at all? Why was anyone? She had been unkind to Fridovigia too. Unkind, uncharitable—and what use was the institution of convent life if not to develop kindness? Love? She sat up, opened her eyes and found Fortunatus standing within inches of her. He had been watching her in her spasm of self-distrust.

"Agnes, you're not happy?"

She denied that she was not.

"You drive yourself too hard."

"Maybe," she agreed humbly. "I . . . She stopped.

"I" again, she thought and mentally stepped on the word as images of the virgin step on the snake's head.

Fortunatus began to speak of some poem he was writing and she half listened, letting him propel her along beside him through the kitchen-garden where curly winter kale grew in hedges thick as a cart-horse's belly and as high. His hand was on her elbow, an unsensual area but which tingled now as though every feeling in her body were dancing on its tip. "Oh God," she thought. "I'm lonely, arid. I need a little human tenderness."

Fortunatus talked gaily and lightly. Surely her incandescent elbow-bone was burning his palm? But no. He went on about his poem. It was about virginity, was to surprise Radegunda when she came out of retreat but would be formally dedicated to Agnes. "Since Radegunda is of course not a virgin." It was a very long poem which Fortunatus had been working on all through Lent and had demanded research. Agnes's mind swam. She stumbled, managed to right and take hold of herself and struggled with the impression that Fortunatus was making little sense. The poem, he was saying, praised Radegunda, made puns on Agnes's name and Agnus Dei, then plunged into the delicious paradox of holy virgins who, because they did not know love, would know Christ, the Mystic Lover. He, born of a Virgin, sought his pleasure only in virginal viscera. "Human love", said Fortunatus, excitedly gripping Agnes further up her arm, "is an image of the Divine! One reaches one through the other. Hence my imagery is the same. The experience is identical. Radegunda has had", he reminded her, "the experience of heat around the heart spreading to her bowels and womb: God's love following the track of man's. A holy hallucination. Knowledge comes to us through the senses only. There is no other door ... Agnes!"

He had pulled her down in the furrow between the hedges of kale. Hands groping her, he whispered, "let's love each other, Agnes!" He talked and talked and moved above her, furrowing and burrowing and she, battered and exhausted by a lifetime of scruples, felt irresponsibility invade her and tension flow from her as he rolled her on the crumbly earth releasing smells of crushed kale and parsley.

"Oh God, Fortunatus, you talk so much!"

"Yes," he agreed. "This is better than talk. But you need talk too. It gives edge to things."

"Sin ..." she breathed hopelessly.

"It's all around. Everywhere. Accept it. Then deal with it. You aimed too high, Agnes."

"Radegunda ..."

"She's out of the ordinary. A touch mad. That's sanctity. It's not for everyone."

"Your poem ..."

"It's a poem: a construct. Myth. Heady. Useful. Edifying. Forget it."

"I must go. Let me."

"Shush!" He held a hand over her mouth. The two novices had come out of the bakehouse and were walking past, two rows of kale away, talking in their impenetrable Frankish. Their pale skirts swept the earth, visible on ground-level under the hedges where the thick, jointed kale stems were bare of foliage. Their voices rose and clashed excitedly and their skirts paused as they grew absorbed in their conversation just a yard from the abbess whose own skirt was now bundled, thick as a wheel, round the axle of her waist. Fortunatus put his other hand between her legs and applied rhythmic pressure. The voices floated in nervous indignation over the kaletips and Agnes, hearing her own name, shuddered convulsively and felt wetness on Fortunatus's fingers. One of the novices laughed and the skirts moved out of sight. Agnes got his hand off her mouth.

"I must go ... go ... Fortunatus."

"Not now," he whispered. "We may as well finish."

"No, no!"

"Yes," he was panting. "As well be hung for a sheep as a lamb. Sin is sin."

"Oh," Agnes began to scream and he put his two hands over her mouth this time, almost choking her.

"It'll be all right," he reassured. "Let me ... once ... then ..."

She lay back, arched on the thick bundle of clothes gathered in a wad under her backbone, stared at the sky and felt a quick, confused sensation of pain, heat, tension and release. The sky was like the neck of a pigeon. Fortunatus removed his hands. "Don't cry," he whispered. "It's the same thing Radegunda feels. Just the very same only she reaches it by different ways. The followers of Dionysius felt it too."

Agnes wept. "Sacrilege ..."

"We can repent."

"*Do* you?" She seized his hand, staring anxiously.

"Not yet."

"With *who* else ...?"

"Nobody. Nobody here."

"Fortunatus ..."

"Agnes."

"Would anyone have done or did you especially ... want me?"

He kissed her. "Agnes," he whispered, "*this* is the real sin: passion of the heart, of the mind. The body is unimportant. Your *mind* should be God's."

"God's too," she said. "God's finally since he made us both. But first I want us to love each other. If not, this is—lechery."

He kissed her several times, then: "Lechery is a lesser sin."

"But a meaner one. Will we love each other?"

"How can we?" Still kissing her, quick dry little kisses now.

"Oh," she turned from him. "You don't."

"Haven't I always?" He tried to put his arms around her. "Weren't we friends?"

"Now it must be different. Look," she whispered. "I know this can't go on. Some day, perhaps soon, very soon, we must repent, stop, ask for forgiveness, but not yet. Not until we have known each other: made a sort of communion out of our love. Else what good was it? You *said* human love led to God."

"And away from him."

"Fortunatus, shall we break off now?"

"No!" he seized her.

She pushed him off her. "Is it lechery?"

"It's everything." He buried his face in her neck. "Everything." He bit her. "Good and bad."

"Can we be happy for a while?"

"Yes," he whispered. "At least for a while. For a dangerous while."

"Love?" she wondered.

"Yes," he promised, "my love."

"Oh God," Agnes whispered. "Thank you."

Chapter Seven

Radegunda was tried by doubts. A.D.

When the Bridegroom was away—what lover stays 569
constantly with his beloved?—they came. Her choice of
convent life had sprung from love—but of what? God?
Self? Peace? Privacy? She had no belief in mixed motives.
Neither she nor her spiritual advisers saw morality in
shades of grey. In arid moods, she threw a blighting
glance at a past suddenly rotten. Her youth stank and the
stench was tonic, rousing her to furnish fresh efforts.

What did demoralize was ambiguity. She could not
cope with good in evil, mixed like light dappled in a forest.
Animals—Clotair—pursuing their inevitable appetites for
flesh and blood were most troubling. All dealings with
him were open to doubt. In his boiling animality, in the
sparky splendour of his youth, Clotair had shown no
signs of having the ability to reason. He had cunning,
but so has a fox and if his reason reached no higher than a
fox's, how could he be held responsible?

And if he couldn't, mustn't she?

In memory, old encounters turned turtle, like capsized
boats. Where once she had seen moral triumphs, she was
now less sure. Tilted, a knife blade will blaze brighter than
captured light, then return at a twitch to leaden grey.

Which was true? Which? She maddened. Had she been
right before? Or now? And why was she unsure? Was God
tempering her? Lucifer, the lightbearer, flashed his
trick mirrors in her mind's eye. There was no criterion.

She was remembering a turning-point in her life: the A.D.
second time Clotair came to try and get her back. Ten 559
years ago almost to the day. It had been spring but an

earlier spring than now. Irises in the convent garden were blooming. Their blue and purple were a luminous counterpart to the Lenten veils in the convent chapel. Radegunda was in that chapel when a nun came to tell her Clotair was in the garden. Waiting.

"*In* the convent garden!" exclaimed Radegunda. "Who let him in?"

"The abbess, mother. She could hardly refuse."

"I suppose not."

Clotair, since his brothers' death, was king of all Gaul. Besides, who else had endowed the convent and brought pressure on the local duke and bishop without whom the buildings could never have risen so fast nor on so grand a scale? But Radegunda was resentful. He had been magnanimous. He had let her go. Why did he have to turn up with memories of their married years? To contaminate her new life? She walked reluctantly to the garden.

The sight of him was a shock. It was seven years since she had left him and although he had tried once to get her back, she had been preserved by a miracle from even having to see him. She thought of the miracle with satisfaction. It ratified what she had done and become.

He turned his head. He looked—was it possible?—pitiable. Red-flecked eyes, face a sunburst of broken veins, bright, pitted, shiny, as though some of the blood he had shed had spattered back on him. Maybe it had! He had murdered his own son and infant grandson the year before. He was, Radegunda remembered, prone to rages of regret.

"Radegunda!"

She saw him quiver, repressing an urge to embrace her. He would have wanted to. Hugs, punches, slaps and kisses were his language. Squeezes, grabs, bites and tickles. Even inanimate things had to be touched. He was always testing the blades of weapons, fondling a stone, crushing a leaf, trailing a finger along a girl's or a horse's neck, dipping it in the juice oozing from a roast or a goblet of wine and sucking it dry. Now she felt his planned embrace reverberate off herself. His hand hung unhappily. He was afraid of her. Awed. Memory of the miracle shielded her still. Charitably, she held out her hands.

"My poor lord! The world has not been using you well."

She felt a shudder stiffen him. Unused to pity. Then the hands in hers went limp.

"No," he acquiesced. "The last few years have been ... unlucky. How long is it since I came to see you?"

"Seven years."

"So long."

It had been at her villa—a villa he had given her—at Saix. She had gone there on leaving him and turned it into an alms-house. Thirteen months later, she heard he was in the district. He was staying at a local estate of his with his court, using up the accumulated produce which it was more practical to consume on the spot than transport to another villa. So there he was with his household, hunting in the surrounding forests, liable, at any moment, to turn up. He had no particular woman at the moment, might even, people guessed, be thinking of claiming her back. She was not young, no longer in the bloom of her beauty but he had been attached to her and besides, having been publicly rejected, might choose for that reason alone to assert his will. Also, wasn't he reaching an age when the sexual impulse grows slack and memory of successful sex better perhaps than fresh adventurings? He might want her as a mnemonic. Radegunda was aghast. Local people agog. News, echoing from mouth to mouth, reached her in the high colour of folk-tale. She bargained with God, knelt all night on stone floors, caught chills, had nightmares and turned to the bishop for comfort. She was a deaconess, wasn't she? *Mustn't* the Church protect her? But the bishop—not Medardus but a local one—was unimpressed. Orders? No woman could be in orders. She was perhaps a nun, he supposed. At most. But of what order? Answerable to whom? It was all irregular. Clotair was his temporal lord and he was just as pleased to keep this Latinized German woman at bay. He was an outdoor man, an administrator, of Gallo-Roman stock, with little taste for excess. Clotair, for all he cared, could claim her and good luck to him. "Render unto Caesar," he quoted glibly. "Your body belongs to your husband." At this news, her body ceased functioning completely.

Rumours of Clotair's coming were so frequent that she had to ignore them. When one proved true there was no time to hide. Frantic, her bowels turning over, she stumbled with Agnes and a girl called Disciola through the kitchen-garden and along the edge of a ploughed strip behind the villa. It was March. Trees were skeletons and offered no cover. A farmer was sowing grain on the bare strip of field. He had already sown half of it and must have been working since dawn. Radegunda, tripping on her mud-heavy hem, shrieked into the wind to him:

"Friend, for God's love, if anyone comes by and asks have you seen us, say no one passed since you started sowing your oats!"

The man shouted back that he would do that.

"How close is he?" Radegunda asked Disciola. She was panting, and drawing breath pained her.

"The portress", began Disciola, "told me to run. That she'd keep him talking, then send him the wrong way, but ... Look!" She pointed across the narrow strip of ploughed field.

He was there. Not three perches off. Looking at them: gash of teeth, eyeballs straining like arrow-heads at the ready. As though she had eaten henbane, Radegunda's eyesight distorted the distance, magnifying him until he filled her field of vision. A great blur of silver-stubbled skin and flame-blue eye descended on her. His long apricot hair flaring in the diffuse sunlight dazzled as she folded at the knees. The wind flung itself about her, pricking her with rain-spittles, rousing her denying flesh until her body tides drew away, congesting like a fist, tightening on her heart until it threatened to explode. The tension jammed her mind. Her pulse stopped. Clotair hovered. The air was turbulent, Radegunda blind. Gradually, she became aware of a release. The humours of her body were flowing back, with a keen and horrid pleasure, to where they belonged.

She opened her eyes and saw a green wave of oat-stalks rising in front of them. The oats had grown, miraculously—how else?—from the farmer's seed to conceal her. Tall as spears, metallic then green according as the wind moved them, they rose sheerly up to foam at their summit in a lacy crest of quivering panicles.

Radegunda reared to her knees. "God has intervened," she cried. "Christ, my Lover, has claimed me! See!" She drew a hand along the harp of stalks, "the farmer's seed," she insisted to Agnes and Disciola.

They were looking at her a little wildly.

"Radegunda, stay calm .... Maybe he only wants ... Radegunda, are you all right? Oh, Blessed Angels, help us!"

"Kneel down," she commanded. "We must give thanks. Don't you *see*?" For they didn't seem to, were still rearing fearfully backwards, staring with far-focusing eyes as though the oat-wall had been transparent. "We've been saved!" she explained.

They had. Clotair understood that heaven had spoken, or so one must presume, since he rode away and did not try to see her again.

Until now.

"Clotair," she said, "that last time, I ... you won't believe me but it pained me that you ... had to go as you did. Without our even having a chance to forgive each other. I had been terrified just before the ..." She refrained from using the proud word 'miracle'. "Even now, this time, when just a while ago they came to tell me you were here, I was afraid. Your name aroused old terrors. I was shaking."

"*Shaking*!" His blue eye focusing on her like a nail. "*You*! You, Radegunda were the toughest opponent I ever met! Tough ... Ah God!" He laughed.

"I used to shake," she insisted. "Secretly. Then nerve myself to seem tough so you would never know how hard it was. I had to resist—in so many ways. You wouldn't have an inkling."

"How did you know about what inklings I had?"

Still staring at her with a twitch of a smile. Bitter though.

"Let's sit," she said socially. They did. She looked at him with confidence, managing calm, even grace. This was easier in that he was looking old. His animal pride, that exuberance that used to act like rubbed amber, magnetizing, drawing her to him when she least wanted to be drawn—was gone. Even his eyes had lost their blue, insolent flame. His once red-and-gold hair was cobwebbed with grey and the rest of it as dull as winter bracken.

"You're not afraid of me now," he said flatly. "I don't rouse you any more. Ah, you were a sexy piece, Radegunda, juicy as an apple or a hunk of fresh beef: all squirty and warm and ready as a mare with her tail up. You couldn't help it and you didn't want to. You pulled away from me as a puppy pulls a stick—so I'd pull you back. I could play you as my harpist plays his harp. But I've lost my touch. I can feel that. I'm not surprised. The spirit—some of it— has been knocked out of me. I wouldn't say this to anyone but you. I, too, have to seem tough, you know. Well you do know, don't you? I suppose you get news here? You hear what's going on?"

"Yes," she said coldly. "We get news. I heard", she said, "of your marriage to Vuldetrada."

"Did you hear that the bishops made me break it up? She's married now to Garivald of Bavaria. I gave her to him. That caused me no heartbreak. It was a marriage of . . . policy. She was my grand-nephew's widow, you see, too young for me maybe, but as I was getting his lands, it seemed . . ." Clotair shrugged. "An insipid little thing. She didn't interest me. Not that my interest isn't as lively as ever, if properly roused." He grinned, his foxy grin. His teeth were yellow like old mushrooms. "You wouldn't want to think otherwise, would you? You wouldn't enjoy resisting a eunuch. Where would be the glory? You like a fight, Radegunda, even if it's only with yourself! Ha, I know you! Knew you since you were twelve years old, remember? I was your guardian, remember?"

"My captor."

"That too. *I* had you educated, turned you into a Roman lady and a Christian. If there's something you've learned that I don't know, well you've got me to thank, right? You can't deny that, can you? I can say I created you as much as any human being can create another. I spared your life. I was a second father to you, and lover. Do you remember our marriage night?"

"No."

"You do. So do I. Ah God, how odd it is! I'm exciting myself. I am. I'm all randy and ready and there's nothing to do with it—where can I put it? Nothing but nuns around me. That's a joke, if you like! Do you know I could hardly get it up for Vuldetrada and here you are, thirty-eight years old and not well preserved either. I'm not reproaching you. I know how you live. Whip marks on that white flesh I'll bet. Is it still white? Have you ruined and tanned it like a slave's backside? And yet you excite me! Well, it's better to have an appetite you can't satisfy than have the satisfaction waiting and no appetite. I know that. I've experienced that. I was lying before when I said I had no troubles with the flesh. I have and that's a bad thing for a man like me: that's death. That frightens you, sends a breath of the tomb through your vitals. Death's a finicky glutton. He takes his first bite of a man's most pivotal part. Well, I'm grateful to you for beating him back a bit for me. I feel less afraid of him now I know he hasn't got any hold on me yet." He was laughing, holding his private parts in his huge hands, lazily, affectionately, as though he held a puppy cupped in his lap.

"Clotair . . ."

"Talk about something else? Yes. Yes, you're right. Better for us both. Did you hear I was back in your country a while ago? In Thuringia."

"Burning, pillaging, murdering—I heard."

"You've no relatives there now, Radegunda! What are the Thuringians to you—ah God, I shouldn't have said that, should I? Considering how ... Yes. Radegunda, I'm sorry. My tongue is like an ill-trained hound. It runs on and scares the game away. Have I done that, now? Have I lost you, turned you against me? Listen." He jumped up, strode away, then back. "I'm going to tell you something you may not believe: I didn't want another war with the Germans! I was all against it, but I had no choice. That surprises you, doesn't it, that I don't always get my way? You won't have heard what happened when I marched against the Saxons? No? No." He turned his back on her and said nothing for so long that she began to wonder was he sick. He was still a big man with no droop to him and his carcass was well padded out. His belly was flat from days in the saddle. Only his rear had spread. It was true, it occurred to her suddenly, that she didn't want to see Clotair humbled physically. The physical world was his domain. He had been a splendid animal in his prime: one of God's successes. Yes, why despise the physical? One could renounce it without despising it.

"Are you ... all right?" she asked. Silence had never been natural to him. In that he was like a child or hound. Waking hours were for action: eating, laughing, fighting, loving. Radegunda's flesh did react now, but she had aroused herself. Experimenting. She made a quick aspiration for forgiveness. Jesus, Mary ...

"I'll tell you," said Clotair whose actual presence she had forgotten. He was more compelling in memory. "I can talk about it to you. To you I can. It was an outrageous thing. Terrible!" He turned an outraged face to her, pink under the hair which still hung loose and long as only the king might wear it, but thinner now and inclined to gather limply in rats' tails. Pale hairs, some white, some still ginger, sprang in tufts from his nose and ears, blazing and dimming as he moved his head in and out of the sunlight. "Outrageous!" What could have outraged Clotair who was outrage itself? Stories of his choicer murders were as popular on a dull evening as any ghost or werewolf tale.

"My own leudes," he was saying. "My own men turned on me." He spat an angry gobbet of spittle on the gravelled path and Radegunda felt something like relief to see that his juices were not dried nor his indignation tamed.

"Tell me," she encouraged.

It was a long story, sour and, she suspected, not often admitted. A story of defeat for Clotair whose warriors had forced him to engage a battle against his judgement.

"They attacked me. Physically. Can you imagine! Me. Their king. They burst into my tent, made ribbons of it and destroyed some of my most precious possessions. An embroidered saddle I was fond of disappeared and hasn't been seen since. Byzantine it was. If I ever see it I'll rip the backside off the thief. I'll put my scramasax up his arse-hole. What was I saying? Yes. They were mad for loot, you see. Rabid. They forced me to fight. They'd have killed me if I hadn't agreed to lead them. So what could I do? I said 'Yes' though I knew it was mad. As I say, a lot of good it did them! So far from their getting loot, the crows got many of them. *I* had to sue for peace and creep home with my tail between my legs. Yes. Well, you don't have that sort of trouble in convents, do you? No. No troubles at all." Staring around him, angry with the anger he had been unable to vent on his rebellious leudes. "Here you're under God's wing," he said, "and I suppose you'll have no troubles in the next life either!" He wiped spittle from his lips with the back of a hand and she noticed the large, pale freckles of old age. "You", he said, "have the advantage of me now, haven't you?"

"I don't . . ."

"You understand me and I don't you. That's the way it is. Like in the hunt when the huntsman knows how the boar or stag is going to react but the boar doesn't know about him. Only with you and me it's the other way round. I'm coming after you. I'm the huntsman—and I don't understand you. I can't soften you. To another woman—to *you* if you were like other women, I might say: 'Radegunda, do you remember when we were young, how we did this or that? Do you remember the mare I gave you, a Thuringian like yourself, with a silver coat, spotted, beautiful and hard to tame?' I might say: 'Radegunda, I see you young again and cosily mine when I see the way your shoulder twitches. Even under that hideous habit your shoulder is talking to me, and your foot when you sit there and it begins to move on its own. It's reminding me of things, moments when things were good between us.' They were, you know. Sometimes they were. You'll deny that though. You'll deny it to yourself—so how can I move or soften you? I can't, can I?" Staring at her from a blunt, astonished face. Had Clotair often acknowledged such a puzzle?

Softened after all, she decided to touch him, reaching out a wooden hand awkwardly to his knee. But he didn't notice. It was too late, too wooden or—if he *had* observed it—too unpleasantly pitying. He took no notice and she pulled it back, letting it hang, as though now misplaced, across her thigh.

"Then I think," said Clotair, "'she's a religious woman. Duty is something she knows about. I'll remind her of her duty to *me*.'" Stepping backwards, he surveyed the convent. "This is a fine place you built yourself with my morning gift? The finest in Gaul I'm told. With *my* morning gift! Ha! There's a joke all right! You give your wife a good morning gift after your first night of love. A generous, outsize one to show you appreciate the pleasure she brought you—and what does she do? Thanks you kindly, uses it to build herself a convent and leaves you alone in your bed. I must be the fable of Gaul. Horny Clotair grew a horn to match his wife's halo. Give me a tune and I'll sing it." His laugh was a bark, loud and desolate. Why did he want her? "I sometimes think", he said next, "that my luck left me with you. I've had knocks, you know. Mmm—mind you," a quick swaggering grin, "I've had luck too. My brothers died and I got their land. That turd, Childebert, croaked in the nick of time.

122

He was conspiring against me while my back was turned. While I was fighting the Germans, can you imagine. But God smote him!" Satisfaction lit the old blue flame for a moment in Clotair's eye. "He was a turd right to the end," he remarked. "May his soul rot!"

"My lord, he's dead!"

"Are you trying to cross me?"

"He was your brother!"

"God smote him! His judgement spoke. You'll agree about that, won't you. You're a religious woman. You agree with God's judgement, don't you?"

Clotair's eyes popped. Like stones in a sling, they looked ready to fly at her: wild, protuberant, restrained only by a frail network of bloody lines. He had often thrown her religion into their fights. Fighting was his talent. He could make a weapon of anything. "A religious woman," he'd roar—she could hear him now—"and a lousy wife! A nun in bed. Wears a hair-shirt but can't come to table on time. The shirt rubs others more than it does herself. Religion's a convenient cover for obstinacy and getting one's own way." He wasn't such a fool, Clotair. Some of his shafts hit home.

"It's easy for you," he said now. "What temptations have you here? None. And if you do commit some sin— eating sausage or whipping your nuns too hard, well, repentance is easy for you, as easy as swearing is for me. It's a habit. Now I can't repent at all. I haven't got the knack. I try. I tell myself I shouldn't have done something and I try to feel sorry for it and then, thinking of it, don't you know, I get carried away. I start doing the thing all over again in my mind. Again and again. I feel the desire to do it gnawing at me. My palms begin to itch. My belly tightens with expectation. My muscles tense. I commit the sin in fancy, over and over as often as I think of it. Then do you know what happens? I laugh. I can't help it. It's funny. I roar laughing and I have to creep out of church with a cloth over my nose pretending I've got an attack of sneezing. My only hope is that God thinks it's funny too. On my good days I think he does."

"I heard you made a pilgrimage of repentance to Tours, to the tomb of the Blessed St. Martin."

"Yes. That's why I'm here. I was so close."

"Ah, you just wanted to see the convent?"

Clotair was silent for a moment. Then: "You know why I made the pilgrimage to Tours?"

"I can guess."

Clotair nodded. His shoulders slumped. "Chramn!" he said slowly. "My eldest boy Chramn—you must have heard how he rebelled against me?"

"Yes. He visited me here at the time. I tried to talk sense to him."

"Peugh!" Clotair blew her remonstrances into the air. His lips clapped like a snorting horse's. "Wasting your breath! He was conspiring with that turd, Childebert. You heard that too of course! Bad news travels fast. While my back was turned. I had to have him murdered. Did you know he took the field against me? Spread the rumour that I was dead—that was when I was in Germany. Hoping to get some of my own men to join him. Some of them did too! Grabbed my lands. Then, when that turd Childebert died, he ran off to rouse the Bretons against me. The Bretons! He'd have allied himself with Lucifer if the fiend had made the offer. I had to have him murdered. You kill a mad dog, a dog who has the rabies, no matter how you loved it when it was sane. Don't you?"

The nun did not reply. Clotair bent forward and caught her wrist. "Don't you?" he heckled, "kill a mad dog?"

"You did not", she said, "have to kill his wife and children too. You did not have to shut them up in a labourer's cottage and burn the lot like wasps in a nest!"

Clotair roared: "Hornets! They were worse than wasps. The children too. His blood was in them. It was bad."

"You had him tied to a bench with a cloth over his mouth and then fired the house. They were helpless."

"Hornets! Hornets! You said it yourself!"

"Clotair," the nun put her hand on his arm, gripped it and pulled him to a sitting position beside her on the bench. His body was shaking, his skin sweating. "Listen," she said firmly. "Calm yourself and think. You said you wanted to repent. You went to Tours to repent, didn't you?"

Clotair leaped up. "I can't repent," he roared. "How can I? I hate him. I'm sorry I didn't pull his heart from his stinking, treacherous body with my own hand!" He spread five fingers, grabbed a heart-sized measure of air and wrenched his arm furiously backwards. "I loved him," he yelled. "I was a good father to him. There was no reason . . ."

"Clotair!" She was standing, straining to control his glance. "Suppose. Just suppose it's Judgement Day and you are before the throne of God. Imagine God looking at you. Suppose God were to ask you, 'Clotair, my son, why did you murder your own son, Chramn, with his wife and little children? Why did you burn them to a slow and painful death when they were already your prisoners and could do you no harm? You have often sinned against me, but I have been forbearing! I never struck you down in your sin as you did Chramn. Why did you do it?' What answer could you give to God?"

Clotair stiffened. He stood, very erect, very serious but avoiding Radegunda's glance. "I would say," he stared unblinkingly at the sun as though addressing it. "I would say . . ." He paused a moment, then burst out angrily: "I would say, 'why, oh God, did you put them in my power when my temper was up? *You knew* how I'm made and what I'd do! If you delivered them up to me it was because *you wanted* me to do it! It's *your* fault!'" Clotair turned to Radegunda. "*That's* what I'd say," he told her. "What could he say to that? Tell me. What?"

Radegunda was silent, then: "We'll pray for you, Clotair," she promised. "The whole convent."

"Radegunda," turning to stare into her eyes. "There's a better, quicker way than prayer. I haven't got much time.

I need help. I need someone with me whom I can trust, talk to. You know I've never been one for prayer or talk. I hadn't time. It wasn't . . . the thing expected. I'm a king. I command. I demand. I take. I fight. I force respect. That's what I've done for fifty years. Fifty years I've been king. How can I learn to do the opposite now? Unless *you* help me, Radegunda. You know that's why I'm here, so why pretend? I need you."

Radegunda was moved. He saw this.

"Not the flesh this time," he promised. "That's not what I need. Anyway, women . . ." he waved dismissively, "are never scarce: servant girls, slaves, ambitious little virgins . . . I have to push them away. They're like the puppies who tease my old hound when he wants to sleep. He bites them but they come back for more, disturbing his rest." He leaned forward. His once arrogant, lean, young man's face was still discernible, still present in the basic bone beneath the half-shucked pod of loosening skin. She scrutinized the map of that skin, but lines tell little. This might have been an old ascetic. If she had not known him, she might have taken the deep dents for the track of suffering. Old men strip off the evidence of dead passions. His cheeks, once bold and bellying like sails in a tailwind, were now trimmed down.

"After all," he argued, "it would be an act of . . . mercy. I know you don't want to leave your convent, maybe you don't want *me* to have the best of both worlds—or any of the other world at all. Maybe you don't think I deserve it? Maybe I don't. But shouldn't you leave that decision to God, Radegunda. Shouldn't you do your best by me? Return good for evil—if that's what you think you got from me! Your nuns can carry on without you. How do you know God wants you here anyway?" he urged, and, seeing a sign of weakening in her, struck: "It's your duty!" he asserted. Triumphantly.

"My duty is here," Radegunda told him with a perceptible tilt of her chin.

"How the devil do you know?" Clotair dropped his

126

suppliant's pose. "You're a proud, obstinate female. Always were! So sure, always so sure, so right, so much in love with yourself! You say you are giving up the world for God but you only give up what you don't want. Your 'charity' is all for lepers and people who have no claim on you. *That* impresses people. Kissing the sores of disgusting old beggars makes a good story. It does the rounds of Gaul and turns up in every harpist's repertory. God's belly, but I'm sick of hearing about you and your lepers! I tell myself it must be a vice! You made more bones about performing your conjugal duties than a wild mare brought to stud! But when it came down to it you liked it well enough! You were a sexy woman, Radegunda, sexier than a lot of whores I've known and I've known plenty. You just liked to be forced! You're not unique. I've known other women like you, only they weren't clever enough to make use of religion to salt their sex. You liked the forcing!" roared Clotair. "*That* was the best part. Now that you haven't got me to force you, you force yourself—to kiss lepers!"

"I see, my lord," Radegunda spoke in an icy, toneless voice, "that I would still have to suffer your abuse if I were to return to you. At least you are not attempting to get me back under false pretences. *Now*!"

"Oh I," roared Clotair, "am honest."

"Not so honest about Chramn!"

"I am! I *am* honest about Chramn! I'm sick about Chramn, sick but not sorry, can't you see that, you cow? I vomit, I bring up my guts when I think of my own son turning on me and of all the things he did and how I had to fight a battle to vanquish him! It was him or me! And how can I be sorry it wasn't me? How? Huh? I'd kill him again if I had to and I'd be right. What kind of a king would I be else? The bishops agree with me, do you know that? They know how the world is run! They said it was like God's judgement on Absalom! Absalom, have you heard about him?"

"Yes," said Radegunda wearily. "But you still went to

Tours to try to repent."

"Because," howled Clotair, "God is unreasonable."

"His reason ..."

"I know. I know. It's beyond us. That's what the priests say, damn them. Well then it's beyond us and I can't be expected to repent! I'm stifling. I can't breath! How can I live? I have all of Gaul to govern and every town is full of conspiracy. Traitors spring up like ragweed in a field. I have to have eyes in the back of my head. Whom can I trust? Tell me that. My men assault me. My brother and son conspire against me. I have to survive, don't I? Gaul needs a king—any king is better than a pack of smaller men tearing at the kingdom like dogs at a carcass! *How can I survive and repent!* How? How?"

"My lord, you've been shouting. People are frightened. Look!"

Clotair turned and saw a row of nuns' heads along the top of the garden wall. Terrorized eyes peeped.

"Ha!" he roared in amusement. "Frightened, are they? Frightened for you?" He walked over to the wall, stared silently at the veiled heads for a moment then suddenly let out a yell: "Boo!" he cried and the heads bobbed down and up again like gulls on a wave. Clotair laughed and slapped the wall. "Don't worry," he told them. "I'm an old dog now. I bark. I don't bite." He turned back to Radegunda. "See," he said, "they were anxious about you. The protective instinct survives, even in a convent."

"All the instincts, my lord."

"All? Would they kill for you?"

Radegunda closed her eyes.

"All right, all right. I'm sorry. Now, you see, to you I can say that. I really am sorry I upset you. You can go," he shouted to the nuns. "Your foundress is safe. I'm not going to take her off. Go off now. Shoo!" The heads disappeared. Clotair laughed more quietly, nodding his head. "It's an old feeling," he said, "one I hadn't felt since you left. You were always making me sorry! Do you know, Radegunda, why I remember you more fondly than

other women? Not for the reasons you might think."
Clotair sat back down beside her on the stone bench.
"No, the reason, Radegunda, is because you had no
children. Are you surprised? I am. I was so proud of my
children. Once. I was like a farmer who plants seeds and
sees them come up: a good feeling. It doesn't last though.
The seeds turn into plants. The plants are alien. They're
not you, not the farmer and not the old plant. They're
a new thing: a rival and they claim the mother's love. I
knew that long before Chramn turned on me. I knew my
children were my enemies. A woman who has no children
mothers her husband. Even you, Radegunda!"

"I", said Radegunda, "have my nuns. They are my
children."

"Then they're my enemies. I've been robbed again!
You took my morning gift and made rivals for me! Ah,
the sour old joke! What a lot of gifts I gave you. I suppose
you remember none of them. Mostly I gave them to you
to make up for some row—when I was feeling sorry.
Every sort of gift. But you've forgotten them! You don't
remember where they are! I can tell you about one. It is
in the Church at Tours. I saw it when I was there on my
pilgrimage. On the high altar. I was trying to pray, standing,
trying to collect my thoughts, feeling wrong, somehow,
out of place. And then, right in front of me, I saw something
familiar. It was a gilt lace altar-cloth hung with pearls
and bits of gold, very intricate, very costly and it brought
something back, some memory of years back. Where had
I seen that lace? There couldn't be two pieces like it. It
was of very special workmanship—and then I remembered.
It was a tunic I'd given you and which you'd offered the
saint. I suppose your dresses are hung on half the altars of
Gaul? My gifts! Think of the memories if I were to go
on a pilgrimage along your track, Radegunda! Well,
maybe they'll do me some good when the time comes that
I need it."

"Clotair," Radegunda spoke gently. "Why don't you
stay here a while. If I can truly help you make your peace

with God, I will see you as often as you like. You have villas in the Poitou. Stay on here and you can visit me. Every day."

"You won't come out?"

"This is my life."

"*Why* is it your life? You were married to me. You lived with me fourteen years. How do you know God doesn't want you to come back to me now when I need you? Doesn't he demand sacrifices from people like you? His special people?"

"Clotair," even more gently, "you yourself saw the sign the last time you came. At Saix. Don't you remember?"

A shyness, a kind of humility prevented her saying the word 'miracle'. But she was sure he did remember.

"What?"

"God showed us both that my place was not with you."

He shrugged, frowned. Did he really not understand?

"The oats," she prompted. "The oats that sprang up and hid us from sight when you came by on your horse! That was why you turned back! They grew up in the space of a few moments and you ..." She waited, "you *knew* then, you understood, didn't you, that it was", again she paused, "a sign!"

He was staring at her distrustfully. "Do you often get dreams like that? Are you talking clever priests' talk—parables and such—or do you really believe oats sprang up and hid you? I mean real, vegetable oats out of the earth?" He had withdrawn into himself, pulled back, shrivelled a bit and was looking at her intently.

"Why did you turn your horse around then, Clotair? Why did you ride off instead of trying to speak to me? You had come to speak to me, hadn't you? And I was within a few ells of you, two perches at most, with Agnes and Disciola!" In her memory's eye she could still see the thick-jointed stems of the oats, their surprising size. She could see the delicate clusters of green-sheathed grains on top, quivering like water in a breeze, yet forming a screen opaque enough to blot out the horrifying image of

130

Clotair. "Why then," she challenged in triumph, "if what I say isn't true?"

He spread his hands. "I was sorry for you. I knew you would be no good to me. I knew it when I saw you huddled between those two children and when I saw you kneel up to pray."

"You saw me kneel up?"

"Of course I saw you! You were like mice waiting for the falcon to swoop. If you'd been a virgin it wouldn't have stopped me. I'd have thought, 'Well, she's shy. She doesn't know me. I'll reassure her.' As one does with a cub one takes home to tame. But I'd been married to you for fourteen years. If you weren't tame yet ..." He threw his hands out again. "So, I turned my horse and left." He gave her a long look. "Did the other two see oats spring up?"

"Yes, yes. Of course. So did the peasant."

Clotair nodded. "Well, it's like repentance. I can't talk to God and he doesn't talk to me."

"I don't believe you," cried Radegunda angrily. "You saw the oats the same as all the rest of us but you won't admit it! You won't because, if you did, you would have to admit that you were wrong to try to see me again after receiving a sign like that! It's easier to say you didn't receive it, to cheat God and try to cajole me into going back to you! I don't know why you want me. You think I can teach you some trick to get you into heaven. But there are no tricks, Clotair. Not for that. You killed all my relatives, you used my body and abused my spirit for fourteen years. You let me have this convent for politic reasons. The Church is powerful in Gaul and it suits you to keep in with the bishops. I owe you nothing."

Clotair stood up. "You are not generous, Radegunda. You care more for your own salvation than mine. Maybe holy people are never generous that way. I won't trouble you again."

He walked away. It was the last she saw of him. Four months later he caught a fever while hunting, died and was buried in the church he had built in honour of Medardus who had died some years before and was now recognized as a holy man and perhaps a saint.

Chapter Eight

That spring Agnes was half mad and knew it. Her sane self kept the other going. Sometimes it seemed a near thing. She felt her skin must erupt dreadfully like the fruit trees which had broken out in a disease of bright pallor, easing themselves in lavish foamings.

"We must be discreet, Agnes. Agnes, are you paying attention?"

She smiled.

He accused: "You look mad!"

"I am."

"Has anyone noticed? Said anything?"

"No. I'm only mad when I'm with you—and when I'm alone."

Madder when alone: Fortunatus constrained her.

"Prudence ..." he recommended.

She managed it, subduing impulses to destroy herself in a number of ways. One would be scandal. Religion no longer hampered her. Everything it promised she had reached in the teeth of it. Since she was happy, God, rising above his own rules, must be approving her. She was not afraid of him. Only of Radegunda who would not understand and for the nuns who wouldn't either. One had to think of them.

"I am prudent," she assured him.

"You", said Radegunda to Agnes, "are my justification. You are happy. I see it in your face."

Agnes said nothing. The two were combing wool. She bent over hers. Yes: the happiness was bursting out of her. Explosively. Shamelessly. She tried to hide it.

"I have visions," Radegunda confided. "But I have

doubts too. Supposing my messages from Christ were figments of a mad mind? I don't believe this but I have no proof other than my own belief. The real ratification of our enterprise here", said Radegunda, "is your happiness." She smiled at Agnes with affection.

Agnes worked, pulling thick handfuls of wool through the iron comb.

A.D. I have been asleep.
587   I feel weak. They have forgotten to bring me food. I have some from before but the lettuce leaves are limp and rotting and the bread is hard. They have forgotten. Something unusual is happening. The bells have not rung. Blessed Virgin, you who succour the lowly, give me strength. Grant me calm. Blessed Radegunda who heard my vows, help me. I am agitated. I cannot pray. My leg is stiff. A pain runs up the bone. Move it up and down. Crouch and rise, crouch, rise, crouch, rise. The pain is worse. Again. Again. Count: six, seven, eight ... Try to reach a hundred. Pain! *Pain!* The movement keeps the leg from growing stiff and the pain may be offered up. Twenty-seven, twenty-eight ... Keep it up. Thirty, thirty-one, thirty-two, thirty-three, thirty-four ... Holy Angels! What was that? What? What can that be? That noise? Surely no one—a demon must be troubling my mind. Pray. St. Martin help me. Help me holy St. Denis! Could the convent be under attack? No, no one would dare. In all their wars, the kings respected the convent. Only once the outlying farms were attacked. But that was a mistake. The soldiers swore that they hadn't known where they were. They were punished, moreover, not that ... Don't think! I mustn't think of that now. I grow agitated when I remember that and I am trying to stay calm. Calm. But I can *see* the blood, the charred wood ... *Don't* think of it. Think of what happened afterwards. Yes. Afterwards the blessed Radegunda mortified her flesh for forty days and nights. She heated a metal blade shaped in the shape of Christ's initials and, when it was

at white heat from the coals, impressed it on her flesh, branding herself a member of Christ's flock forever. Or did she do that some other time? I forget. I know what she said to us. "Sisters," she said, "when you hear what happens out in the world and even on our own estates, can you feel that our cloistering here is a great sacrifice? Is it not perhaps an act of selfishness? Of self-love?" The nuns were confused by that question. What did it mean, they wondered. Did the foundress want to open the convent and send us back to our homes—those of us who had homes? There was a lot of agitation. Nuns wept and questioned the chaplain and the abbess and prioress until, finally, Agnes, the abbess, called us all together to explain. The foundress, she said, was only asking us to consider our own good fortune and reflect on how we must try to merit it by accurate and joyful observance of our Rule. The Rule itself, she reminded us, was not harsh but gentle as a linen robe. The abbess could always restore serenity.

It is dark now. The cracks of light have gone.

There *is* something wrong. The bells have not rung for several days. I am sure of that. Besides, my bread ... Why are they not bringing me fresh food? The noises I heard before were ... Were? No, I cannot be sure. Demons play tricks on me. Maybe I was asleep or unconscious and let my food go stale? But where is the fresh food then? Eat. It is when I am weak that the demons grow strong. Suck the hard bread. Chew a little garlic and swallow the rotting lettuce. Maybe it is not rotting? I cannot trust my senses. Sometimes I have seen monsters, felt their hairy, scaly touch or the bite of their teeth. Those were figments and devilish artifices. Oh Lord, into thy hands I commend my spirit!

"From her first entry into the convent, as the East can attest and the North, South and West can confirm, Radegunda diligently begged and amassed a vast quantity of relics .... When she heard of a new relic she drank the words as greedily as though they were quenching a thirst in her or as

though she were a sufferer from dropsy whose thirst grows and worsens the more he satisfies it."

Sister Baudonivia, *De vita sanctae Radegundis*

A.D. 569 Maroveus, Bishop of Poitiers and Radegunda's spiritual overlord, was talking to his secretary. The bishop was in his habitual state of gentle inebriation, having been drinking Chian wine for several hours.

"Who am I?" he asked his secretary. "Do I exist at all? Is Radegunda bishop? It looks like it. Being queen wasn't to her taste. She prefers to be Bishop of Poitiers. She is her own carver and *I* might be dead for all the notice she takes of me. Dead! I can taste the charred coal in my grave. My mouth is dry with it. Give me another glass of that wine. My saliva has stopped flowing. Have one yourself. You'll be better company."

"My lord, she has sent asking you to officiate. This time you can't ..."

"I can't what? I can't refuse? Is that it?"

"She needs you now, Monseigneur. She needs you to receive the procession bringing the fragment of the True Cross back from Constantinople. It *is* a historic occasion. She wants you to be there."

"She wants me the way she'd want a man's head stuck on a pole outside her convent. She's a head-huntress like her ancestors. She wants my presence to complete her own glory. Not my active participation. Not my advice. Let's not even mention my authority: just my head on a pole."

"My lord, she's a holy lady ... Known for her purity, esteemed ..."

"Holy, pure!" the bishop groaned. "Lucifer was pure! Purity is a dangerous virtue. It engenders pride. That woman is stiff with both. And, in case you were thinking of it, don't mention miracles. You don't believe in that sort of thing, I hope. It's useful. It's inevitable. We can't do without miracles. We have to compete for people's minds, hearts, etcetera. We're all agreed on that. We don't have to be too credulous ourselves. You are a Gallo-Roman, my secretary, and a man with a career to make in the Church, so don't talk to me about miracles."

"Gregory was telling me the other ..."

"Gregory, you don't need me to tell you, has the mind of a nine-year-old and that's all right. He doesn't have to be intelligent. I forget how many of his uncles are bishops? Half a quorum in most councils. His career is assured and his mental processes barbaric. His mother must have got him off a serf. It's the only explanation. A man of his descent! Well, they tell me he's writing a history of the times! It would be doing posterity a good turn to burn it. If they judge us on poor Gregory's evidence, God help our image. If I had the energy myself, I'd scratch down a few aphorisms, but our blood is tired. Tired, Florius. We've been in the saddle too long, men of our race! We have saddle-fatigue. Except for Gregory. His energy is another sign his mother got him on the wrong side of the sheet. Off some Frank no doubt. The Franks are roaring with energy. They're like the pirate bird that terrorizes other predators into disgorging prey then eats it ready chewed. That's what they did to the Visigoths. To the Burgundians. Terrible people. Fatiguing. Like all the Germans. Like Bishop Radegunda. She even wore out Clotair. Ha, that must have taken doing! They say he slept with six kitchen-maids a night trying to replace her. Now she wears God out with her antics. Oh well, I suppose *his* energies are tireless too. Eugh! I've made myself tired thinking of all those energetic people, all those little battering rams. Where's that wine? You know, I think I need a rest. A trip to my country estates to taste the new vintage and mark the casks that are worth keeping. That always does me good. Besides, if I don't go, the serfs drink it up before I can get the casks counted. Tell Proculus we'll be leaving tomorrow early. I'll ride the silver mare: a Thuringian like Bishop Radegunda. I can imagine I'm riding *her*, driving my spurs into her flanks. Gee up, Bishop Radegunda!"

137

"And the True Cross, my lord?"

"Florius, I am going to my country estate. I am as good as gone. You can think up any excuse you like. I even give you permission to tell Bishop Radegunda the truth, which is the following: she has consistently acted as though I and my office did not exist. I and my office—and it is the office which matters, Florius, the office, not the man! She saw fit when she first installed that abbess of hers to go over my predecessor's head and have the blessing administered by the Bishop of Paris. Since then she has been sending her agents back and forth to the four corners of Christendom collecting relics without any inquiry as to what I thought of this practice."

"A holy one, surely?"

The bishop moaned. "A form of high-class butchery. She sends—thanks to her money and connections—to Eastern churches for her relics because she knows that here in the West we do not hack up saints' bodies to give out ears and fingers and less mentionable parts to passing pilgrims. She has collected the most imposing charnel heap in Gaul. Really, when one sees what the Germans make of Christianity, one wonders was it worth converting them. Each trophy has a story, of course. St. Mamas's finger flew off its metacarpus when her agent turned up in Jerusalem. Other relics transported themselves to her convent from a villa where she happened to have left them. God has obviously nothing better to do than to go round picking up after Radegunda! Smug—oh my God! That I should have have to deal ... Here—pour me some more wine. *And* yourself. I shall believe you are insensitive if you don't take the odd dose to blur the edges of perception! The sheer triviality of it—why did *you* enter the Church, Florius? Silly question. Ignore. What is it you've been trying to say to me?"

"You *did* grant the pilgrims your permission to go to the Emperor Justin and ask, in her name, for a fragment of the True Cross!"

"Oh, I did. I did. I granted my permission because,

before she'd even asked me, her son-in-law and my temporal lord, King Sigibert, had already granted his. How could I refuse? But I will not turn up and applaud her having gone over my head and forced my hand. She doesn't respect my authority so let her do without it."

"But who will take your place?"

"Nobody will. The city gates will remain closed and the procession may proceed where it likes. Florius, don't argue with me. I'm within my rights. This is my diocese, I believe? Yes. And, as you were so usefully reminding me a moment ago, several councils and synods have laid it down that "the government and direction of monasteries and their inmates are the responsibility of the bishops of the diocese in which the monasteries happen to be." The words of the Council of Arles, I believe? Held in 554. Similar stipulations were made by the Councils of Agde and Epaone, if my memory does not deceive me. In case it does, I'd like you to look up the relevant canons. A letter will be going off to our friend Radegunda, to remind her of a boring little virtue called 'obedience' which is not one she cultivates with enthusiasm. I am not doing this from petty motives, Florius. The Church is an institution and it is my duty, as one of its officials, to see that it survives as such, which it won't if individualism, meddlesomeness, German anarchy and childless women are allowed to sap it. That woman does whatever comes into her head and her head is as changeable as one of those horses' craniums pagans stick on poles with their jaws wedged open. Crows pluck out their eyes, their flesh shrivels off the grin of their teeth and the wind whirls them, yet country people think they have powers. They think the same thing about Radegunda because she too whirls and rattles in a way that strikes the imagination. Her head's half Romanized and the body's German still. They repel each other: hence her restlessness, her crazes and fancies. The latest is this need to send off to Constantinople to get a bit of the True Cross, to change the name of the convent to Holy Cross and to get that tame poet of hers to write a hymn to it. It's all very close to idolatry, Florius. Dangerously close. The German mind likes the concrete. If it isn't a horse's cranium it's a bit of the True Cross set in a bejewelled gold triptych."

"It stimulates religious feeling, my lord."

"A rapacious religion, but I suppose that's something. I suppose so. Her other fancies too. They delight the people. She has her uses. Maybe they'll make her a saint, make Gregory a saint, make her abbess and that poet of hers a saint. Maybe you and I will be the only anonymous forgotten ones—or reviled ones if Gregory puts us into his history. Our taste will have been too good. We will have refused to enter their circus where one may perform miracles or—since miracles must surely be rare—tricks. Mind you, the circus is a dangerous place: challenging. People have mislaid their minds there, come out mad, demonic, sick and/or sainted. But at its best it lacks taste. And Christianity has another side."

"But is first of all an institution?"

"And an institution needs support, you are going to say, Florius? Needs the crowd and to get the crowd what must one do? Join the circus. Put on my best vestments and receive Radegunda's procession with appropriate pomp?"

"I didn't say it, my lord."

"No. I did. I said it myself. I am a churchman. I should not let personal distaste for her sort of piety get in the way of my duty, should I, Florius?"

"No, my lord."

"But neither should I allow my authority to be flouted?"

"No, my lord."

"No, and as there seems to be a clash of principles here, it would seem that I *can* take my choice. I can see that the Radegundas and Gregories are going to have things their own flamboyant way for a while. Discipline and order are ghosts. Even memory is dying, do you realize that? Do you realize that the younger generation, your generation, hardly reads? Can't read, is illiterate. It is an odd feeling to be alive at a time like this, to watch the slow destruction of a whole mental universe and to be incapable of saving it. Oh, I suppose if *I* were writing history instead of poor, muddle-headed young Gregory with his dazzled eyes like a rabbit caught by a boy with a torch ... but it's too hopeless. Why try? I shall go into mourning for the passing of reason and drink a toast to the age of miracles which is upon us: the kingdom of the imagination. I drink. What else should I do? The imagination is the barbarian of the mind and, wed to the spiritual, can produce unhealthy offspring."

"My lord, if I might voice ... ?"

"Voice, voice it whatever it is. It'll be safer voiced than fermenting in your brain."

"You said, my lord, that Radegunda was proud."

"And I am proud too, is that it?"

"Yes, my lord."

"Yes. It's true. I admit it. I am proud and I am not angry. Watch me, Florius. One of the last men of reason. What would a Frank do? What would the late King Clotair or the present King Chilperic have done if you were to turn his argument round and catch him in the net of his own garrulity?"

"Quite possibly kicked me."

"Very possibly, Florius. It's an aggravating trick. Yes, I'm proud, proud with the pride and lucidity of despair. Maybe Radegunda and I will burn in the same part of Purgatory, eh? The Purgatory of the proud. Not that I believe in Purgatory. It's a concept, a symbol, a place of the mind. She believes in it as a place she can and will touch with her live flesh. Poor Radegunda: pursued by physical horrors! I am only pursued by mental ones. Who is happier? I am already in my purgatory, burning, Florius, burning. That's why I drink. But I shan't meet her procession. There's a clash of principles, Florius, a clash. Maybe that's for the good of the Church, what do you say to that, Florius?"

"The good, my lord? I don't understand."

"I'm not drunk, Florius. I was just thinking of clashes,

141

you know, between my kind of Christianity and Radegunda's and how clashes make sparks and sparks throw light. You have to have two sides so that they may clash and correct each other. *My* pride is humbled—a salutory experience—by having to deal with miracle-mongers and believers in a horned Satan who smells of shit—that *is* what they believe, you know. You haven't been out among the people yet, Florius. You've been living in your father's villa with your volumes of Euclid, your swans and partridges and your hot baths. A lost world. Living in the past. How many of your kind do you think exist today? You'll learn—and maybe you'll take a little comfort from this good Chian wine if they're still importing it when your day of need comes. Do you know that in our own diocese within the last few years a man was sacrificed to the devil? That there have been scalpings ... Maybe you're right after all and Radegunda can communicate better with these people than I can. Maybe you're right. But I shan't meet her procession. She may learn something from my refusal. And the city gates shall not be opened."

"My lord, she may call on the king."

"She may. She will. Let her play her part. I'll play mine. Good-night, Florius. I'm leaving for my estates in the morning."

Maroveus struggled upstairs to his bedroom and the secretary called to a servant to put out the red terracotta oil-lamps which stood in every room in the church house, flickering in draughts, smoking and throwing twisty shadows some of which were not at all unlike Satanic horns.

Chapter Nine

Although the next decades were to be bloody ones for Poitiers, the event of that time which future generations would commemorate was neither a siege nor the lifting of one. It was the coming of the True-Cross fragment from Constantinople.

For weeks beforehand rumours, omens and domestic mishaps kept people in a fever which spread to the animal and even the spirit world. Cows went dry, hens laid monstrosities and there was no doubt but that the demon population of the town was in a state of malignant terror. Demons were even seen within the convent walking, in the shape of small goats, across the refectory wall, but when the blessed Radegunda raised her hand to sketch the sign of the cross, they turned into smoke and evaporated. She was acting with her accustomed tenacity on two fronts. On hearing that Bishop Maroveus had so unaccountably taken to horse and left for his estate, she sent word to the bearers of the Great Relic telling them to turn back. She did not want to welcome the cross in a hugger-mugger way and was resolved that it should not enter Poitiers until another bishop had been found to receive it. Accordingly, she prayed, kept vigil, wept and wrote letters to King Sigibert. While awaiting the outcome of these endeavours, she advised the bearers to seek hospitality in the male monastery which she had founded years before on a visit to the town and shrine of Tours. The monks received the relic with joy, proper pomp and a chanting of psalms which they kept up for the whole time of its stay. This was not prolonged, for Sigibert acted with all speed in persuading Eufronius, bishop of Tours, to accompany the relic to Poitiers. The ceremony devised by Radegunda was of a splendour never before seen in Gaul, as befitted the welcoming of spiritual riches such as Gaul had never seen. The Emperor Justin had generously added several lesser relics—bones, hair, nail-parings, teeth and strips of the dried flesh of martyrs and apostles—from his personal collection. The power of these, although enclosed in an iron-clad box, sent tremors of violent joy and terror through bystanders and even penetrated into surrounding houses, where many sick and bedridden people were afterwards found to have been cured of their maladies and haunted or uncanny rooms to have grown salubrious. The box was borne at the head of the procession by the clerics who had brought it from Constantinople. Behind walked local priests, chanting and carrying a great profusion of lighted tapers whose glow seemed to pale and multiply as they walked through open spaces, then to blaze like knives in the darker gulleys of the town. Incense was burned and scents scattered whose fumes astonished the simple citizenry, many of whom had to climb on the roofs, as the procession itself took up the whole width of the streets through which it passed. It was said afterwards that several people had fallen and been found miraculously intact and other wonders too were witnessed, although, no doubt, the high point of the day came when the procession reached the convent. There, on the walls, the nuns were waiting, looking, in their white, fluttering habits, like doves ready to fly up to heaven. The iron box was opened and the relic shown in its naked glory. It was in five pieces arranged in the form of a double-barred cross on a plaque of lapis lazuli. The crowd fell to its knees and, as it did, there rose, first gently, then booming and echoing from all sides, the strong strains of Fortunatus's new, now famous hymn whose martial syllables so splendidly celebrate the pain, power and paradox of the cross:

Vexilla regis prodeunt,
fulget crucis mysterium,
quo carne carnis conditor
suspensus est patibulo.

Chronicle

Agnes and Radegunda were travelling across Gaul. Pale skies, dark woods, summer rains, nights spent sometimes in the comfortable annex of a bishop's house—at Bordeaux and Saintes—at others in wretched improvised quarters. Days of jolting one's bones in a four-wheeled *raeda*. Now they were in a boat. A second one behind carried their baggage and escort. Gliding. The waters of the Garonne stretched, absorbed light and hardened, icily opalescent as a mussel-shell with a dark-blue rim: the wooded horizon where a storm was threatening. Agnes felt light caressing her, felt her own secret paleness, the paleness of a body she had only recently learned to know, burn in the vigour of the late summer air. Her skin was hyper-sensitive and she had begun, secretly, to wear a silken undergarment beneath the rough wool of her habit. Fridovigia had provided—who knew how? Possibly a stolen altar-cloth? Agnes lay back, stared at a mild, cloud-specked sky and felt no guilt. She loved. She was in accord with a love which she felt in the air's delicate glitter, in the river's movement, in the crew who were busy steering the boat between islands of purple loosestrife, meadowsweet and reeds. Surprisingly, her scruples had evaporated faster than Fortunatus's.

"That's why I'm good at running the convent," she had said to him before leaving for this trip "I take a decision and stick to it. No point in half doing something. I love you. Wholly. How can that be wrong? I see God in you. Don't be frightened."

After all, Radegunda had taught Agnes that knowledge was something one reached directly and with immediacy. One knew God, sin, one's own calling in one illuminating instant and by intuitive—God-given—grasp. Rules were swept away when the soul was enraptured and Agnes was sure hers was. By sweeping away Radegunda's rules, was she not being faithful to Radegunda's spirit? Not quite—but then surely God's way would not be the same for every soul. Agnes had continued to do her work at the convent and these had been busy months. The coming of the True-Cross fragment from Constantinople had brought all sorts of changes. There was the reception ceremony to be planned involving one of those upheavals which disrupt community life. Radegunda was ebullient at the news of the arriving relic, stunned when the bishop inexplicably refused to welcome it, fired at last by energy and defiance: all disruptive emotions. She wrote letters, sent ambassadors to King Sigibert, wept, prayed, tortured herself, received the king's assurance that the Bishop of Tours would be sent to take Maroveus's place and preside over the ceremony, then once again wept, prayed and tortured herself. Other nuns, infected by her emotion, also tortured themselves slightly but showily and grew incompetent. Agnes kept her head and temper and the convent on an even keel during the difficult months.

"Because of *us*," she told Fortunatus. "I draw strength from our love. I need a human intermediary between me and God. I am an efficient but dependent person. I need love. Before you I loved Radegunda. But her love is all turned towards God. It consumes her and does not warm others."

"Do not go forth into the world," quoted Fortunatus bleakly. "Return into yourself. Truth is in the inner man." He grasped her to him with what she feared was cold lust. "She's right, you know," he said.

"Your truth", Agnes told him tartly, "won't turn up in other men's books. You are all divided, Fortunatus. You're like one of those corpses the pagans mutilated to keep their spirits from haunting them. Your head is buried in one place—usually a book—your body elsewhere and your spirit can never get itself together."

"Every human being is bound to the living corpse of his own body."

"Is that a quotation too?"

"From Aristotle."

"I am making a penitentiary", said Agnes, "with scales of penalties to be paid by you every time you talk with another man's tongue. The least will be making love to me

146

right away, wherever we are and without delay."

"Dangerous."

"So don't quote," she said. "You owe me two lovings already."

She loved him as a pony eats an apple: skin, juice, seeds and all, rotten bits too if there are any. Easily and with pleasure, nuzzling, ready for more. Wanting to be loved back the same way. And at first he had—who had begun it all? The furtive chanciness of their meetings meant that they never left each other sated nor met too soon again. He was always ready, always tremulous—but he disliked this. There was the difference between them. He was humiliated, feeling caught in his own body as in a trap.

"That's a quote too!" she accused.

"No, it's how I feel."

"Liar! Welsher! Come on. Pay up."

Ebullient, she could carry him with her for a short while, just as she carried the whole convent. And that was surely a sign of her rightness? Her being in control. It was she who had encouraged Radegunda to make this journey to Arles where they were to visit the convent of St. John which had been functioning for fifty years and, having been founded by St. Caesar, a bishop and papal vicar, enjoyed exemption from later episcopal authority.

"It's the only sensible thing," she explained. "If our own bishop won't be responsible for us, what we'll do is adopt the Rule of St. Caesar and the exemption going with it. The Rule will guide us. The exemption will protect us. We can visit the convent and learn how their system works."

Since leaving it, this was to be her first return to what nuns call 'the world'.

Letters had been exchanged, gifts and messengers sent. Fortunatus had alerted friends and bishops along the way, recommending the two nuns to their care. Their journey led through three Frankish and one Visigothic kingdom. Borders were vague. Gaul was like a painted chessboard whose inks have run. The nuns had provided themselves with an armed escort and wore around their necks small receptacles containing dust from St. Martin's tomb at Tours, a present brought by the bishop of that diocese, Eufronius, when he came to Poitiers. It was a sure specific, he assured them against the dangers of the road. Which was all very well but, Agnes noticed, a storm was coming up. The surface of the river had darkened and grown choppy. A breeze was rising and the sky turning a luminous but dangerous pale green. She called to the helmsman.

"Will we reach Agen before the weather breaks?"

"I don't think so, Mother. Currents." He shrugged.

"Where can we spend the night then?"

Another shrug.

Agnes turned to Fridovigia who was in the prow of the boat behind. "Find out is there somewhere we can stay tonight," she called. "Somewhere close. A church, a house. Ask the boatmen. They should know. They're local."

The river banks were hairy and wild with dark brambles and soaked overhanging beards of grass. No sign of a road. The breeze was clattering the branches of the trees together with that dry warning which comes just before a storm. Agnes shivered. She had been feeling so unguardedly at one with the landscape that its sudden change was like a rebuff. A drop fell on her cheek and rolled down like a tear. Be rational, Agnes. The weather did not lend itself to rationality. Lightning ripped its rent in the sky. She clutched St. Martin's dust and braced herself for the thunder.

The church house where the party finally found lodging was a small one attached to a village church. The nuns' party was not the only one driven here by the storm. A pair of Syrian merchants were already installed when they arrived and, although the priest was quite prepared to put them out in favour of the new arrivals, Radegunda forbade this. Radegunda, whose energy came in spurts then died down like a fire covered by wet slack, now took over. This was something for which Agnes always had to be prepared. Radegunda, who thought she left control and responsibility to Agnes, was not even aware of what she was doing. Authority was part of her. She had to make a conscious effort to get rid of it as she had rid her diet of meat, fish, fruit, eggs and wine. When she forgot, her directions were immediately obeyed and often ran counter to some arrangement made by Agnes. Now, she chose to be charitable. The merchants must stay. Travel suspended convent rules and were these not ·doubly in abeyance anyway since the convent was about to adopt a new Rule? Besides, how send a Christian out into a night like this? Agnes reflected that the merchants could well have slept safely in some stable, and prepared for an embarrassing evening. Radegunda would not eat, would fall into one of her semi-trances in which she was perhaps quite simply conserving the energies which she insufficiently nourished and would be unaware of what was around her. What was around, Agnes had quickly noted, was a half-drunken priest, a housekeeper who was not of canonical age, and a sense of something interrupted. There was a cauldron of some herbal mixture on the fire and a number of bottles and and phials had been arranged on a bench but were now being put away by one of the Syrian merchants. Merchant, she wondered, or doctor? There was a Syrian colony in Bordeaux where they had spent a night on their way here and where she had heard strange tales about these Easterners. "Syrian" was a vague term used, she knew, for any Christian of Eastern descent. They were thought to have curious, perhaps diabolical lore. Their knowledge of surgery, philters and inexplicable cures made them suspect. The Bishop of Bordeaux—who had told her of all this—was of the opinion that the only medicine a God-fearing Christian should seek for bodily ills was the application of a relic. Yet, Agnes knew, the old Romans, probably even her own ancestors, had had medical knowledge which was now largely lost. Or had it been gathered up by these acquisitive Syrians who travelled the trade-routes buying and selling whatever they could market? Greeks? Persians? Armenians? Their quick foreign eyes flashed messages at each other and they moved to a distant corner of the smoky room where Fridovigia was unpacking the food. Minutes later the two were in conversation with the old woman. Agnes closed her own eyes and tried to imitate Radegunda who carried her cloister with her and was totally withdrawn from the obscurely sinister scene. Agnes sat up and tried to face down her own reaction. Why 'sinister'? Wasn't it just poor? The oil in the lamps was of an unpleasant cheap variety and the wicks must certainly be of elder-pith. No, it wasn't that. There was something not right about this house. Secretive: that was it. There was a secret here. The priest and the Syrians had been interrupted in the middle of some activity they did not want known. Well, it was no concern of hers or Radegunda's. They would spend the night, shelter and move on tomorrow, leaving their hosts to finish whatever it was they were up to. She shivered. Absurd! How absurd it was! Her cool confidence in herself—the competent abbess—her control had simply gone. She felt vulnerable here off her own ground. It was just as though she were a mollusc which had been scooped from its shell and exposed. Her skin moved on her back. The simplest young girl, she thought, knows more about the outside world than I. Glancing over, she saw the two Syrians' eyes fixed on her. Fridovigia was whispering something and she saw one of them signal the old woman to be quiet. They had been discussing *her*. Or was Fridovigia just haggling over spice or garum? But there was curiosity and a flicker of something—something like pity?—in the younger Syrian's eyes. Then Fridovigia said something else and they detached their gaze.

Agnes sat with Radegunda and the abbess of St. John's convent, Mother Liliola. Outside the window lay Arles, a pale stone city surrounded by marshes and wild birds. *Duplex Arelas,* the twinned town that had been Constantine's before he founded his own, rose on two sides of the River Rhône on a scale astonishing to the nuns from Poitiers. Its pontoon bridge, theater, arena, baths and circus were still monumentally intact but, as they rode in, they had passed evidence of the pillagings and plunderings which it, like other cities, had suffered from the recent civil wars. They were talking about this and about the Rule of St. Caesar which they had come here to learn.

"Moderation", said Liliola, "is the basis and kernel of our Rule. An abbess must guard against extreme behaviour of any kind."

She was clearly in doubt as to whom she should address. Agnes had been presented as abbess. Radegunda's fame had reached here and did not, Agnes suspected, dispose the Provençal woman well towards her. Her words, after all, were a condemnation of Radegunda's way of life.

"Penances of a dramatic or theatrical sort", said Liliola, "may be of use to the individual in her search for perfection. They can never be other than harmful to the community as a whole—and that", she looked at Agnes, "must be an abbess's first concern."

Mint, fennel and rosemary bushes scented the air. Shade was provided by cypresses, those dark rigid trees which stretched in close formation at regular intervals across the surrounding landscape. Packed in straight-lined phalanxes, one expected them to start marching like the ghost of an old Roman patrol: one two, one two. But they simply stood. They were windbreaks, sometimes woven together by reeds, so menacing was the blast of the wind they must withstand.

"There's something I have to tell you," said Fridovigia. "It's no use my putting it off. The opposite in fact. You're quick with child."

Agnes failed to take this in.

"Pregnant," said Fridovigia. "You're going to ask how I know. Well, I know and ..."

She talked. The strong scents flowed approvingly over

151

Agnes. So did sunlight and the marsh-wet air. So who was approving her? Herself? A white stone caught the light dazzlingly. On the low wall a lizard was sunning itself. Fridovigia mentioned the Syrian doctors. Ah, so they had been doctors? On the way back, said Fridovigia, she could arrange a meeting. They would be expecting a message from her. At Bordeaux. Or Auch.

"Obviously", said Fridovigia, "you must act now. This journey is a heaven-sent opportunity."

The words clicked like the last piece of a puzzle in Agnes's brain. She understood what Fridovigia had been saying.

"Do you think so?"

"What?"

"That this is heaven-sent?"

"This? *What*?" Fridovigia asked.

"I shan't return by Bordeaux," said Agnes. "I shall persuade Radegunda to return by the Rhône valley."

"Suit yourself," said Fridovigia. "But you'd better think hard about your situation."

"The situation of an abbess", Liliola said, "is rather special. There can be conflicts between her personal search for salvation and the needs of the convent."

She was showing Agnes around the grounds. St. John's, flanked by two churches, rose on the ruins of two temples dedicated, one to Diana whose cult the nuns, in their own way, perpetuated, the other to the Phrygian goddess, Cybele. This was the highest corner of the city and commanded a view of the flatlands beyond its wall.

All the doors but one, Liliola explained, had been sealed up by the convent's founder and the keys to that were in the abbess's possession.

"The abbess", said Liliola, "is answerable to God for the welfare of the whole community. Her authority must be preserved at the expense, if need be, of her humility. She may secretly repent if she has committed faults, but it would be a mistake to ask pardon of those subject to her. Even if she has unfairly punished one of her nuns."

"How should nuns be punished?" Agnes asked.

"As in the Old Testament," Liliola told her. "Thou shalt beat thy son—and so therefore thy daughter—with a rod and deliver his soul from hell. Proverbs, 32:14. It is in our Rule. We are having a copy made for you."

"And how is the abbess's soul to be delivered from hell?"

"It is harder for her," Liliola said. "I believe there are monks in Ireland who have worked out a scale of secret penances by which sinners can pay for their sins without the scandal of a public confession which—naturally—besides being unadvisable for persons in authority, can only be made once in a lifetime."

The Abbess Liliola swept ahead, showing the way. She was propped and enlarged by the solidity of her convent, her Rule, her certitudes. Agnes was supposed to be like her. But I'm not, she realized. I'm not. The competence in which she took such pride, her success at running her own convent was a nervous, doubtful skill compared to this woman's. Decidedly, Liliola had been 'called'. Her ear was clearly tuned to a superior certitude. Not like Radegunda's. No. Liliola was simply sure of herself. There was no straining, no flame. She was very solidly here and sure of her use.

"Those Irish penitentials", she said now, "do, I suppose, fill a need. But our bishops don't like them. Neither, I hear, does yours. Here in Arles", said Liliola, "we hear news sooner than most places. This is still the hub of some of the main trade-routes. Of course there has been a decline ... "

Trade-routes, bills of lading, penitentials, scales and schedules for prayer and punishment—Agnes had the feeling that the world around her was the figment of a meticulous madman. Why—no, not why: *how,* how could it be like this? Precisely like this and no other way? Laid down. Fixed. Birds flew, lizards crawled, the sun rose in the east and always would, grass could never be blue nor sin innocent. One was confined within one's

153

skin. Like a parcel. When one lost it, it would not be to mingle flesh deliciously with a lover's, dissolving together like two coinciding rays of light. It would be only to get it back in an even more meticulously planned otherworld where one paid many times over what had not been paid here. Carnal lovers, in one account of hell, were attached by their genitals to swiftly spinning wheels. I will repent, thought Agnes. I have always meant to. But how will I know I am forgiven? She plucked an aromatic leaf, crushed and held it to her nose. I can't quite believe, she thought, in *anything*. I must be going mad! Carnal passion has fogged my brain.

"Recent news", Liliola was saying, "is bad ..." She went on to discuss an event which was over a year old but now having repercussions all over Gaul: the murder of Queen Galswinthe of Neustria who had been found strangled in her bridal bed a few days after her wedding to King Chilperic. He had returned forthwith to the arms of his concubine, Fredegunda, and was being harried by his dead wife's sister, the wife of his brother, King Sigibert. Their wars were intermittent, bloody and an especial threat to Poitiers which both kings claimed. In the last year it had changed hands twice and neither was likely to give it up for good.

"But you'll be safe in your convent," Liliola consoled. A convent was a sanctuary rarely invaded. "We must try to merit our privilege," she said. "We escape the world's dangers ..."

These were real enough. Look at Galswinthe. Even the luckiest women in the world must face pregnancy, death in childbirth, miscarriage and the fear of all these.

"We escape ..."

But Agnes had not escaped. Like children playing the game of "sanctuary", she had stepped out and had been caught. Caught by the trap of her own body—who had said that? Her heart stopped and started fiercely up again. It was not of hell she needed to think but of what she could do now! I am mad, she thought. What was I thinking of?

154

"Human love", said Liliola complacently, "is never ..."

Agnes fell rather than sat on a bench. No! her brain was shouting: no! She could not listen to this.

"Galswinthe," she managed to say, "passed through Poitiers on her way to her wedding. In a silver-plated car. Someone who saw her told me she looked sad."

Liliola let herself be steered back to gossip. "Yes, poor little queen ..."

The someone who had seen Queen Galswinthe was Fortunatus. He was writing a poem for her death: a delicate venture since Chilperic was a patron and must not be blamed. But the subject could not be passed up. "Think of it," he had said excitedly to Agnes. "I *saw* her!" Cutting himself a new pen.

"Aren't you sorry for her!"

"Of course. That's why it's such a good subject! Don't you see? Heaven-sent!"

Heaven sent odd gifts. Oh, Fortunatus, are *we* a good subject? Oh, what can I do? If only you were here! At least half of me would be consoled.

"You", Liliola was saying, "are a woman of sense."

Senses?

"Balanced," said Liliola. "You'll make a good abbess. Our Rule, you'll see ..."

"I am less worthy", Agnes rushed out a half confession, "than may appear. I ..." She was tempted to unburden her sin.

"What *appears*", said Liliola, "is what matters. You are God's representative to your nuns. For their sake, so as not to trouble their faith, you must appear worthy."

"But I—supposing *I* sin? Who will forgive *me*?"

"Do not judge yourself too harshly. Excessive remorse can hinder the performance of God's service. It is the service which matters."

But it was not a matter of judging or not judging. It was a matter now of deciding what to do. An abortion— Fridovigia's solution—was unthinkable. So was a pregnant abbess. God's service could be helped by neither.

155

"God help you!" Fridovigia had whispered last night when bringing Agnes the sleeping-potion without which she could not sleep. *Was* it a sleeping-potion? Agnes, seized by distrust, had poured it on the floor. "Oh my lamb!" the old woman had muttered as she cleaned it up. "If it were as easy as that! At two months gone! Two—or may be three? There *are* abortifacients. I'm not saying there aren't. But I'd put scant faith in anything taken through the mouth. No. There's some use clysters though, or sit in a bath of linseed, wormwood and other herbs. Or do exercises ..." She paused artfully. "No? Well I wouldn't count on them anyway. If you'd only come to me earlier. If you'd come *before*! There's plently of help I could have given you then, my lamb. Unguents to smear on the matrix. Not hard to get either. Such simple things: honey, old olive oil, the juice of the balsam tree or even a lock of wool ... So easy, my plant. But would you tell old Fridovigia? No, not a thing. And taking no precautions. There's virtuous women for you! The worst fools. Well, the scalded cat fears cold water and I'll lay it won't happen to you twice. What you should do now if you'd be led by me ..."

"That's enough, Fridovigia."

"You think it would be such a terrible sin—but there's less to it than killing a mouse. Than killing a wren. They're no bigger than that!" Fridovigia measured off a length of thumb. "If it came out now it'd be no bigger than what brought it in!"

"*Fridovigia!*" A shriek.

But she had lost all authority over the old woman. Joying in her special position as confidante—coveted for so many years that Agnes could almost believe she had laid a spell on her—Fridovigia was milking the circumstance for all it was worth.

"All nuns do it. God help you but you're innocent! I was talking to a pilgrim yesterday"—Fridovigia spent hours in the basilica atrium talking to people who were washing in the fountain or resting or eating between prayers—"who told me about a convent in his home town.

I forget the name but it had a pond behind it that had to be dried for some reason and do you know what was found in it? How many infant skeletons? In the mud. It seems the mud preserved them though some say it was a miracle. They were white, perfect. Like a pile of shells or necklaces. All white. Thrown there by the nuns. I tell you they all do it. It's no worse than killing rabbits—and those were full-term babies. But those Syrian doctors ..."

Agnes covered her ears. "Go away," she shrieked. "I want the baby. I want it, do you hear? Now leave me alone or I'll go mad. I'll go crazy, out of my mind and it'll be born an idiot. Pregnant women should look at beautiful things and think happy thoughts and instead what do I have to listen to? If I give birth to a monster, it'll be your fault, Fridovigia!"

The old woman had gone off. Just as happy really. She was still in possession of a secret, was probably already laying plans. But Agnes lay awake all night—regretting the sleeping potion which she had poured away—and wondered had she meant what she said? She did not think she was sleeping but next morning was convinced she must have been for how, while awake, could she have entertained such lunatic fancies? She had imagined herself and Fortunatus fleeing to Italy or even the East, abandoning nuns, Radegunda, responsibilities, everything to live and love together with the baby: a family. A lunatic dream. Or was it? They would live happily, die and rot in hell spinning from the wheels that tortured carnal sinners. Or repent? No, how could they repent?

"Do not judge yourself too harshly," Liliola was saying. "Or abstain too much from sleep or food." She was looking hard at Agnes's scorched eyes. "That", she said, "can be a mistake. Some would say a temptation of the devil. I prefer to say a mistake."

She thinks, thought Agnes, she thinks I am tempted by sanctity.

"You mistake me, Mother," she told Liliola. "I am not too fervent."

157

Liliola gave her an evasive look. "I doubt if you are lukewarm either. Remember," soothing voice. "If you ever were to fall into sin, you must not despair. The suffering itself would bring you near to God. You *would* suffer for, unlike ordinary nuns who may unburden themselves by confiding in their abbess, you would have to carry yours. But that in itself—the suffering—might save you. Downright sin can be better than a life of tepid virtue. The shame of the sinner brings him back to God. *O felix culpa!* Remorse is God's last lifeline thrown to the sinner."

Agnes stared at Liliola. What had she guessed?

"Come," said Liliola. "I want to show you our herb-garden. One can make excellent cordials . . ."

The two abbesses returned to manageable matters. They were women who allowed for incursions of the irrational—how could they not?—but knew and cultivated techniques for keeping these to a minimum. One was to turn one's mind to spheres where it could be effective.

"Beware of fervour," reminded Liliola, handing Agnes a crushed sprig of lemon balm. "The crushed herb", she remarked, "pleases the senses best. We are God's plants but should not seek to destroy ourselves before our time."

"Oh, a fox!"

It streaked through dew-white grass, speedy, red and three times its static length. The farmer's enemy. Predatory and nocturnal: the very carnal manifestation of nature's turbulence, it briefly gave the land an untrammelled look. But the sun was up and it would be making for the safety of its underground tenement. Beautiful as sin, thought Agnes, astonished at her own image, it served its sentence daily in its smelly catacomb.

The nuns were proceeding home by the Rhône valley. The air was heady. Grapes fermented on vines. Autumn was ripening and putrefying in the hot valley hollowed by the slow passage of the river. Blackberry time. Leaves were turning a transparent yellow. Crab apples and nuts grew on common land. Late peaches fell softly and bubbled amber-sweet sap where insects had pierced them.

Radegunda carried a crucifix and the two women prayed before it wherever they stopped for a night or even for food. Radegunda had taken to reciting a few lines she had learned off by heart. They were by St. Augustine.

"Thus the soul is guilty of fornication," recited Radegunda, "whenever she turns from You and seeks from another source what she will nowhere find pure and without taint unless she returns to You. Thus even those who go from You and stand up against You are still perversely imitating You."

The lines reminded Agnes of Fortunatus, whose habit it was to take the evidence of his senses and turn it on its head. Good became bad, pleasant sensations a threat. He looked at daily events as though they were fodder for poems and of no interest until *he* had fabricated some surprise out of what had seemed quite straightforward. As though the word "no" were a guiding principle instead of a mere check. Trees must be lopped, saplings twisted, leaves crushed, spices pounded—how bored she was with the whole sad stock of images. "The loppèd tree doth best and soonest grow!" Did it? Did it always? Some of these wild unlopped crab-apple trees and chestnuts were doing very nicely by themselves. The *raeda* swayed and jolted. Agnes could feel Fridovigia's eyes on her. Hoping still for a miscarriage? A lopping? No, old friend. She smiled at Fridovigia who smiled back.

Fortunatus had written a new poem just before they'd left: a hymn to the cross, it turned on the most basic Christian paradox and he had written it to celebrate Radegunda's obtaining the fragment of the True Cross from the Emperor Justin. It had been sung by the procession which had come to deliver the relic, sung by the nuns receiving it, sung again so often Agnes could not get bits of it out of her head:

Forward go the kingly banners.
Forth the Cross's mysteries blaze,

Here as flesh the flesh's maker
On this tree of pain was raised.
Harsh the spear that rent and spilt
Blood to wash away our guilt!

O felix culpa! He would love blood washing away guilt. So surprising. Life was like winter meat. It needed spice.

It should have aroused a disincarnate awe. But it didn't. Not in the least. There was something brutal in the bargain: a blood-price being paid for man by God-made-man during the transaction's length. Dislikeable. Familiar. Were not thieves' hands lopped? And where had she heard that in parts of the East adulteresses might have their noses slit so that the fissure secret in their bodies be figured by a disgracingly visible one?

Agnes's fingers flew to her face. Her moods changed like the wind. They said here that the local wind made people mad. It was a melancholy hot wind from Italy. She looked across at Fridovigia but the old woman had fallen asleep. Radegunda was praying or in a trance. Agnes was alone.

At night now she accepted Fridovigia's sleeping draughts but polarities pursued her in dreams animated by daytime images of this harsh country with its blazing light and shadows blue-black like bruises on the ground. Monuments passed on their journey spelled out harsh messages. They had seen one Roman arch where toga'd victors triumphed over bound and kneeling Gauls. Someone was always being subdued. Christian churches preserved the same vengeful drama: picturing the damned on one side of their painted walls being devoured by beasts, the saved rising weight-lessly on the other. No half way. "Those who are neither hot nor cold," said Christ, "I spit them out of my mouth."

And into the devil's.

A few mornings ago Agnes had woken to see a black carapaced creature on her bed. Its two waving claws and tail aimed straight at her and grew in the magnifying prism of her sleep-dulled eye. A devil. She shrieked and Fridovigia rushed over and killed it.

"It was only a scorpion."

"A what?"

Agnes had never heard of such a thing. What a hideous place! Besides, nothing was only anything. Everything meant, threatened and signified something more and other than itself: signals, omens, divine or diabolic warnings. The black, mutilated body on the floor, crunched and split by Fridovigia's foot, revealed itself as full of grey egg-like things. She buried herself in Fridovigia's fat and comforting embrace.

"Fridovigia," she whispered. "I think I'm going out of my mind!"

She was thinking more and more—even when indisputably awake—of her dream of running away with Fortunatus. She would take Fridovigia with her, she decided. She couldn't leave her. But where would they go? A runaway nun was liable to imprisonment anywhere in Christendom. But would Radegunda denounce her? She would. She would. Radegunda would always sacrifice a body—anyone's—to a soul. It was a mad, bad fantasy but she couldn't rid herself of it. Not, anyway, until she'd shared it with Fortunatus.

"Your condition", said Fortunatus, "must have affected your brain! I'm assuming it has and that I have to think for us both."

He and Agnes were once again in the rose-arbour of the convent henceforth to be known as Holy Cross. It was the first time they had managed to be alone since her return.

"Can't you get that woman of yours, Fridovigia, to help? Those old women are as handy as any physician. How long is it, can you tell?"

He launched questions through which a faint touch of masculine distaste seeped as pus will through an ill-adjusted bandage. No. It was she who was all pus and wound. She was the unhealthy figure in Fortunatus's tidy world. He was unsure how to treat her. She felt this. He could not just cast her off. She was not disposable. Not a wench with whom he might have satisfied a passing lust. She was the abbess of Holy Cross convent, a figure of lasting importance in his life. Fortunatus had no desire at all to leave Poitiers with or without her, nor had he any to forfeit her friendship. She could see his regret at having let it slide into the unmanageable and marshy regions in which it was foundering now. His astonishment. Theirs, he had convinced himself, had been a mingling of spirits figured forth by a few carnal acts of as little importance, really, as metaphors. Now, somehow, as in one of his own paradoxes, everything had turned upside down: the carnal was the real and affirmed itself in a way impossible to ignore. *Amor, dilectio, amicitia,* had all those courteous, monastic tropes, been masking—no, certainly not. She saw his head twitch backwards like a shying horse's. With dual vision, she watched the man whom her body craved and her mind was judging. And her heart? Ah, the heart was the body's fool. Minutes ago, she had asked him to take her to Italy. He was a layman and free. In times like these no one would know or come after them. The sin would be all hers. She had seen him cringe, his mind casting cautiously about for ways of calming her folly while keeping alive her good will for himself. Ah God, she whispered, have you sent me this lucidity as a punishment?

"My poor sweet lamb,"—*agna*, his pun on her name—"it must have been terrible to have to box this secret up yourself! No wonder you're a little beside yourself! What you said just now was mad, you know? If only I had been there with you to share the anxiety. Thank God for Fridovigia! Didn't she suggest anything? By the way, I thought Radegunda said you had to ride part of the way? I should have thought the jolting . . . ?"

"Excuse me," said Agnes. "I must go. I feel ill. My condition, you know . . ." She left him, with a touch of vindictive pleasure, to his bad conscience. The jagged ending of their interview would irk the poet in him. She hoped. At the very least.

Chapter Ten

Many sins have become impossible since I became an A.D.
anchoress. Despondency and lassitude are the two against 587
which I must still be on guard. Lassitude breeds idleness,
drowsiness, restlessness, instability of mind and curiosity.
But even of these, several are without scope in my cell.
To keep my mind stable, I try to pray or count or stretch
my arms to feel the wall all about me. I count the jutting
hewn stones in the wall, starting from the ground and
reaching up as far as I can. The number is always the same.
I have not grown since I immured myself although I
might have, for I had just turned fourteen a while before.
Or if I did grow a few fingers' thickness, it was not enough
to reach a further row of stones. Besides, I stretch less
easily now than before. I have become a little hunched.

There is that noise again! Noise!

Could it be thunder? No—that was a scream. I hear a
clashing. Metal. Men's voices. Breakage and what might be
a battering-ram at the outer door. Noises crash through
the cloister close to my wall—God, what was that?

A light flashed past my slit. A flame? What? Oh My
God, what? Blessed Radegunda, how can you be letting
this—what?—happen? That light again. Smell of burning
resin. Metal on stone. A weapon rattles in my slit. It does.
It does—God if it will serve you I am ready to die. Or
live ... God? Are you there ... God? God, God! The
noises ... Are they real?

Radegunda spent more and more time in her cell. A.D.
Protected by the fragments of the True Cross, her nuns 570
needed her less. The Great Relic hung in the chapel in a
reliquary set with garnets and green paste. Its brightness

was quelled by shadow but the wood within regulated life in the convent as surely as a hidden moon controlled tides, seasons and the rhythms of women's blood. Lesser relics abetted it, some from as far off as Jerusalem. Trusting in their influence, Radegunda felt free to isolate herself from the community for weeks on end.

She was seeking that union with God in which she had often experienced the separation of her spirit from her body and an energizing peace. At those times her spirit had been swept up, charged by the currents of a life-giving power, then annihilated like a river pouring into the saline reaches of a great and turbulent sea. On returning to herself her chief sensation was disappointment and a longing to return to the rapture. She had been unable to reach it for a long time now. Why? Why had God turned from her? What had she done wrong? She raked her conscience and was brought up short each time by a single name: Clotair. Had she—as *he* had said she had—chosen her own salvation over his? *Was* he in hell and, if he was, was she to blame? She mortified herself and offered the mortifications for his soul—but the divine favours did not return. Neither did peace of mind. Remorse, biting and rebiting at her brain like some tunnelling insect, was an impediment to prayer. She began to believe it came from the devil and fought it. Her suspicions were strengthened when a little novice was found paralytic with terror after seeing a devil run up and down her dormitory pulling at the hair of the sleeping nuns. Devils in convents were common enough. Their tricks were part of a strategy with which the religious must cope if they were to merit heaven. Virtue offered a challenge and this made the devils' attentions almost reassuring. What frightened Radegunda was that her visions should have stopped. Life was a menacing carnival, a booby-trapped maze through which the blind soul groped looking for the light. Humble souls took a straightforward, ground-level path through this. They only ran the ordinary dangers of temptation and sin. She—presumptuously perhaps?—

had tried for immediate knowledge of the unseen powers. She had taken flight towards God. Her soul now was in suspense and open to folly, figments, failure of nerve and always the machinations of the devil who could deceive by taking on the appearance of his Great Enemy. God might allow this. Those who tried for the most were tested most. The soul setting forth into rarely charted spaces must be prepared for diabolic as well as divine encounters—and for a dangerous uncertitude as to which was which. With the interruption of her visions, Radegunda's confidence began to fail. She was not even sure now that *any* of them had been from God. Proof that they had could only lie in their outcome: her life and works. But she was—quite lately—beginning to wonder about these. It was only a crack of doubt but, coming at such a time, it threw her into a near panic. She had refused Clotair for the sake of the convent. Did it justify her? She wasn't sure. It was not she who ran it. Slowly, it was borne in on her that the nuns were terrified of her. She had no real contact with them at all. They froze or scattered at her approach. She loved them, but it was a disembodied, prayerful love. She could pray for but not talk to them. Shy, shifty, twittering creatures, she watched them from her cell window and realized that their femininity was as alien to her as Clotair's maleness had been. They giggled. They poked each other. They pinched, twitched, joked in a way she could tell quite well, from the distance of her window, was hardly verbal at all but more a kind of pooling of energies, an overspill of mood and humour into a current which held them in its orbit as rubbed amber might silk or a lodestone metal. There was nothing improper about this friskiness but it was something in which *she* couldn't join. She needed Agnes as a go-between to understand her nuns. Unfortunately, Agnes had been sick and confined to a sick-cell for several months. After the return from Arles, she had fallen ill. Fridovigia had nursed her, discouraging visits, but insisting that, with the help of a course of remedies devised by herself, Agnes would pull

165

through. She did. By Candlemas, Fridovigia pronounced her out of danger and by Shrovetide Agnes was back in the common dormitory and carrying her full load of duties. This was a relief. The slackness Radegunda had sensed during the abbess's sickness disappeared. The nuns had a more contained look. Tensions seemed to have gone. That was all reassuring. What was less so was a change which seemed to have taken place in Agnes herself. Radegunda could not put her finger on it. She was not, she realized a little sadly, at all good with people. She would not dream of asking Agnes what the matter was but seemed to know that the abbess's character was convulsed: closed in. It might be a result of her illness. It might pass. Radegunda prayed it would but was hurt to feel Agnes had withdrawn from her. Being incapable of making quick contact with people, Radegunda needed them to make it with her. She valued Fortunatus's easy conviviality. The daily chats which she and Agnes had enjoyed with him in the convent garden were important to her. Now that Agnes was well and the fine weather starting, she had assumed they would begin again. But Agnes did not come. She never said she wasn't coming; on the contrary, she usually promised she would be along but the time would pass, the bell for Compline ring, Fortunatus be obliged to leave and there would have been no sign of Agnes.

"I'm sorry," she would say later to Radegunda, "I thought I could get away, but ..." And of course she never lacked excuses. "Tomorrow," she would promise insincerely.

Radegunda was hurt.

"She's snubbing us," she told Fortunatus.

"She's probably very busy."

"No. She's snubbing us."

"I'll write her a poem," he promised.

Two days later he produced it.

"Read it," he said, "I wouldn't like you to think I was conducting a secret correspondence."

Radegunda took it with amusement, expecting to read one of his light Latin jingles about an indigestion or colic brought on by eating too much of some titbit Agnes had sent to his quarters—though now that she thought of it, Agnes had given up sending titbits to his quarters. Odd. The poem too was odd. Agnes, whom so many of his other verses had described as a little maid or 'maidenlet', *virguncula*, or as a lamb, *agna*, was here hailed as Fortunatus's "mother in religion and sister in friendship". Like an epitaph, thought Radegunda wonderingly, and went on to read a declaration that the poet loved Agnes with a love free from fleshly complicities—surely there was no need to say so? "I call Christ and the Holy Apostles to witness . . ." the poem went on and then went on further to empanel half the heavenly population. This was religious rhetoric rolling in its rut and Radegunda was not disturbed until she met a mention of "evil rumours" which Agnes must ignore.

"Have there been evil rumours," she asked, "or is this a figure of speech?"

Fortunatus said he thought something might have been said to make Agnes think so.

"Why", he asked heatedly, "would she avoid us? That woman, Fridovigia, has a poisoned tongue. I wonder that you tolerate her here!"

"I wonder at your intolerance."

"Forgive me," said Fortunatus. "This has been driving me mad, burning me up! People who soil things. I . . . Look, I'm sorry I mentioned it. It's irrational of me. Perhaps I'm wrong besides. I beg you, say nothing to Agnes."

"But why should anybody think such things—whatever they are?" Radegunda was perplexed. But did not, she knew, understand people. Nor really want to perhaps.

"My poems, I suppose, are open to interpretation."

"But Fridovigia wouldn't know about your poems."

"No, no, I suppose not."

Radegunda made the best fist she could at telling all this

167

to Agnes. "I really couldn't make out what he was saying," she said. "But he is upset. Very. Hurt too. I think you should join us once or twice. He *is* upset."

"He's clever," said Agnes who looked rundown. She must, Radegunda resolved, be persuaded to supplement her diet by a little fowl-meat.

"Clever? Oh you mean the poem?"

"The poem too."

"What does he mean by 'evil rumours'?"

"A literary device."

"Will you join us tomorrow?"

"If you like."

Later Radegunda chanced to go into the kitchen as Agnes was throwing a scroll of papyrus into the fire. She was throwing it with an angular, almost theatrical gesture—an upward vindictive jerk of the wrist—and Radegunda thought she recognized the scroll on which Fortunatus had written the poem. She could not, of course, be sure.

Next day the three met in the garden. Fortunatus read them some more verse. It was a dour account of childbirth intended as a foil for his celebration of chastity. He had tipped the scales.

> The virgin's wise—he read—she doesn't weight
> A torpid womb with cumbrous weight. . . .
> When bellies bloat and skin's distent,
> The mother's spirit's all but spent,
> And mewed-up embryos, which burst
> Out through to life, may meet death first.
> Pain-stunned, the woman turns her eyes
> To where a stillborn infant lies.
> No virgin now—nor may she claim
> The honour of a mother's name.

There was a lot more. He was clearly affected by his own arts for his voice shook and he had twice to wipe his eyes. Radegunda, who had run a hospital for the sick poor, could have supplied him with more harrowing detail. The subject did not shock her. His zest for it did. The nimble meters struck her as flippant when used to package this anatomy of her sex at its most vulnerable. Woman, in the performance of her essential function, had no dignity here. She was so much matter: grotesque, turgid, torn, a numb lump of it. Radegunda was repelled but, recalling the poem's purpose, could only applaud its success. Agnes's reaction struck her as aberrant. The nun had a sly and, Radegunda could have sworn, malicious, even triumphant expression. Fortunatus, taken up with his own feelings, did not seem to notice. By the time he had recovered his calm, Agnes had composed her face.

"Well done," she said. "Very nice. How useful life is: a compost heap for the garden of verse."

"Have you no pity?" Fortunatus asked.

"I suppose," Agnes said, "people's first pity must be for themselves. I am not", she forestalled Radegunda's protest, "denying the need for charity. But don't you think one must first love oneself if one is to love others and care for them?"

Radegunda thought no such thing. One must, it was obvious to her, destroy and remake one's identity in God's image. One must transcend the given self. But Agnes knew this. So did the last little novice in the convent. Her wild statement was aimed somehow at provoking Fortunatus. It was clear that the two had quarrelled. Radegunda did not choose to know more. It would blow over. What it did show though was that Agnes was less far along the path of spiritual perfection than had appeared. Her acerbity might be a result of her sickness—or might mean that Radegunda had made a mistake in forcing her to enter the convent. For she could not deceive herself about this: she had left Agnes no choice. How could a twelve-year-old have resisted her? Agnes had given her life to Radegunda who had given it to God. But into what better keeping could she have given it? Fortunatus's poem supported her. Could that be why Agnes disliked it? Might her bad temper, her repugnance be for convent-life itself? The thought was horrifying. Radegunda reassured herself. It wasn't possible. Agnes had been a perfect abbess until now. Even Liliola had been impressed by her. A life of virtue didn't suddenly crumble—oh but it *did*. There was the devil, and the devil put his pride in suborning virtue. That sly mockery Radegunda had glimpsed on Agnes's face could very well come from him: the father of lies and source of all mockery. Radegunda saw that here was a battle which must be fought by spiritual means. She resolved to drive a bargain with God.

Agnes and Fortunatus were alone. Sooner or later this had to happen. Chance. Pure chance, she told herself and tried to quell the hammering in her head.

"I heard", he said, "that our Mother has been inflicting even more horrible mortifications on herself."

"Yes," said Agnes. "She has."

Radegunda had tied chains around her middle some months before. They were so tight that now the flesh had grown over them and would have to be cut through if they were to be removed.

"I hear", said Fortunatus, "that parasites have lodged in the rotting flesh."

"Oh," said Agnes, "this is for the biography? Pain fascinates you, doesn't it?"

There was a silence. Then he said:

"You're thinking of my poem. The one about childbirth. I'm sorry you didn't like it. I can see—now—that you mightn't. I've been thinking of you, you see, and now I do see—but, you know, it was meant as an offering to you."

Agnes laughed sourly. "Oh I knew it was for me. Fridovigia tells me that there are old women who restore virginity to girls who need to make respectable marriages. They use oak galls and the like. Astringents. Your poem was trying to give me back a spiritual virginity, wasn't it? But the Mystic Bridegroom would hardly be deceived, would he? God is not mocked."

"I was trying to show that I knew you must have— suffered. That I'd felt for you. Writing the poem was a ... a sort of trying to live through it with you."

"What I thought", said Agnes, "was that it was telling me that married life would not have been all roses."

"Agnes . . ."

"You want me to grant you absolution, don't you? To say, 'Forget it, Fortunatus; all is forgiven and forgotten.' That is what you want, isn't it?"

"What can I say?"

"Nothing. That is what you want. But it's not possible. You see the child was not born dead and I—mentally—broke my cloister-vow. I was ready to leave. As to the other vow I broke . . ."

Fortunatus was white. He covered his eyes with his sleeve.

Suddenly, she was tired of baiting him. Tired of the knife-blades in her own voice and eyes. She had seen them reflected in the looks the nuns gave her. She had grown cutting, harsh—but mostly cut herself. She was like those snakes metal-workers traced on buckles, and monks in the margins of manuscripts. They writhed, wound but always ended by biting their own flesh. Their venom flowed in a closed circuit. Pity, Agnes. Try to find some. She did try: a mental exercise. She summoned the Agnes who had been happy sitting in a boat on the Garonne. She fixed her mind on the scene, willing it to bring back an old mood: gilded water, pale air, coot diving into widening rings of darkness, calm . . . No good. The memory mocked. Happiness slipped through. The black rings widened to enclose the whole scene. That Agnes was dead: worse, a ghost who would continue to haunt and sadden her. So would the other, the worried, still deluded woman who had ridden up the Rhone valley in a jolting *raeda*, tormented by the mechanical clack of crickets, a wooden sound made, she had been told, by the creatures rubbing their limbs together. She had dreamed then of a dangerous existence fleeing through Italy under an assumed name with this man who had no courage. Softened after all, she touched his sleeve—their first touch for over a year.

"It's all right," she told him. "The child is being looked

after. She's a girl. Fridovigia found a family for her. It would be better", she absolved him, "if they were left to bring her up on their own."

Radegunda argued and struggled with her Mystic Bridegroom.

"I want to die," she complained. "I want to leave all this and follow you. You bade me have no care for the body and you know I have none—and yet you will not release me from it. I would joyfully release myself and join you. I long to. There is nothing I long to do more—yet you forbid me. You have forbidden self-slaughter and I must abide by your will. I must live on in a failing body in a world of flesh which I understand less and less—for my spirit strains only towards you. You. It longs to burst its bonds. It yearns to shed this body which is like an old husk gone dry, foul, senseless and ill-fitting, so that the spirit itself can see less clearly and hear less sharply through eyes gone blear and ears desperate for the sound of one voice: yours. I am neither here nor there. I am hungry for your presence. I hanker for the great blaze of your glance which, when you turn it on me, will burn out the husk of my body and draw my soul to you. This is what I covet and crave, what I have been longing and living for since I was a girl. You deny me. I submit. You deny me, too, the sense of your presence here while I am still in the body. You no longer visit me. I submit. I abide by your decisions although they are harsh. I am neither soul nor body now, neither fully of this world nor yet of yours and my fellow mortals find me a queer, blunt creature. I submit to all this. But *there is one thing* which *you,* since you are justice itself, *cannot* deny me and that is the salvation of my sister, Agnes, whom I entrusted to your love. This," she insisted, "you owe me."

When she had said this she began to wait for some sign that she had been heard. Obstinately, she stood, concentrating her will and energies in a taut current directed towards God. Every last mite of herself was channelled into it and towards him. She had emptied her mind of every thought but this: that she must compel his response. She thought of him and she thought of the force flowing from her to him, speeding hotly through space, burning with the speed of its passage, burning with the heat of his presence as it approached him: the source of all light and power. Light, she thought, burning, and, opening her eyes, saw the air furry with a red glow. Now there must be a response. The flow must turn and come back to her. She braced herself, emptied her mind, waited, saw herself as a receptacle waiting for light, a lamp waiting for the oil and the wick and the tingling, searing flame. Several times she imagined she felt the wave of premonitory heat flow through her—but these were illusions. She lost count of time. Her limbs were cramped, her brain dry and wooden and her skin, she discovered, testing it against the cold flags of her floor, had grown quite cold. It was when she saw that the glow in the air was a reflection of the dawn sky that she grew impatient and, going downstairs and across the convent yard, entered the kitchens where she collected a brazier full of live coals and brought them back to her cell. Here she took a pair of tongs and, grasping a red-hot coal with it, applied it to her bared thigh. For a moment she felt nothing. Then the shock of the pain almost made her swoon, did indeed make her half swoon, but even though her mind was shrieking like a mad animal inside her and her flesh was raging, her will and the hand holding the tongs kept to their programmed decision. She did not move the coal until it had burned a hole deep in her flesh and its own bright, luminous edge had dimmed. Carefully, she put the coal back. Then, taking from a bench which stood in front of her personal reliquary, a monogram of Christ which had been cut in metal, she thrust it deep into the red center of her brazier. She waited for this to heat, staring into the heart of the fire with eyes as dull as the eyes of a statue. Once or twice her body contracted in a spasm, then gradually relaxed and once she let out the words "Jesus Christ". Then, when the monogram was glowing so vividly that it looked translucent, she took hold of it with her tongs and applied it to her other thigh. She held it there until it had burned its letters indelibly through the skin then, removing it, applied the still-hot metal to her arm, branding herself as she had seen slaves branded with their owner's sign or name. She let the piece of metal fall, dropped the tongs and dragged herself over to her bed. Carefully she settled herself on it so that no area of burned flesh was touching the sheets. Holding herself down with her hands, she tried to prevent herself from writhing.

"Now," she panted, through clenched teeth, "you cannot deny that I am yours! I have burned your hot caresses on my body! I have opened a passage into it. I have forced you to accept me for your own!"

She closed her eyes and the bright monogram danced on the red screen of her lids so that she felt they were burning too. She opened them but the luminous image floated in front of her gaze still, following it a little unevenly as she swung her glance right and left so that the vivid flower-like shape lagged and lurked briefly in the corners of her eyes.

"Haven't I?" She challenged. "Can you be so unfair, so cruel as to deny me now?"

She continued to challenge and scold the Bridegroom for his harshness and remoteness, though sometimes she changed her tune and thanked him for doing her the supreme honour of testing her and assured him that she would be found worthy. The pain was still acute, particularly from the first wound she had inflicted on herself with the coal and very quickly she found she had grown feverish and her forehead was burning. She heard bells ring for the nocturnal and early morning offices and, straining her ears, caught the sound of a psalm being sung in the chapel. She herself was in retreat, so nobody would come to her cell until about noon. More than once, for a brief moment, she was sure she felt the Bridegroom lying beside her as he had done in the past. At other times

174

it seemed to her that he was inside her head speaking and challenging her to make the most supreme of all sacrifices and give him up: to embrace hell for love of heaven, to merit him by destroying her love for him.

"I", he said using the voice inside her head, "went down to hell to bring up Moses and Adam and even Eve the first sinner. Can you not choose to give me up for love of me? Why are you so grasping in your love?"

"If I went to hell for you," she cried, "I would love you still and my love for you would force you to follow me. My love would protect me and put out the flames and lighten the darkness and make a heaven of hell."

When noon came, Radegunda was quite delirious. She was aware that the novice who had come with food and water was trying to speak to her, but she could only vaguely determine what the girl wanted. She was aware that her own answers were not directed at the girl's questions but she could not make the two jibe. The girl, she decided after making a massive effort of will to try and concentrate on what was being asked, wanted to know, wanted to know . . . what? The meaning which had been just within her grasp twisted capriciously away. She reached out after it again, had the sensation of touching it with the tips of some apprehending mechanism of her mind, had the conviction that she held it, knew it, was about to deal with it and again, somehow, found it had eluded her. It was not, she was quite sure, at all important. That was why her mind would not hold it. More important was the conversation she had been having with the voice inside her head. She could not deal with this and the novice at the same time.

"It is all right," she heard herself tell the girl, "hell's flames must not be put out nor should we pity the damned in hell. Their sufferings are necessary to them. They assuage their terrible, unimaginably crushing guilt at having sinned against God. They are happier in their flames than they would be with unpaid guilt," she told the girl while realizing that this was not what the girl wanted to be told at all. It *had* something to do with flame though. Something to do with burning. "I'll be all right," she told the girl. "Leave me alone."

Later, when the girl had gone, it seemed to her that her pains had too. She felt airborne, faintly giddy and elated by the sun which was now opposite her window and pouring inwards on beams hung with a dazzle of dust motes. These blazed and dimmed as they sailed on a tremor of noonday air. She watched their coruscations and felt a responding shimmer along her skin.

Slowly, she became aware that someone had entered her cell and was standing in the track of the light so that his hair—for he was a man of, she judged, about twenty-two—flamed glassily and his shape was half effaced by the radiance. He stepped closer and she saw that he was solid and disturbingly seductive: virile but with the entrancingly supple grace of an ungrown hound. There was something of her dead brother in him and she felt an urge so stinging that her fingers were twitching to caress him as she had failed to caress Chlodecharius on the night of his murder. Almost at once the sensation changed and she recognized a surge of the old sensual tides which had so humiliated her when she was married to Clotair. The young man stepped over to her bed and put his hand on the raw, uncovered burn of her thigh. His touch did not hurt but she cringed away from him in shame. Her spine was quivering like a divining rod and the erogenous parts of her body were unquellable. The young man's hand plunged deeply into her wound. Radegunda opened her mouth to scream but the sound stayed jammed in her throat. Her wound was not hurting but was responding in spite of herself and with rapturous relish to a gratification which seemed to be a brew of all those perceptible to the bodily organs. It was febrile and languid, voluptuous, delicate, icy and hot, honeyed and tart, salty, spicy, aromatic, pungent, niveous and vivid, mellow, vigorous, an irresistible ravishing which she was, however, trying to resist, when the young man said:

176

"Don't resist me, Radegunda. Don't you enjoy my touch? Doesn't this give you pleasure?"

"Go away," she whispered. "Go! Go! Go! Christ," she screamed, "why have you abandoned me? Jesus help me!" She tried to roll off the bed in order to kneel on the stone floor or even grope her way towards her reliquary, but the young man held her back.

"Radegunda," he said. "You are burning with desire for me."

"No!"

"Yes! You have been imploring me to come and now that I have come, you don't know me. *I* am your Bridegroom, Radegunda. You begged me to come and now I am here." The young man lay down beside her on the bed and took her in his arms. Radegunda's tormented body gave a spasmodic leap then slowly relaxed. "You must surrender yourself to me, Radegunda," whispered the young man. "Relax. Give yourself. Be the plaything of my love. This is what you wanted, isn't it? It was for this that you were made. Human love is only an image of this. Give yourself totally, Radegunda. Let me gratify myself at your expense."

When Radegunda returned to herself she found evidence that she had indeed been made love to. Her wounds, moreover, no longer hurt her at all. The depression in her thigh remained deeply visible however for she had burned away tissue and the monogram of Christ would be branded on her body as long as she lived.

In the days following this vision she felt full of vigour. It was, she told herself, as though a wave of power had poured from the Bridegroom into herself, a wave so intense that it had penetrated her inmost soul and merged it with the divinity. Her doubts about Agnes were dissipated. It seemed to her now that they had been morbid, ungrounded in fact and a result of her own inner weakness. Agnes was all right. The convent was run as perfectly as ever, more so indeed thanks to the completeness of the new Rule. Radegunda herself was a new woman: energized and prepared to use her new strength in action. She gave up staying in her cell and began to occupy herself as she formerly had with the routine of convent life, taking on other nuns' tasks—over Agnes's protests—and, when there was nothing left to occupy her rage of diligence, sitting down to write long, dissuasive letters to the kings of Gaul who were warring against each other again. These —Guntram, Chilperic and Sigibert—were her own step-sons. She had known them well when they were growing up and the exhorted them in a variety of styles. They replied—or the Bureau of Scribes which each kept in his palace replied—with formal punctuality. The wars, how-ever, went on and were to see many murders and to devastate Poitiers more than once in Radegunda's own time.

Chapter Eleven

Agnes threw herself into her work as if she were throwing herself away. She had slipped once into the arms of human tenderness and they had not been reliable. She hoped the thing would not recur, avoided seeing the child, listened only reluctantly to Fridovigia's accounts of how it was doing and half hoped it might die. What future had it at best? It was a girl: Ingunda. She had not chosen the name. Fridovigia had. The old woman's starved motherliness fastened on it, leaving Agnes herself to a cold peace.

She let the old woman take all the clothes, food, vessels and remedies she chose from the convent store. It was the least the family who were raising Ingunda could expect and, being poor, their right to convent charity was unassailable. Agnes was relieved at being prevented by the Rule of her cloister from visiting them and did not encourage Fridovigia to bring the child to her. Here too the Rule alleviated responsibility. Children were not allowed inside the convent walls until they were seven and then only if they were expected to become nuns.

Once, however, when Ingunda was four and another civil war had sent the forces of King Chilperic's son, Theudebert, to gut areas around and even inside the city of Poiters, she judged it humane to permit convent serfs to come for refuge within the cloister. Among them was Ingunda's foster-family.

While trestle tables were being set up to feed the refugees, Fridovigia caught Agnes's elbow, drew her forcefully towards a gaggle of children and, picking up one blackberry-eyed, dirty-faced little girl, whispered:

"Look at her. Isn't she a beauty? The spitting image

of ..." Fridovigia's gaps and pauses could be more intrusive than speech. She gave this one its due, then: "I make sure she gets her share. She's well fed, as you see. She knows me, don't you pet? Don't you know old Fridovigia?" Wagging her ecstatic old head and dodging mirthfully back and forth behind Agnes's. The little girl laughed and Agnes felt a fossil hollow contract somewhere inside her.

"Yes," she said reluctantly and with what might be fear. "She's pretty."

She walked off, her head swimming. She couldn't cope with whatever she was feeling and didn't want to know more about it. Later, when she was giving bread and pottage to the families, she found herself watching the woman who was Ingunda's foster-mother. She was ordinary enough: a serf and the wife of a serf, strong-bodied, older-looking than she probably was. She seemed to have several other children as well as Ingunda and the little girl seemed comfortable with her. That was as much as Agnes could tell. She did not dare watch too long. Did the woman guess whose child she was raising? Fridovigia had sworn to be discreet but would have hinted at the girl's noble blood. Her own contacts with the convent were obvious and public. Even a peasant woman could make the connection.

Agnes walked away. Fridovigia, however, was not going to let her off. She came after her, panting more than she used to. She had some respiratory sickness which got worse in the winter and her eyes were runny and red. She might not, it occurred to Agnes, live long. Who then would keep up the frail link between Agnes and Ingunda? Or was it as well to let it snap?

"Well?" Fridovigia's breath knotted in excitement. "Well?"

"What?"

"You've seen her!" The words escaped in strained, painful little spurts. "Doesn't that change anything for you? You've seen how she lives—or you can guess. I could tell you, I ... " Fridovigia was having to learn to save her breath. Ironically, it had been an old threat of hers. Now she paused for a few puffs, her glance pinning Agnes the while to where she stood. "A child", she resumed painfully, "of a senatorial family—on your side. Even on the other, she ... Well ... good enough stock I suppose. They've put her to work now," she said. "Watching geese. You can't blame them. It's what they do with their own. But she's not like their children. She's sensitive. She ..." Fridovigia's breath caught in her chest and she had to stop.

Agnes closed her eyes. "St. Caesar", she recited, "has said 'As holy vessels cannot serve for human uses or be taken back once given to the Church, so no nun may be involved in obligations towards her relatives ...'" She said it the way she might have thrown a small stick at a charging animal: hopelessly and because it was all she had. As she had expected, it failed to arrest Fridovigia.

"Listen!" The old woman's breath rasped in her throat but the impediment only magnified and gave more moment to her speech, "... to me," she coughed and caught Agnes fiercely by the arm. "That child is defenceless. She's weak and she's yours. She didn't ask to be born. Your friend, St. Caesar, didn't ask for her to be either, did he? So forget about him and do your best for the girl."

"What can I do?"

"Make a nun of her!" Fridovigia creaked like a bellows, the breath oozing weakly away. "Take her in. It's not much of a life, God knows, but maybe it's the best there is nowadays. Your mother and grandmother had a better life, but what's the use remembering the past? Make a nun of her. No," she put a hand up to stop interruptions, "I know it's too soon. She's better where she is for now. But in a few years, take her. You have girls in the convent who are only seven."

"But ..."

"No 'but'. I may be dead by then. I'll die easier knowing she'll come to you. You know that woman she lives with? Her 'mother' as she calls her? Do you know that woman can't eat meat? Hiltga her name is. When I started taking it to her from the convent kitchen, I couldn't make out why she never ate any but gave it all to the children. 'Have some yourself, woman,' I used to say. 'There's plenty more where that came from,' I'd tell her. 'The nuns don't eat it unless they're ill and have a dispensation. It's their Rule,' I said. I was explaining to her, you see. It's hard for people like that to understand why anyone would give up what they never had. 'They have it', I told her then, 'for the sick and the poor. So you're poor, aren't you? And you may as well profit. Eat some yourself, Hiltga! It'll do you good!' Well, one day she got so fed up with my trying to force the meat on her that she opened her mouth and said, 'Look at my teeth!' So I looked sure enough and, do you know, they were all ground down like an old cow's, like some underfed old cow's that would have been chewing coarse roots for years. All flattened and crooked and worn down to the gums from eating woody roots and the bark off trees during the famines they've had here. Well," Fridovigia paused but her upheld hand showed she was not to be interrupted, "after that," she went on after a moment, "I said to myself: Let Ingunda be a nun. Anything's better than this! Anything. They're not bad people, God help them, but ..."

"All right," Agnes cut her short. "I promise. When Ingunda is seven or eight she can come here."

At this time the Bridegroom made another visit to Radegunda and told her she must sacrifice her dearest wish. She must allow the sanctuary which she had so painstakingly built up for herself and her sisters to be violated. Peace, he reminded her, is not of this world. Radegunda was not surprised. She knew that human wishes, even the best, were likely to be opposed to divine ones, that earthly happiness was currency for buying its counterpart in the other world and that sooner or later the sacrifice least to be foreseen was likely to be demanded. Indeed, the warning reassured her. She had had doubts about the celestial origin of her vision. Its human effects were so real. In memory, the faces of Clotair and Fortunatus kept alternating with that of the Bridegroom, whose actual features she found impossible to recall. They had been luminous and elusive and, as time passed, her certitude that she had seen them at all became weaker. She was ashamed to doubt and equally ashamed at the thought that she might be misled by a self-aggrandizing fancy. In the circumstances, the demand for a sacrifice could only be a relief—the devil did not ask for sacrifices. She begged the Bridegroom to forgive her doubts, wiped his feet with her hair and promised to do whatever he wanted. This time he stood with his back to the light and, as she was excited and had tears in her eyes, she got an even less clear view of him than before.

"You may imagine", he told her, "that if I have given you such proofs of my love, it is because I have a mission for you. You may be asked to do things which may seem strange or shocking: to violate your own cloister and undo your own work. Do it in obedience to me."

"How shall I know when and what to do?" she asked submissively.

"You will know when the time comes," she was told.

A bad year for Gaul. Pilgrims who paused in Poitiers A.D. brought news of floods, an earthquake in Bordeaux, fires 580 and summer hail in several areas and, most terrifyingly, the plague. Fridovigia caught it when it first started in August and suffered badly from pains in the kidneys, a heaviness in the head, pustules, fever and vomiting. She directed her own treatment, had cupping vessels applied to her legs and shoulders and sent Ingunda, who was now a novice in the convent, to the fields for herbs which were then brewed and decocted according to Fridovigia's own recipes. They seemed to bring her relief for a while but just as she seemed to be on the mend, she worsened and died. Ingunda and Agnes cried and, for the first time since the girl had come to the convent, found themselves alone

183

together at the old woman's bedside. Keeping vigil.

Agnes stole glances at the girl, who must by now be ten years old. She was pale, a contained little person with freckles under her eyes which would have come from working out of doors. She was crying. For Fridovigia. The child caught and acknowledged Agnes's look.

"Mother!"

Agnes started.

"Mother Agnes, you loved her too, didn't you?" Nodding at the dead woman.

"Yes," said Agnes. "She was my nurse."

"She was the person closest to me."

"I see."

The two were silent for a long while. But vigils were processes dangerous with memory and too tiring not to be interrupted with some talk. Agnes, to seem natural, questioned the little girl. Cautiously. Keeping on the subject of the dead woman.

"I had hoped", the girl whispered, "that maybe, one day, she might tell me—who my parents were. Now..."

"You think she knew?"

"Oh yes. She knew." The girl had a blunt resentful look. "She was mean about it though. Wouldn't say a thing."

"Maybe she couldn't."

"Why?"

Agnes foundered. "What good would it do", she said feebly, "if they were dead?"

The child looked impatient.

"Or maybe", she ventured, "couldn't acknowledge you?"

"I'd know," the girl said, "I'd know more about myself. Whether I was wanted and that. What the trouble was— there *has* to be some trouble. I'd like to know what kind. Fridovigia", she added, "said I had 'good blood'."

"That means nothing in a convent." Agnes reminded her. "This is your family now. You have two hundred sisters. We are all equal here." That, she realized, was absurdly untrue: theory, not practice. Ingunda was

184

probably made to feel her irregular origin by better-born nuns—and who would not consider herself better born than a girl brought up by serfs? "You'll miss Fridovigia, won't you?" she said, realizing that the old woman must have been a protectress in many ways. While despising convent hierarchy, she had known how to deal with it and made full use of her special relations with its abbess. Ingunda must be feeling very bereft. "You'll miss her," she acknowledged. "Won't you?"

"Yes. I'm alone now."

"Don't you visit your—family?"

The girl shrugged just perceptibly. "Yes."

Those ties too were loosening. What would a family of serfs have to say to a nun? Rashly, Agnes said, "We were both fond of her," nodding at the dead woman. "If you're lonely you must come and talk to me about her. Come tomorrow afternoon. You can help me work in the sacristy. It's work she used to do sometimes."

"All right."

The next day, however, Agnes was unable to keep her appointment with Ingunda. She was half glad. She needed time to contain a rush of feeling which had come on her while Fridovigia's body was being carried to its burial place outside the cloister. Agnes had stood at the convent wall watching a hasty little group bundle the bier on its way. No mourners. The nuns could not leave the cloister and fear of infection had kept any friends Fridovigia might have had among the tenants from showing their respects. The bier was piled with strong-smelling herbs but, from the way the bearers craned from it, Agnes could tell that the decomposing body had begun to stink. It was a vulnerable moment and the one in which the dead woman came nearest to winning her old war against Radegunda— maybe she did win it. Certainly, a ghostly version of the nurse's voice had begun debating with Agnes's inner thoughts: a wily one which granted that Agnes's first duty was to avoid the scandal which could only destroy herself, the convent and Ingunda too. Allowing that much, argued the voice, leeway could and must be found for the feeling Agnes had managed to suppress as long as Fridovigia was there to do her mothering for her. Now, said the pleader, it must be given an outlet. Occasions could be contrived, words found to channel towards Ingunda a tenderness capable of consoling her without betraying itself. How? Well, why not take over the novice-mistress's duties? At least some of them. This would allow Agnes to devote time and attention to her daughter *without appearing to single her out*. That was the pitfall to be avoided. Ingunda was lonely, her affections turbulent. *She* could not be expected to be prudent. Agnes must be prudent for two.

The last of Fridovigia's little funeral procession had disappeared. Agnes left the look-out place and went into the chapel. Her head was light. Instead of praying, she found herself dreaming up and discarding moves which were either too awkward, extreme or likely to alarm the child. There must be no suddenness, just a growth of intimacy such as might happen between any teacher and pupil. The planning was pleasant. Agnes indulged herself and found that the old obstacles had turned into assets. Without the ten years of restraint and being a stranger to her child, how could she have felt this keen anticipation? If her daughter had been everyday fare to her she would not put such value on the girl's response. If she had known her as a baby she would not be confronted by a whole person whom she must learn to win. This surely was a challenge worth meeting, a love of a different order to the milky reflex linking mothers to the parasite just detached from their own organism? She remembered wondering, almost eleven years ago, about how soon a foetus was ensouled—that was when Fridovigia was suggesting a visit to the Syrian doctors. She had never found out the official doctrine of the Church but had reached her own conclusions: ensoulment surely took place over years. An infant was only potentially of a higher order than a cat or dog. Fridovigia had sensed this since she had been ready to help Agnes abort yet solicitous of the child once it survived and began to grow. Childhood was the time Fridovigia liked best. She was a wet-nurse by vocation, had been Agnes's and would have been Ingunda's if she could. Even in her old age, she had provided a warm chrysalis of affection for the girl and had prolonged her own life, thriftily stretching it just long enough to see Ingunda through childhood. Now Agnes and the girl must struggle to know each other as adults. Agnes wondered, dreamed, mourned, though not painfully, for Fridovigia and noticed that her old scruples and shame had gone. Perhaps ten years' dutiful attention to the convent needs had absolved her? Civil law allowed for such workings off of guilt for injuries done. Why shouldn't God's?

She left the chapel in a mood of exhilaration. She was eager to get to grips with this new challenge, but was impeded.

A nun had come to look for her. There were visitors at the convent gate. Important ones who would not be put off.

It was still early. The garden foliage was white with dew and the sun had not finished burning the haze from the tops of the vines below the convent walls. Who could have come with such imperious needs outside convent visiting hours? Someone, it appeared, from the royal palace at Soissons. An emissary from Queen Fredegunda herself. Poitiers had been under the rule of this queen and her husband— who was also under her rule—since its former king, Sigibert, had been murdered five years before. Popular opinion credited Fredegunda with that murder but then half the murders in the kingdom were laid at her door.

"Who is it?" Agnes asked the portress when she reached the gate. "Did they give a name?"

"Bishop Bertram of Bordeaux."

"No less!"

This bishop, whose already shady reputation had not been improved by recent rumours of a scandalous intimacy with Queen Fredegunda, was not in his own diocese and Agnes under no obligation to receive him. However, she handed her key to the portress who opened the door.

A bull-like man with heavy jowls, not much neck and dressed more like a soldier than a bishop was outside on horseback backed up by a train of armed and mounted men. A girl, also mounted, was beside him but her head was bent and Agnes could not see her face. The bull-faced man inclined his torso a little, identified himself as Bishop Bertram, and began to speak.

"My lord," Agnes cut short his compliments. "I should be grateful if you would state your embassy briefly. Our Rule permits us only the most necessary dealings with the world outside."

"Admirable, Mother!" The bishop raised an eyebrow then bent his head. The two gestures seemed to annul one another. "How I envy you!" He paused, then, injecting a careful dose of insolence into his tone, said, "My mission, as it happens, is holy and delicate. If you would allow me to unfold it to you in some place more discreet...?" Another pause. "It concerns", he decided to admit, "a vocation." Nodding at the girl beside him who did not look up. "I can say no more here."

"All right," said Agnes. "I shall see your Grace in the reception room then. With the postulant. Nobody else."

The bishop bowed. Agnes withdrew. She went for a moment to the chapel to prepare herself for what was coming. Bishop Bertram would not have made the journey from Soissons simply to escort a nun. Agnes wished she could have consulted Radegunda but Radegunda was in retreat. The only other person familiar with courts and politics was Fortunatus. How thoroughly she was cured of him! She had not thought of him once during the vigil or funeral. Now his name came to mind in a worldly connection—appropriately, for he was a worldly man. He had become a priest four years ago: a late, tepid vocation. But he did know about court intrigues. He would be able to help her. She left the chapel and gave orders that a peasant was to be sent to the poet's quarters with an urgent request that he come to the convent. Then she went to the parlour. The prioress was waiting at the door and followed her in:

Justina. She was the niece of the Bishop of Tours, not the one who had come to the ceremony for the True-Cross relic but his successor, Gregory. Justina was the most likely of all the nuns to be able to give useful advice. Besides, the presence of another nun was required at all visits. Bishop Bertram did not waste time.

He was a coarse-faced creature with a nose as fat as a fist knuckled into the flesh of his cheeks and as thickly riddled with blackheads as a March seed-bed is with grain. He began to speak with some ceremony—a purely vegetable ooze or crackle might have surprised less—but without conviction and as though he had been hastily drilled in fine phrasing which he did not find congenial. He scratched himself once or twice during his speech, gabbled it through at speed and reserved his considerable power of expression for the grunts and groans which must have been his own addition.

"Mother Agnes," he began, "as you so usefully reminded me just now, your convent is cut off from the world and you probably do not know the latest news from court? No? ... I thought not! Well, it's not good. It is particularly painful to the princess here, so, if you'll allow me, I'll make my account of it brief. Yes: this is Princess Basina, King Chilperic's daughter by his ex-wife, Audovera, who, you will recall, withdrew into a convent on the princess's birth. The reason for that was that she had been imprudent enough to baptize the child herself —the usual story, she had taken bad advice. Well, that made her her own daughter's godmother, her husband's godsip and thus, by Church Law, ineligible to continue as his wife." The bishop waved a hand impatiently at these theological niceties. "There was controversy about all that but the upshot was that she *chose* to renounce the marriage leaving His Majesty free to marry Queen Fredegunda. I remind you of all this because there have been some ... developments. Audovera has just been murdered in her convent. The assassin's identity is un-known. You will appreciate the shock this was for her daughter here. Indeed for us all. A terrible thing. It has contributed to the girl's distaste for the world and her eagerness to join your flock, Mother Agnes. There are other circumstances, too. The girl's brother, Clovis, has killed himself. He was found with a dagger in his chest and his own hand on the hilt. An unstable family, as you see. He was her last remaining brother. Two others had already ended violently. I would rather not go on with all this in front of the princess. It must be painful for her to hear. Perhaps she might withdraw? I say this purely from sympathy, Princess Basina, though I know I'll get no credit for any with you. May she withdraw?" he asked Agnes.

Agnes nodded and Justina took the girl out, then returned alone.

The bishop immediately dropped his official manner. He continued in a confiding gossip's voice with which he was obviously more at ease. It was a voice which evoked winks, cynical leers and digs in the ribs, but the bishop managed to keep his ponderous face straight.

"The truth is", he told Agnes, "that the step-family—this girl and her mother and brother—are suspected of having poisoned Queen Fredegunda's sons in the hope of obtaining the succession for themselves. True or untrue," the bishop shrugged, "what matters is that the queen believes the story. She had several maids tortured when her sons died. The doctors said the boys died of the plague but royalty", again the sly insinuating tone, "don't like to think their own kinsmen can die as serfs do: of natural causes." He paused as though expecting a laugh. "Well," he resumed briskly, "some of the tortured maids were persuaded to blame the step-family and say that they had paid them to poison the children. This may be true and it may not. Either way the girl is unsafe at court and Fredegunda doesn't want her there. The maids", said the bishop meditatively, "took back their story before dying—but what does that prove?"

"Are you seeking", Agnes wondered, "a sanctuary or a prison?"

"Does it matter?"

"Yes. If the girl doesn't want to stay, I shan't have her."

"And what if she ends up like her brother? With a dagger in her breast and her own hand on the hilt?" The bishop waited a few moments, then: "It will have, in part anyway, Mother Agnes, been put there by you!"

"All these stories", said Agnes in some agitation, "bring in here a world which we do not understand and with which we do not know how to deal. You're trying to make use of us, Bishop Bertram. I don't know if it is a good use. I don't know at all. We did not leave the world and its..." she looked for a strong word, "sewer in order to have it follow us here. Our office here is to pray. We attempt to live in harmony—I wonder if you know how hard that is, Bishop Bertram. We offer our harmony to heaven. We recite eighty psalms a day. We try to mediate between God and those who have less leisure to pray than we do. We pray for our own sins", Agnes told him, "and for others'. That is our function. If we begin to act as the prisons of the realm we will end up performing both functions badly." She panted nervously—angry at her own anger. She should be in better control!

"You prize your peace! Mmm! It is true", the bishop remarked, "that you're lucky here. You have never, I believe, been pillaged by one of those ragged armies our kings are forever hurling into battle against", the bishop rubbed his fat nose in amusement, "each other," he finished disbelievingly. "Remarkable luck really! Have you even seen any of our soldiery close up? No? Horrifying scum, Mother Agnes. Not paid at all of course. They are expected to pay and feed themselves with whatever they can grab from the populations whose lands they pass through. They tend not to distinguish between Church property and the rest. A convent is no different to them from a bordello. A lupanar. Forgive me, mother, the word slipped. Yes. We bishops have to deal with matters of the world, you see and—what was that word you used just now? 'Mediate'? Yes, we mediate between such holy persons as yourself and the world. We can become some-what foul-mouthed. I do hope you'll forgive me. Pray for me even." The bishop shook his jowls. "As I was saying, these armies are quite uncontrollable. You've no idea. The officers follow as a huntsman does his dogs. When they're too late they find the hounds have torn the prey apart. You've been lucky here!" He drilled his glance into hers. "You'll agree you have?" he harried her.

Did he think her a fool? Probably. Agnes refused to react. "We pray for the soldiers too," she said.

The bishop shook himself. "Prayer..."

"My lord," she interrupted him. "It is almost time for our next service. Do you want me to question the princess."

He shrugged, nodded, closed his eyes. "Why not?"

"Justina?" said Agnes.

The prioress left. The bishop and the abbess stared in different directions. The prioress returned with the girl. Agnes beckoned her. She moved forward, crabwise. Her face was tight with a look of dislike which she turned impartially on the abbess and the bishop. Agnes guessed that she was about eleven.

"Do you know", Agnes asked her, "that convent life is austere and often disappointing?"

The girl considered her own foot. "My mother", she told it in a flat voice, "was in a convent. She kept me with her for a while. I know about convents."

"You may not know about ours. We make no exceptions for persons of royal blood. Our foundress is Queen Radegunda whose husband ruled all Gaul, but she treats herself more harshly than anyone else here. We own noth-ing. There are no chests with keys. Nobody has any personal possessions. Everyone sleeps in a dormitory. There is no privacy."

"You don't want me?" The girl sounded surprised.

Agnes scrutinized her: dull-eyed, dull-haired, pale, suspicious, sly-looking, possibly stupid, certainly unhappy, presently in a state of shock. Hardly a good recruit for community living. Poor child! Yes, but it was Agnes's business to look out for the community.

"Do you think you'd fit in here?" she asked. "We are two hundred sisters. We live and work together. Each must take her place and no more than her place. Each must move at the pace of the others. It can be a harsh life if one has not a vocation. Boring." She fixed her eyes on the girl, "difficult if one already has difficulties of one's own."

"You don't want me either then?"

"Either?"

The girl shrugged.

"We want you if God wants you. Only you can know that. Has he called you?"

Another shrug. Basina's face was as expressionless as a plate of porridge.

The bishop was tired of this. He crossed the room. "Basina," he put a professional hand on the girl's arm. She looked at it as though it were a slug. "The abbess", he said briskly, "is not trying to discourage you. All this is routine. She would not", a faint grunt of amusement here, "want you to be able to say . . . *afterwards*, that you didn't know what you were taking on. The vow", his voice hardened, "is binding."

Mute, Basina stared at the floor.

"You will be safe here," he encouraged. "You can pray for your mother and brothers."

The girl whipped from his arm and into a corner. She dug her back into it and screamed, "Why don't you kill me too? Be done with it? Aren't those your orders? Shove her into a convent and turn the key. Kill her if she refuses. Or are three murders too much for even Fredegunda—and my father?"

Poor child! Yes. The girl's own father—Fredegunda's husband after all—must be involved too! Agnes repressed her impulse to comfort the girl. All this would have been planned by Bishop Bertram and with neither the girl's nor the convent's good in mind!

"My dear," she remarked instead, "if there had been an

193

intention to murder you, it would be more difficult now to carry it out. Besides, your way back to Soissons leads through the kingdom of King Guntram. You could seek refuge there."

The bishop gave Agnes a furious look.

"It seems to me, Mother, that you are curiously ready to encourage this child's delusions! They have been malignantly and deliberately induced. Surely such receptivity is dangerous in an abbess. It makes me wonder do you have many mad nuns here? Many who receive visits from demons? Incubi?" He bared his teeth. They were yellow, waspish, veined with black.

"We do", said Agnes insolently, "have unsolicited visits we might have preferred to forego. Perhaps this one might now be terminated? The girl has clearly no vocation."

"You refuse to take her?"

"I do."

"The queen will be curious to know your reasons."

"Tell her the girl has no vocation."

"The queen is convinced she has."

"With respect, this is a matter over which the queen's jurisdiction does not extend. I must be allowed to decide for myself."

"Might I remind you..."

"No, my lord. You have reminded me already of too much. You have brought with you the smells and schemes of a world we pity but in which we do not choose to live. Please convey my obedient respects to the queen and tell her we remember her in our prayers."

Agnes turned away. She and Justina were leaving the parlour when there was a thud on the floor beside her. She felt her feet being clutched. Basina had flung herself across the room and was now prostrate, groping and scrabbling at Agnes's skirts.

"For God's love," she whispered, "let me stay."

Agnes glanced at the bishop but could not detect any complicity in his face. It was caught as though in undress: half way between the rage of a moment earlier, surprise and a slow, congealing irony.

Agnes tried to raise the girl but she refused to budge. "Keep me," she begged. "Please keep me here. I want to stay. I'm sure I have a vocation." Weeping, whimpering, her nails scraped the stone floor and her body seemed as flat to the ground as a sheepskin rug.

The bishop challenged. "Well, Mother Agnes?"

Agnes hesitated. "You may leave her", she told him, "for a few days. I shall look further into this. I warn you: I am giving no undertaking at all that I shall let her stay longer."

He inclined his head and left.

The two nuns took—they had almost to carry—the shaking girl to the store-room where an infusion was prepared for her from herbs, cinnamon, pepper and cloves. Several nuns gathered round murmuring the news to each other and trying to sooth Basina.

"Hush now," they whispered. "Drink up. It'll do you good. Don't cry. You're safe here. Safe."

Her anxiety reassured them. The world was as bad as they had hoped. They had made no mistake in giving it up. The good life was really here behind the high convent walls with the tidy flower-beds, the scant food and furniture, and the day divided perhaps too symmetrically by canonical offices. The flatness of their life needed just this contrast to give it flavour. This shuddering resonance from the harsh storms outside enhanced the value of their own bland existence.

"Poor, poor child," they repeated. "Think of it: Fredegunda's stepdaughter!"

Here in their own store-room was a creature of fable: a princess ill-used and menaced by the jumped-up serving-maid, Fredegunda, who was a probable murdress and possibly even a witch. Basina's story was interesting too with suspense. What now? Agnes, who had other things to do, left the girl to relax a while with the younger nuns.

"And had you no friends at all at the royal palace? No one who was good to you?"

Several of them were crying in sympathy. Basina was

dissolved by the lens of their tears into a denizen fit for their utterly fanciful notion of a royal palace. They had all entered the convent when they were little girls no older than ten. Their imaginings must have been vaguely liturgical, based on the way the chapel looked at its best when gold cloths were draped on the altar, wreaths of spruce stuck with flowers hung on the walls and lights massed on every available surface: a brilliant, flickering place dangerous with dark corners and condensations of passion.

"Had you no one?"

Basina sobbed. "There was a maid ... Austrechild—but Fredegunda had her tortured. She had them shave her head and tie her to a pole and whip her until she said ... said my brother had asked her to poison Fredegunda's sons. Afterwards she said it wasn't true, but no one would listen to her then. She was burnt." More sobs. "She looked," whispered Basina, "... in the end, like ... a hunk of butchered meat!"

"And your brother?"

Basina lifted her head and wailed like a hound.

It was almost too good. Here was evil undiluted and ill-used innocence available for rescue and comfort. The nuns were euphoric. They petted and caressed Basina, raided the dispensary-room's stores of dried fruit and fed it to her. They took delight even in her appearance. Her dull hair and pale, shifty eyes were more satisfying than beauty.

"You've only to look at her to see how she's suffered!"

Her fears lest she be sent away became the fears of all.

"Would the queen really have her killed?"

"We'll put in good words for you with the abbess."

"We'll pray for you."

When Agnes came back the girl's resolution to remain had been stiffened many times over. Agnes's warnings about the austerities of convent life no longer frightened her: were if anything a spice added to the welter of sweetness with which she felt surrounded. When Agnes repeated that royal blood earned no privileges at Holy Cross,

Basina was undismayed. Her interesting story, as she had already seen, would.

"But what made you change your mind?" Agnes guessed vaguely at the unhealthy excitement the girl had aroused, sensed, as she had from the beginning, that she was not a good element to introduce into a community. She was violent—that scream at Bishop Bertram, that thudding fall at Agnes's feet—and violence clung about her. An aura of blood, by her own fault or not, of drama, of disturbance followed her. Agnes could feel the change of temperature in the convent, knew that Basina's was an explosive presence, regretted already having allowed her to stay even as long as she had. "Why?" she asked.

The girl shot a glance at her: furtive, Agnes noted, leery.

"I saw you were on my side."

Agnes was stricken. The child was defenceless. Her mind shifted to Ingunda, blending the two girls' histories, then tried to anchor on the undoubted fact that her duty was to think first of the convent as a whole. But her affections were in a receptive state. A crack, thin as a hair, had been opened in her defences. Her usual good sense had to struggle with a maternal secretion lately released and unfamiliar enough still to throw her off balance.

"Child," she appealed, "we will help you reach sanctuary if that is what you want. You would be safe at the courts of your relatives, Queen Brunhilde or King Guntram. They are Queen Fredegunda's enemies. But you must not try to make use of God. If you become a nun, you will be his bride. You must love him unwaveringly. He can't be second best to you, you do see that, don't you?"

Basina looked quickly at and then away from Agnes. "Can anyone be so sure, Mother? Were you? Have you never wavered?"

Agnes staggered. She looked hard at the girl wondering where she got the intuition to deliver such shafts? Could some supernatural voice be speaking through her? But the girl had the same obstinate, lumpy look as before. She expected hostility, had always lived with it. Probably, she could be—very gradually—won out of it. Her pale eyes gave nothing away. Like individual globules of frog-spawn before the tadpole has developed, they lay scummy, torpid but, Agnes suspected, secretly alert, in the ambush of her face. Agnes made some vague answer— she could not afterwards remember what—and put off the rest of the catechism for another day.

It was evening before Fortunatus appeared in answer to Agnes's summons. Since he was now a priest, his connection with Holy Cross was more official and visiting-hours flexible. They met in the parlour. He apologized fussily for the delay. It had been caused by Bishop Bertram. Fortunatus's voice was peculiar and he had a hunted look.

"The bishop", he said, "arrived at the same time as your messenger. I had to entertain him. He just left. He's spending the night with Bishop Maroveus. He has landed me with a . . . a problem. Shall I tell you about it or do you want to tell me yours first?"

"Tell me yours."

"It's confidential. We'll have to be alone."

Agnes nodded to Justina who was in the room with her as usual. "You may wait outside the door," she said.

Fortunatus licked his lips, took several breaths and suddenly spoke in a loud, unnatural voice. "First let me show you a poem I've written." He produced a short scroll and handed it to her. She recognized his handwriting but it was shaky and the papyrus was covered with blots. "Basina's brother", she read, "is not dead. He is wounded, may recover and is presently in my lodgings. Nobody knows this except Bishop Bertram, myself and now you. Basina mustn't be told or Queen Fredegunda get wind of it. Can you hide him somewhere on the convent estate? He'll need nursing. *This is highly risky!*"

Agnes opened her mouth. Fortunatus put a monitory finger on his own lips, handed her a small piece of charcoal and indicated that she should write a reply.

"Why", wrote Agnes, leaning on a chest, "should the bishop do this?"

Fortunatus took the scroll and charcoal and wrote: "Keeping in with both sides. The boy, Clovis, is now heir to Chilperic's throne." He grabbed the paper back almost before Agnes had read it. "The thing is", he said aloud, "that the bishop has left me no choice. It is not possible to back out of a thing like this . . ."

"I shall show your poem to Radegunda," Agnes said as Fortunatus put his scroll back in his pouch. "I shall have to interrupt her retreat anyway to tell her about Basina—but you of course know all about that. The two things are . . ."

"Yes," Fortunatus jumped up nervously. "Let's not talk about that now. I do know about Basina. Bishop Bertram told me. Yes. No problem there, surely? I mean comparatively."

"I have to think of the convent," Agnes told him. "I always have! Your suggestion is totally . . ."

"Not now! Not now!" Fortunatus was putting so many fingers to his lips he seemed to be applauding or warming them or to have gone utterly demented. His eyes rolled. He made silent grasshopper leaps in his anxiety to stop Agnes speaking. "We'll," he mouthed the word 'speak' then finished aloud "tomorrow. Show Mother Radegunda my poem."

"She won't like it."

"We'll see. We'll see. You never know. I have to get back. You may imagine." He spun out of the parlour.

Chapter Twelve

"... tedium ... is akin to dejection and especially felt by wandering monks and solitaries ... disturbing the monk especially about midday, like a fever mounting at a regular time, and bringing its highest tide of inflammation at definite accustomed hours to the sick soul ..."

Cassian

A.D. 580 Radegunda had been waiting for some years for the mission which the Bridegroom had told her would present itself. It had not done so. This was a trial. She accepted it. However, it had jolted her calm. Since the mission was to endanger and perhaps destroy the convent, she found it hard to give the convent her old devoted enthusiasm. She tried to divert her energies towards prayer, but here too met with obstacles. She suffered from morose delectation. Her mind, in seeking to dwell on God, found itself approaching him by a path littered with disagreeable impedimenta. She felt driven by a force in which the carnal was, to her dismay, intimately entwined with the spiritual. She struggled to separate these elements and to conceive of the deity in fleshless terms. But the recipes of the Areopagite and St. Cassian were not geared to her sensibility. She tried valiantly to leave the senses and the intellect only to find herself, by some process as irresistible as gravity, forced down when she would have gone up. She did lose herself in ecstasy, did achieve trances which burned, thrilled, even made her swoon with delight but, afterwards, she was humiliated at the precision with which she was able to detect the sensual element involved. If she had been a virgin she might have been deceived. At the same time, was it not the height of arrogance to have

200

a revulsion against the form taken by the divine favours? Was she not in the position of one who says "Take these away, Lord, I prefer another variety"? At this point in her reasoning, she would start to torment, and frequently reduced herself to such a state of frenzy and exhaustion that she began to fear for her sanity. It was then that she felt most need of reassurance from the outside world and that, coming full circle, her mind began to munch and chew on the notion of the mission which was to be hers. Why had it not come? Could she have failed to recognize it? When? Where? Should she have sought it actively? How? Her letters to the kings of Gaul had not mitigated the wars and ravagings to which these monarchs continued to subject the population. Yet *they* were her own stepsons. Clotair's charge that she had brought good to no one but herself and a few well-born women rankled. It was many years since she had washed lepers or administered charity. She longed to perform some labour which would hasten the coming of God's Kingdom on earth. She prayed for an opportunity.

Agnes came to Radegunda's cell shortly after noon. The nun was standing at her narrow window staring out at a plane of vineyards and crops. She looked caged. Autumn again. Trees were tattered and brown like old aurochs. The horizon, dissolving in illusory liquids, flamed and broke in a scatter of bright sherds. Planes of light shifted. A pair of goats cropped in the foreground and a child herded geese away from someone's lettuce patch. The sun was a raging disk. Last week the grapes had been gathered and crushed to make wine. I too, Radegunda decided, I too must be crushed so that I may ferment.

Agnes told her about Basina and her brother. "My own feeling", she ended up, "is that this is something with which we should have as little to do as possible."

"Where is your charity?" Radegunda turned a dazzled face towards Agnes. "If God sent us these children it is so that we may save them. Did you say the boy is the heir to the throne of Neustria? And in need of nursing?"

"Yes and hiding. But I don't trust ..."

"Trust, Agnes. Trust in God."

"But the only really safe hiding place would be *within* the convent," said Agnes and waited in mounting panic. "That surely", she hoped, "is unthinkable?"

"Why, Agnes, why? Special circumstances call for special measures!" Radegunda's eye-sockets brimmed with reflected sunlight. The eyes themselves were lost in the great scoops of glitter which overflowed and fractured on a bubble of opalescent spittle on her lip. Agnes felt unable to argue with her. Holy certitude and good sense had no common ground. She turned to leave. "I", Radegunda called after her, "will nurse him myself."

"Where?"

"Here. He's a boy, isn't he? We mustn't be narrow in our interpretations of rules, Agnes. We mustn't be like those Byzantine monks who refused to have nanny-goats or cows within their cloister! Even hens!" Radegunda laughed ecstatically. "How old is he, anyway?" Her head as she turned to the retreating Agnes was lit by the sun pouring from behind her. It fell and broke through the folds of her white veil. "He can dress as a girl. A postulant. We can give it out that this postulant has the plague. That will keep people's curiosity in check! We will keep him isolated," Radegunda planned craftily.

"As you wish," said Agnes to whom this mixture of glee and exaltation was distasteful. "He may still be beardless," she admitted, "and being a royal prince will have long hair."

"You see!"

"Yes." She paused. "It won't be for long?"

"We must take things as they come."

"I suppose then we keep the girl too?"

"Well, for now, don't you think?" Radegunda seemed to have forgotten the girl.

So two new 'postulants' joined Holy Cross. One was officially plague-stricken, both, in Agnes's view, were tainted by an obscure worldly contagion. Not that Basina was not exemplary. Too much so. At every turn of path or corridor she seemed to lie in Agnes's way, looking pious, diligent and always equipped with reasons for being where she was.

"Sister Disciola sent me with a message to the bell-ringer ... I was going to the field to collect autumn crocuses for saffron ... to help Ingunda pick hazel-nuts ... Chrodechilde card wool ... to the chapel to say a prayer ... to Sister Justina for a reading lesson ..."

They all made too much of her. Could she be blamed for making as much of herself? Her piety was theatrical. Sobs were heard at night in the dormitory and when Agnes came to see what the trouble was, there was Basina lying prostrate on the freezing stone floor.

"Why aren't you in bed?"

"I was praying for my mother."

Well, her mother had been murdered. One could not deny that Basina had been touched by fate. Yet she did nothing to make herself inconspicuous.

"If you get ill," Agnes told her chillily, "someone will have to nurse you. You are part of a community, Basina. Peculiar conduct is not tolerable. Get into bed."

Basina did. But the ordinariness and routine which Agnes wanted to impart to the workings of the convent did not return. Perhaps it had not been there in the first place? Perhaps Basina's presence was not the disturbance which threw it off keel but merely an indicator, something like a mason's plumb-rule which reveals departures from the true vertical? There were currents moving in the convent and they gathered around her. These women, who called each other 'Mother' and 'Sister' and were neither, were so many stoppered bottles. Emotion fermented in them. Their tenderness was turned on a distant, inconceivable infant: the babe of Bethlehem, an image just persuasive enough to set the milk of human affection moving in their body ducts. They longed for reality. Any reality. Basina, young, plain, and menaced, was a godsend.

Five minutes after Agnes had left the novices' dormitory, a figure slipped across it and into Basina's bed.

"Shshsh!" A hand pressed on her mouth. "I've come to comfort you. Don't make a sound."

Basina wriggled but didn't.

"I", whispered the girl who was lying with her chin pressed against Basina's shoulder, her mouth funnelling reassurance through Basina's hair, "am your cousin, Chrodechilde. Not cousin the way they say 'Sister' in this place! I'm your real blood cousin. I'm King Charibert's daughter and you and I have the same grandfather: King Clotair. We must be friends, Basina."

Chrodechilde talked. Basina listened. Other ears in the dormitory did too but nothing was said or reported of this to Agnes. Chrodechilde, although only fourteen years old, was a force among her peers. She was six feet of pallid flesh, freckle-flecked as though she had exposed herself to sieved sunlight as she perhaps had in some forest. There was something feral about her: a spikiness, an obtuse, potential violence. The other novices were afraid of her. She had the reddish hair and the temperament of King Clovis's descendants—though what had reached her was perhaps even a peculiarly fierce fermented strain of this. Her father, King Charibert, had had many prickly dealings with the Church, having been excommunicated for marrying Chrodechilde's mother, an ex-nun and, on another occasion, sending a recalcitrant bishop trundling home to his diocese in a cartload of thorns. He had died, as Chrodechilde now informed her cousin, leaving her no inheritance at all.

"Just like yourself, poor darling! We're in the same leaky boat: birds of a feather and our plumage sorry at that."

Inherited land followed the spear not the spindle. Females had no claim and, after the kingdom had been divided among her uncles—"Your papa got the lion's share! But I don't hold that against you!"—Chrodechilde had been tossed from pillar to post, being brought up

204

haphazardly and more or less heartlessly by a succession of foster-families. They found her unendearing—"Well, maybe, I was!"—and foreseeing small return for any affection they might have given, gave none. "So I owe nobody anything!" finished Chrodechilde with satisfaction. "It's the other way round!" By law, all a female could hope to inherit was "the spoils of her mother's neck".

"They even robbed me of most of those! Gold collars . . . rings . . . Well, what good would they be to me here? Unless I were to offer them on the altar as Radegunda offered her jewels. The miracle is that I'm not dead. I'm telling you this to show you how much we have in common."

Basina wept in sympathy and self-pity and the strong hands caressed her neck, her back, her bottom.

"But you didn't die?" Basina was entranced, taken out of her own woes, gathered into this new cousinship. "Tell me", she begged, "more."

No, Chrodechilde had not died. Regard for her royal uncles—"again: one was *your* papa!"—who, though they had forgotten her existence, might at any point remember and be displeased to find it ended, had made the foster-families minimally careful of her.

"He forgets my existence too!" Basina whimpered.

"Fathers do." Chrodechilde, an aged fourteen-year-old, had watched life from inside too many families to be anything but cynical. It was in no sacrificial spirit that she had decided to enter the convent at the age of eleven. Her current fosterer had been relieved. Her uncles had put up the spiritual dowry and that had been that. She did not mention the hopes she had concealed on entering Holy Cross, nor give the less flattering facts about her background. Her blood was mixed, for her mother's father had been a weaver and that mother had died as a result of the excommunication pronounced against her by Bishop Germanus, after her sacrilegious marriage. Since Germanus was now a saint, there was no gainsaying

205

his judgement nor the spiritual stain which lay on Chrodechilde. Her looks, too, were mixed. She had a badly
undershot jaw which from some angles made her look
grotesque. From others it was countered by her bright
abundant hair and the compelling mackerelled eyes which
swam above her cheek-bones like lazy fish. Early on she
had learned that hierarchies are precarious. She who had
been brought low might yet rise as her mother had.
Since this looked unlikely to happen by marriage, she had
decided on a spiritual career. Radegunda's story had
influenced her. It struck her as encouragingly close to her
own. Radegunda, a king's daughter, had also been brought
low but was now acknowledged on all sides as a living
saint. Chrodechilde pondered the aspects of this satisfying
tale. To her it represented the triumph of the meek by a
bending of unpromising rules. She discounted its spiritual
implications. If *she* became a saint it would be in order to
triumph first in this life and get her own back on the saint
who had excommunicated her mother. After thinking
lengthily about this, she began to believe that her plan
was fated to come into effect, and reached Holy Cross fully
imbued with the expectation that Radegunda would know
and recognize in her a spiritual sister endowed with a
destiny parallel to her own. She expected the foundress to
make some sign that this was so. Later, looking back,
Chrodechilde felt acute relief that she had confided this
hope to no one. What she had done, one day when she
could bear to wait no longer, was to leave some tedious
task which had been assigned to her, climb the stairs to
Radegunda's cell and walk in without permission. It was
an unheard-of violation of convent etiquette, for Radegunda was the community's link with God. Other nuns
had strict timetables and when summoned at any hour of
day or night were expected to drop what they were doing,
whether job or prayer, in deference to the obedience which
was the nerve and sinew of the whole monastic enterprise.
Other nuns but not Radegunda. She was felt to live as much
in eternity as in time. Nobody interrupted her. Ever. But

Chrodechilde, then eleven years old, had come to believe that she too lived outside time. She was a child of strong imagination and no discipline at all. She pushed open the door and saw Radegunda sitting very ordinarily on a chair.

"Hullo," said the foundress in a matter-of-fact voice. "Who are you? A new novice? What's your name?"

"Chrodechilde," she said, shocked and wondering was this some sort of test, "Mother."

"Well, Chrodechilde, were you curious about my tower?" Brisk but indulgent. "Nothing much to see here, is there? I suppose it would be a good idea if I were to meet all the new novices but, recently, I have withdrawn rather from the community. I have", Radegunda prevaricated outrageously, "been ill. However we've met now, haven't we?"

They had. On a humiliatingly mundane level. In her state of overstimulation, Chrodechilde could only suppose that the foundress—who of course had supernatural insight and knew all about Chrodechilde—had deliberately staged this scene so as to humiliate her. She began to blush the maddening, prickling blush of the red-haired. "I'm sorry," she said inadequately.

"Don't be," said Radegunda. "I'm glad we met. Pray for me. The prayers of the innocent are precious."

Chrodechilde genuflected, kissed Radegunda's hand, mumbled something and fled.

She did not hold this failure against Radegunda whom she continued to admire. Later, however, when an attempt to win Agnes's affection—Chrodechilde, like a stray dog, tried for allies wherever she could—had also failed, she turned fiercely against Agnes. What happened was that she intemperately courted the abbess and, when it was pointed out that ordinary respect for convent rules, which she despised, would be more pleasing, took bitter offense. She was lonely, desperate for immediate approval and now, since the two women who represented authority, had refused this, resentful. They had better look out. She would bide her time. She was their enemy, she decided, and had survived through the next years in the convent very satisfactorily, living a life which was half real and half in her head. The real part had to do with the other novices, some of whom she cowed by violence while others she won by charm. Basina was being treated to the charm.

"You'll be all right here," Chrodechilde told her. "It's not perfect but it's safe and we're trying to make things better. You must help. We'll explain. Oh, don't be alarmed. There's nothing here as bad as in your stepmother's court. What an animal that woman is!" she whispered, stroking Basina's neck and terrifying her by her daring. "An obscene beast! They must have a hot place waiting for her in hell! No, nothing like that here. There are just little things that need changing—like our having to take orders from a woman who is neither royal nor even of our own race. You know who I mean. A Gallo-Roman nun. Well, who runs Gaul? Who conquered it? Mind you, while the foundress is alive you could say that she's only relaying *her* orders and so we—you and I who are of royal blood—are not demeaning ourselves by obeying since the foundress is a queen. But when she dies? Did you know that she burns holes in her flesh with live coals and . . . oh, am I frightening her, little squirrel? All right, I'll say no more. But the point is Radegunda can't live long at this rate, can she? And then we'll be left with old Agnes. Some of us are thinking of complaining to our relatives. You could help there. We won't write to your father, perhaps, since things are tricky for you in that quarter, aren't they? But we could both write to our uncle, King Guntram of Burgundy. I wouldn't mind Agnes not being of the blood royal if she had any leadership, but she's just a stickler for rules. So dull. No feeling. Feeling—for me anyhow—is the very pulse of religion. I can tell *you*'re the same. Passionate! The spirit kindleth and the letter killeth—or something like that. I can never remember words. I'm not a word person at all. I'm too spontaneous. I think that's a strength. I mean, instead of looking up old words in books—and I see you have as much trouble as

I do learning to read—instead of that, we look into our hearts. We invent for ourselves. I think that's better. I'm sure I'd make an excellent abbess. You know Agnes was about my age when she became abbess? Radegunda didn't want power herself, you see. I admire her immensely. A passionate woman! Have you heard how she burnt herself with coals? They say the smell of burnt flesh came right into this dormitory ..."

Basina rose the next day aware that she was sought after and that there were little poles of power, nets of intrigue, all that was needed to give life zest within the convent walls. Although weaker than her cousin, although utterly passive in her affections, she was less easily won than Chrodechilde might think. Precisely because she was passive, she was faithless. She began to wonder did she prefer the abbess to her cousin. Would she not rather be in the camp, since camps there were, of the woman who was abbess than of this clearly dangerous cousin of hers who only aspired to be?

Basina began to court Agnes, the only nun who held out against her. That it was a question of holding out and not of indifference she was sure. She had seen something on Agnes's face when she had asked her whether her love of God had never wavered. The question had been random—but not innocent. Basina was not innocent. She had been reaching purposefully though uncertainly for a weapon and Agnes's reaction had shown that she had found one. Now she set out to see could she break through the abbess's defences.

Agnes took over the duties of the mistress of novices. It was in a writing class a few days later that she discovered that several of the girls were unable to hold their pens. Why?

"Show me your hands."

A show of shyness. Then the palms were shown: bleeding and scabby in imitation of the stigmata.

"Where else?"

Their feet of course. Scratched more or less vigorously

209

with a nail. One child had yellow pus on hers.

"What about the wound on Christ's side? Did you imitate that too?"

No. They hadn't thought of that. Or perhaps, since the fifth wound would not have been visible, had not felt it to be worthwhile. Imitating the exploits of great saints—as small boys did those of great circus performers—they stuck to externals as actors must. It was a form of homage. There was no mockery here. Agnes saw that. More than a game, it was a rite. As other children might play with dolls, these, reared for the cloister, were seeking an equivalent. The equivalent though was dangerous. Nobody can take a doll for a baby but a nail-scratched palm can deceive an imaginative girl into believing she has been marked out by heaven.

"Whose idea was it? Who did it first?"

Silence. Solidarity. But she could guess.

She made mild fun of them, preached sound sense—and was undermined by Radegunda. The children declared they wanted to confess their sins. Publicly. A deputation went to Radegunda, explaining that the abbess, because of the mildness of her nature, was being too lenient with them. They themselves felt the need to unburden.

"For the sake of our souls, Mother Radegunda, prevail on the abbess."

Radegunda prevailed. The game intensified. Among the shadows of the draughty chapel where oil-fumes mingled with the rankness of evergreen garlands, the little girls, ceremonially, one by one, prostrated themselves on the mosaic floor and cried out their guilt with the art of practised actresses.

"I blasphemed. I pretended to have received the favours of Christ. I scratched my own palms and feet until they bled a bit and then pulled off the scab when it formed. It didn't even hurt much. Now I am afraid I have endangered my soul. Please give me a penance."

"I used menstrual blood."

"I didn't copy the others but my refusal came from

pride. I felt superior. My sin is worse than theirs." This from Ingunda.

"I", Chrodechilde confessed, "thought the whole thing up. I am the worst sinner of all."

And on and on. Boasting. Competing. An orgy of it. Radegunda sat listening, her face stiff with charity. How silly she is, thought Agnes sadly. She encourages zeal and all she gets is theatre. Some of the older nuns looked bewildered, even stunned. This sort of thing was new to the convent.

"All right." Agnes stood quietly in the chapel. "We've heard your confessions now." She turned a quelling look on the flushed excited faces. Eyes glinted; lips were licked; tremors passed among the adolescent herd. They had intoxicated themselves, keyed their nerves to a pitch of collective expectancy and were ready for anything—except to be let down. The bright, drugged eyes implored Agnes: "Something," they pleaded. "Prescribe something violent. Strange. Anything. Only don't, please, force us back into our imprisoning separate selves."

Agnes spoke in a dousing voice. "There is nothing," she told them flatly, "which prevents feeling like shamming it. Pretence", she insisted, "dries up the heart. Now I cannot be sure but what I think is this: that you have been playing with religion and that the repentance you all expressed just now was also play: a sham. If it was, you had better admit this to yourselves, because the hearts you dry up", she warned, "will be your own. You may go."

There was a silence. More: a kind of vacuum as the girls grappled with the probability that nothing more was to come, nothing to happen after all.

"That", said Agnes, cruelly mild, "is all. We shan't discuss this incident again."

They left, slowly, shrunkenly, dragging themselves and she, touched by their dejection, felt distaste for what she had done. Wasn't it like rubbing soot into the eyes of a peacock's tail, sham eyes but which have delighted many? She had broken the current uniting them, quenched and shown up the sad spuriousness of their fantasy—and what else had these girls got? Why had she done it? In the name of a genuine but perhaps unavailable experience? *She*, certainly, had never enjoyed religious ecstasy and had no tips as to how to achieve it. Or had she been aiming for order and the sort of conduct with which community administration could best cope? And was refusal of sham emotions—resignation to a narrow life not just as likely to dry the heart? Hadn't it perhaps dried up her own?

"Well," said Chrodechilde to Basina. "You saw. She has no temperament."

"I'd have said", Basina answered, "that she won that game."

Next day she went to see the abbess who was making wreathes for the altar.

"What you said about pretence, Mother," she said, "moved me. I think I have tendencies to be pretentious. I . . ."

"Think of your work," Agnes told her coldly. "And think three times before starting a sentence with 'I'. Work will save you if you want to be saved."

"May I help with yours?" Basina picked up some laurel branches which Agnes was bending into circles.

"You'd do better to practise your writing. If you're going to stay with us, you'll have to learn to write."

"If?"

"If."

Basina began to cry. Deliberately? She was a great crier. But what difference did that make, Agnes asked herself. She knew the root complaint of these little girls who alternately disguised and paraded it: a need to be loved. Small birds thrown early out of whatever cold nests had hatched them, they grabbed what cover they could. Like rejected nestlings too, many were unappealing. The God in whom convent-Rule invited them to sink their separateness was a comfort to the very few. For others he fell apart in the mind: a scarecrow-lover put together from scraps and hazy images of a world in which they had no place. The best thing for them would be to love each other in a mild and not too individual manner. Or so Agnes felt—and failed to act on, for she picked up the crying child, kissed her and told her she could stay.

Basina kissed her back, noted the smell of verbena from Agnes's clothes, fell in love with her and thought she might warn her against Chrodechilde.

A bell rang.

"That's for me. I have to go," said Agnes. And so was not warned.

Later that day Agnes and Ingunda finally met to work on the sacristy vestments. Agnes was shy of the girl and at first planned to let her talk. But the girl did not talk so Agnes had to start questioning her if she was not to let the hour go by without either of them opening their lips.

"Do you get on", she asked, "with the other novices?"

"Not well," said Ingunda. "They're from better families than I. You know—I speak bad German and worse Latin. I'm improving ... but slowly—besides, they remember what I was like before."

"Did they *ask* you to join—to pretend you too had the stigmata?"

"Oh, they asked me all right. They were all doing it together. In the dormitory."

"Weren't you tempted?"

"No." There was a pause. "Don't think I'm better than they are," said Ingunda. "It's more the other way round. I'm more down to earth. I mean, can you imagine the family that brought me up, my foster-sisters, doing a thing like that? They'd think it daft. It's like fasting. They never heard of it. When you had food you ate it—or saved it. You don't think of depriving yourself of something you don't have half the time!"

"Are you ... happy?"

"I'm content."

"But you miss Fridovigia?" Agnes fell back on the

213

acknowledgeable link. "Don't you?" she begged.

"Oh, I was sorry for a bit when she died. But, after all, she was old. She's better off dead."

Agnes felt rebuffed. How much easier it would be to get close to Basina who came rubbing up against one like a spoilt cat. This girl ... Agnes looked at her: intent face, closed. A touch of the peasant who gives nothing away. Well, what had she expected?

"Time for compline," she said.

"Yes."

"Will you come again tomorrow?"

"All right."

Chapter Thirteen

"I tell you," said Fortunatus, "I have lost my appetite. I A.D. can't eat." 580

Agnes was impressed.

"Not a thing. I can't swallow!" Hand to recalcitrant throat.

"That is bad!"

It was. She knew. The seat of his energies was his mouth. Its functions combined beautifully.

"I", he complained, "have never aspired to be important. Or heroic. Or saintly. You know that, Agnes. My God!"

Was God nodding, one wondered? He was supposed to note the fall of a sparrow and here he was sending a lark on a hawk's errand!

"All this about", Fortunatus lowered his voice and cupped a hand funnel-like about his mouth, "the prince is not my kind of thing at all!" They were standing by the convent wall which dropped sheerly below them into empty open countryside. On the inside was the garden which did offer some cover for possible eavesdroppers but Fortunatus had checked every bush.

"Well," said Agnes, "Radegunda has things well in hand. I mean: nobody sees him."

"How long can that last? I ask you. With two hundred women fluttering around. He's like a cock in a barnyard. They'll *smell* him!"

"She's with him all the time. And she has marked the door of his cell with the tau cross: the sign of the plague."

"And suppose she goes off into a trance? What then? What worries me is Bishop Bertram. What's he up to? Which side is he on? What's his game? He's an intriguer, a tricky customer, slippery, deep. God knows what he's up to. Anyway he left me no choice. Can you imagine my feelings when he arrived in my place with the wounded—for all I knew, dying—prince? I couldn't throw him out. That might cost me my life—he *is* Chilperic's son. But keeping him was almost as dangerous. Bertram has a hold on me now. Do you think that's what he wanted?"

"Why should he want a hold on you?"

"There's always dirty work to be done. They always need someone to do it. They could have anything up their sleeves. Anything. Saints Hilary and Martin guard us! It's all very well for Radegunda. She's a queen. She's a saint. She probably wouldn't mind being a martyr as well. Might welcome it. Though you probably don't know it—it's shocking how little people do know of their religion!—self-slaughter has been condemned by two Church Councils. Two, wilful martyrdom is a form of self-slaughter. Ergo—but women never understand theory." Fortunatus walked up and down, gulping in air as though it might save him from drowning in some element which his splashing movements made present even to Agnes. "Oh," he cried and was so clearly aghast that she would have caught and calmed one of his hands as one does a bird which has strayed desperately indoors—but how could *she*? Safety, she knew, haunted his mind. He had left Italy in search of it.

"Fortunatus, is there something you want us to do?"

He flung up his hands prayerfully. "Agnes, for your own sake, for my sake, for the prince's sake, *be careful*! Have you got him dressed as a nun at least? Shaven?"

"Yes. Yes."

"He's not dying I suppose?"

"He's recovering. Radegunda has applied poultices and..."

"Mmm!" Fortunatus waved away medical detail. "Now comes the tricky decision: do we get him out of the convent and slip him off somewhere and, if so, where? If any harm came to him, we would be responsible—and he *is* heir to the throne of Neustria. On the other hand, if Fredegunda ever

216

heard that we had helped him it would be the rope and pulley for me."

"We can pray."

"Oh, by all means pray. Pray. We can ill afford to forego any available support!" He spoke with violence. "The question is where could we send him? It's a bad moment. Usually the kingdoms are at each other's throats and refugees from one safe in the others. Not now. Right now there's a reshuffle of alliances. Everything's up in the air. Until lately, it was clear enough." Fortunatus sliced the air into segments. "Chilperic was on one side, Guntram and Childebert on the other. That was after Guntram adopted Childebert as his heir. But the latest word is that Chilperic is also thinking of adopting Childebert as his heir. Great family spirit, what? Childebert may be an orphan and a minor but no one can say he lacks fathers. And Chilperic's fatherly feelings have evidently been saved for now. After all, it's largely his own fault if he's heirless— or thinks he is, since he doesn't realize that you know who is in the land of the living. If that little fact were to leak out, Fredegunda would soon make it past history. In the twinkling of a knife. She's more of a man than he—he only plants the royal seed; she reaps it. She's trying to grow some more of her own at the moment, according to reports. She's desperate to get pregnant. Going to witches, sorcerers and Syrians of every stripe. Rubbing herself with ointments, dosing herself with potions. She doesn't neglect the saints either. They say she prepares steam infusions and—saving your presence—vaginal douches with scrapings from St. Denis's tomb. A woman of eclectic belief. She's on a diet of she-rabbits and dandelions from what I hear: sympathetic magic. Maybe she'll produce a buck rabbit."

"You sound well informed," Agnes spoke with distaste. He sounded, it occurred to her, in better spirits too. Gossip restored him. "Well," she said, "what now?"

"Nothing," decided Fortunatus, "for the moment. We'll have to sit tight."

217

Radegunda had become attached to her patient. He was not the child she had supposed. Time flew. He was fifteen and a veteran of several campaigns, but weak now, harmless and amenable to good advice.

"Peace", she told the prostrate prince as she dressed the wound in his chest, "is something we would all enjoy if young men like you would refuse to fight."

"Refuse? I", he told her, "spent most of my wars running away."

"That's nothing to be ashamed of. The Bible says . . ."

"Who's ashamed? It's a matter of luck. I mean if an army suddenly surrounds the place where you're sitting with your stepmother drinking perry—well, you run. Or take the time I was sitting in Bordeaux over my lunch when a fellow I'd never seen in my life appeared outside in the street roaring that he was going to hunt me like a deer. He was an ally of my late uncle, Sigibert, who was on bad terms with my father and he swore he'd chase me across Gaul with horns and trumpets like a deer. Did you know that stags used to be tutelary animals—no, I suppose you wouldn't be interested. Anyway, he didn't say 'stag' but 'deer' and like a deer I ran. And he followed. Just as he'd said. With horns and trumpets. I still dream of them at night. Painful. It would be doing me a kindness, since you don't sleep much, to waken me when I bell."

"Bell?"

"Like a deer. Like this." The boy began to roar.

Radegunda clapped a hand over his mouth. "For God's sake. You're in hiding here. You're supposed to be sick."

Clovis apologized. "I've hurt my chest," he complained.

"Did you try to poison Fredegunda's sons? Did you poison them?"

"Those poor brats? Why should I? They were never meant to live. She smothered them in affection—as well have smothered them between two tics. She has the evil eye."

"Did you have someone else poison them?"

"I did not. They died of the plague. She was furious.

218

She'd hoped I'd get it, you see. I used to find strange bits of clothing stuck under my sheet at night: rags from plaguey corpses. She had me sent to the villa at Berny where it was raging. My father consented. Poor man, he's like an extra limb of hers. Between them they make up a human being. She's the head, guts and liver, he's the penis. Sorry if I've offended you."

"Do you want to be king?"

He tried to shrug, hurt his wounded chest and grimaced. "If it comes it comes. Right now the omens point the other way."

"Will you fight and burn the country if you become king?"

He laughed sourly but carefully, not disturbing his dressing. "Are you wondering whether I'm worth saving? People come to that sooner or later. I see them weighing me up. 'What are his chances?' they ask themselves. 'Shall we keep in with him? How close to his father is he?' In your case we can substitute 'God' for 'father', am I right?"

"Oh, I intend to save you anyway. My professional pride is involved. I ran a hospital once."

"It's a lucky wound isn't it? A touch nearer the heart and I'd be dead. I suppose they think I *am*. Except for Bertram. I keep wondering why he saved me."

"You don't believe he might have had a virtuous impulse?"

"I believe you might. But I know Bertram. I've been working things out as I lie here and what I think is this: there has to be an opposing party, some group who would like to have someone—me or another—to put up against Fredegunda. So this gives me market value. Bertram can keep or kill me according to who bids highest—Fredegunda or the others. He'll be haggling over me now with Brunhilde and Childebert and maybe with the nobles who don't care much for our family anyway. Possibly even with Guntram, though *he* has nothing at stake. He has no heir of his own."

"You don't believe *we* would kill you?"

The young man had a crooked, mirthless smile. "You

don't have to know what you're doing. You'll hand me over to Bertram and he'll do his own dirty work."

"I could", Radegunda had an illumination, "tell him you were dead."

"And what would you do with me then?"

"Hide you. Here. You could dress as a nun. Would you feel demeaned?"

"To be a woman? I suppose not really. I'm not proud, you know: not of my sex or race or even stock. I've had no reason to be. I belong to the stepfamily. Everyone who wanted to keep in with Fredegunda treated us worse than they did the palace dogs. My two eldest brothers died in stupid wars, wars about nothing. As for being a woman— well, the toughest human being I've ever known was a woman: Fredegunda."

Radegunda looked at the weak, young face and re-membered Chlodecharius, her brother. She was convinced this situation had been sent. What she meant to do with it, she did not yet know, but this would be revealed to her. The first step was clear: Bertram must be deceived. The boy's survival would be a secret from all but Agnes and Fortunatus. She would keep him alive as she had failed to keep her brother alive, teach him and maybe one day he might be instrumental in bringing God's rule to Gaul. It was a mad idea but surely that proved that it had come from that more receptive part of the mind to which God talked directly: the feminine part which waited, humbly and uncritically, to be fecundated by divine decisions which are unfathomable and must simply be accepted. Behold the handmaid of the Lord, be it done unto me, she prayed, according to thy Word. What word though? How would she know it when it came?

"My tutor", said the boy, "was from the East. Very knowledgeable. He taught me some anatomy. The womb, for instance, consists of seven cells or pockets. Men are born in the three right-hand ones which are warmer, being near the liver; women are born in the colder side: the left. Hermaphrodites are born in the middle cell and they, my tutor held, though in some ways monstrosities, are in others the most perfect of humans, being conceived in the most temperate and balanced heat. The golden mien, the point of equilibrium where an object hovers so that it falls neither to right nor left is the ideal spot. Mentally, my tutor, said, we should all strive to be hermaphrodites, being neither over-choleric like men nor over-passive like women. Unfortunately, his training of me did not get far. We never reached the point of equilibrium."

"What happened?"

"Fredegunda thought he was a sorcerer. She was afraid he was making me too clever and besides she doesn't like foreigners. When my father put his eye on and another part of him in a slave girl with whom he had been recently presented, she decided this must be the result of sorcery and my tutor must be the sorcerer. The slave was Eastern like him and that was enough for Fredegunda. She had my tutor castrated with live coals and then strangled. I apologize for the grossness of the tale."

"God rest his soul," said Radegunda. "He must have been an admirable man and his theory bears out my own: the ideal human being is sexless. Now you have had some training in striving to conform to the ideal. If we keep you here and dress you as a nun, the experiment can be continued. We shall see if we can breed masculine faults out of you without breeding feminine ones in. You might be the saving of Gaul. You must", she fixed him with fiercely focusing blue eyes, "swear to me that you will neither reveal nor attempt to make use of your masculine attributes while you are here. If you do, I shall be obliged to get rid of you at once."

"Whereupon Bertram or Fredegunda will get me. Obviously", said the boy, "I am in your power."

"I need more than your passive agreement. I need your active collaboration."

"You have it," said Clovis. "I swear by the True Cross."

"Nor", Radegunda warned him, "may you reveal your presence here to your sister or anyone else."

"I won't."

"Swear."

"I swear."

A.D. 587   I have been asleep again or in a faint. The two are more and more similar now. I thought I smelled resin a while ago and heard armed men moving in the cloister. One rattled his scramasax in the slit of my wall. Franks. They were shouting in some patois I hardly understood, shouting— God forgive me, I *thought* I heard: "Where is the abbess, the old she-fox. We'll run her to earth yet and cut off her brush!" Surely *that* was a demon? Yet it might not be. Sanctuaries have been violated and profaned before now. Silence. Where are they? Gone? But the convent is large. Sounds carry badly through these thick walls. I hear nothing. My mind is plagued by ignoble thoughts. Agnes ... God, may not mortification of the mind find grace in your eyes? My mind is a sewer. Cloacal. The sewer smell is the devil's. Many saints have recognized him by his sulphurous exhalations. But he has penetrated into my mind! God *is* this your will for me?

There have been anchoresses who were visited in their solitude by celestial visions. Some—our chaplain told us— were visited by their Heavenly Spouse who shone so brightly that the cells and dark places where they were immured were lit up as though by noonday sunlight. His light penetrated their flesh. I never dared and do not now dare to long for such visitations. I do *not* complain of my own baseness. I never thought to be a saint. I chose the wall willingly.

The lewd fancies are coming back. *My* visions come surely from hell. They buzz and torment me like summer flies. Those men ... laughed. Their weapons clinked on my wall. They shouted and I thought I understood that they were threatening to strip the clothes off the abbess's back and take their pleasure from her front and rear. One yelled—I heard him distinctly: "The old sow must be fifty! A fifty-year-old virgin is tough as an old thorn bush.

Best use your scramasax if you don't want to skin your prick!"

Did I *hear* that? The words echo in my skull. My mind is as filthy as the vault I live in. I try to fix it on holy things but it slips as my feet do in the muck.

My God, let me be mad. I consent to be mad, damned even, rather than that these men should truly exist.

Where did I get such foulness? I always knew foul words, being brought up by serfs who lived, through no fault of theirs, much like their own animals. When they took me in the convent, they taught me new things but could not efface the old. I could never be like the girls who came from villas and palaces. Yet I too had good blood. I knew this but was used to the poor people who had brought me up. When I left them I cried. I clung to my foster-mother and for a long time regretted her. I could not get used to the silence of the convent. I hated sleeping alone. I used to cry for Merofled, Theudebert and their small brother, Marileif. I cried when I remembered how the four of us would snuggle together to keep warm and how, when the really cold times came, we would go into the animals' stall and sleep between two cows. The heat of those big creatures seemed the most consoling thing in the world and even the smell of cow-dung seemed sweet.

How could I talk about this to anyone at the convent? The abbess used to try and comfort me. Sometimes she asked was I lonely and why? But what could I say? I said nothing. I must have seemed like a half-wit or as if the rough-coated, silent animals had passed a little of their nature on to me. Well, I was suckled by cow's milk when everyone else is suckled by a woman's. That must have had some effect. The other novices sometimes cried too when they came first. They used to talk about the luxuries they missed. How could I say that what *I* missed was sleeping with cows and on straw? I lived for the days when I was allowed to take food from the convent kitchens and visit my foster-family.

Then, with the years, I grew used to the convent. I

changed so much that my foster-sisters and I began to feel shy with each other. None of us could help it. We'd grown different. They were working on the land and had grown and developed, while I was still a shrimp. At the age of twelve they looked like women and used to tease the men by tying their skirts high around their waists and letting them see their thighs when they were weeding or gathering in crops. I still came to see them and brought them food but by now it was the food and not myself that interested them. I would sit watching while they ate what I'd brought and they would talk and mention secrets they couldn't tell me because I was a nun. Once or twice my foster-mother gave a kind of chuckle and threw me an odd look saying that nuns were not so different from other Christians as people thought. "Even abbesses," said she. Her husband had died and her tongue grown bitter. Once when I mentioned something our chaplain had said, she exclaimed: "Ha, there's a good one, the fox preaching to the hens!" She often made disparaging remarks about the convent, but then she made them about everything and everyone.

No!

I won't. Won't think. Not now. My mind escapes, like a ball bounced out of its cup, dangling on its string, swinging. My periods of blackness are more frequent now. My thoughts flow off like escaping sheep, turning, escaping under fences, sliding back along old tracks. An anchoress may slip into lunacy with the speed of a lost animal losing its footing in a bog. Sometimes I have felt the threat encircle me and the soft mud of madness rising round me. Sometimes I have been tempted to let it come.

Chapter Fourteen

Chrodechilde and Basina were winding wool.

"Hold your arms out stiff," said Chrodechilde, "it tangles if you don't."

"My muscles are sore."

"Offer it up." Chrodechilde imitated Agnes's voice. "You like our lady abbess, don't you?"

"She's all right."

"She's up to something. *You* wouldn't notice but there's something going on. A change. A whiff of fishiness in the air." Chrodechilde wrinkled her freckled nose then laid a finger along one side of it. "I can tell, but shan't. You're not to be trusted."

"Me? Oh Chrodechilde, what can you mean? Tell me."

"Arms stiff. No. I'm not sure anyway. Only on the scent. I may tell you when I find out what I find out—then again I may not." Chrodechilde pulled several rounds of wool from Basina's wrists. "It's cold," she shivered. "This convent is always cold. They should light more fires. At night my feet are perished. I have two new chilblains." Again she imitated Agnes's voice: "Offer it up, dear!" Then, in her own: "If you come to bed with me tonight, I may tell you something."

"It's against the rules."

"Rules!"

Chrodechilde suddenly began to spin on her heel, whirling faster and faster so that the wool she was holding wound round her as she turned. Basina, her two hands stiff out before her as though in the stocks, had to start running round her to keep the wool from breaking as it pulled off her wrists, got caught, tautened and drew the skein into a tangle.

"Stop, Chrodechilde, stop!"

Chrodechilde stood still laughing and Basina proceeded round her more slowly now twenty, twenty-five, thirty times, trying to gather the wool back on to the skein which held her arms as though handcuffed so that she could only grasp the thread of wool with the tip of her fingers.

"Now why did you do that?" she grumbled furiously, the tears starting from her eyes.

"To see what you'd do. You could have dropped the skein. It would have made far less mess. But you're such a timid little sheep, playing by rules and you see where it gets you. I shan't tell you anything."

"I'll come to your bed tonight."

"Who wants you?"

Chrodechilde, whom Basina had now freed like an unwound spool, dropped the ball of wool she had been holding and left the room.

Maroveus held up a goblet of wine and observed a transparency within a transparency: the glass was milky, the wine pale gold. New vintage: the colour of morning light or the last blanched leaves on October vines. A little young yet but a good year.

"What are you after?" he asked and sipped and closed his eyes the better to savour the liquid's passage first to the front of his mouth where his tongue dipped, bright as a blackbird, in the delicious bath then, after a swift bilateral swish into the puffed cheek-hollows, down the reaches of his throat. The successive sensations recalled the movement of a hand drawn across a harp: the acute, almost painful pleasure of the high notes yielding to gradual relief as the sound broadened. The wine was from his own vineyards. One day it might be a match for imports from Italy. If so, the merit would be partly his. There would be something of himself in the liquid he had laboured to produce: an anonymous aroma which posterity—his kind of posterity— would recognize. Would it? The vineyards might be burnt again as they had been in an invasion some years back. He opened his eyes and took another less pleasurable sup.

"What is it you want?" he asked.

He stared at the puffy-faced poetaster who hung round the nuns of Holy Cross and had finally become a priest a few years ago. Why? He was thick with royalty. Probably he'd been promised a benefice. Maybe Maroveus's own? Well, Maroveus was not about to die to convenience him. If the poet had been on fire, Maroveus doubted if he'd have pissed on him to put it out. The fellow had come here with a lot of talk about Church unity and gabble about politics. Some convent intrigue too. Those nuns at Holy Cross seemed to have finally got their fingers burnt. Something about King Chilperic's daughter having become a novice and his now wanting her out again to marry the King of Spain's son.

"Nothing to do with me!" said Maroveus. "I mind my own onions. I have no jurisdiction over Holy Cross! Let the nuns fry in their own fat."

The poetaster looked sly. Talked about how Chilperic had no heir and how the province might before long be fought over like a bone. It had happened before. Burned vineyards. Yes. Disagreeable prospect. Maroveus couldn't see for the life of him what *that* had to do though with King Chilperic's daughter. Obviously some secret the poet thought he might know. He was being sounded.

"If there should be an invasion of Poitiers . . ." The poet spread hands soft and white as raw dough. Maroveus observed them with dislike.

"What? Why should there be another invasion?"

"My lord," the poet told him, "there is an army on the march and headed this way. I've had news from Tours."

"What do you mean 'on the march'? Whose army? Why? How far have they got?"

"It's King Chilperic's led by Duke Desiderius. There has been looting and destruction of property."

The bishop sighed. "There always is. But we're loyal to Chilperic. He knows that. He'll respect the city."

"Some say he's heard a rumour that the men of Poitiers

were negotiating to hand it over to King Guntram. There is also a ... possibility that Chilperic may be intending to revenge himself on the convent which refused to give up his daughter."

"Daughter? Daughter? Nobody ever yet fought a battle over a daughter. If it were a son were hiding there, now, I might understand your fear, especially as Chilperic, since the death of his sons, has no heir. But as he hasn't he hasn't. Why are you so peaky looking? Can't you hold your wine, man? I don't know what you're trying to tell me. If there's an army coming, let it come. *I'll* deal with it. I've done it more times than you've said mass. I only hope my vineyards don't get burned or trampled before they get here. I'll put on my vestments and wait for their messengers in the basilica. If the worst comes to the worst I'll break up a gold chalice and pay them off—throw a sprat to save a salmon. You go and tell your nuns to sing psalms and stop bothering their holy heads about politics. Tell them to pray for me." Maroveus bowed Fortunatus out. "Oh, and thank you", he called after him with some reluctance, "for letting me know the news. If you're as well in with heaven as you are with the courts of Gaul, you need have no worries."

Chrodechilde's jaw was remarkably undershot. It extended like a drawer packed with teeth which seemed to nibble the air with sharp hunger. A dormitory of novices were watching it do this in silhouette against a combustive sky. She turned from a window through which she had been watching houses burning on a distant part of the convent estate. It was cold. On the low vaults of the ceiling, shadows stooped like mewed-up hawks. The flame from the single lamp was warped and the smell unpleasant. Wicks and oil were short. They had to come from the port of Marseilles and roads from there had been impassible for months: the war. But now the war was here.

"Some sin has been committed in this convent." Chrodechilde was whispering. "Some secret sin. Else why should God allow my uncle Chilperic's soldiers"—she dropped the royal name with relish—"to burn our lands? There are no accidents for God."

Feelings in the dormitory were tense and she struck chords on them. She knew how to weave connections between the novices and the 'world' which, by cloister-Rule, stopped at the convent door. Even arson and murder could be committed on the convent's own estates, yet concern the novices only as further reasons for prayer. But Chrodechilde could make them feel intimately involved.

"Maybe *we* could expiate that sin—whatever it was—and stop the war. Unless", she jumped down from her look-out point, "the only reason for the burning is that the king is annoyed at not getting back his baby here. He wanted her out, you know, but she refused to go." Chrodechilde walked to the bed on which Basina was lying and ran a long lean forefinger around the curve of her cousin's buttock. Basina's shift was thick but to novices alert for the faintest fleshiness, the gesture was disturbing.

"Now who's being sinful?" one wanted to know.

"Think so?" Chrodechilde wagged the offending finger, then, abruptly, bit it. Her teeth left two tracks like beaded crescents. "See!" She held up the wounded digit as the tooth marks filled with blood, then disappeared, overrun by a flux which dripped on Basina's shift. "I would expiate any sin I committed. Would each of you?" She sat on Basina's bed. "As I see it," she took a handful of her cousin's hair and began to plait it, "all of us are here because we weren't wanted by our families: rejects. Which is not to say", she added, "that a reject can't become a saint. The last shall be first. I intend to be first—although I am not the last." She had plaited Basina's mane into two tresses which she now held like reins, tightening them so that her cousin was forced to raise her head. Chrodechilde jerked the head several times, then let the hair go. She looked around the dormitory. "What's the matter with her?" she asked, tilting her jaw at Ingunda who was lying on her own bed. "Why's she crying?"

A novice whispered. "She's afraid the soldiers may have killed her foster-family. Tenants on the estate. The flames are just about where their house must be."

"Serfs?" whispered Chrodechilde. "Oh, I suppose she's somebody's bastard then? Poor thing! And she's crying for the foster-family?"

"Yes."

"She's a dim creature, isn't she? Crying for a foster-family. God, I shouldn't have minded if *all* my fosterers were put on one pile and roasted like oxen. It would be quite a pile too, I can tell you. I wore them out."

"There's no doubt", Fortunatus told Radegunda, "the army was looking for the prince. Only the leader knew. Duke Desiderius. Luckily he was willing to be bought off."

"For how long?"

"For good. He'll tell the queen he searched the convent and found nothing. Afterwards he won't dare go back on his lie. He's an easy man to deal with: greedy, I had to give him more than I'd expected. Almost all the jewels you let me have. He confirmed what we guessed. The talk about Basina was cover for their interest in her brother's whereabouts. They rather believed he *was* dead but wanted to make sure. Desiderius promised that we needn't worry any more." Fortunatus paused. "There was something odd about his manner. He kept hinting, then stopping himself. I had a feeling something else was up and that he was wondering whether to take me into his confidence. Something—I'm guessing now—dangerous. Desiderius has no particular loyalty to Chilperic or Fredegunda. I had the impression he was about to change sides—but not in favour of either of the other kingdoms. He managed to give me to understand that some totally new endeavour was under way. He as good as told me our prince—whether dead or alive—was no longer important."

"Odd."

"Very. With two of the kingdoms of Gaul being without

230

an heir and the third ruled by a minor, how *could* a legitimate heir lose importance? Unless...?"

"A Byzantine move? The Emperor Maurice?"

"Or the Frankish nobles? They resent royal power and this is a good moment to challenge it—or both together."

"But have they *another* pretender?"

"Well," said Fortunatus. "There is Clotair's bastard, Gundovald—if he *is* Clotair's. All princes of the royal blood, legitimate or not, have a claim to succeed."

"Clotair", said Radegunda, "always denied Gundovald was his son. *He* said he was the son of a serf."

"But the Emperor Maurice gave him hospitality all these years—that gives him some credibility."

"Well," said Radegunda. "He may be God's instrument. We shall see. I doubt it though. There is something about *our* prince—I don't think I'm deluding myself. I can feel a calibre in him, some chosen quality. But, obviously, the moment is inopportune. We must keep him hidden. I want him trained morally and mentally in case he should be called on to rule part or even all of Gaul. I want him moved to a cottage on the estate. You must be our go-between. Another invasion is unlikely."

"You know the extent of the damage left by this one?"

"Agnes told me. She seemed disproportionately upset. What happened was terrible, of course, but might have been worse: a few rapes, one or two houses burned, some looting, no death. It is horrible but worse happens every day somewhere in Gaul. There is something shortsighted about Agnes's grief. As though she could only pity wounds she could feel with her hand. Like Thomas Didymus. We must," said Radegunda, "take the longer view."

"Two of the girls raped were foster-sisters of one of the novices here," Fortunatus told her. "I forget her name. It seems she had some sort of collapse."

"The flesh"—Radegunda sounded impatient—"is weak."

"Yes."

"To go back to the prince: I want you to take his education in hand. I have drawn up a reading list..."

Ingunda was in bed with fever.

On the day after the army left the area, she had begged Agnes's permission to take food and medicines to her foster-family whose house had been destroyed. The steward had brought news that worse might have happened and Agnes had been unsure whether to let the girl go, but Ingunda pleaded energetically and Agnes was struck to see her daughter's face suddenly change. The sullen flesh had come alive. Its heaviness gone, it flickered, mobile as fluid.

"Can I go?"

"All right."

"Ah!" The girl sighed. "Thank you." She smiled.

Agnes lent her a mule, then awaited her return with some anxiety. But the girl was away for hours and Agnes had things to do. Returning from checking a long inventory with the cellarer, she found the dispensary sister waiting for her. Ingunda, she was told, was back, had fainted, had been given an infusion of herbs and had vomited it. Now she seemed delirious. What should be done?

"I'll look after her," said Agnes. "Just help me get her to the sick cell."

Alone with Ingunda, Agnes studied the delirious face as she had not dared to do before, looking for resemblances Fridovigia had claimed to find.

"Your mother's nose," Fridovigia had said. Was it? Perhaps. "His eyes! Blackberry eyes and she has a dimple when she laughs like your father's father whom you wouldn't remember, but..." Memory permeated Fridovigia's emotions and, now that there was no Fridovigia left, carried those emotions along with it when summoned. Scrappy images from Agnes's own half-forgotten childhood and Ingunda's unknown one mingled like coloured beads in a shaken container: the marbled villa, the peasant's hut, a ball-game played with some faceless companions, a stretch of vaguely perceived mosaic where dolphins swam among geometric patterns, water, geese—why geese? Ah, Fridovigia had said "They've put her to minding geese."

232

Yes. Had they been rough with her? They would have been. They were rough. But it would have been their norm and hers too. She would not have been aware of suffering particularly. Now, perhaps because of that roughness, Ingunda was hard to get to know. A peasant. Were peasant responses different? How? More limited? Extreme? Or only slow? Fridovigia had said they had those throaty voices from shouting at each other across fields and into the wind. Must one shout at them to be heard? Or was their deafness protective? A blocking out? The girl was asleep now, drugged by the second infusion the dispensary sister had managed to make her swallow. Agnes touched her face.

Ingunda recoiled. "No!" she cried, "No!" She tossed and clawed at the sheet. "Don't. It's not my fault. Not mine . . . They've raped her! She's all torn . . . But how could we . . . Don't touch me."

Thinking of her foster-sister. Agnes sat down. Time passed. Her own mind lapsed into emptiness then was jerked back. Ingunda was moving again. The drug was wearing off. She spoke a few phrases. Clearly and precisely. Her diction was perfect, her vocabulary good, but Agnes could make no sense of her ravings.

"Soup," whispered Ingunda.

Agnes leaned close. "Do you want some?"

"Please, Merofled, don't look at me like that! Take some. It's not my fault. It's made with meat. Her mind's gone," said Ingunda distinctly. "She'll never be the same again. None of them will—not even me. We're like that pot. Cracked. No, don't throw it away. It'll serve. It can hold dry beans." Then she broke into a nonsense-rhyme, a skipping song. And in a little girl's voice: "They don't want to play with me. They don't like me. But it's not my fault . . ."

Agnes tried putting a hand on Ingunda's forehead and this time was not pushed away. For a while Ingunda was quiet, then said very calmly and as though she had pondered this: "They've thrown me out." Then seemed to sob.

"Ingunda!" Agnes stroked the girl's cheek. "Please, stop it. Please!"

Ingunda looked at her. Her eyes focused, gathering clarity. "Mother Agnes," she recognized. "Why are you crying?"

"For you," said Agnes incautiously.

The eyes clouded with almost suspect speed. A tremor shifted across them. "Oh God," Ingunda groaned. "I can't, bear any more." She turned, tossed herself onto her stomach and hid her face.

A.D. 584 *At this time a son was born to King Chilperic who sent him to be brought up on a country estate where he might be safe from sorcerers ... That same year Chilperic was murdered by an unknown man, and King Guntram of Burgundy, establishing the infant, Clotair, over his father's kingdom, made himself its regent. Guntram was now the most powerful man in Gaul but his power was not to go unchallenged.*

A group of nobles, made restive by the overweening conduct of the kings, now brought the Pretender, Gundovald, to Gaul where bishops and leading men from all three kingdoms rallied to his cause. At news that Guntram had sent an army to crush the Pretender, many of these, taking fright, deserted him and he was obliged to seek refuge within the town of Convenae. This was stocked with a rich store of provisions and might have resisted for many years if Gundovald's supporters had stood by him. This, however, they did not do and, although he bitterly reproached them for luring him to Gaul with false oaths of fealty, swearing that but for their coaxing he would never have left the East, they now resolved to betray him in the hope of saving themselves. Speaking with honeyed tongues, they persuaded him to go out of the city to parley with Guntram's generals, claiming that these had sworn to use him with honour. As soon as Gundovald had walked through the gates, the nobles who were with him drew back inside and closed them fast. Guntram's men fell on Gundovald and, pushing him over a cliff, hurled a stone on his head and pierced his murdered body

234

with their spears. His beard and hair were plucked out and his body left unburied where it had fallen. The treachery of the men of Convenae brought them little profit for, although the rich managed to hide their treasure, the poor, even those who were priests, were put to the sword so that, in the end, not one of such as piss against a wall was left alive. The buildings were burnt and many laymen among the leaders killed. As for the bishops who had supported the Pretender, they were put on trial by their peers at a council held in Mâcon.

Chronicle

It's wet here. A wet womb, tomb. My mind is slipping. Those men I heard—no, not them. Black. Shut in. Pray. Say the words of a prayer. Words hold the mind as skin holds bones. *Credo in unum deum patrem omnipotentem factorem coeli et terrae visibilium et invisibilium* ... All invisible here. There is an anxiety abroad, demons in the air. On certain nights God lets them loose to tempt men. As a furnace tries gold, temptation tries the righteous. If no temptation, then no merit. Were the holy anchoresses led by their nature to choose the solitary life? I had to lead mine, had to beat and wrestle with it as one might with a mule. It is a buoyant nature, stubborn. Good at simple things. I might have been a good wool sister or cellarer or looked after the convent kitchen garden. I did work there for a bit and another time I worked with the convent bees. I liked that. Twice, since I have been here, a bee has strayed in through my slit. One paused at its outer aperture so that the sunlight lit up his furry body and the transparent petal of his wing. He stayed for as long as a minute although there can have been nothing here to tempt him—and how could I not see his visit as a sign? Yes, in all humility, I feel sure he was sent to give me courage. He was the only creature I saw since I came here and, when I choose to, I see him again as distinctly as though he had just flown away. Perhaps I had never looked as carefully at anything as I did at that brown bee. He brought with him the trumpet shapes of flowers he must have visited and the stillness of those days when the earth breaks into winding cracks and lizards sun themselves on stones. I cried when he left: not from regret, from happiness at the image he left with me. All my other memories are blurred or chopped. Sometimes I try to recall exactly how the convent gardens are laid out. But it is as though my eye had shrunk. I can see only a small part at a time with any clarity. Sometimes I try to see a face, but this too comes only in fragments. I am trying to see the sweet face of Agnes, but it is twisting up into a grimace. It is becoming the face of ... no, oh no, now it is the face of one of the damned souls painted on the wall of our chapel, one of those tormented creatures all twisted like knotted rope who try to escape the devil's pitchfork. Why should I see such a sight? God, you are letting me be tempted by despair. You allow the demon leeway. You loosen his bonds and let him tempt me with sick visions. How can you be sure I will not succumb? Do you think me so strong that you can try me in the hottest furnace? I will be. With your grace I shall resist, shall not go mad, shall not despair and neither shall I spare myself. I shall return and plunge myself into my most horrible memories. I offer them to you once more with their pain and shame. In atonement. I shall force your mercy. I shall defy you to withstand my prayer.

It was when I was fourteen. The territory of the city of Poitiers had been invaded by the Burgundians and also by Chilperic's men. They had been back and forth several times in the last few years—so often that the horror had become almost normal. We had heard so many stories that none surprised us. Death raged and epidemics reached even into the convent. Outside, people were making bread with pounded fern-roots and grape-seeds. Some, in order to eat, had sold themselves into slavery. Others had eaten green roots, swollen up and died. We distributed food and rationed ourselves so as to help the starving. Some of our nuns had had relatives killed in the civil war, but none of us had seen it close up—and then it burst into our own estates. We saw the flames one night and by next day the invaders had gone. They had been just a handful of men and nobody could tell why they had come. Some said it was a mistake but one fact was sure—our steward brought the news—Merofled and Theudechild—my foster-sisters—had been raped. It was decided that I should load a mule with medicines and provisions and go to them at once. I did. I remember that the effort—I had trouble getting the mule to move—and the rush as well as the shock of the news dazed me and at first I did not feel much. I was in suspense: waiting to feel. I kept poking the mule and shouting at him. Perhaps I was trying to keep the feeling off me? When I reached the vineyard near my foster-family's farm, I began to smell smoke and cinders: the same woody smell as an autumn bonfire. But it was not a bonfire. The vines were gone—nothing left but a mash of black stumps. The house was gone. It had been made of wood and mud and wattle and must have burned like straw. Now the cinders were being blown away on the wind. In a few months there would be no trace of it at all. Then—no; I can't—*must, must* go on. I had turned to leave when I saw a figure on hands and knees, scrabbling in the cinders: black-faced, filthy, all mutters and tatters, wheezing, muddy buttocks, a wild goatish eye. It stood on two legs and I recognized Hiltga, my foster-mother. She was holding a clay pot which she had dug out of the ashes. I tried to put my arms around her but it was like putting them around—a tree. She had the same empty look of the refugees who came for sanctuary: sightless, wide, struck blind like the pearly eyes of a dog—but of course she was not blind. I asked her questions and she mumbled, not answering but talking about her clay pot. "Tough enough!" She held it up. "Won't ever be the same though. That's all I found. Imagine!" I asked again about her daughters. "I've brought some food and stuff", I said, "from Mother Agnes!"

"Mother Agnes!" She peered at me. She could see

after all. "It's you, is it." she said.

"Yes, Hiltga. I've brought things for Theudechild and Merofled. Won't you tell me where they are? I have food for them from the convent."

"The convent!" Her eyes narrowed. There was a spark in the singed middle of them as if someone had blown on a pair of nearly burnt-out coals. "The convent!" she began to lilt, singing at me in her rage of mockery. "The soldiers didn't go there, did they, oh no, no! That's holy sanctuary. The crow doesn't pluck out the crow's eye but poor folk bear the brunt. *You* were safe while my girls suffered!" She staggered. There was a stream of spittle flowing down her chin. Her eyes were flecked with red. I tried to steady her but she pushed my hand from her. Violently. She was muttering again, but now I could make out the drift: it was the sort of old lament that tenants take up in bad times, a familiar, repetitious, ready-made railing. She was angry because the convent had collected all the crops into the convent barn and the soldiers, finding nothing, had been maddened into raping her daughters. "Gentle folk and convent folk are always safe!" she raged. "Sanctuary forsooth!" Then she began to sing an old rhyme which I'd often heard before about a tenant who didn't pay the eggs he owed and was punished by the lord. "He was caught," she sang, "he was hung. He was buried in the dung. That's the place for poor folk, isn't it?" she shrieked. "The dung! The dung! The dung!"

I thought she was mad. She was. Dangerous too. She kept running cindery hands over her face which was a mess of spittle and black soot.

"I'll go and look for Merofled and Theudechild!" I told her and managed to pull my mule from a bush of scorched leaves he had been eating. I prodded his rump and dragged him off. A howl came from behind me. "Who hides their dung?" she was shrieking. "Who? Who covers up their dirty doings? We do. I did. But when troubles come the convent whores are safe! Their sins are visited on us!" She rushed at me and shoved her face

238

into mine. Her breath was sour. "They burnt the house," she screamed, "looking for treasure. *Treasure*! 'This may be a convent estate', I told them, 'but the convent hides no treasure with us!' All it hides with us is its bastards! I should never have taken you in, you nun's get!" She was leaning on top of me, pressing me back against the mule. I could feel his stomach pulsing behind me and the fever in her body in front. I was as helpless as corn between two quernstones. Her words fell on me like hail and I didn't take them in. I was afraid she would hit or strangle me. Suddenly, she stepped backwards, fell silent and, some moments later said in a new voice, an empty, worn whisper of a voice: "I never did tell you, did I?" she asked. "I kept my bargain and little good it did me. Yes, you're the abbess's bastard, Mother Agnes's by-child." She turned away. Speaking over her shoulder, in the same dull tone, she told me where to find my sisters. I poked the mule forward and went to look for them. What else could I do? I dreaded being alone and dreaded going back to the convent.

That's it. I've remembered it all, or the worst bits anyway. Remember, God, I did it deliberately. I offered it to you. I brought it on myself. I am broken again. The horror comes back. My vision is porous. When I put myself together—as I have done, as I will—carefully, delicately, the way one rivets and sticks a smashed plate, the mended object is always more fragile than before. There are little joins which don't join, little splinters lost, holes and hollows through which certainties leak. I have never been certain since. My certitude was the convent and the convent hinged on the abbess. Like the axle of a wheel, she was its centre. Behind her was Radegunda who talked to God, but it was the abbess who kept us together. What Hiltga said tore a hole in my world. Oh, I am calmer now, infinitely calmer. I didn't reason then. I didn't know what I felt—love for Agnes, pity, horror, fear? It was all mixed up with seeing my poor sisters and the burnt-down house. It was a shock.

My spine buckled. My eyes were dazzled as though I had been looking at the sun. When I woke up in the convent sick-cell—they told me later I had collapsed on getting back and they had put me there—when I woke up the abbess was nursing me. She was all charity and gentleness. She was sweet. She was damned. She was my mother and I couldn't tell her I knew without shaming her. I was glad of the fever which kept me from having to talk to her. When it wore off, she left me alone in the sick-cell and I lay awake, hour after hour, thinking about her and wrestling with the question which I could ask nobody since I couldn't ask her who was my spiritual superior—*was* she damned? Could she be saved? How? I remembered every sermon I had heard about how a sinner could be reconciled to God. St. Caesar, the composer of our Rule, did not believe a public penance was necessary, but other saints were stricter than he. The abbess—my mother— might count on his words and be deceived. Yet how could she, an abbess, perform a public penance, covering her head with goat hair and sprinkling herself with dirt? There was martyrdom. That brought remission of all sins. But why should the abbess be martyred? There were no martyrs in Gaul now, and I didn't want her martyred. I had rather be martyred myself. That was how I thought up my bargain: my life for her soul. I could not die but I could give up my life.

Chapter Fifteen

Fortunatus was dining with Bishop Palladius of Saintes. It A.D. 585 was the kind of occasion he enjoyed. The bishop was returning to his diocese after attending the Council of Mâcon and must be apprised of some of the gutsiest gossip in Gaul. The only obstacle to pumping it out of him was that Palladius himself had been a trifle too close to the action. He had compromised himself with the Pretender, and it must have been touch and go whether King Guntram would accept his apologies. There must have been humiliating moments. One did not like to probe—or rather, yes, one would have liked very much to probe if only one were not seen to do so. Probably, Fortunatus told himself with some amusement, the bishop's servants would have been the people to ask about it all. They were probably spilling seamy details in his own kitchen at this moment. Sooner or later, these would reach his own ears. Meanwhile, he kept the bishop's glass filled and the talk on safe, peripheral aspects of the Council. Bishop Praetextatus of Rouen had apparently read some prayers of his own composing.

"Edifying, I suppose," said Palladius, "but ghastly Latin. Well, I needn't tell you. You can imagine."

Fortunatus could.

"Talking of Latin," said the bishop, "we had one hilarious sample of the darkness which is upon us. Can you believe that a bishop, who must in all charity be nameless, asked were women to be included under the general description 'man' in the Bible and, if not, whether they had souls at all? It was discovered, after some probing, that his doubts came from his ignorance of the distinction between 'homo' and 'vir'. The pitfalls of semantics!

241

As one brother-bishop pointed out, the gospel description of Jesus as 'son of man' would, if narrowly interpreted, mean 'son of woman' since Mary was a virgin and no man involved at all. This should have been enough for our episcopal rustic but perhaps, like most rustics, he was a misogynist and eager to unsoul the sex. Anyway, no more was heard from him."

"A Frank, I suppose?"

"Oh, a Frank!"

The two smiled.

Fortunatus sighed. "Ah yes! Can I give you some more wine? It's from Provence. Bishop Theodore", experimentally, he dropped the name of the most compromised of the bishops, "sent me some casks a while back."

Palladius held out his glass. "He was arrested," he said. "No respect shown for his cloth. Rathar was sent to Marseilles to arrest him. Foreseeably, Rathar seized the opportunity for a little pillage: Church property."

"Has Rathar", Fortunatus risked, "been stricken by some heavensent disease?"

"It's not funny, Fortunatus! It's grave."

"Graveyardly in fact—terrible joke. Forgive it."

"I suppose you want to know the worst?"

"If you can bear to tell. I hope—well I see, as you're here, that all went well in the end."

"The end", said Palladius, "seemed imminent more than once. All our ends. My colleagues put up a terrible show. Shameful. King Guntram was there in all his royal glory, proud as a dog with two tails and outspoken as a northwester; the bishops behaved like schoolboys quailing from their teacher's stick. Not one had the nerve to stand up to him for as much as a minute. The stick—men at arms, etc.—was much in evidence and of course some, like poor old Praetextatus, have felt it very literally in the past. You can't expect nerve in a bishop who knows what it is to be flogged and exiled." Palladius banged his goblet down furiously. "At one point the rumour was that *two-thirds* of us would be exiled for having either supported

242

Gundovald or failed to oppose him. That didn't happen but the abbot of Cahors—a most holy man as you know—*was* excommunicated and the Bishop of Dax, an appointee of Gundovald, demoted. The three bishops who consecrated him are to pay him an annual pension out of their own pockets. I'', said Palladius bitterly, "am one of the three. All this was voted by the bishops but the decision was Guntram's. He's never been so arrogant: like a cock on his own dunghill. Bishops jumped when he farted. Like trained dogs. *I* had to put up with the grossest insults. Before the Council met at all, he summoned us to Orléans where he abused us at his own table. Bertram of Bordeaux is, as you know, my superior and I thought it my duty to cover for him and take most of the blame for the Bishop-of-Dax matter. Small thanks I got from Bertram who turned on me in the most viperish way. The man has no sense of solidarity. In the end Guntram seemed to have calmed down. He allowed us to bless him and we thought everything was forgiven if not forgotten. As a sort of kiss of peace, it was decided that I should say mass the following Sunday. Well I started to and, suddenly, in the middle of mass, the king began to bellow at me—I was, of course, at the altar—interrupting the sacrifice, stamping his feet and behaving like an overgrown infant or a lunatic. I could hardly believe my ears. He was howling the most embarrassing abuse. Right in the middle of church. Saying he would not hear the sacred service recited by a perjurer and a liar. No point in repeating his other fulminations. The man is unbalanced. I had to leave the altar while the others calmed him down. Have you ever heard of such a thing? He's a savage, an animal. All our kings are bestial. I say 'all' even though Clotair of Neustria is still an infant. We can be sure he'll be as bad as the rest. How could he not be with a mother like Fredegunda!''

A vein pulsed furiously in the bishop's forehead. His lip trembled against the rim of his wine goblet.

Fortunatus shivered. "In a way," he observed, "you were lucky to be churchmen. If you'd been laymen he

243

would by now have seized your property, cut off whichever part of your anatomy his whim settled on and then finished you off in some imaginative way. The Frankish imagination runs to butchery. Think of what happened to poor Gundovald and Mummolus. God rest their souls. Don't think I'm not sympathetic. I'm sure your motives were excellent but you were involved in a political plot and—well, that game has its stakes and you lost."

"You clearly are not sympathetic!" said Palladius sharply. "I suppose you feel that as churchmen we had no business engaging in a 'political plot' as you call it. Let me ask you something, Fortunatus. What is the function of the Church?"

"Seriously?"

"Very."

Fortunatus laughed nervously. "What have I got myself into now?" he wondered. "Look, Palladius, I didn't mean to upset you. I apologize."

"Apology accepted. Now answer my question."

Fortunatus turned his hands upwards, fingers spread as though sifting grain. "Palladius, I'm not a theologian. Are you feeling me out for traces of heresy? If you find any, they'll be rooted in ignorance, not malice. I'm afraid much of my reading has been profane. You're not", it occurred to him to wonder, "considering me for a diocese?"

"You may be joking," the bishop told him. "But that's not inconceivable. If you serve the Church well."

Fortunatus shook himself. "You are serious, aren't you? I get nervous when I'm promised something. There's always a quid pro quo."

"Who's denying it? And the quid would not immediately follow the quo."

"No, the Church prefers payment in advance. Fair enough. Things temporal should be paid in temporal coin. A diocese these days is very temporal, isn't it, not to say temporary. Vis Dax."

"You didn't answer my question."

244

Fortunatus repeated it: "'What is the function of the Church?' I'll say 'to save souls'. Uninspired but orthodox."

"Yes. And what is the commonest obstacle to the saving of souls?"

"Oh, it's to be an interrogation? Things are serious. You don't want me to say 'sin', I suppose? Or 'the Evil One'? I thought not. I must be practical. Technical if I can manage it. Let me see: what would I expect you to say? 'Disorder'? 'Indiscipline'? Am I getting hot? I know you look longingly back to the days when Church and Empire were merged in the great unity of Romanism: one of your pet phrases, Palladius. I am a parrot. Why not? The wise man parrots a wiser master. 'Lack of political unity' then. God knows I agree with you if that's your answer. How could I dispute it here in Poitiers where the cathedral priests are hard put to remember for which king's health they're supposed to be praying and the bishop never knows to which Council of bishops he belongs. He's been shuttled back and forth every time the town changed hands. Well— one has to find some excuse for Maroveus, apart, that is, from his devotion to the grape. Have some more yourself?"

Palladius ignored the offered wine and didn't bother to smile. "But", he said, "you think bishops have no business engaging in politics?"

"Ahh!" Fortunatus exclaimed. "I see a drift. Do I? No, I don't. That is to say I would if I thought your plot had aimed at bringing back unity, good government, the *pax romana* and what have you. But your man, Gundovald, was at best another Frank, another descendant of Clovis—if his claims had anything to them at all—endowed with the same anarchic, licentious, bloody temper as the rest of the royal spawn. One more of *them* on the scene would have meant one more greedy snout snuffling in the wretched pig's trough which is Gaul today."

Palladius considered his fingernails. "A weak king," he said musingly, tilting his hands to the light, "dependent on the Church, ruling a united Gaul, financed, at the beginning anyway, from Byzantium, needing to reconcile the local notables ... the formula might just have worked."

"Was that the aim of the plotters?"

"Of some. A conspiracy is like one of those snow balls children roll downhill. It gathers dirt and whatever lies on its passage. Gaining size it loses purity but, you see, Fortunatus, one learns by past mistakes. If we make a fresh snowball we can direct its path more judiciously."

Fortunatus stood up restlessly. "Let's move nearer the fire," he invited. He picked up a bowl of dried fruit and nuts. "Have a walnut," he offered. "A fig? They're good. The nuns from Holy Cross sent them over ..." His voice died. The bishop was drilling his stare into him. Coal-black eyes, unwavering mouth. "What *is* it, Palladius?"

"How is the prince?"

"Prince?"

"Clovis."

"Oh!" Fortunatus stuffed a handful of nuts into his mouth, chewed on them quickly, and began to cough. "You mean", he choked, "Chilperic's son? The one who killed himself?"

"He didn't."

"What?"

"No. Bertram brought him here and left him with you. Alive. I *know* this, Fortunatus. Bertram told me."

"He died", Fortunatus looked Palladius straight in the eye, "of his wounds after Bertram left."

"I don't believe you."

The poet shrugged. "Well, if you don't trust me ..."

"You don't trust me", said Palladius, "or you wouldn't lie!"

There was a silence.

"What can I say?" Fortunatus made offers of figs and nuts. "Some Gaza wine then? It's good. No? No." He moved to the fire, fiddled with it, sat down finally and faced the bishop.

Palladius had the tone of someone humouring a child.

"*If* Clovis is dead," he said patiently, "we'll find another

246

Pretender. Young. Of the royal blood. Whom we can make totally ours—'we', you understand, are the Church—and present to the people when the moment comes. This may not be for years. We can wait. We have to do this. It is our duty: a mission laid upon us by history. We want our next king to be a true son of the Church, suckled by it, unweaned from it, his pulse beating with its rhythms. Ours", said Palladius violently, "is the only institution which can impose order on the country and until it does it can't have order in itself. Is it possible, Fortunatus, that you don't see this? Surely you see that as long as a corrupt bishop can bribe a secular ruler to support him, the Church cannot be purged of her unworthy sons? As long as a venomous overlord can demote a bishop, as Guntram just did, and Gaul itself is governed not as a state but as the spoil of royal robbers, peace and justice will be joke words! We", Palladius made the goblets jump on the table, "intend to make Gaul safe for Christianity!"

Fortunatus seemed mesmerized by the wine in his goblet. He twirled it slowly, watching the firelight play on the transparent liquid.

"Say something," said Palladius.

"You've said everything."

"There's a lot to be done. Can we count on your help?"

"I told you . . ."

"I'm not talking about the prince. I have something in mind for *you*."

"I'm not a man of action, you know! Are you sure", Fortunatus asked carefully, "that I'm the man you need?" He buried his nose in his glass.

"Tell me," asked Palladius, "is there any other man whose welcome is as sure as yours in each of our Gaulish capitals? Any other as well thought of at the court of *each one* of our mutually suspicious, murderous, terrified monarchs? Yours is the only face, Fortunatus, in which neither Childebert nor his mother, Brunhilde, King Guntram nor even the sorceress, Fredegunda, is ever likely to imagine they see the face of their assassin. Not one of them would imagine the poet, Fortunatus, murdering them. Not even for a moment—and, as a moment's panic is long enough to kill a man, it follows that *you* are the safest man in Gaul."

"If I listen to you," Fortunatus told him, "I can see that *that* will soon be in the past tense: 'Here lies Fortunatus, the safest man in Gaul until he let himself be talked into God knows what bloody scheme by his Grace, Palladius of Saintes. R.I.P.' You're not planning for me to assassinate all three I suppose? Or are you? With respect, Palladius, I have the feeling that your experiences in Mâcon have left your blood a touch heated. You should perhaps apply leeches," said Fortunatus excitedly. "Or is it my wine which has affected you? To return to the murder hypothesis: would I be expected to kill them serially or at once? I'm known to be a glutton. I suppose I could procure a poisoned cake and invite them all to partake of it at some ceremony to be devised. You'll hardly have counted on my using force? I've never killed a chicken. My largest kill up to now has been a bluebottle although I usually stick to fleas. As *they*'ve usually had a go at me first, I argue I'm mostly shedding my own blood. As we're mixing politics and religion, why not go whole hog and let me say mass for the three monarchs? I could poison the blessed bread— or would that upset you?"

"Fortunatus . . ."

"Blasphemy? Forgive me, my lord bishop. It was my horror at what I took to be in your mind that troubled mine." His hands were trembling, his pulse stampeding. Angrily, he wiped his face.

"You have a poet's imagination," observed Palladius. "I mentioned assassinations only to point out that the monarchs fear them and, fearing, become themselves dangerous. I did not mean that we should engage in such business."

"I am relieved."

"The trouble with talkers", Palladius's tone, now that he had upset Fortunatus, had grown level and cold, "is

248

that their own rhetoric convinces them. They also think that once they've mentioned the need to do something it's as good as done. A while ago you mentioned the woes of Poitiers and, having deplored them, poured yourself some more wine and changed the subject. When I urged you to join in practical action you were shocked. But the men of Poitiers are none the better for your talk, Fortunatus. And don't think that I don't know precisely why you've been spinning this fantasy about my wanting you to commit a triple regicide. Rhetoricians are first cousins to magicians. You were weaving your jokes and blasphemies, your magic formulae, around me so as to prevent my making a request it might embarrass you to refuse. You know I will not ask you to commit murder. You fear I may ask you to do something more feasible. You're trying to gag me—but I won't be gagged. I will ask and you will have to answer with a simple 'yes' or 'no'."

"What is it you want, Palladius?"

"Two things. I'll tell you the second first: you are to tour the courts, spend time in each, hear the gossip, sift the rumours, take the royal pulse. You can write a few more panegyrics. Praise Fredegunda's chastity, Brunhilde's meekness, Guntram's loyalty. Create a counter-truth; it may confuse them. Caught like metal between magnets, in the tug between your praise and their passions, they may let down their guard. Be watching. Report to me."

"Then?"

"Come back to your nuns. Stay a while. Go back to the courts. To and fro. As often as may prove useful. Your mission is less to spy than to become commonplace. People must say 'Here's Fortunatus returned with the swallows,' and think no more of it. When the moment comes for action, you will be told what to do. You see your value lies in the fact that men of words are not taken seriously today in Gaul. A Roman ruler would have known better. So would an Ostrogoth. Think of Theodoric! Words, he would have realized, have meanings and, sooner or later, the man who plays with them hits on a dangerous one and becomes inconvenient. Such thoughts do not trouble our kings. Your verse beguiles their digestive hours. Doesn't this provoke you?"

"I am more provoked to find a man I respect trying to manipulate me!"

Palladius mimed conciliation. "Fortunatus," he coaxed, caressing curvacious air—no identifiable curves as far as the poet could see, unless perhaps a dog's head and neck?—"I respect you. I envy you. I would have preferred to live like you. I believe you have found the perfect formula: poetry, pottering, a little prayer, chat with your nuns, wine from admirers like poor Bishop Theodore. It's ideal: a Christian version of Horace's Sabine farm. For his courtesans you substitute holy virgins. Your soul is safe."

"But there's a 'but'!"

"Indeed!" The bishop leaned off his seat. "How dare you, Fortunatus, enjoy this bliss and safety in today's world? In a world where bishops ... but we've been into that. The point is", Palladius was forceful, "that when Horace withdrew to his farm there were plenty of others to offer civic service. Who is there today? And yet you, a man trained in one of the last Roman schools, devote your talents to writing about milk puddings and making acrostics on the name of Christ—a virtuous activity, Fortunatus, but insufficient to stem the tides of chaos."

"I do not write ordinarily about milk puddings, that was ..."

"It was unworthy to mention it. I know you have written rousing religious verse, truly committed verse. I would quote it to you if I thought you needed convincing that I could. And, having quoted it, I would ask: 'How can a man who writes like that refuse his rôle in the army of the Cross?'"

"Army? Who else is with you? Is anyone, Palladius?"

Palladius's eyeballs shifted. Firelight bounced off them, giving his already compelling glance a livid edge. "We are not divulging more than two names to any one

250

supporter. I am assuming you are a supporter, Fortunatus! The risks are high. Torture. We have to take tight security measures. I'll give you one name now: Gregory."

"Bishop Gregory?"

"Yes. He is your most generous patron, isn't he—within the Church I mean? I know you and Maroveus ..." Palladius made a dismissive gesture.

"The other name? You said two. Bertram, I suppose?"

Palladius shrugged. "Bertram is ill, said to be dying. God have his soul. He was a wretched Churchman and unreliable for this sort of venture. No. The second name brings me to my other request. You remember I said I had two? The first—in time merely: it is a very minor service to ask—is that you should procure an interview for me with Radegunda. Tomorrow. She, if she joins us—and I am counting on her doing so—will be your second name. Apart from my own."

"Radegunda—you're counting on Ra–, Palladius, you must really and truly be out of your mind! As to your seeing her, that's out of the question. She's in retreat. She sees no one, she ..."

"I know she is in retreat. That is why I need your help. Just to let her know about my mission. Once she hears of it, I don't doubt that she will be ready to waive her arrangements. We have already had some contact with her."

"You have?"

Palladius smiled. His black-opal eyeballs sparkled. With what? Glee? Energy? Scorn? Fortunatus had begun to feel acutely uncomfortable. "Why else", Palladius asked, "do you suppose I would have been so unguarded with you?" Laughing, his teeth glistening, his tongue lolling insolently between the rows, the bishop held up his goblet, "Maybe I will have some more of that wine of poor Bishop Theodore's," he said.

"No!" said Agnes, "I won't allow it!"

They were all looking away. Scandalized. What possible

251

motive could she have? She saw Radegunda's bewilderment, Fortunatus's mild surprise. The girls—Chrodechilde, Basina and their band—were slyly jubilant. The nuns were divided into camps: her own and Chrodechilde's. How or even when this had come about Agnes could not have said. Too taken up by her own anxieties, she had hardly noticed the start of the little cabal. Now, with the age of its members, it had matured.

"They're waiting for the foundress to die," Justina had warned her. "There will be trouble then, mark my words. That Chrodechilde has ambitions. She wants to be abbess. She could stir up support for herself inside and outside the convent!"

"Abbess!" Agnes had scarcely listened, but the word echoed later in her skull. Eyes were looking at her now with malice. Sharp, avid, they drilled their suspicion through the murky light.

"Is there", Radegunda had to ask, "some reason we don't know?"

Minutes ago, Ingunda had announced her decision to the community. She wanted to become an anchoress. She would not be the first at Holy Cross. A nun called Disciola had been immured for several years already. Such seekers after exceptional grace brought a convent prestige and—if one had the faith to believe this—spiritual wealth.

"I am asking permission from the abbess and Mother Radegunda", Ingunda had said, standing in front of the altar, staring ahead with glassy eyes which refused to meet Agnes's, "to withdraw into a cell as small as may be allowed. I wish to be immured and live as a recluse."

A tremor had shaken the congregation. This rare feat, a stroke of bravery with which a girl played her whole life, was as chilling and marvellous to them as the sight of gladiators fighting had been to their great-grandparents. Indeed the exploit derived from the circuses where early Christians had been martyred. It was a form of death willingly embraced. The hundredfold reward was granted to martyrs, according to the Church fathers, the sixtyfold to virgins and the thirtyfold only to the virtuous married. What more reasonable than that a girl who had aspired to the second prize should now desire the first? The nuns gazed on the prodigy their convent had produced. Hands were clasped, gasps stifled. Through Ingunda, all were briefly caught up on a cresting wave of excitement. The younger ones, her contemporaries, swayed with exaltation. A single grin splashed their faces. Unrepressed, apparently spontaneous, the accolade burst from them: "Gaudeamus—let's rejoice!"

Agnes jumped to her feet. "No! I won't allow it!"

Silence. Astonishment.

"Is there some reason?"

"The girl has been ill." Agnes blundered, groping for words. Tears were pricking from her eyes, blinding her and she daren't be seen to wipe them. "Her foster-sisters", she tried to explain, "were—had an ... accident. She is not herself. She doesn't know what she's saying. We mustn't keep her to this!"

"Well, of course," Radegunda agreed, "she must be given time to think. Her resolution is a noble one and must be free." Radegunda smiled tranquilly. She might have been a mother whose daughter was unsure whether to trim her gown with fur. Agnes felt a sensation of hardness in her chest as though something were pressing its way out. Did she, she wondered for a half second, hate Radegunda?

"How *can* she think?"

Ingunda's face was taut and white. It was composed but the eyelids were puffy and Agnes knew the girl had been weeping herself to sleep every night. She had visited Ingunda's dormitory several times in the months which had passed since moving her from the sick-cell. Each time, Ingunda had pretended to be asleep but the face on her pillow had been streaky as bacon: swollen as though with welts, dingy with wiped tears. She would not talk to Agnes now at all and every time the abbess managed to catch her eye, a heavy dullness closed it quickly down.

"*How* can she think?"

Agnes's voice leaped from her throat. Around her the nuns' faces menaced. Featureless, like rows of maces, they armed the darkness. She blinked the wet from her eyes and focusing hard, perceived quite close to her Chrodechilde and a group of friends. Their skin was flushed and glistening, their teeth, triumphantly bared. They seemed to her carnivores who would press Ingunda to keep her promise, would make a human sacrifice to satisfy their own appetites for wonder. All these foiled lusty young women were as dangerous as an army of Visigoths. Her vision muddied. She swayed and the nun beside her had to catch her or she would have collapsed.

"Calm, Mother Agnes," whispered the prioress, Justina. "Better discuss this some other time."

"All right."

She let Justina help her from the chapel.

But it was as she had expected. Ingunda avoided her. When summoned, she was monosyllabic. Eyes on the floor, she repeated obstinately that she felt called upon to make this sacrifice. Yes, she was sure. No, she did not think she was being emotional or theatrical. She did not understand what the mother abbess meant by that. No one had forced her. She had thought of it herself. It was her own decision. She would obey, of course, if the mother abbess refused her permission.

Agnes did refuse but would not be able to stick to her refusal. Radegunda would not agree. Other nuns would be scandalized or ready to turn the incident to their own use. Already, she knew—reports had come in after the scene in the chapel—she was being described as 'tepid', 'unspiritual', 'worldly' and 'lacking in vision'.

The girl maddened her. She could have struck her—the Rule allowed whipping—but the absurdity of that impulse brought her back to her dilemma: what she wanted to exchange with Ingunda was not blows but love or at the very least, words. Besides, the girl, in her present state, might have welcomed the punishment—and she was within her rights. It was her own life, now, to throw away. Suicide had been condemned a century before at the Council of Arles, but reclusion was not suicide. It was only a living death.

"*Why*, Ingunda? Tell me. Please. I beg you. I am worried ... for your sake. Are you unhappy here? This is such an extreme decision."

"Sister Disciola made it. She chose that way."

"Yes. She had visions. She was a little ... strange. I didn't think you were like that."

"Must one have visions?"

"No. There are no 'must's. It's just that sometimes one is so close to something that one can't see it. It blots out the light and talking it over with someone else might make it look quite different. Couldn't you talk—just *talk* about this with me, Ingunda? I thought we were friends. Have you forgotten? Can't you trust me? Look at me even?"

Silence.

"I would", Agnes risked wildly, "help you leave the convent if ... if you wanted?"

Ingunda glanced swiftly at her: a furtive, astounded glance.

Leaving the convent was impossible on pain of excommunication. But Agnes would have risked that. Would have ... oh how absurd, how hopeless and helpless not to even know the rub which was driving Ingunda to this folly! Yes, Agnes had to suppose, 'I *am* unspiritual. For me it *is* pure, witless folly and self-destruction. And she gets that desperate impulsiveness from me. I, too, persist doggedly for years and then, quite suddenly, am ready to bolt. Is that timidity?"

Aloud, she accused: "You are not really drawn to this. It horrifies you. I can tell. You want to force yourself into a position from which there is no retreat. But why? Why *must* you punish yourself, Ingunda? You are not responsible for what happened your sisters!"

For, of course, that was the source of this madness. Ingunda had not been the same since the day she had returned from visiting them. Her fever had lasted only about a week, but the aftermath of her sickness was still with her: a kind of hibernation in which her blood seemed colder, her eye duller, her face paler. She seemed somehow stunned. Agnes, watching her as a cat stalks a bird, had not seen her laugh or joke with the other novices; she took part in no recreations and she had not again visited her foster-family.

"Ingunda," pleaded Agnes, "say something."

The girl said something reasonable, even trite. Something which was acceptable currency in this convent and all other convents founded on the principle that this world is a vale of tears and real life begins after death. Agnes took no notice of it.

"Is something wrong?" she harried.

"Yes."

"What? Tell me."

Ingunda burst out crying. Agnes took her in her arms. The two clung to each other. For minutes Agnes gave herself up to the relief, to the numbing melancholy of this precarious unison. Smell of clean hair, wool, taste of tears— she held the girl gripped tightly, almost brutally.

"There are", she heard herself plead in a tense whisper which seemed to be coming from her lips without her own volition, "other ways of measuring reality different to what we've taught you here. You've taken our teaching too literally. Maybe it's not even true." But what was she saying? Did these words mean anything? "It's to do", she tried to focus her mind on Ingunda's troubles, "with your foster-family, hasn't it? Can't I help at all?"

"No. You can't."

"There are things I could tell you which..."

"*No*!" Ingunda looked terrified. "Don't *tell* me ... anything ... I..."

"What?"

"Anything. Look!" Ingunda drew away from her.

"Can't *you* trust *me*, Mother Agnes? Have *you* always been right?"

The same question Basina had asked her once. Agnes felt her flesh weaken. "No," she admitted, "but that's exactly why I'm trying now to explain how one can go wrong and..."

"Please, please, then, let me make my own decision."

"To? To—are you still going to..." She couldn't finish.

"Yes, I must. And you must let me. I don't want special treatment. Please, it's my life. I'm almost fifteen. I know what I must do!" She was almost shouting.

Agnes let her go.

She tried to talk to Fortunatus. He was leaving on a visit to the court of Rheims and only gave her half his attention. She had been ready to tell him who Ingunda was—old prides had shrivelled and didn't matter now. What mattered was to get his help. But how address the confidence to the abstracted, self-important creature he had become?

"You are the convent's spiritual adviser," she reminded him instead. "This girl should be dissuaded."

"Why? What does it matter? She'll go faster to heaven."

"She may simply go mad."

"Divine madness..."

"How do we *know* it's divine and not demonic. And anyway, we must think humanly. Think of the life that child is contracting for. I mean *think*, Fortunatus, of the reality. How can you be so callous? Do I have to describe it for you?" She scrutinized his face, looking for a flinching or any softening in him to which she might confide.

He shrugged, annoyed at her insistence. "Look Agnes, my substitute can talk to her. I have to ... oh well, all right. I'll say a few words myself. I disapprove of this sort of thing anyway. People who aim to high go for a fall. The sin of Lucifer. Angelism leads to its opposite. I think I have a sermon on the subject. I'll look up my notes."

"Notes!"

Agnes's breath stuck like a lock of wool in her throat. She coughed, felt the tears in her eyes and knew she had never been less compelling. "Not a speech, Fortunatus!" she managed to say. "Find out what's the matter with the girl. Something is. I can't . . . she won't confide in me. . . . Fortunatus," Agnes nerved herself, "do you know *who she is*?"

"A novice, fourteen years old. Agnes, forgive me," he sighed, gabbled, "but I, very much against my will I assure you, am embroiled in urgent enterprise. Great interests hang on it. There are risks. Thought of it chills me. Worry addles my brain. I've been meaning to ask you for your gargle of ginger and oregano to purge the head passages. I . . . I'm constantly upset, nervous. This matter weighs on me. Teases my nerves. I think for that matter of your novice, my substitute would really do a better job, handle things better. He has more time. Shall I send for the gargle or will you send it to me? I'm leaving in the morning."

Agnes went to see Radegunda. But Radegunda was now impermeable to appeals. Words bounded off her like hail from a polished surface. Only a very few subjects could hold her attention. Her face was blank, her use of language different from other people's: she trafficked less in immediately intelligible meaning than in clangorous symbols and allusions to what could not be said but must be allowed imperative significance. To Agnes, all this was like the empty movements of a conjurer's hands. Radegunda claimed to have visited hell and perceived its reality with all her senses: taste, touch, smell.

This was not someone from whom Agnes could expect sympathy for her view of Ingunda's decision. Even if Radegunda had known—perhaps all the more if she had known—the girl's parentage, she would have approved of her immurement.

"Radegunda, I'm worried for her!" The poor everyday

words cowered on Agnes's tongue. "I'm in anguish," she blurted.

"Attachment to creatures", Radegunda replied, "is as much to be dreaded as hell itself. Creatures are frail and fleeting. I mean *particular* attachments, Agnes. We may work to bring peace and justice to earth but finally it is in God alone that. . ."

Agnes turned and rushed out of Radegunda's cell. It was in one of the turrets of the old city wall which had been incorporated into the convent building and the stairs leading down from it were twisting and narrow. Agnes lost her footing on these. She threw out her hands, clawed at the wall, missed it and slid the rest of the way on her back, banging her head on several jutting steps as she did so. She knocked herself out, injured her spine, and had to be taken to the convent sick-cell where she lay for weeks.

When she came to herself and was sufficiently recovered to receive visitors, a number of nuns—some with malice, others with sympathy or innocence—described the ceremony she had missed when Ingunda had been bricked up in a hollow of the cloister wall. The nuns had held lanterns and sung hymns while the masons worked. Radegunda had presided and the girl herself had kissed all her friends and taken her leave from them with exemplary steadfastness. Others had wept but not she. Her cell, by her own wish, was much smaller than Sister Disciola's: too small to allow her to lie down.

Chapter Sixteen

A.D.
586 Agnes was different when she recovered. She looked older. Her temper was short, her mouth sharp and she was sometimes so unreasonable the nuns whispered that she was going through an odd phase and that, really, Chrodechilde was not so wrong in saying she should be replaced as abbess. Not wrong at all.

But who was to do it? Radegunda was now completely cut off from convent life and the chaplain, Fortunatus, spent more and more time away. When he was around, he shuttled between Radegunda's tower and a cottage on the convent estate, where some wondered if he kept a woman. The nuns grew lax, ate meat, played chess, backgammon and other board games, gossipped and wondered was something in the wind.

Rumours seeped into the cloister through the kitchens—to which tenants brought soap, wax, honey and garbled news—and from the steward, who had recently returned from Marseilles with a load of spices and some odd stories picked up along the trade routes. The Bishop of Rouen, famous for having stood up to Queen Fredegunda and treated her without fear or favour, was stabbed in his own church on Easter Day. During the Divine service. Fredegunda had come to gloat and, as the bishop wasn't dying fast enough, offered him the services of her physician. The bishop had cursed and accused her of having armed the assassin's hand. All churches had been closed throughout Rouen in protest.

"Queen Fredegunda", said Justina, the prioress, to Agnes, "has never been so unpopular. All Gaul is indignant. Killing a bishop! They say when she offered her own physician, the bishop said 'Now I know that God means me to die!' The woman's mad. She must have the devil's help to have survived so long. They say she sent assassins, too, to kill the monarchs of the other kingdoms but they were discovered. That shows her guilty conscience. She's afraid." Justina lowered her voice. "Now", she said, "would be a good time for a move." She knew something of Radegunda's plans.

"Shsh!" said Agnes.

"Oh, I wouldn't say a word. But my uncle was saying . . ." Justina's uncle was Bishop Gregory of Tours.

The two were working in the dispensary, making up medicines. There had been an epidemic and other signs and portents had been observed. "Which is no wonder," said Justina. "Priests and not stones are the foundations of the Church. Priests know God's meanings. They make Christ's body with their words. With their mouths they make it. If they are to be killed and the killer go free, what will we all come to? They have the key of heaven. Without the keys no man can reach it, or woman either."

Agnes could not deny this. It was orthodox. But Justina's certitudes grated on her. Fortunatus was a priest. And to what had he ever held the key? She shook herself, trying to empty her mind of the images gnawing at it. Like vermin they gnawed. Her dreams were more bearable than her waking moments. Something always happened in the dream. Some precipitation of event, some change, even a horrible one was better than the endless nullity of her waking hours, the endless knowledge of that suffering mad presence in the convent wall.

The painful thing was that, looking back, it had become clear to Agnes that her life had for years been narrowing until now she was caught in a vice: truly and finally unfree. It was only now that she saw how much freer she had once been and that there had been moments when she might, with more grit and nerve, have saved herself and Ingunda from the impasse to which prudence had led her. Like a sheep nipped at the hocks, she had let herself be nudged and pushed into this dead end, this negation of life which was worse than death. It was not only the waste of Ingunda's life which tormented her for that waste was the result of her own. She was forty-six: old. Everything was over and what choices had she made? She had backed away from choice. Crouching in her haven, she had imagined Gaul stretching around her menacingly: tumid with blood, greed, a bristle of dark forests and malevolence. But the haven itself was poisoned. She should have struck out. Weak, penniless women had come in off the roads to the alms-house where she had once worked and had set off again. They—some of them—survived. And was survival so desirable anyhow? Life had played an ironic trick on her. She had been given survival and safety, the things she had seemed to prize, in their most naked misery. "If", she thought, "I had had five years with Ingunda and then died, wouldn't it have been better? One year."

"Queen Fredegunda..." Justina was whispering. Her voice slithered in her throat.

Fredegunda excites people, thought Agnes. Just as Radegunda does. They would say that one horrifies and the other exalts but that is not it at all. People—the nuns—watch life as they might a chess game. The black queen thrills by her blackness. Each of our queens has her own sort of power. Radegunda's is concentrated on herself. She can reverse reality, starve herself and taste honey on her lips, freeze herself and feel heat around her heart. Heat and honey are the rarest things in December when last year's stores are low—but she has them. Might Ingunda too? Perhaps she is more Radegunda's daughter than mine? Perhaps she can find what she wants in her wall? I don't believe that.

Justina had stopped speaking. Interrogative echoes hung in the air.

"Yes," said Agnes.

"How 'yes'?"

"I thought you said...?"

"What I said was...." Impatiently the voice chugged on. The note of annoyance with Agnes who had not been

262

listening gave way to a more general outrage and the pleasures of indignation. "That Fredegunda...!"

The black queen! Their counter idol! They protested but, underneath, were perhaps excited at a woman killing a bishop. After all, no woman could be a priest and make Christ's body, as Justina had just said, with her mouth. But she could kill one.

Agnes was tired. She tired easily nowadays and did nothing but the most mechanical tasks. Now she was grinding cloves in a mortar. The smell was hypnotic. It sent her faculties to sleep. Only her nostrils were active and drew in the hot, powerful spice-particles. Probably she had failed to answer some question. The prioress was weighing measures of costum and galingale and putting them in bowls with a suffering air.

"Did you say something?" Agnes asked. "I'm sorry. I didn't catch."

"Nothing," said Justina then, unable to let it go: "They say she killed a nobleman who dared reproach her. Killed him there and then with a poisoned stirrup-cup."

Death was the most exciting theme of all. Naturally. Behind death's curtain lay everything the nuns had given up in this life, all the pleasures thriftily postponed in the hope of getting them back a hundredfold. Death was their dominion. Radegunda dreamed of it constantly, claimed to have seen her own place in heaven in a dream. Would Ingunda be better off dead? Killed? Dispatched to heaven? Now?

Agnes had got up from her bed several times in the last weeks and months and walked downstairs to the cloister. Passing the chapel window, she had stared in to where a few tapers glowed on the altar and a nun was keeping vigil. The window was wet with rain and the light from inside broke through the drops, shattered and spun lacey symmetries in each. When she left, the pallid patterns came with her so that she was looking at the sky through a damp, glass-like grille. She had walked over to Ingunda's window. It was unglazed, no more really than a slit practised diagonally in the thick stone so that Agnes could see nothing. She had stood there until her pulse subsided and she began to hear the girl's sleeping breath. "She is less wretched now," she had whispered to herself. "She is dreaming perhaps. I shall not wake her. What would be the use?" She stood so long listening to the breathing that it began to seem as though it was coming from her own body. Then she had left, moving her numbed limbs with difficulty. Each time she came the girl was asleep. Anyway what could she say to her now that she had not said before?

"Chrodechilde..." said Justina.

"What?"

"She's on her high horse again."

There was criticism here. Not only of Chrodechilde: of Agnes. Agnes had gone too far, the prioress considered, or not far enough or too far to then balk at going further. She should be on her guard. "She's dangerous," said Justina. "I can't begin to tell you half of what she's up to. Ever since..."

Agnes shrugged and poured yellow pimentos into her mortar. She worked the pestle around and the thin dried pimento skins broke like parchment, the pith soaked into the pestle. She had whipped Chrodechilde—to both their astonishment.

"You let things go," Justina criticized with gentle persistence. "Then suddenly you swoop! That enrages them. They grow confident and then they're indignant if you stop them at all. A tight rein would be better: tight but steady."

Yes, Agnes was no longer steady.

"It was while you were ill, of course, that they grew unmanageable. I said it to Father Fortunatus, but..."

"Yes." He would pay no attention. He was absorbed in his larger intrigue and had no eyes for the small ones being played out in the convent. Chrodechilde had tried to draw him in but he had paid her as little attention as he had Justina or Agnes. Only Radegunda could rock him and, on Easter Sunday, had.

On that day Radegunda had spoken to the nuns in chapel.

"Ordinarily," she had said, "nuns are called on to keep their vows and..."

Agnes had seen Fortunatus's anxiety. His mouth twitched and she, who had been letting the words flow over her, was alerted to their oddity. Why "ordinarily"? A "but" was implicit.

The foundress's speech wove on in classic phrases which crested with the regularity of waves. Only Fortunatus and Agnes waited for the sudden reversal, the turn in the tide. The other nuns were passive, perhaps not really listening? Agnes watched with curiosity. Radegunda had changed over the years. Growing thinner, she looked even taller and had taken on a mannish air. The virile silhouette of her warrior ancestry jutted beneath the white veil. Stiffened by will-power, bent as an old weapon which has been leaned on too much, her body was all points. The candles on the Easter altar threw shadows from every angle so that her great white frame looked riddled with holes. Her voice had grown hollow too and, in moments of excitement, wheezed.

"There are times", she said, "when what appeared to be a life-long vocation turns out not to be, when a noble choice proves to have been countermanded by God and when the needs of our poor world must be satisfied at the expence of remoter spiritual ones. *If* we could bring the Kingdom of God to earth," said Radegunda, toppling towards her congregation of nuns as she fixed them, one after the other, with her zany eye, "should we not do so?" The eye blazed like the small pure blue flame which sometimes appears in a coal fire when a cracked fragment has released a puff of gas. "If a dying man", she cried, "were to be flung by soldiers at the door of our church, should we not leave Christ on the altar to bring help to Christ in the man dying at our door?"

Even now, Agnes noticed with detachment—since she had suffered all the suffering life was likely to hold for her, she had grown detached and now, with detachment,

265

noted—that the nuns seemed to observe nothing peculiar about Radegunda's speech. Hearing what they expected to hear, they did *not* hear that Radegunda was inviting them to break their cloister-Rule, if need should arise, and sacrifice heaven-in-heaven to heaven-on-earth. Mildly, they stared at their ecstatic foundress. Harmoniously, they sang the hymn at the end of her talk. Persistently, they denied, when Agnes questioned them afterwards, that Mother Radegunda had said anything memorable at all.

"She said we should observe our Rule, pray, be charitable," said Justina. "Yes, she was passionate. But she is often passionate. Eloquent. I was moved."

"You needn't worry," Agnes told Fortunatus afterwards. "They didn't understand a thing."

"How many did you ask? How can you be sure? They may not say what they think. Besides, next time it may be worse. She's mad," said Fortunatus violently. "Mad, mad, mad!" He walked to the sacristy door—they were in the sacristy where he had not yet removed his vestments after saying mass—opened it, inspected the corridor, closed it, lifted a tapestry, delivered a violent punch at a hanging curtain.

"Madness", Agnes shrugged with some malice, "is close to godliness. Divine folly you yourself once..."

"There's folly and folly. This sort is dangerous." He dropped his voice and gabbled in a furious whisper, "Senility perhaps? Who can tell. But she's different. Perhaps she's tormented her body to breakage point? She's transformed anyway. She frightens me. She keeps pushing me to hurry the bishops. She's afraid she'll die before the..." Again his voice dropped, so low now that he was hardly making a sound. His face writhed like a clown at a fair. "The prince," he mouthed and tilted his head.

Agnes stared at him dispassionately.

"What does she say?" she asked.

He washed his hands in invisible water, walked back and forth, ground his teeth. "What does it matter: cogent things enough but that the premise is mad ... That God helps those who help themselves—that's what she says when I tell her it's the wrong moment. That there's personal cowardice in hiding behind a spiritual stance—that's her reply when I say that the whole thing is a matter for laymen. Pride, she says then: there's pride in electing to live and act on a spiritual plane only. What use, she says, is there in nuns accepting humiliating tasks—cleaning kitchens, etc.—if they will not accept direct participation in worldly events? 'The world', she says, 'is grubby and we should be prepared to get our hands dirty.' And so on. She's never at a loss for argument. Words flow out of her. There are moments when I think it's the devil, the father of lies, who has deluded her. It wouldn't be the first time such a thing happened. Saints are vulnerable. They're tuned to dangerous regions, inhuman. We know that. What she wants really is power, power in this world, in this country, now. Oh, how did I ever get myself involved in all this?" He was sweating. A reek slunk from him. He wiped his face with his stole. "I can't back out now. The others, naturally, would protect themselves." He turned to Agnes. He was trembling. A tic twitched in one of his eyes. "She may do anything—and when I tell the others, the bishops, they don't believe me. They have no confidence in me. They think I'm an alarmist and inventing this to give myself an excuse for backing out. They think I'm a coward—well, I am. But what we heard this morning would worry *them*! Only they wouldn't believe it if I told them. I'm caught between her and them." Fortunatus munched his lower lip. "Oh, I could beat myself. How did I let this happen?"

"You had no choice."

"I didn't. Oh, my God. I'm a man of words. I could write a poem about a conspiracy—but *run* one, oh God!—and they give me responsibilities! I'm so terrified, I refuse to carry any papers on me, yet they use me as a courier. I learn things off rather than have papers, then I get so frightened my mind goes blank. If I told you where I do carry papers you'd—you'd be disgusted! Talk of grubbiness. God have mercy on me." Fortunatus threw himself on his knees.

"Get up!" said Agnes. "Why should your prayers be heard?"

"You're harsh, Agnes!"

"I've seen you before now recover from a fall which destroyed . . . others. You land on all fours like a predatory tomcat pushed off a balcony." She heard her own voice with surprise. Bitterness gave it an edge, a life which she had thought gone out of her. A kind of cold, slow pleasure flamed through her.

"You hate me?"

"I have forgiven you but not myself for listening to you. I wish none of us had ever listened to you. *You* brought the prince here!"

"Shshsh!" Fortunatus goggled at her, mouth and eyes gasping. "For God's sake!" He repeated his round of the door, the tapestry, the curtain. This time he climbed on a stool and stared out the window.

"Am I the only sane creature left?" he lamented. "Listen," he opened a coffer, inspected it, poured some wine he found there, drank it and sighed. "My motives, Agnes, are not selfish. Truly. I'm afraid for myself, I'll admit. Why not, for God's sake? But I'm afraid for this convent too and for Gaul. It's my adopted country. I don't want to see it mangled again—I've seen more of war than you, you'll admit?"

"But *you* first introduced the prince!"

"Did I have a choice? I wish I'd smothered him. He", Fortunatus leaned towards her, caught her shoulder, let his breath—wine-laden now—play hotly on her ear, "is not to be relied on either. He's nervous, like a horse who's been too long in the stall. He'd do anything. He's—well, what would you expect? He spends his time disguised, dressed as a woman, gardening. From boredom. Studying Latin with me. He has no sense of reality. How could he have? He needs a woman too. He's growing up. The family of Clovis, you know—hot blood! He should be got out of here."

Fortunatus's face ballooned too close. Agnes could not see or focus properly. It was a puffy face now. Wine had thickened it and age—he was well into his fifties—twitched and pinched it into cruel little lumps and udders.

"I've told the bishop," he said, "and they say it's my affair to keep him in check! 'In check'! 'In check'! It's easy to say. Here I have a mad saint and a randy youth on my hands. I should get him some whore—keep him from breaking into the convent. That's what I'll end up as: a pimp. All in the noblest cause, you know, but causes have a way of mobilizing the oddest elements. Change is tricky. Throw something up and it may fall back in your eye. One can't predict. Perfection is not of this world—that's an axiom. It's dogma. So mustn't it be wrong to seek it?"

"Seeking safety", said Agnes, "is not always the way to find it."

"You're always reproaching me, Agnes. I'm weak." He sighed.

"I know."

"Also," he straightened up somewhat, "I have some sense. I know more about what lies outside these walls than you do. *There was nowhere to go*, Agnes. We were safer here."

"Safer!"

"Happier—well, we might have been. If you had wished. But you're stiff: an extremist. I always hoped you'd relent, come back to me after..."

"After the child was born?"

"But you closed me out. Suddenly you—like Radegunda —were playing all or nothing. But *we*'re not like that, Agnes, you and I. We're not all-or-nothing people. My God!" He began to laugh and plead at the same time. "Our whole story was born under the sign of compromise: a love affair in a convent. I was your second choice, Agnes. You had already chosen God. I only did that years later—*He* was mine. I pray He'll forgive me. Our affairs had to be secret, had to be cautious, preferably a little light-hearted. I tried to tell you that, Agnes. We had to divide ourselves ..."

269

"You can't divide a child!"

"Did it die, Agnes? Was that it? You never told me—and I have wondered."

"You never asked."

"I was afraid to. You had closed me out."

Agnes's jaw felt frozen: held in a clamp of ice. With a wrench she opened it. "She—the child—didn't die. She grew up and became a novice here. Now she expiates our sin. She is the recluse: Ingunda." She steadied herself.

He turned away. Bent shoulders, a bent head, silence were all she was presented with and a soft, hooped back. "He is suffering," she thought and wondered was she pleased? Sorry? Triumphant? Somehow justified? No. None of these. She probed herself: nothing. His suffering had come too late to alleviate hers. Why had she told him at all? An experiment perhaps? And why had she said that Ingunda was expiating their sin? Did she believe that? In a way, a confused way—but which sin? Having loved or of not having loved enough? She sloughed off such niceties? What did clarity matter? It might have helped once. Now it was too late. Life was almost over. The world, she felt obscurely, was almost over too and Radegunda's conspiracy absurd. The soft, hooped shape in front of her was shaking. So he could still feel? Maybe after all he was more generous than she? Younger too. He didn't feel things were over. He could worry. He could cry.

"Fortunatus!"

He didn't turn.

Tears. Easy response. She envied it. She left him to it. Standing there, she exiled herself into nothingness as she had learned how to do and waited five, ten, twenty-five minutes? She couldn't have said. Finally, he turned.

"Why didn't you . . . tell me?"

"Because. . ." Why? There must have been reasons. They receded, eluded even her memory. She should have. Of course, she should have. Fortunatus, the eel, the back-bending, flexible courtier, might have ferreted out ways and means to help. But Agnes—as he said—had been too

270

stiff. She had refused to deviate from her rejection of him, from her response to his rejection of her. Stiff! Her throat felt stiff now. She couldn't swallow. It felt like dry stone. She was, had been a stone for a decade and a half. He had stunned her.

"Agnes!" His face, all grimy lines, a gleam of tears, pain, was knotted and concentrated on her. "Agnes! We can still do something!"

"She won't listen. You think I didn't try!" The protest ripped at her throat, came out in tatters of sound. "You think I . . . I . . ." Now she was crying too. "Besides it's too late."

"Listen!" He came close, held her. She let him. "When we finally launch the . . . attack. When the prince is produced, there will be great confusion, comings and goings, war. I can use the time—our forces, disguised maybe, I'll work that out—to kidnap her. Take her off somewhere where I can talk to her, reason with her, try to show her a wider world than the convent . . ."

"She won't . . ."

"She may . . . We must try, Agnes."

"When?"

"Soon. I'll push the thing forward. I know I can. Radegunda wants me to anyway. So does the prince. I'll persuade Palladius. Agnes, don't cry."

"The sin . . ."

"Holy Virgin, Agnes, you think too much, say 'no' too much! It won't be *her* sin. Let it be our sin. We can take it on ourselves. We owe it to her and . . . to *us*."

"Who?" Ice was receding from her dead emotions, freeing the ragged-edged wounds so that they hurt again. "I am too old," she cried.

"You are a greater coward than I!"

"Yes."

"There's always a middle way: slow, foot before foot. But you leap or hold back entirely! You lacerate yourself!"

She pulled away from him, put a finger to her lips, jerked her chin towards the door, turned and began to fold vestments in the coffer behind her.

Fortunatus moved with silent caution to the door, then whipped it open.

"Well?" she heard him say. "I thought I heard something. Where are you supposed to be at this time?"

"I ... came to see you." Chrodechilde's voice. It quavered, then reasserted itself.

The door concealed the two women from each other. Agnes did not move.

"Why?" Fortunatus asked in a flat voice.

"I represent a body of nuns. I'm their delegate. We have no one else to turn to. The foundress is so absorbed..."

"What about the abbess?"

"It's about her!" Chrodechilde began to recite: "We, not in any malevolent spirit but because we have the good of our holy convent at heart, feel obliged to bring to your attention the fact that our abbess is no longer able to carry out her duties. We feel her illness has troubled ... her mind? At any rate," Chrodechilde was producing her words faster and more nervously, "we have", she said, "drawn up a list of charges. I and my cousin Basina in particular feel that we are not being treated as we should be. We are the kinswomen of kings and for all the respect shown to us we might be the daughters of low serving women. The food and clothes we are expected to ... you don't take me seriously, Father Fortunatus?" She interrupted herself. "I can see you're not sympathetic. But these things are not as trifling as they might seem. They interfere with one's devotions—besides, rank is rank even in a convent. Certain things are due to it and the abbess has never acknowledged this. Listen, before that peasant girl, Ingunda went into the wall and became a recluse—she was weak in the head, poor creature, so perhaps that was for the best—can you believe that the abbess paid more attention to her than to any other novice? As if she were trying to humiliate us! There are many irregularities in this convent—may I come in? The corridor is not a safe place to talk."

"Come in," said Fortunatus.

272

Chrodechilde walked in, saw Agnes, and stopped. "You trapped me!" she reproached Fortunatus.

"Go to your dormitory," Agnes told her.

Chrodechilde left. Agnes watched her walk down the corridor then turned.

"Do you think she heard anything?"

"I'm not sure. It didn't look like it. But she's clever. This is another reason for moving fast."

"Yes."

"Could you," he asked, "keep her locked up for a while? Isolated?"

"Yes."

"Be firm."

Agnes was so firm the convent was shocked. Chrodechilde was the first nun ever to be punished by publicly receiving twenty lashes of a strap on her shoulders. The beating was administered by the abbess herself and afterwards Agnes sentenced her to stay in an isolated cell. Justina would bring her her food until further notice.

"It shook her little following," said Justina afterwards. But I'm not so sure that's a good thing. They have a grievance now!"

Chapter Seventeen

A.D.
587 "Happiness", Radegunda pinched the loosening flesh on her arm, "is shucking off the body. I have known it. I've been outside mine. My freed soul looked down at this body which is blood-nourished like a tick in a dog's ear. There was nothing it wanted less than to return to it. That is why it did."

She was walking in the convent garden with Fortunatus who, for once, was not listening to her. He was thinking of a message he had sent the bishops of Saintes and Tours. His genius for Latin acrostics had come in handy for he had inserted the dangerous message vertically and slantwise in a hymn. The key was in a seal which showed an X and a Roman cross superimposed. None but the bishops themselves, who knew his liking for such learned tricks, would notice the design. "Security here weak," he had written. "Delay dangerous. Prince should be moved now."

"I could not", Radegunda was saying, "believe at first that God wanted me to sacrifice our peace here for the peace of Gaul. I had intimations, but how could I believe them? They might have come from the devil."

"Indeed," said Fortunatus inattentively. He could see the road down which a messenger would come. It was white and parts of it, in the faltering air, seemed mobile. Soon a messenger must appear. He would be small and white at first, hardly bigger than a puff of dandelion-down bowled along by a breeze. When he arrived, he would be as dusty as a miller. Fortunatus had already discerned three imaginary moving specks.

"The safe course always", said Radegunda, "is to say 'no'. But is safety God's way? 'Leave all and follow me' surely meant leave safety too?"

Her face was unhealthy. He was only half listening to her. Already, he had decided not to tell her the bishops' answer. The best thing would be to get Clovis off the estate without her knowing. The other problem was Chrodechilde.

"I hunger for action," Radegunda sighed.

Fortunatus shuddered. "Have you", he asked, "grown tired of prayer?"

"I despise prayers which try to wring concessions from God."

"Pride!"

"It is my besetting sin," she acknowledged. "It is the devil's own and he is clever at disguising it. I had thought I was renouncing it by engaging in action. Action risks failure."

"Do you want", Fortunatus let his horror sound in his voice, "to fail?"

"You don't trust me, do you?"

Her eyes had sunk in her head. Their fierce, burning quality was put out by the sunlight. For the first time, the poet realized that she might die soon. She was sixty-seven and had led a life of extraordinary privation. No, he did not trust her.

"Tell me", she said, "about the prince."

"His Latin is coming along. He's intelligent."

She shrugged; her face sharpened. "I mean what's he *like*? His temperament? His character? Have you managed to restrain that richness of the blood that all his family have? I think of poor Clotair. The boy is twenty. What does he do for sex?"

"I thought you had cast the body off—forgotten such things."

"Don't be foolish. We're all stuck with and in a body. And the body *he*'s stuck with has probably got violent appetites. Like his grandfather. What's he doing with them? He should eat little if he's hoping to quell the flesh. Especially meat—he should abstain from that."

Fortunatus had a suspicion the prince was doing something highly incautious about those appetites. There were

275

plenty of girls working on the convent estate and Clovis, being dressed as a female, had easy access to them.

"Have you asked him?"

"Yes. No. I think he's all right?" Her sudden, ridiculously late, practicality threw him off stroke.

She had turned from him and was shading her eyes. "There's someone on the road," she announced. "A rider. Are you expecting a message?"

"Yes. Actually."

"Have you given up confiding in me?"

"I don't bother you with details."

"Details are just what I want to know. It's definitely a messenger. He's moving fast. Why don't you go down to the gate so as to stop him. If you don't, he'll go into town to look for you. I'll wait in my cell." Her tone was as alert as it had ever been. "Bring me the news", she said.

Fortunatus bowed. Before moving out of sight, he turned to look at her. She was standing with fists pressed together so that the knuckles showed white. Under her loose habit, her limbs bulged like tent pegs, each slightly out of place as though a fist had wrung and twisted her the way one wrings a wet cloth. She was, he remembered, often, if not always, in pain.

He climbed down the steps to the convent door, walked out and settled himself on a bundle of wood at the edge of the road along which the rider must pass. Yellow celandines grew in a hollow by the roadside. Glossy-petalled, they reminded him of the gold which the bishops were amassing for the coming uprising. Some had come from Byzantium. More would be supplied by the dissident nobles who had been mobilized and alerted. Several of these were more violent than the kings whose power they resented, and one or two bishops had expressed doubts about relying on them.

"We are not relying on them," Bishop Egidius of Rheims had retorted to Bishop Palladius whose idea would have been to keep the conspiracy small. "We need military men and are using them. Once the present government is removed, a period of confusion intervened and our prince

276

has presented himself, it will be appropriate for us to hail him as the God-appointed heir who can unite our unhappy country. *We* need only surface in the role of healers."

Astute enough, thought Fortunatus, but such a plan depended on tight security and that no longer existed. Rumours leaked in all directions and probably only the fact that they were garbled in the telling had preserved the plotters until now. Speed and stealth were no longer to be hoped for. Fortunatus regretted the years of poetry, piety and pleasant dalliance with the two nuns who had been seeking nothing but peace when they founded their convent. What had gone wrong? Personal matters aside— he banished *them*, could not now cope with their implications although, from time to time a black halo fringed his mental images, corrosive as a scorch, and reminded him that in his own life too there was something to be faced. But he managed to dodge confronting *that* until it could be dealt with. Aside from it then, what had happened here in Holy Cross? How had the temporal—even the expedient —come to count so much? Or *was* Radegunda's interest in the immediate matter at all? A woman whose view trembled off into eternity, could hardly accommodate her eyes to the close at hand. Maybe the plot was only a pawn's move in some very long game played with God? She might be offering it, giving them all as martyrs. Anything. Fortunatus felt a shiver of panic. She might indeed. Her rage for self-laceration might have begun to nibble all round her. She did hate the world. He stood up. This was fanciful. He would do better to worry about the active plotters. Some new recruits were very queer fish indeed. But when you spread your net wide that *was* what you caught: scavenging fish and crabs who might tear holes in it. Duke Rauching for instance. Fortunatus had been shaken to hear they had enlisted him. He was a brute, a barbarian who had buried two of his serfs alive because they had dared to marry. The two had sought refuge in a church, refusing to come out until Rauching had given the priest his word that he would allow them to live together "until death". Rauching gave and kept his word—in his own way, by burying them alive. Fortunatus had used the story to try and teach Clovis the difference between the spirit and the letter of the law.

"The trouble with Frankish laws", he had tried to explain, "is that they have no unifying spirit at all, no concept of equity. They're like a housewife's repair kit: so many patches for applying here and there to stop the more obvious holes, to keep disorder in check. But they have no guiding principles, not even a concept of honour. Look at the laws protecting women. If I violate a girl, the Frankish laws don't consider I have offended honour. They consider I have offended against property because she belonged to someone and whoever it is, guardian, betrothed or husband, will want monetary compensation according to her worth. If she is an embroidress or of child-bearing age, I pay more. If I only picked up her dress and uncovered her, I pay less. A little more if I uncovered her backside than if I only looked at her thigh and less again for the knee. But a Roman would have either killed me or closed his eyes to the matter. The offence is absolute. Honour is not measured in inches of leg."

Clovis's interest had noticeably sharpened with the mention of backsides and legs. "I think our laws are more humane," he said. "Fancy killing a man for violating a girl, who maybe liked it."

"Well that has fallen into disuse," Fortunatus admitted.

"The Church's laws are like ours," Clovis had argued. "Sins are graded, aren't they, by the amount of flesh one makes free with?" His hand stroked fat air.

No power to conceptualize! A Frank. Still, the boy was bright enough. Fortunatus had a feeling he didn't believe in much—which was what came of keeping him inactive and making him think. Bad? Good? Better than making him a bigot probably. And how inactive was he in fact? There had been a trace, a smear of femininity about the cottage sometimes when Fortunatus came. Something

278

impossible to pin down: a bunch of wild flowers in a cup, some oaten or spelt bread which had not come from the convent kitchens, an air of tidiness, something.

"I want to see my sister," Clovis had said recently. "If the plot is ever coming off it'll be soon, from what you tell me. I should see her before I leave here. After all, I might be killed."

"All the more likely if you let people know you're alive."

"Five years you've had me boxed up here like a monk," the boy complained. "How much longer?"

"Do you know how Gundovald died?"

"Do you know how often you've told me?"

"I thought you might have forgotten."

"I'm not a coward. I'd rather die than live another year— another *half* year in this place."

"It'll be soon now," Fortunatus had promised. It had better be. The boy was impatient. Radegunda was impatient. Chrodechilde was, in her own way and for her own reasons, a danger. She had come to him again, complaining about her mistreatment at Agnes's hands. She had been half hysterical, threatening to run off and enlist the help of the kings—"my royal uncles", as she called them. They were unlikely to take any notice of her but he couldn't take a chance on this. It was no time for a royal inspection. He had managed to calm her, promising—he had no idea what. She was twenty-one years old or thereabouts, a lusty, violent creature at the top of her energies. The whole convent was a tinder-box. The long, over-long gestation of this plot must come to some sort of outcome fast. There was Ingunda too ... What a time that rider was taking. The road wound back and forth below the town and they had sighted him when he was only a blob of dust, but still ... Impatiently, Fortunatus stood up and began to walk in the direction from which the man must come.

The rider, masked in surrounding clouds of dust like some descending Olympian, almost ran him down.

"Fortunatus! The man I'm looking for. Have you had

279

the news? What are you doing on the road?"

The rider was Palladius himself.

"I haven't," said Fortunatus, "but I can see it's bad."

"God save us, but it's bad!" The bishop looked right and left, back then forth again. The country was flat and open. "Everything's over," he said in an exhausted voice. "Disaster! God, but I'm tired. I can hardly breath. And saddle-sore. This dust." He began to cough. "I came alone," he managed to say between coughing and spitting and wiping his chapped mouth. "Mad! I might have been killed twenty times on those roads, but ..."

"Don't try to talk," Fortunatus told him. "We'll get you a drink at the convent. We've got to go there. Radegunda saw you arrive." He wondered whether to warn Palladius about her but decided not to. He would see for himself. *She* might be cooled by the look of him. The bishop looked wild-eyed. His face was streaked with filth and his horse probably not long for this world. A shawl of froth covered its withers and blood streamed from its mouth. Fortunatus led it slowly towards the convent gate. "Are we in danger?" he dared to ask. "The prince I mean?"

"No. I don't know." Palladius coughed again, swallowed with difficulty and leaned forward over the horse's neck to whisper, "Rauching was taken: butchered. But he had no time to talk. *Someone* talked but we think whoever it was knew only about the nobles—the laymen—not about *us*. He knew, whoever it was, that King Childebert was to be murdered by Rauching and tipped the king off. When Rauching came for an audience, he found Childebert surrounded by a bodyguard. The audience went off quickly. Neither Rauching nor the king said anything of note. We know this from a man of ours who was there. Then, when Rauching walked out the door, he was tripped up, swordsmen leaped on him and hacked his head into a smear of brains. 'Like spilled porridge,' said our spy." The bishop's whisper was hoarse but level. He showed no feeling. Weariness, sustained shock and perhaps sheer repetition had taken the nerve out of his voice. "The body", he went on, "was stripped and thrown out of the window. The king's venom saved us. His anger. He should have had Rauching tortured and tried to get names out of him. Instead, he had him butchered on the spot. Our allies, Ursio and Berthefred, who were to have moved in with troops and taken over the palace, were warned in time and managed to flee. They've withdrawn to the town of Woevre. Meanwhile King Childebert has gone to Andelot to strengthen his alliance with his uncle, King Guntram. There's going to be a purge among the dissident nobles. With any luck, *our* connection—the Church's—won't even be known. But your prince had better be kept out of sight. What was your message about 'weak security' for? What's been happening here?"

"Nothing. Nothing that matters now," Fortunatus told him. "Don't mention the murders to Radegunda. She couldn't take that."

"The news", Palladius told him, "is common knowledge along the trade routes by now. It wasn't my intention, I assure you, to have so much blood. The thing got out of hand. Once Rauching was brought in..." He broke off again to cough. "The dust," he coughed.

"Leave your horse here," Fortunatus told him. "We'll get you a drink."

Radegunda and Palladius faced each other: two white figures. Hers was the vertical whiteness of her habit which fell in flat folds from her shoulders. The bishop was white from road-dust which clung like a fungus to his surfaces, buried his eyebrows, disappeared in the chapped pallor of his lips. He had told her his story—less than he told Fortunatus but enough, it was clear, to shock her into realizing that the endeavour to which she had lent herself was not only defeated but had been impure from the start.

The bishop sighed, groped for a bench, remembered he had not been invited to take one and straightened up. A moment later he was sagging again. His hands foundered. "Unity", he said wearily, "is the bloodiest word in the

lexicon. One makes ... concessions to it. It becomes ...
the main end. And then, nothing cements like blood.
Literally speaking. Masons tell you that. When one
starts making ... concessions, the extremists take over. *I*
tried to hold out, ..." His hand fell in discouragement.
"You ask why we chose Rauching. We didn't. We all said
we would *not* have him and then, somehow, I don't know
... it became accepted that there was dirty work to do ...
someone dirty needed to do it. Rauching ..."

Radegunda held herself as stiff as a stake. Her nose
menaced the bishop like a knife-blade badly sheathed in
its aged and thinning skin.

"Bishop Palladius!" She summoned and quelled his
glance. "You deceived me and are now attempting to
deceive yourself. You talked to me of the City of God.
Now you talk of having dirty work to do."

His hands flew, froze.

"No!" She quashed their implications. "Things are and
must be clear. They must be right or wrong. I blame
myself. I should have known when Bishop Bertram asked
us to violate our cloister that sin leads to more sin. You have
been so busy brewing and stewing in the hope of distilling
good from evil that you no longer know one from another.
I can see that. You and your fellow-bishops are now the
devil's workers."

The bishop let his hands fall. He opened his mouth,
closed it, shrugged and drooped. He had been through
bad days and nights and expected to go through some more.
His horse was perhaps dead. Only a fraction of his attention
was alert. "It is more complex," he pleaded.

"Complexity," she told him, "is of the devil."

Palladius coughed. "You lack charity, Mother. You are
not humane." He coughed again, so that tears came to his
eyes, fell on his dusty chest and rolled down carrying the
dust with them and making lines like long black cuts.
He had not been given the drink which Fortunatus had
promised. "Perhaps", he said, "I had better take my leave."

Radegunda closed her eyes. Palladius started to go.

"I'll come with you, Bishop Palladius," Fortunatus offered.

"No!" she stopped him. "I need *you!*" She looked impatient. "Send the steward with the bishop." With an obvious effort she turned her attention back to Palladius. "Extremism was not your mistake," she told him. "Impurity was, and that comes from worldliness. You should have purified yourself in the furnace of terror and solitude. But you wanted the support of a crowd, a ... crowd of Rauchings. Where was your faith? With faith you would not have used *human* methods. You would not have become —as you have, my lord bishop—indistinguishable from your enemies. It was because your methods were human that this all took so long, so long!" Her voice rose. "Where was the fountain of strength which explodes in a man's soul when God has touched him with his grace? If we'd had that, we would have moved long ago, sped by the winds of holy impetuosity. Even now ..." Her voice lightened. "*If* you could rely on God's strength, we, the faithful among us," she was cajoling, coaxing, almost smiling at the astonished Palladius, "by ourselves," she begged, "we might act. If God gives us a sign. Shall we ask for one? Fortunatus!" She pointed to a chest on which lay a gold box. "Take out the Epistles. We shall give God a chance to speak to us. We shall consult the auguries. Bishop Palladius," she cried to him, "will you consent to consult Holy Writ? To be led by it? *Will* you?" She was suddenly mobile, alert, almost quivering and the opalescent transparencies of her aging face—blue-veined, green-bruised, flecked with brown and chillblained with pink—were suffused by a girlish flush. Radegunda was aflame again with hope and urgency. "*You* must open it, since it is you," she told the bishop, "who have need of reassurance."

Her excitement crackled in the air after she had stopped speaking. The two men were very quiet, hunched into themselves as though waiting for thunder. Fortunatus held out the Epistles. Palladius half shrugged, then spoke in a quick, cautious voice:

"You want me to do this?"

"I do. I do."

"Well. . ." He opened the book Fortunatus was holding "1 Thessalonians," he read in a speedy, reluctant tone. "Chapter five, verse three," he gabbled, ". . . they shall say Peace and Safety; then sudden destruction cometh upon them, as travail upon a woman with child; and they shall not escape." Then, as though the meaning of what he had read had just caught his attention, he repeated it: "and they shall not escape." His mouth slipped sideways and he released a sound which might have been on its way towards laughter. ". .not escape," he said again.

Radegunda walked over, read the verse herself and turned away. After a moment she turned back: "Forgive my keeping you, Bishop Palladius. I realize you must be tired." She nodded his dismissal.

The bishop left.

"Fortunatus!"

"Mother Radegunda?"

"The bishop's comfort", she told him, as though answering some protest, "is not important. Neither is mine nor yours. Small things must be sacrificed to greater. Bring the prince."

"Here?"

"Yes. We must not be fussy about breaking a small rule now. We—through those associated with us—have broken big ones. The blood of the wretched Rauching and of who knows how many others will be on our consciences. All right," she made an impatient gesture, "dress him in something—anything. Women's clothes, a priest's, whatever you can so as not to give scandal. But bring him."

She turned from him, stiff as a board, upright as the leg of the great crucifix in the convent garden, moved two paces from him and collapsed. Fortunatus ran to her and raised her head. Her mouth was edged with froth, her eyes emptily dark like the holes sparks burn in cloth. "Go," she told him. "Justina will look after me."

He went. On the stairs he met Agnes. "Keep the nuns away," he told her and explained quickly why.

"It's their recreation time."

"Well, change it. Keep them on the other side of the building for the next hour."

He rushed off.

Left alone with Justina, Radegunda agreed to lie down but would not be silent. "It's all my fault," she groaned.

Justina protested.

"It is," Radegunda insisted. "You don't understand. The bishops' was the temporal part. Mine was the spiritual. They were to plot and I was to pray. I should have swayed God, I should have charged the act with nobility and had faith for all. If there has been a murder it is because my prayers were not insistent. We are part of the same net. Pull here and it twitches there. Weaken here and the weakness spreads like rot. It's my fault. Christendom", said Radegunda, "is one."

Justina brought her some water. "You can't carry the world," she said.

Radegunda drank and closed her eyes. "I can," she said. "If I believe I can, I can."

Justina went to the small cell window and looked out. The sun was going down and she could hear Agnes calling the nuns in another part of the convent. A bell was slowly ringing. She watched the light ripen from blonde to rose as the sun slipped the last fraction of its way towards the horizon. Swallows were flying around the tower. Or were they bats? The light was behind them and she couldn't tell. Back and forth they swooped like lacemakers' pegs, down and up, leaving black after-images on the pale, perforated sky.

A voice, quieter now, came from the bed. "Bishop Palladius", said Radegunda with assurance, "misunderstood the text. 'For when they say Peace and Safety,' she quoted, 'sudden destruction shall come upon them.' He thought this upheld his decision to abandon our plan. But it means the opposite. Exactly the opposite! We should

285

not have said 'Peace and Safety'! We should have said 'Suffer and seek the impossible' for the gate is strait and Christ brought not peace but the sword. It was a sign", she said calmly, "and he misread it. We should persist, you see, don't you, Justina, don't you see that?"

"Try to rest."

"But you see, don't you, that we *should* persevere?"

"Yes," said Justina. She could see Fortunatus and the prince approaching. They were walking across the vineyards below the convent garden and the prince—she supposed it must be he although she had never seen him—was dressed as a cleric. Fortunatus was speaking, making gestures and the two were moving fast. When they came closer, they moved out of her view but a minute or so later emerged into it again as they crossed the convent garden beneath the tower-window. She could hear their voices now although she could not distinguish their words. Suddenly, as they passed a thick clump of bushes, two nuns skipped out from behind it as though to head them off. Their backs were to her.

"Father Fortunatus!" a high voice challenged. Justina recognized the abrasive tone as Chrodechilde's. "I have a complaint," it shrilled. "You *must* listen this time! Our rights are not being respected here. The Rule is not respected. Our recreation just now ..." Justina strained her ears but Chrodechilde had lowered her tone and she could make out no more.

Justina glanced at the bed. Radegunda's eyes were closed. Taking a stool, Justina stepped up on it and managed to crane her neck out the small window. She saw Fortunatus push Chrodechilde quite roughly out of his way and draw the prince quickly past her. "The Foundress", she heard him say, "is ill, possibly dying and we are bringing her spiritual succour. This is no time for trouble-making."

But while he was addressing himself to Chrodechilde, the other nun—it was, Justina saw now, Basina—had approached the prince. "Holy St. Hilary," thought

286

Justina. "He's her brother! She'll know him!" The two were in fact staring intently at each other. The prince put his hand on Basina's arm and must have asked her something, for Justina saw her open her mouth to reply. Abruptly, Fortunatus wrenched the young man's hand away and propelled him ahead of himself towards the door of the tower.

"Father Marius!" Fortunatus called loudly after him, "Hurry ahead and tell our Holy Mother I am coming." He turned to the two nuns. "Go and join your companions at once! Tell them our Holy Foundress is dying and to start singing psalms and praying for a happy release of her soul." His voice was peremptory. "Go!" he let out a roar. "At once!"

Justina saw the two nuns back away in fright, turn and run around a corner out of sight. As they disappeared, Basina clutched her companion's elbow and Justina had the impression that she was panting out information. Fortunatus followed the prince.

"Mother Radegunda!" Justina stepped down from her lookout point. "Are you awake?"

"Yes," Radegunda rose from the bed and, moving unsteadily, joined Justina at the window. She looked out.

"A cindery sky," she remarked. "We must be prepared for further suffering."

Justina asked, "Are you in pain?"

"I welcome pain," said Radegunda. "I welcome disappointment. I offer it up. It may be my last offering. What matter whether *I* see the success of our plans so long as they do succeed? As they will," she told Justina. "I know it. Sooner or later Gaul will be united under one king annointed by the Holy Church. The project is a seed. It will take root." She lurched and Justina caught her.

"Sit. Please, Mother. I can tell you're dizzy!"

"Pain keeps me lucid. I shall stand." Radegunda clutched her chest and stared at the empty doorway. "Are they coming?"

Justina walked through it and down the stairs. "They're coming," she called.

When the two came in from the well of the dark stairway, the light from the window was in their eyes. Radegunda was standing with her back to it so that reflections mirrored in the open pane fell on her veil and rippled redly down its folds. She seemed to have difficulty directing her tongue. She clutched herself, panting as though the air were burning her throat. "Prince Clovis," she managed in a scorched voice, "I shall not live to see you King of Gaul nor even ... Neustria. I shall not ..." Her breath came in gulps. She staggered, motioned the others to keep away and said, "guide you, but I want to say ... Clovis, I am your spiritual mother. I am the mother of Gaul, I ... no don't stop me, I ... must say this ..." There was a long pause. "Beware", she managed finally, "of pride. It is the most corrosive sin. Her breathing was growing rougher. "Do not", she croaked, brutally forcing her voice, "think of God as a source of ... power or a ... counterpower who may help you ... on this earth. Clovis..." Her hands still repelled the others' dancing, tentative impulses to advance and help her. Outstretched, palms forward, they might have been those of someone wondering how to swim or eager perhaps to test some new, quite unfamiliar element. "I willingly renounce," she said, "I ... will ... Clovis, remember always that we sacrificed the greatest—sacrificed oneness with God to try and ... help you. Clovis ... I, I..."

Her breath strangled. "Fortunatus!" she called. "Justina!" She fell forward into their arms.

Chapter Eighteen

Radegunda's body was being taken for burial to the church of St. Mary Outside the Walls. The bier was moving slowly, borne by clerics in vivid vestments. It was cold. Windless. Sunlight spattered piercingly from the metal cross at the head of the procession. Ceremonial order prevailed. The procession wound down among orchards which had only lately shed their blossom. Late-blooming pear-trees were still fluffed with white and, high on the convent walls, the community of nuns clustered: white too like a gathering of gulls.

Outside the basilica, lunatics and cripples had been waiting all night in the hope of a miracle. Excitement and a sense of their public had sent several into fits. At word of the procession's coming, these increased in extravagance. Disordered movements shook the patients' limbs. Heads rotated. Spines contracted, froze in concave arcs, then clapped forward in convulsive spasms.

Fortunatus, light-headed from worry and fatigue, had a momentary impression that all were dead and this place hell. The faces of the sick poor—dry as papyrus, grey as old sticks—had a raw animation alien to any faces he knew. Wens, warts, boils and nasal hair sprouted with fierce strength from skin no hand had touched with cosmetic intent. Nature surged here untrammelled and cankered with its own excess. Weakly anarchic, they disgusted and horrified him. Gauls or Franks, they were alike in that their minds had abandoned the struggle to quell their flesh. He drew away from them, reproved himself for his lack of charity and attempted to sustain the blistering, sucking stare of a woman holding a child out to within inches of his face. Obviously, she wanted him to touch it but it was deformed, had no fingers and smelled so terribly that he almost fainted before managing to get by. Another creature—how human were they?—had crawled forward between the legs of the crowd and managed to park herself on the edge of the path where the bier-bearers must pass. Suddenly, with a dog-like leap, she was up, touching and then clinging to the bier. She was pulled off, laughing then roaring that the devil within her was vanquished, must go, *was* going back to hell. "To hell," she yelled in the voice of the devil, a hectoring, furious, male voice. "I'm going back to the stink and pain!" It bellowed and spilled from her in globules of spit and sweat as though she were a boiling pot shedding the spirit within her in a steamy overflow. The voice cursed the saint, then the woman fell quiet and, moments later, in a thin, doubtful, reedy whine asked, "What happened? Where am I?" Bystanders reassured her. "You're delivered, Leuba! You're yourself again. The saint. . ." They were shouting "A miracle! A miracle!" as the procession moved away from them and in through the basilica portico.

Fortunatus turned to look back at the convent before going in. The nuns were still on top of their convent walls. His eye ranged over them, over the garden below where he had so often sat with Radegunda, down past further walls to the road which led out of the city. A group of white-clad figures moved along it, identical to the ones above. Nuns? Impossible. An optical delusion? He screwed up his eyes, trying to focus better. They did look like nuns. Perhaps two dozen of them. They couldn't be. How could they have got out? The abbess had the key to the only gate. The sun glowed. Perhaps it *was* a mirage? A reflection of the white figures above? He was holding the procession up. He turned and walked into the basilica.

By the time he came out again it was early evening. The sun shot oblique rays through a copse of young larches luminous as a cut lemon. Low-flying swallows portended rain, darting like shuttles through a warp of dusk. The ceremonies were over. Radegunda had been placed in a double sarcophagus, an old Roman one scraped and re-used. It would be scraped some more.

"Bishop Thaumastus's sarcophagus", a priest remarked to Fortunatus, "is perforated. Literally. They've scraped holes right through it. Like Vandals! They", he nodded to the crowds of pilgrims cooking and eating in the basilica atrium, "make medicines from the scrapings. They drink the stuff, gargle it, make poultices and fomentations. It's supposed to be sovereign against toothache and fever."

"And why not, why not?" A monk had overheard. "You're not doubting, I suppose, Father? You're not doubting our holy saint's powers?"

The priest shrugged. "Do you think, Brother, that all the people's beliefs are to be taken seriously?"

"Who said 'all'? But Bishop Thaumastus . . ."

"Is in your parish! He brings trade, pilgrims . . . I know."

Fortunatus moved off. He had not slept in days, had been keeping vigil before the body of Radegunda. Now his head was light. Words shot through it and refused to knit into coherence. He was tired, might well say something imprudent if he wasn't careful. He had, of necessity, pushed his anxiety to the back of his head but the vigil with its smoking lights, giddy-smelling herbs and endless gazing on the dead woman's face had reduced his mind to a kind of gentle frenzy, a waking dream. Parts of this had been nightmarish. At one point, the nuns had crowded into the dead woman's small room, filling the narrow stairway since only a few could actually squeeze inside and Fortunatus and others nearest the bed had had to hold hands and press backwards to try and keep from being precipitated onto the corpse. Later, the nuns had begun a wail which gathered momentum as they beat their breasts with clenched fists and stones which some had brought in for the purpose, calling out that they too wished to die so as to reach heaven under the guidance of the saint who had first assembled them here. Agnes and Fortunatus had been obliged to resort to physical force to quell the hysteria. The nuns had been sent off and told to get on with their regular tasks which were, or should have been, prayers in themselves. Only a few had been chosen to keep vigil. Among these was Chrodechilde, picked so that she might be under Fortunatus's eye. Justina had undertaken to keep watch on Basina.

Some time in the small hours of the second night while they were alone together by the dead woman's corpse, Chrodechilde had spoken to Fortunatus. About the succession. She wanted to be abbess. Now.

"I warn you," she had whispered. "I have suffered sufficient ill-treatment in this convent to justify anything. I warn you, Father Fortunatus, that you would do well to come to an agreement with me. I think you know why."

"How", he whispered, "can you talk like that in her presence?"

They were standing on opposite sides of the bier where the dead woman lay.

"I have waited", she answered him, "until now from respect for her. She was a holy woman and a queen but she did not know what was happening right here. ... I am warning you. I have discovered things which some might not like revealed in high places. I am of the royal blood. I can talk to my relatives and ..."

"Hold your tongue and pray."

"It was a friendly warning."

"Listen," he whispered. "We have put up with you until now from respect for her, but I swear that if you make one single move to disturb the peace of this convent which she worked all her life to build, if you lift a finger to disturb it, I will lay violent hands on you. Would you", he whispered through his teeth, "care to be the convent's third recluse? A reluctant one? To be walled up in a small cell? If it seemed necessary for the wellbeing of the rest of the community, I would not hesitate to advise the abbess to have this done—and I, Sister Chrodechilde, am the convent's spiritual adviser. Think about that and stop harping on your royal blood which is as cheap as the waste seed of your goatish relatives."

She had not replied. He saw a quiver in her undershot jaw, a pressure in her fists. It was open war now. God knew what she was meditating. He had been sick with anger against her and against himself for letting her provoke him into an outburst disgraceful in such a place and at such a time. The strength of his fury had astonished him. He had sometimes believed himself incapable of sustained feelings but lately they had been lodging in him as parasites will that slip under a man's skin so that they suck his blood and grow and can only be removed by surgery. There was the black private anguish which he had swept into the murky corners of his mind where it boiled and threatened to break out. There was his fear and now, flaming in him with the same sour vigour as it did in Chrodechilde, there was rage. Perhaps some of the energy which had been stored in Radegunda's body was seeping into his? He hoped it was not seeping into Chrodechilde too. He tried to calm himself by staring at the dead saint. Nobody questioned her sanctity now that she was dead. Her clothes were being preserved as relics. Her hair, nail-parings and even objects she had touched were being saved for distribution or put in reliquaries. Several minor miracles had happened within an hour of her death and news of others kept coming to the convent. Stone-cutters on a nearby hillside had heard angels arguing as to whether she should be restored to life to placate the grief of her wailing nuns.

"No," the angel carrying her soul upwards had been heard to reply. "It is all over now. We cannot bring her back. It is consummated. She is already in the Paradise of the Spirit. Her friends must not mourn. They must rejoice that she is at last with Him towards whom her soul was straining all the years of her life."

The stone-cutters claimed that they had heard the angels' dialogue coming from a low-flying cloud-formation which some of them described as chariot-shaped and others as like a boat.

293

Palladius was signalling to him.

"Let's walk back together."

"All right."

The two men had had no chance to speak since Radegunda's death. Palladius had officiated at her funeral as Bishop Maroveus was, by chance or design, absent from Poitiers. They walked in silence until they had left the basilica and its outbuildings behind. When they were in open country, Palladius said:

"The kings are cracking down on all prominent persons suspected of disloyalty. A purge. So far all affected have been laymen. The bishops' rôle is not known."

A cleric from Trèves who had come for the funeral had, however, brought fresh and disquieting news. Three of the conspirators had taken refuge with bishops. Sanctuary. There was nothing suspicious in this. But the sanctuary had not been respected. One of the men had seized Bishop Magneric of Trèves and, barricading him with himself in the church house, declared that he would hold the bishop hostage for his own life. The king, caring nothing for the bishop's safety, had set fire to the house and the clergy had had the greatest difficulty rescuing their leader.

"Which", said Palladius, "shows how the wind lies. That was an innocent bishop. Think what they would do to a guilty one!" The prince, he repeated urgently, must be got rid of. "Could you do the job?" he asked Fortunatus.

"What kind of a job?"

"Get him out of Gaul."

"And into heaven?" Fortunatus spoke with blunt and nervy heat. "If you've got another Rauching lined up somewhere you'd better say so. I won't be part of such a scheme."

Palladius touched him lightly on the shoulder. "Nor will you be asked to. Just get him to Marseilles, Fortunatus. There will be a boat waiting. It can carry him to Byzantium where all good pretenders go and grow. He'll be safe. We have connections there. He may even live to try another day."

"I'll think about it."

"You'll have to think fast."

"Yes."

They were inside the city wall now. They fell silent again, walking slowly, taking the wall when they passed people. Fortunatus held a crushed bay-leaf to his nose. He had taken it from the bier and was sniffing it to drown the stench rising from the open sewer which flowed with a stale, scummy slither down the middle of the road.

There was a message awaiting Fortunatus at his house. It was from Bishop Maroveus and urgent. Fortunatus was to come to him at once.

He found the bishop in an unusual state of agitation.

"What in God's name", he wanted to know, "is going on in that so-called convent?"

Chrodechilde, it appeared, had broken out during the funeral. A score of young nuns had followed her—it seemed they had managed to steal Agnes's key—and had presented themselves boldly at the bishop's house.

"There they were when I got back from my diocesan tour! Forty or so nuns from an enclosed order, having broken their vow of stability, sitting under my portico like so many trollops!"

"What did they say?" Fortunatus felt himself invaded by a despair which was curiously relaxing. He felt numb, cold and at the same time at rest for the first time in months. So it was all up then! Chrodechilde would have told what she knew. Maroveus would inform the kings. Wouldn't he? Of course he would. He hadn't been invited to join the conspiracy and now had a chance to prove his loyalty to the triumphant kings. Besides, he had never cared for Fortunatus or the convent. What a justification for him! Why didn't he get on with it then? Was he trying to torture Fortunatus by his delay, to play and torment him as one plays a fish? Curious that the torpor Fortunatus could feel in his own senses seemed to have seized the bishop too. He seemed to move like a man walking through water. His lips nibbled air and no sound came. "What did they say?" Fortunatus managed to repeat.

The bishop's answer took some moments to reach Fortunatus's understanding. When it did, it dispelled the numbness and brought back the itch of fear.

"Say!" the bishop had exploded. "You don't imagine I *listened*, do you? I told them I'd have them whipped through the town like public women, since that was how they were behaving, if they didn't get back inside their convent within half an hour."

"You *didn't listen* to *anything* they said?"

"Not a word, I ..."

"And did they go back to the convent?"

"That's what I want you to tell me!"

Maroveus was intending, it seemed, to take the convent in hand. He did not, however, want to be blamed for the mismanagement he expected to find there. He would not involve himself yet.

"I've never had dealings with them, as you know. Their choice, not mine. Their decision. I let them have their heads. If something's gone wrong it's no responsibility of mine. They *should* have been under my authority, of course, but Mother Radegunda claimed that St. Caesar's Rule carried an exemption from episcopal jurisdiction. A very questionable claim. Very. In St. Caesar's own diocese of Arles he could make what exemptions he liked but you can't export things like that. Mother Radegunda of course—well, she's dead. Better not speak ill of her. I hear she's credited already with as many miracles as St. Hilary?"

"She *was* a saintly woman."

"No doubt. No doubt. She was also a queen. Her successor isn't. I shall have to look into convent affairs more closely in future, but I want to know the lie of the land before I intervene. I am told there are factions? Very disagreeable. Two of those trollops say they are related to the kings?"

"They are."

"And it seems they are threatening to go lodge some

complaint with their royal relatives. *I* wouldn't listen but that's what they told my deacon. I should have had them locked up. Sorry I didn't now. I wanted to avoid a scandal, but if they head for one of the courts we'll have a worse one."

"You could", Fortunatus suggested anxiously, "send a party out to look for them. Mounted men would catch up with them easily in an hour or so."

"Because you don't think they went back to the convent?"

"I doubt it very much indeed, my lord bishop!"

Maroveus gave him an appraising look. "I think you'd better tell me what has been going on there," he commanded. "Frankly, Father Fortunatus, and in full. You, too," he thought fit to remind him, "will be working in closer association with me and my authority from now on."

"And so?" Bishop Palladius's toe, leatherclad and nervous, followed mosaic designs on the floor: interlocked squares which deceived the eye or perhaps were not regular. "What did you tell him?"

"The minimum. The necessary."

"A lie?"

"No. Too risky. An incomplete truth."

"What?"

"That the girl's dangerous, a bit mad, likely to create unsavoury scandals—as bad for him as for the convent. He *has* neglected his duties towards Holy Cross. The kings wouldn't like that. He didn't even attend Radegunda's funeral and she was a relative of theirs. They'd take it as a slight. He has to be careful. He asked me," Fortunatus paused in astonishment, "did I mean the girl was 'some sort of saint'?"

"Meaning that Radegunda ..."

"Was herself a bit mad? Precisely. Maroveus is oddly impervious to the spiritual. For a bishop ... Well ..."

"He intends to take things in hand?"

"Yes. He's sent out men to look for the runaway nuns.

297

He is ignoring Agnes. He should, normally, have consulted her. He may be thinking of supporting a change of abbess. A clean slate, you know."

"But Radegunda left a testament naming her."

"Yes. I don't think he could go against it. He will try to interfere more than he did though. The abbess, whoever she is, will be under his authority."

"The prince", said Palladius, "has to be gone when those nuns get back. All trace of him. Then Chrodechilde can say what she likes. We'll say she's mad. Malicious. You must leave tonight. I'll tell Maroveus you've gone on a mission for me."

"What mission?"

Palladius twitched his supple spine. "I'll think up something. You could have gone to receive a relic coming from Byzantium. Off a boat. At Marseilles. That way if you're seen . . ." He didn't bother to finish. "I'll lend you my own retainers. No time to find others. Besides, they're reliable. If Maroveus feels slighted I'll calm him down. He's going to need episcopal support when he starts trying to bring the convent under his rule. I'll promise mine. Quid pro quo."

Later, in the dark, Fortunatus, on his way to the prince's cottage, passed close beneath the stricken convent wall. A sour blast of kitchen air exhaled from a grating and assaulted his nose with fumes of woodsmoke, fat, soap, turning milk and burning oil. Two nuns were sitting at a window. Pale silhouettes, they were puffed, he could tell in the starlight, like a pair of anxious hens. Rustling. One held a bowl of something—nuts? Grain? She was whispering and eating and nudging her companion. Continuously: nudge, eat, whisper, nudge. The hand flew from bowl to mouth. The elbow pulsed and poked like a striving but ineffectual wing. Talk burst from her in vehement congested clots and although Fortunatus could not hear a word he had a fair idea of what was being discussed.

Chapter Nineteen

It was eight days since the fugitive nuns had left Holy A.D. Cross. It had rained. Mud foamed in every hollow and had 587 yellowed their woollen habits to the knee. Soiled below, white on top, they struggled across country, advancing with the gait of bedraggled and frightened fowl. They avoided main roads. Not daring to present themselves at inns, much less at the religious houses along the way, they had slept one night in a pile of hay, another in a shepherd's hut. Only in Tours, where it had been assumed that they were going to return to their convent, had they had decent lodgings. Once they had been lost for half a day while they tramped doubtfully back and forth through fields of soft mud. Later, they managed to get a boat down the Clain. Chrodechilde paid for their passage with a piece of cloth taken from the convent, but had not much left for bartering now. Bishop Maroveus of Poitiers had given them short shrift; Bishop Gregory of Tours shorter still.

"Which we might have expected!" Chrodechilde observed bitterly. "A friend of Fortunatus's! But we had to try. We tried the proper way first. That'll be remembered in our favour."

"What other way is there?"

"We'll find one."

The nuns wept from vexation, cold and fear. Their feet were blistered, their hands chilblained and several had had to throw away their broken shoes.

"Holy Christ, we were mad to follow you! Raving. Mad as poor Nantilde."

One nun had lost her mind. It had been a weak fluttering thing at best. Now it had flickered out. She became incontinent, subject to fits, and drooled and babbled. But they tolerated her. They *must* stick together. Chrodechilde had persuaded them of this.

"If we leave her and she's found, how long do you think it'll be before they find us? Besides, she might do anything! We'd be blamed. Best keep an eye on her."

By now the Counts of Tours and Poitiers must have set men on their trail. Bishop Gregory had threatened that they would be rounded up like cattle if they did not return to Holy Cross.

"You can bring whatever charges you have against your abbess before a properly set-up Ecclesiastical Court," he told them. "But until you return to your convent and obedience to your superiors, I won't listen to one word you say!"

But they were afraid to go back and as for appearing before an Ecclesiastical Court—who knew what penalties it might inflict on them? Their voices dropped, muttering in morose, horrified excitement. Thoughts of the soldiers who might be seeking them along the main roads both thrilled and appalled.

"What do they do to people like us?"

No one knew. They could speculate though. A nun who had lived in the royal palace as a child remembered how "One Ash Wednesday the bishop preached such a violent sermon against the sins of the flesh that it was decided all whores were to be whipped in the palace courtyard. The men who had lain with them were forced to hoist them on their shoulders. The women's skirts were thrown over their heads and they were whipped until they were as raw as butchered meat. I was six but I've never forgotten the sight."

"If you'd been more than six maybe they'd have had you up there too!"

"Whipping's the least we can expect. They might brand us with a hot iron!"

"They might immure us!"

"Cut out our tongues!"

"That's enough of that talk," said Chrodechilde. "We're on our way to the court of King Guntram who is uncle to Basina and myself. If we can reach him, he'll see we get justice. He'll protect us from the bishops. *He's* never been afraid of them."

"Well, why are we going south then? Isn't his court in Orléans?"

"Didn't you hear them say in Tours that he is staying on his estates near Avignon? Once we get to him, he'll load us with gifts and new clothes and see we are properly treated."

"But meanwhile we have to pass back through the Poitou! What if we're caught?"

"We're out of the Poitou now," said Chrodechilde who was not sure of this. In the last day or so things had leaped out of her control. It was as though she had started a precipitation, something like a mountain slide when all she had meant to do was to dislodge some small stones. In the first place she had not planned to leave the convent at all. She had tried to get the ear of the bishop who had come to officiate at Radegunda's funeral—a thing she had a perfect right to do by convent-Rule. In the case of grave infractions, an appeal, it stated, might be made to a bishop. And the infraction was certainly grave. Basina, on recognizing her brother in the convent garden, had realized that she must have seen him once or twice before dressed as a peasant woman. At the time she had dismissed the notion that the tenant seen delivering produce to one of the convent kitchens could possibly be her dead brother even though the resemblance was striking. Now she knew better. *He*—he had been unable to conceal his emotion—had recognized her.

"Why didn't he let you know before?" Chrodechilde had wondered. "Are you sure?" she insisted, being eager to establish this major irregularity as firmly as could be done.

Basina was sure. "What I think", she decided after considering half a dozen other explanations, "is that Clovis is having a love affair with some nun. That means he cares

301

for *her* safety more than he does for me! Oh," she had cried with vexation, "to think how I cried for him when I thought he was dead! I could hit myself. But maybe it's not that. Maybe there's some other reason? I can't think of one which would keep him from telling *me* he was alive though. Blood's blood. Who do you suppose is his paramour?"

"The abbess." Chrodechilde chose the most dramatic hypothesis.

"She's too old."

"Old meat is gamey! Anyway who else could make all the arrangements to have him hidden?"

That was what Chrodechilde had tried to tell Bishop Palladius.

He had pretended not to hear. Astoundingly, he had walked away. Chrodechilde had run after him and he had turned on her and hissed between his teeth:

"Sister, I advise you to keep your mouth shut if you value your own safety!" Seeing her astonishment, he had produced with speedy unction "Woe to her by whom scandal cometh! I say to you it were better that a millstone were hung about her neck and that she were drowned. Or", he leaned his face venomously into hers, "that her evil, babbling tongue were slit!" Suddenly, he put his forefinger and thumb into Chrodechilde's gaping mouth, caught her tongue and gave it a harsh little pinch. Then he turned, with a swish of purple silk, and sped off at top speed.

It was only then that Chrodechilde knew the matter was grave. Up to now she had been half playing a game, testing her luck, groping and guessing her way around a world in which she was not quite at home and whose rules she had not quite learned. There had always been something of a game in her opposition to Agnes. Always, she had expected that at some moment one or other would call 'pax' and come to an agreement. She had boasted that one day she might be abbess but clearly the boast had something theatrical to it—like the stigmata which she had persuaded the other novices to join her in faking when they were children. She was twenty-one now but her life had experienced no break. The events which shake a girl out of childhood had not come her way. Betrothal, marriage and motherhood were not for her. All she knew was the convent and life there was lived at one or more removes from reality. Brides of an invisible Bridegroom, the nuns wore white and wedding rings as little girls do when they play at being brides. Religious ritual prolonged childhood play. The convent was full of correspondences. Radegunda's burning Christ's initials on her flesh was more violent but of the same order as other rites aimed at finding sensory symbols for the secret rapture of the soul. Inner outer, hidden public: opposites called to each other and, as the nuns were assumed to be taken up by a perpetual inner dialogue with their Spouse, so their calendar was a succession of meaningful ceremonies, and their sacristy as brimful of props as a circus tent. Wednesday was Christ's birthday, Friday his death day but also—since paganism had not been forgotten—it was Venus's and Frigg's day and a bad day to start anything. When everything had as much meaning as this, doubt could not but arise as to whether anything had any meaning at all. Reality, Chrodechilde felt, was fugitive as a fish. She reached for it and it wriggled slick in her grasp. She played with words, but was never sure quite how serious they might be. "The abbess has a paramour," she hazarded, "there is something going on in this convent!" When she discovered that indeed there was, she could not cope. She tried to talk to Bishop Palladius and he threatened her. She turned to Bishop Maroveus and he refused to listen. Unable to let go now, she urged her following to make the trudging trip to Tours to see Bishop Gregory. Only when she got the same response from him did she begin to measure the cynicism of the world outside the convent: the world proper. In that unknown 'world' she had one asset: her blood. How good was it? She did not know but had to find out. She persuaded her following to turn back, after heading north to Tours, and head south for Avignon and King Guntram. Guiding themselves as best they could by the sun—since they were keeping off the roads—they were hoping to reach the Garonne and a boat.

"Chrodechilde! Water! A river! Look!"

"The Garonne!"

"Or the Dordogne!"

"Surely we passed that?"

"Rivers wind. This might be another loop of it."

"Pessimist! Death's head! God, I have a thorn in my foot. Someone help me get it out. Please."

"Holy St. Caesar, how hungry I am! Are we to beg or what when we reach a town? One where we'll be safe I mean?"

"I hear men! Hide! Quick!"

The nuns scattered. Most reached the cover of dense undergrowth. A few laggards plunged and crouched precariously inside a near-by hazel thicket. Moments later a boar hurtled past, belly to ground: a bristling streak of terror so close they could have touched it. It was followed so hard by dogs that one seized its hindleg as it passed the thicket. At once another—a bitch, as they were able to see in a moment—had the animal by the neck and then the whole pack were fastened into it and rolling like a tug-of-war team as the creature rushed and charged in its last, hopeless efforts to rid itself of its attackers. The stragglers among the dogs failed to gain any purchase for their jaws and raced about yelping and being trampled as the compact mass ebbed and heaved like a single multi-limbed creature. The nuns clutched each other.

"Holy Saints! It's coming in here!"

"Sushsh!"

"I've got blood on me! I'm bitten!"

"Shut your mouth, will you?"

But their shrieks had betrayed them before they realized that the pack of dogs had been followed by a pack of huntsmen. These, turning their attention from the dead boar, were now staring with interest at the thicket.

A fur-cloaked rider nudged his horse sideways towards the thicket and slowly thrust a long lance into the middle of it. The girls backed away from the weapon, pushing and toppling over onto each other. Chrodechilde, being in front, was pitched out of the bushes so that she landed on hands and knees almost under a horse's hooves. The horse's rider reined back, stared at her and began to laugh.

"Well by God we've come on odd game!" he told his companions. "Are there any more in there? Haul them out!" He jerked his chin towards the thicket. Several men had dismounted and were already probing the greenery which was soon a turmoil of shrieks and scratches, squirms and hisses, lunging and spitting like any moil of maddened cats.

Chrodechilde stood up, brushed her skirt and lifted her over-prominent jaw.

"I", she stated, "am the Princess Chrodechilde, daughter of the late King Charibert and a nun at Holy Cross convent in Poitiers. I am in search of sanctuary. Who are you?"

The rider looked amused. "I am Duke Childeric the Saxon and no respecter of rank or sex as you would know if you knew anything. No respecter either of trollops who make up fancy lies." He stared with curiosity at the women who were being dragged out of the bushes.

"I think they *are* nuns, my lord!" said a huntsman. "Maybe we'd better not make too free with them?" He nodded at a man who had lifted one of the nun's skirts and was sliding his hand along her thigh. The nun was in tears, wild-eyed and clearly too bewildered to try and defend herself.

Another man laughed. "What if they are nuns? Nuns aren't snails. They don't carry their cloister on their backs. Outside their convent they're fair game."

A third made an appreciative noise, smacking his lips together as the first one found and showed off the nun's crotch.

Childeric lifted a long-tailed whip, swirled it and

fetched the man assaulting the nun a smart cut on the cheek. "Enough of that," he said.

The man clapped his hand to his cheek. When he removed it, his fingers were dripping with blood.

Chrodechilde grasped Basina's elbow and propelled her towards Childeric. "If you're duke here," she told him, "you owe allegiance to King Chilperic's son. This is his daughter, Princess Basina."

The duke looked at her. "Basina?" he wondered. "Ah yes, Audovera's daughter. Yes. I remember the story. She was forced into a convent all right! I suppose you might be she. Well," he grinned, "you can't blame us for your reception. Who'd expect to find a herd of holy ladies hiding like conies in a thicket?"

He stared at Chrodechilde. "You needn't be so afraid," he mocked.

"We could not fight you," Chrodechilde told him contemptuously and her jaw rose like a weightless scales. "But you don't frighten us. In our convent there was as much bravery as you could know. Our foundress was the holy Radegunda who burned her flesh to the bone with live coals for Christ's love. Would any of your men do that?" She stared fiercely around her. "Why", she poked a disgusted toe at the boar's dismembered carcass, "did you not whip off your dogs? Can't you even discipline *them*?"

"We like to remind them what the chase is about lest they forget the function for which nature made them," Childeric's grin widened, "as happens to women in convents!" He roared with laughter and the men around him took up the roar. Through his laughter, the duke kept trying to outstare Chrodechilde. The nuns watching felt the two glances lock like fists. Chrodechilde's nostrils flared. Her eyes were pale, wide and steady. The duke stopped laughing. "Proud," he remarked. "Sinfully proud for a holy nun. Well, we may have interests in common. We'll have to look into that. If you'll forgive the impetuosity of my men just now and agree to ride one with each of them, we may just have enough horses to get you back to my villa. What do you say? You needn't be afraid. You said you were seeking sanctuary. My wife and her women are there. Will you come with me?" he asked Chrodechilde.

She scrutinized him, trying to understand what was behind the noisy challenge of these men and what value they put on her. It was Basina whose title had impressed the duke but it was herself he had invited to mount his horse.

"Yes," she said.

"What about the others?" he challenged her. "Will they follow?"

Again her chin jerked waywardly up with the movement of a restive mare's. "Do the limbs", she asked, "refuse to follow when the head commands?" Without a further look at her companions, she put a foot into the cupped hands of one of Childeric's men and swung herself up behind the duke.

"You thought the king was in *Avignon!*" Childeric had been drinking heavily through and since dinner. His thick diction and tangled thinking astounded the nuns who, having almost all entered the convent at the age of seven, had no experience of drunkenness. "Avignon!" he repeated and laughed stupidly. "So that's what they told you in Tours! What ignorant people! Avignon! Ha!" He drank some more wine and the nuns stared anxiously at his wife. But she too was drinking and seemed unconcerned. Her eyes were swimmy and she had a pleased, lazy smile on her face.

Childeric belched contentedly. "Andelot is where the kings are," he said. "Both of them. Not Avignon! Andelot! It's the other side of Gaul. This is the south-west and Andelot is in the north-east, see?" He made laborious marks on the table with his knife. "See what I mean?" He pulled at Chrodechilde's sleeve and gushed a blast of breath heavy with wine, garlic and coriander into her face. "The kings", he told her, "went there on very important business. They discovered a plot to oust them and they are meeting to sign a pact at Andelot. Yes," Childeric screwed his face up portentously and nodded it at Chrodechilde, "it's in the north! Beyond Dijon. Beyond Langres. It's in Austrasia. You'd never get there. There are mountains between here and there, forests, wolves, brigands, bears—and bishops." Childeric began to laugh. "Bishops are the worst of all, aren't they, little nunlets? Don't they make your holy hair stand on end, eh?"

"Did you say there was a plot?" Chrodechilde asked.

But Childeric had begun to sing an interminable Frankish song and took no notice of her. His wife had fallen sideways in her chair. Her eyes were closed, her mouth open and she was beginning to snore.

The next day, however, the duke was sober.

"Tell me about your convent," he asked Basina and Chrodechilde. "It's rich, isn't it? Radegunda was very rich. She got a lot of gifts I'm sure? Eh? Gold ornaments? Embroidered cloths? Jewelled chalices?"

"Yes."

"It's probably the richest convent in Gaul?"

"Yes," said Chrodechilde. "I think so."

"Hm!" said Childeric.

"Some of the others", Basina told Chrodechilde, "are likely to slip into sin if we don't leave here. At night the men ..." She lowered her voice and whispered. "The sin", she told her cousin, "will be on your soul."

"Mine? Why on mine? Why not on their own?"

"Can anyone blame a limb for acting as the head commands?"

"Oh, you're angry because I said that. But you know I didn't mean I commanded *you*! You know I think of you as my twin, my second self!"

"A two-headed body can hardly be well regulated. I'll not divide the guilt with you," Basina retorted. She stared angrily at her cousin. "I rue the day ..." she began.

"Sweetheart," coaxed Chrodechilde, "I know things will come right in the end. I have a secret weapon, a relic. Look." She lifted her outer tunic, opened her bodice and produced a small bag from between her breasts. It was tied with a string which she quickly unknotted. She emptied the bag into her palm."

Basina screamed. "God's blood! Where did you get that?"

"It's Radegunda's! I took it just before the bier left the convent. Nobody knows. The body was covered with bayleaves and herbs so nobody noticed what I'd done. It's the most powerful relic. I cut it off with a sharp knife from the kitchen while Fortunatus was out of the room and I was alone with the bier." Chrodechilde held up the sawed-off finger which was already darkening and had begun to dry out. She pressed it to her lips as Basina winced. "It's her right index finger," she whispered. "It'll bring me her power."

"When you get back," Childeric the Saxon told the nuns, "it will be thought that you are all whores."

The nuns, whom he had summoned, saying he had important news for them, were sitting in a row along his trestle table. Their hands were folded in front of them just as they had been used to folding them when listening to Radegunda or the abbess. Most of them were looking down. Childeric's wife was sitting beside him on the other side of the table. She kept casting quick glances at her husband then at the nuns or carrying a goblet to her mouth and holding it there as though to mask it.

"Tonight", Childeric said, "will be your third night under my roof. Now I, as my wife will tell you, have a very bad reputation throughout Gaul. My men are known to be scum: drunken, lecherous devil's spawn. Did you know that the devil's semen is said to be cold? I don't know whether these fellows' is. Maybe some of you could tell me?"

He gazed about with a great show of keenness. A

nun blushed. Chrodechilde glared furiously at her.

"I", said Childeric, "don't care what you've been up to. What I'm telling you is that you'll be taken for whores and bawds even if you're pure as the driven snow. *Seeming*, in these matters, is as bad as being. You might get the death penalty."

The nuns' eyes, which had been downcast, jumped to scrutinize his. He nodded at them. "Oh, indeed. Adultery and playing the harlot are punishable by death in almost all the law codes. Burgundians smother the adulterous woman in mire. Any Burgundians among you? No. Well, the Franks have similar provisions, I'm sure. I realize that you holy ladies come under Church jurisdiction and I'm not too well versed in Church law. I would imagine though that a nun who cuckolds her Divine Spouse is much the same as an adulteress. That's how I would expect churchmen to reason. But you needn't take my word for it. You'll have a chance to find out for yourselves before long. You disobeyed *three* bishops, did you say?"

Several nuns were now loudly sobbing. Childeric waited to let his words take effect, then leaned forward.

"I might be able to help you," he said and paused again. "Your case is desperate and desperate cases call for desperate remedies." Another pause, then he began to speak with urgency. "My proposal", he told them, "is this. Let me and my fellows come back to your convent with you, capture the abbess and her advisers and force them, at sword's point if necessary, to agree to whatever it is you want. I don't pretend to make head or tail of your woes." He was addressing himself now to Chrodechilde. "But we can get her to sign anything you want. Better still, if, as you say, the abbess has a paramour concealed in the convent, we can get the other nuns to tell us what they know. Then she will be completely in your power. You can force her to intercede for you with the bishops, force her even to give you her place if that is what you want."

The nuns were moaning like a funeral chorus. Chrode-childe jumped to her feet.

"Stop that!" she shouted to her nuns. "Why", she asked Childeric, "would you do this for us?"

He shrugged, grinned. "Sport," he suggested. "You could call it 'sport'! And the convent is rich. Maybe when you're abbess you will reward me? Maybe your royal relatives will? Or—I *could* pay myself!"

"No!" said Chrodechilde.

"Are you mad?" Basina had leaped from her bench and thrown herself like a wild cat on her cousin. Nails flailing, eyes stark, she lunged. Her fists closed on Chrodechilde's shoulders. "Has the devil taken your wit?" she screamed. "This is our one chance. Our last. You said yourself we have no hope of reaching the kings. Neither can we stay here without disgrace. You heard what he said, didn't you?" She turned to Childeric. "It's 'yes'," she told him. "Our answer is 'yes'. *They* all agree." She pointed at the other nuns. "Yes, yes and yes! Don't you?" she harangued the dejected women.

"Yes?"

"It's our only hope."

"May the saints defend us!"

"He'll tear the place apart!" Chrodechilde shouted. "He's a pirate, a cut-throat. He says it himself. You fool!" she slapped Basina's face and gave her a push which sent her down on her back. "We'll be in far worse trouble if we take up with him!" she screamed. "Can't you see that? Can't you?" she challenged the nuns. But they were hunched into themselves, too depressed to take any position on anything; timid and accustomed to being directed, they were waiting for someone to take control of their destinies this time too. Suddenly, Basina was on her feet again.

"*You* got us into this trouble," she yelled at Chrodechilde. "You've got to let him help us now!"

Cautiously, she dodged away from her cousin, keeping the trestle table between them.

"Have you any other plan?" challenged Basina. "Have you?" She kept circling away from her cousin, bent in her direction, challenging her with her words and stare but afraid to come too close. "Well?" she cried. "Have you."

"No," Chrodechilde admitted wearily. "I have no more plans."

A fine rain fell, darkening and cooling the air. The procession of riders moved briskly along the road between Bordeaux and Poitiers. The horse in front of Chrodechilde raised its tail, paused and dropped a shower of golden manure. Hot air billowed from his hindquarters and a sweetish, grassy smell reached her nostrils. Gold. A good omen. She was determined to take all omens henceforth as good. Even Basina's revolt—silly, tremulous Basina, who had never dared oppose her cousin before in anything —even that must be a nod from Fate, a kind of humorous wink meant to remind Chrodechilde that help could come from the oddest quarters. She had scrupled to accept it from Childeric. Basina, the weakest of mousy cowards, had managed to force her into accepting it. All right then. That was a sign, a sign that Chrodechilde was meant, by hook or crook, to be abbess.

A small hard object pressed and pained her inner arm when she tightened her grasp on the reins: Radegunda's finger which she had inserted into a slit in the flesh just above her elbow. She had cut a deep flesh wound, buried the finger in it and, closing the lips of the wound, strapped a swathe of linen round her arm to hold it until it should heal. It would bring her force. Like it or not, some of the dead saint's power and virtue was now imprisoned in Chrodechilde's body. She was determined to use it well. She would manage somehow to restrain Childeric and his men. She had no doubts about their intention which must be to rob the convent. But perhaps she could buy them off? Offer them some of the convent's wealth in return for a promise not to pillage? They were uncomfortable allies but having found even such allies as they was so near miraculous that she felt confident that her luck must hold. Experimentally, she pressed her wounded arm to her ribs and felt the hard, painful, thrilling pressure of the relic. Yes, she *would* be a great abbess. She would be as energetic as Radegunda had been but *she* would direct her energies into administration. She would keep a tighter rein on the male monastery founded by Radegunda at Tours and on the basilica of St. Mary's Outside the Walls, both of which had hitherto been allowed to run themselves. She would be an administrator, judge and planner worthy of her kingly ancestry. She would preach sermons, too, and make sure that the convent was run properly as it had not been up to now. She would be famous—not as Radegunda had been but in another way. She would not give herself up to private communings with God but to establishing a great institution. Noble young women from all Gaul would come there to seek a haven from the savage world of Childeric and his kind. Chrodechilde's breath swelled excitedly in her chest as she thought about all this. Excitedly, she tapped the horse's sides with her heel and it bounded forward. She tightened her reins and the horse began to dance angrily.

Childeric the Saxon looked back over his shoulder and laughed at her.

"You're giving contradictory signals," he warned. "Look out or your horse will throw you."

Chapter Twenty

Agnes was awoken by a shriek then briefly sucked back into dream. Ingunda was screaming. Her face hung, bloated, on dark waters like a weed-anchored lily. Rotting. Another shriek. In the dissolving dream, Agnes started to knock the wall down stone by stone, then woke up and climbed on her bed to stare out the dormitory window. Lights were moving below in the cloister. Other nuns had been roused.

"What's happening?"

"Is it time for the office?"

"Sh! I think the convent has been broken into?"

"Who . . ?"

"Shh!"

"Could it be Chrodechilde and the others come back? They had a key."

"*They* wouldn't use lights .... Did you hear that? A *man*!"

"We'll take sanctuary in the chapel."

Down the dark, turning staircase, groping as they groped every night, recognizing irregularities in the plaster as they always had when making their way down for the nocturnal offices which were chanted while the mind half slept.

Justina and the nuns from her dormitory were in the chapel before them. They had come through a passage which gave onto the cloister and overheard the invaders as they passed.

"Roaring", whispered an agitated Justina, "at the top of their voices. Drunk. Making no effort to be quiet. There must be hordes of them. They're Childeric the Saxon's men from south of the Garonne. They've come to rob—and", she told Agnes, "to kidnap *you*. We heard them say it. Several of us. They were sent", Justina's teeth were chattering, "to capture the abbess. By Chrode-childe! ... Yes. I'm sure. Sister Gunsildis heard it too. And Gerberga. Didn't you, Gerberga? She did. Listen, you must hide." She caught Agnes's elbow. "No time for talk," she told her. "Come ..."

Agnes hung back. "I shall never ..." Her mind rattled like a broken weathercock. Had she heard that shriek— Ingunda's shriek—really this time? She lurched towards the cloister. Several hands caught her.

"You must!"

"For the sake of the convent, Mother Agnes."

"There's no reasoning with ruffians like that."

Bodily, they propelled her up the nave, past the cancelli and into the presbyterium. The curtains of the ciborium were drawn. Inside, beneath its canopy, was the altar on which a single oil lamp burned. The opaque folds of the altar-cloth formed a smaller tent inside the larger one and it was under here that Justina insisted on bestowing Agnes.

"This is no time for argument, Mother Agnes. You *must* hide. It's your duty to us all. I'll say I'm abbess. They'll want to be out of here by daylight. By the time they discover they've got the wrong woman it will be too late to come back. I doubt if they'd risk a return before nightfall. As soon as it's morning, you can get help." Justina turned to the rest of the nuns. "Get back to the nave," she told them. "Sing and keep your eyes off the altar."

On hands and knees, enclosed in a space not much bigger than Radegunda's sepulchre, Agnes crouched, doglike, and heard men burst into the chapel. The nuns' singing wavered, stopped, took up again, then dwindled off. Agnes heard shouts, metal clashing and a nun's voice— Justina's—shriek that her sleeve had been slashed and she had nearly lost a hand. Then a male shout. Then Justina—firm-voiced now—demanded the invaders' names and mission. There was no need, she pointed out,

315

for violence since the nuns were defenceless. She, she stated, was the abbess here, Mother Agnes.

A nun shrieked: "They're tearing off her clothes!"

A man bellowed that the nuns should shut their mouths. Another that he would slit Justina's throat if she or anyone moved a finger.

"Just like you'd wring a chicken's neck, holy lady! I'll wring yours the same way if you give trouble. Remember how one kills chickens, do you? Chuck, chuck, eeek! Well, keep thinking of it. I'm damned already so I've nothing to lose."

"So this", roared another, "is the randy abbess? Where's her paramour? Skedaddled? Maybe she'd like a stand-in? A ready cock?"

The noises grew unrecognizable. Agnes guessed at acts which made her stuff a corner of her skirt into her mouth to keep from crying out. She clenched her teeth on it and a flavour of fatty, unbleached yarn trickled down her throat until she needed to cough. She managed not to but her body heaved with dry spasms. Nobody came near the altar.

Briefly the nuns began singing once more and were told to stop. A man asked where the gold ornaments were kept but did not wait for a reply.

"We'll find them easily enough ourselves!"

Someone shouted an order. The nuns were to be locked up in one of the towers. More clanks, then silence. The chapel was empty. Time passed. Agnes's joints had begun to ache. Lights seemed to flash before her eyes but she judged them to be imaginary. The heavy altar-cloth reached to the ground all around her and she did not dare lift it. She strained her ears, wondering did she hear sounds and from where. They seemed to be coming from the kitchens. The men must be eating. Drinking, too, for she heard steps make for the wine cellars. She moved her limbs with caution, feeling as though they must crack, lifted a hair's breadth of the altar-cloth and saw a stretch of grey and later of yellow light. Day. But the noises

316

persisted. The men had not left, as Justina had expected, before dawn. Now, they would wait until dark returned. Were any visits due from friends of the convent today? She racked her memory but could think of none. Fortunatus was on his way to Marseilles. Palladius had gone back to Saintes and Bishop Maroveus was avoiding the place. But surely the townspeople would notice the silence of the bells and guess something was up? The steward too was away on a journey—but mightn't some of the convent tenants notice what was happening and give the alarm? Was Chrodechilde mad? Stark out of her mind? How could she hope to get away with such sacrilege? Without punishment? Mad. Yes, perhaps she was. Agnes could not now be sure the sounds she heard coming from different parts of the convent were not in fact within her own head. She shook it vigorously in an effort to rouse herself for she was numb with cramp and cold. But she could still hear the same noises: dim and teasing like those heard in dreams. But they were real enough, only muffled now since it was day and the invaders would be leery of being heard by passers-by outside the convent walls. Oh God, let them be heard! Let someone inform the count or Bishop Maroveus. Please, please God ...

Suddenly, kneeling numbly in the ignominy of all fours, a thought struck her like a blow: earlier, a soldier had shouted something about the 'randy abbess'. What could he have meant? Surely he ... How? No, it must, could only be a chance word from a foul-mouthed thug? Unless God had put that word into his mouth? And for God there was no chance. For God there were slow, unfolding patterns, unpardoning scrolls of which the living only saw a measured stretch. These thugs could be his punishing instrument, this invasion a penalty for Agnes's sin. She had never welcomed religion's bleak arithmetic any more than she had looked for its disembodying flights. But now, here, caged under the marble altar-slab like an answer under the line of a sum, God's book-keeping began to look inescapable. She should have prayed but suddenly couldn't. The guilt to be repented was too old, dead and detached from herself: like cut nail-parings. Was her conscience dead then? Gone insensible as her breasts had after the infant, Ingunda, had been taken from her and her milk dried up? They had been her most sensitive bodily organs and had lost all sensation so that now she could twist or pinch them and feel as little as if she were twisting the ends of her hair. Ingunda, she thought. The name shot giddily through her mind. Was the girl to be punished too? Had she perhaps already been hurt? How could the men have found her? But there *had* been a shriek? Then again, she sometimes shrieked for no reason —or for some reason private to her dark loneliness.

It was evening and pink reflections were falling on the mosaic floor where emblematic animals—peacocks, fish— were framed in squares scarcely smaller than her own hiding-place, when the chapel door was once again flung open. Agnes dropped the hem of the altar-cloth. Feet tramped up the nave and this time right to the altar. A man leaned on it and his toe intruded into the space where she was crouched. It landed on her skirt, pinning it so tautly that she could not move. If the foot were to come a thumb's breadth closer it must touch her body and discover her. Hampered and muffled by the intervening altar-valance, the toe's snout probed and menaced.

"What about taking this cloth?" a voice wondered. "It's fine heavy linen."

"Are you thick? This is no farmhouse. It's *rich*! Full of gold! We can't carry the lot, so leave the trumpery and take only the best!"

"Well, then, what about this cross here? Solid gold. Is that choice enough for you?"

"Too conspicuous. Anyone can tell it's church property. It's too big, too—hard to break up. Come on. There'll be better stuff in the sacristy. Gold cups. More negotiable..."

The foot withdrew. Agnes fainted.

When she recovered it was pitch dark. Night again and the altar-lamp had been allowed to go out. Had the men left? She listened for a long while, heard nothing and eased herself out from under the altar. Hobbling with difficulty, for she had a cramp, she groped her way out of the chapel and into the cold, starlit cloister. Before she knew it she was at Ingunda's slit. She listened. The girl's breath was rougher, louder and more uneven than usual. It could have been the wall itself breathing.

"Ingunda," Agnes whispered.

A scream burst shockingly from the wall: "Wa-a-ater!"

"Shsh!" Agnes felt as though the breath had been knocked from her own body. She gasped for air, listened, heard nothing. Were the nuns still locked up then? And the men? "Shsh!" she repeated. "For God's sake, be quiet. I'll get you water."

She moved cautiously into the bright middle of the cloister. No sounds. She managed to reach the well and draw water from it without making more than a few faint, rustling noises, paused, ladled some liquid silently down the side of the pitcher which was kept there, and carried it back to the shadow. The girl's water-pouch was dust-dry. Even before the invasion, the sister in charge of her rations must have forgotten to fill it. But maybe that sister was one of the renegades? No, their duties had been reapportioned. But, undeniably, order at Holy Cross was breaking down. She slid the the filled pouch into the slit.

"Ingunda," she whispered, "this is Agnes. You *must* be more quiet. It's dangerous to scream. I haven't time to explain, but . . . do you understand me, Ingunda?"

Silence. But the breathing had grown quicker. Feverish wall. Who had said 'Priests, not stones, are the foundation of the Church'? Ah, Justina.

"Ingunda. You have been screaming, haven't you? You realize that, don't you? Are you feverish, Ingunda?"

Again she waited. Then: "I absolve you from your vow of silence. Answer me, Ingunda. This is the abbess."

"Demoness!" It was a rasping crumble of sound.

"Ingunda . . ."

"Tonight demons are abroad. They try the righteous."

Agnes tried to sound matter-of-fact. "Yes," she agreed. "The convent has been broken into. But by men, Ingunda, men, not by demons. You mustn't let them hear you. They're dangerous. I think they've gone for the moment. But they may come back. So please, Ingunda, be quiet."

The breathing in the wall was almost a rattle. She's ill, thought Agnes, and remembered Fortunatus's plan to get the girl out. Had she time to do it now? Could she? She tried to rock the stone immediately below the slit but it was firm. She'd need help. Some of the younger nuns were strong. Besides, she should release them. She ran quietly over to the tower where she had heard the men say they were going to imprison them. The door was nailed up. She would need some sort of a lever to remove the boards which had been nailed across it. She walked back into the cloister and was making for the kitchens when she heard sounds at the outer gate. Her way was cut off. She backed into a leafy thicket which rose next to the well. By daylight, it might not have hidden her, but in the darkness she would be safe enough. After her day's terrified hiding, Agnes was beginning to develop the selective listening-techniques of a blind woman. She sensed the men's arrival in the cloister before she heard them. They were being more cautious than last night. There were only two or three of them and they had taken off their shoes. A mule brayed and a man cursed softly.

"Tie him up here. Give the bastard some hay or something. Where's that barrel of pitch? Roll it over near the well. No, keep it away from those bushes. We don't want to burn the convent down. And keep the loot at a safe distant. Right? Set a light to it then."

"Keep that mule quiet, can't you?"

There was a spark, then a flare as the pitch barrel took fire. Agnes pressed deeper into her bushes for the flames were so close that a spark fell on her and the middle of the cloister was suddenly as bright as day. The men, too, seemed dazzled for a moment. There were four of them, she saw now, and two mules. Agnes recognized the animals as convent property. Bags had been tossed across their backs and two of the men had started loading them with gold cups.

"Hey Droctulf, why not flatten these? They'd take up less room. We'll be selling them for the gold anyhow. They're no good this way: all covered with crosses and Latin. Might as well have the word 'stolen' all over them. We can do it quietly. Wrap the mallet in cloth."

A straw-haired fellow had been standing all this time beside Ingunda's slit. "Hey, let up a minute, will you?" he called to his mates. "I hear something. In this wall."

The one addressed as Droctulf made a smart reply but stopped hammering. The straw-head raised a hand and leaned his head towards the slit.

"Anyone in there?" he called.

Agnes felt her body freeze. There was a thundering in her ears and she heard—did she *hear*?—Ingunda's voice. Yes. Yes, the voice was coming from there. It was lilting. "Dung," Ingunda chanted, "Ding, dong, dung. No bells today. I expiate my mother's sin. What's that light? The demons are come. Their eyes are red. Shitty fingers are bright too. Pearl-and diamond bright. I am rich and I can pay. Pay the demons for my mother's sin. Come, demons, I can pay. I am Mother Agnes's bastard. I have rings on my fingers ..."

The straw-headed man thrust his scramasax into the slit. There was a cry.

"What's in there?"

Droctulf and the other two had joined the first man. Jostling they tried to peer into the slit. One ran back to the pitch barrel, took a hold of a burning piece of wood and returned holding it aloft. He tried to cast its light in through the slit.

"No good," said the pale-haired man. "It's deep and it's at an angle. I didn't hit anything either. The scramasax won't reach."

"There might be treasure in there. Those nuns are crafty."

"We'll see about that."

They began to dislodge the stones in the wall, poking at the mortar with the handles of their swords, then levering out the stones with a bar which seemed to have been lying with the rest of the loot. No more sounds came from the hole. Agnes wanted to scream at them to go gently but her mouth seemed to have gone numb. Her mind however was racing like a trapped mouse. Maybe they're demons, she thought. Maybe they are, I don't care who they are if only they free her. Free her gently, gently," her brain screamed at them but her tongue bulged like a piece of dead matter in her mouth and her jaws were locked. "I'll pray to you," her brain told the men. "To you."

When the hole was wide enough, one of the men stepped through it. His companion held up the torch. Agnes had crept heedlessly out of her thicket and was only a few paces behind them but they were all staring at the hole and didn't see her.

"Well, what's in there?"

"Shit mostly. It's a small place. There's a woman here —or a child. I can't tell. She's in a bad way. Here. Catch."

The man held up an armful of bones and tatters, a limp, live creature whose breath kept coming more and more loudly, wheezing and rasping and thudding through the cloister with such astonishing volume that it seemed to be the breath of the whole building or to be a freak organ, a heart which had grown while the body around it had shrunk into a mere receptacle or casing for this vigorous, beating pulse. Agnes glimpsed a pair of dazzled eyes but there was nothing individual about them and she wouldn't have known them. She herself was standing right behind the men now. She stretched a hand between two of their bodies to touch the area around the two light-mirroring orbs. The men were too absorbed to notice. She reached Ingunda's hair—it was dry and thorning—and one of the men pushed her hand blindly aside without wondering where it came from.

"Are you sure that's all that's there?" he asked, taking

322

the wheezing bundle from his companion and leaning so heavily across it that Agnes could hear Ingunda's breath being crushed. The man craned towards the hole. Agnes put a hand between his heavy body and the frail burden which he was about to flatten. She poked his belly with her elbow and he leaped backwards, dropped Ingunda and, involuntarily, kicked her cranium with his heavy boot.

"The devil," he cursed in surprise, "I've cracked its skull." He backed away, staring at the fragile creature at his feet. Blood was pouring through the sparse hair. "As well finish it off," he remarked and bashed it in with a flat blow of his scramasax. There was a sound of bone being crushed. "Queer looking, isn't it?" he said as he cleaned the short sword on his tunic. "Hadn't much life in it, I'd ..." Then he saw Agnes. "What .."

Before he could say more, she had snatched the scramasax from his limp hand and plunged it at his lower belly. He howled and doubled up. The man beside him swung round, saw her holding the weapon and raised his own.

"Stop him!"

Chrodechilde and Childeric stepped into the light. "Don't let them touch her," shouted Chrodechilde." Save her. It's the abbess."

Childeric was holding the man's raised arm. "Easy," he soothed.

"You're all animals!" Chrodechilde was shaking. "Oh Christ! You've killed her. Killed the recluse. Look: Oh Jesus, God!" She shook and swayed in a lament that spilled from her like blood or vomit or some overflowing humour. "Oh Holy God, what have I done? It's my sin! Mine," she spurted. Her undershot jaw gnawed the air. Her tongue got in the way and the words fell out like clots of wet, angry matter. "Did you hear, did you? The recluse was her child! Hers. You've killed her, you'll have no luck. We'll all be damned. Damned! We'll burn!" She screamed at Childeric. "Your men are devils!" Her mouth wobbled and a spray of white spittle foamed out of it and across the face of the man whose weapon arm was still frozen in mid-air.

The man jerked angrily and Childeric, who was still holding him, pulled him backwards. The man Agnes had wounded was still bent over, holding himself and groaning.

"She's castrated him!" shouted the fair-haired man. "Let's kill the bitch. Both of them!" He glared furiously at Chrodechilde. "They're mad," he said, "mad, bloody women!"

"Leave them alone!" Childeric turned to Chrodechilde. "I thought you wanted to be abbess yourself?" he said. "Didn't you? Well, now you've got her where you want her. When the bishops hear she had a child . . ."

"I was wrong!" Chrodechilde flung herself on her knees and began to embrace Agnes's. "Forgive me," she whimpered. "Punish me. You're my abbess."

Agnes stood rigid, dry and dead-eyed. She took no notice of Chrodechilde and did not even look at the broken-skulled bundle which had been Ingunda. She waited until Chrodechilde's outburst had dwindled into a sobbing mumble then said dully. "I am not your abbess. You can take over now. You or . . . another." She stepped carefully around the two bodies twisted on the ground and walked towards the hole in the wall. "I shall go in here," she said. "I shall take her place in the wall."

Fortunatus and the prince rode south. For the first two nights Fortunatus had not slept fearing that the bravoes supplied by Palladius might have orders to kill one or both of them. But they had reached Saintes, Bordeaux, Agen, Toulouse and crossed over into the territory of the Goths without any attempt being made on his or Clovis's life. The bravoes had become familiar by now. He knew their names, listened to their talk and had grown to trust them. This might be foolish but he could not believe that it was. Reaching the south his spirits rose and when they got to the sea, the southern sea which recalled his youth in Rimini, he had a feeling for a moment that he was young again and emerging from a long passage underground and into the sunlight. He saw it first on a hot morning at the bottom of a sloping field of thyme and lavender, swelling and bellying like a great scaly reptile toasting itself in the sun. A breeze moved the leaves from green to silver. The sea-scales shifted. Crickets made a sound tiny and busy enough to fit the surface quiver of the visible landscape. Fortunatus struck Clovis on the shoulder.

"Look, you Frank!" he shouted. "Here is a country which should sooth even your boiling and spoiling for fights!"

"You wouldn't want me soothed *now*, would you?" laughed the prince.

The boy thought he was being brought to join an army of supporters who would help him gain the crowns of Gaul. He treated the armed escort as his first henchmen, looked on them with emotion and had confided to Fortunatus that he intended to find a good position in his armies for their leader. Poor deluded wretch! Whose fault? Fortunatus sloughed off the discomfort he felt every time the boy talked of his hopes.

"Don't talk about that!" he said, frowning.

Clovis took on a look of discretion and responsibility. His mouth twitched with joy.

"Oh the devil!" roared Fortunatus and turned his horse down the slope to the sea. He drove it into the waters until they were delicately nibbling at his heel. The boy would have to sail for Byzantium. There was no help for it. He would be told, on boarding the ship, that it was taking him to join the bulk of his army at some likely port, then, once at sea, he would be told the truth. Not by Fortunatus. Fortunatus would be on his way back to Poitiers where he would wait for a bishopric to fall vacant. As they hadn't killed him, they must reward him. There were only two ways to treat a dangerous man. A man who had been dangerous. A man eager for retreat. Fortunatus bent over his horse's neck, caught a scoop of sea water and splashed his face with it. Life would be quiet now, he thought as he straightened up. Agnes would be supreme at

Holy Cross. She could release Ingunda as she wanted. The matter of the renegade nuns would be easily settled. Bishops Gregory and Palladius would see to that. Radegunda's white-hot spirit had dissolved and lost itself in the light of the godhead. She was gone, lost like one of those long-tailed falling stars which appear from time to time, inexplicably burning the air around them, then finally fall and bury themselves leaving a crater where they sink: a space, a hole, a nothingness, thought Fortunatus, looking with a needle-thrust of melancholy at Clovis. At best an afterglow in a few memories.

"Race you up the slope!" he challenged and prodded his horse to a gallop with a quick-tapping heel.

"You cheated!" shouted Clovis, taken by surprise.

While the kings were still in conference at Andelot, news reached them that the convent of their holy kinswoman, Radegunda, was without an abbess. The foundress herself had but lately thrown off her fleshly body to enter the heavenly kingdom and her spiritual daughter, the Abbess Agnes, had been moved by grief to become an anchoress. Being filled with solicitude for the nuns thus doubly orphaned at a single stroke, they sent pressing directions to Maroveus, Bishop of Poitiers, recommending that he choose as abbess a young nun, wise beyond her years, the fame of whose piety and probity had already reached across Gaul. This was Chrodechilde, a kinswoman of their own whose virtue was as noble as her lineage. This was done and Chrodechilde proved a worthy successor to the holy Radegunda for she ruled with zeal and perseverance showing as much energy in punishing the wicked as she did modesty in consoling the weak.

Some years later, Maroveus, being old and full of days, died and was succeeded as bishop by the poet, Fortunatus."
Annals of Holy Cross Convent

VIRAGO MODERN CLASSICS

The first Virago Modern Classic, *Frost in May* by Antonia White, was published in 1978. It launched a list dedicated to the celebration of women writers and to the rediscovery and reprinting of their works. Its aim was, and is, to demonstrate the existence of a female tradition in fiction which is both enriching and enjoyable. The Leavisite notion of the 'Great Tradition', and the narrow, academic definition of a 'classic', has meant the neglect of a large number of interesting secondary works of fiction. In calling the series 'Modern Classics' we do not necessarily mean 'great' — although this is often the case. Published with new critical and biographical introductions, books are chosen for many reasons: sometimes for their importance in literary history; sometimes because they illuminate particular aspects of womens' lives, both personal and public. They may be classics of comedy or storytelling; their interest can be historical, feminist, political or literary.

Initially the Virago Modern Classics concentrated on English novels and short stories published in the early decades of this century. As the series has grown it has broadened to include works of fiction from different centuries, different countries, cultures and literary traditions. In 1984 the Victorian Classics were launched; there are separate lists of Irish, Scottish, European, American, Australian and other English speaking countries; there are books written by Black women, by Catholic and Jewish women, and a few relevant novels by men. There is, too, a companion series of Non-Fiction Classics constituting biography, autobiography, travel, journalism, essays, poetry, letters and diaries.

By the end of 1986 over 250 titles will have been published in these two series, many of which have been suggested by our readers.

Also of interest

THE LOVE CHILD
by Edith Olivier
New Introduction by Hermione Lee

At thirty-two, her mother dead, Agatha Bodenham finds herself quite alone. She summons back to life the only friend she ever knew, Clarissa, the dream companion of her childhood. At first Clarissa comes by night, and then by day, gathering substance in the warmth of Agatha's obsessive love until it seems that others too can see her. See, but not touch, for Agatha has made her love child for herself. No man may approach this creature of perfect beauty, and if he does, she who summoned her can spirit her away...

Edith Olivier (1879?-1948) was one of the youngest of a clergyman's family of ten children. Despite early ambitions to become an actress, she led a conventional life within twenty miles of her childhood home, the Rectory at Wilton, Wiltshire. But she wrote five highly original novels as well as works of non-fiction, and her 'circle' included Rex Whistler (who illustrated her books), David Cecil, Siegfried Sassoon and Osbert Sitwell. *The Love Child* (1927) was her first novel, acknowledged as a minor masterpiece: a perfectly imagined fable and a moving and perceptive portrayal of unfulfilled maternal love.

"This is wonderful..." — *Cecil Beaton*

"*The Love Child* seems to me to stand in a category of its own creating...the image it leaves is that of a tranquil star" — *Anne Douglas Sedgwick*

"Flawless — the best 'first' book I have ever read...perfect" — *Sir Henry Newbolt*

"A masterpiece of its kind" — *Lord David Cecil*

THE SHUTTER OF SNOW

by Emily Holmes Coleman
New Introduction by Carmen Callil and Mary Siepmann

After the birth of her child Marthe Gail spends two months in an insane asylum with the fixed idea that she is God. Marthe, something between Ophelia, Emily Dickinson and Lucille Ball, transports us into that strange country of terror and ecstasy we call madness. In this twilit country the doctors, nurses, the other inmates and the mad vision of her insane mind are revealed with piercing insight and with immense verbal facility.

Emily Coleman (1899-1974) was born in California and, like Marthe, went mad after the birth of her son in 1924. Witty, eccentric and ebullient, she lived in Paris in the 1920s as one of the *transition* writers, close friend of Peggy Guggenheim and Djuna Barnes (who said Emily would be marvellous company slightly stunned). In the 1930s she lived in London (in the French, the Wheatsheaf, the Fitzroy), where her friends numbered Dylan Thomas, T.S. Eliot, Humphrey Jennings and George Barker. Emily Coleman wrote poetry throughout her life — and this one beautiful, poignant novel (first published in 1930), which though constantly misunderstood, has always had a passionate body of admirers — Edwin Muir, David Gascoyne and Antonia White to name a few.

"A very striking triumph of imagination and technique... The book is not only quite unique; it is also a work of genuine literary inspiration" — *Edwin Muir*

"A work which has stirred me deeply...compelling" — *Harold Nicolson*

"An extraordinary, visionary book, written out of those edges where madness and poetry meet" — *Fay Weldon*

PLAGUED BY THE NIGHTINGALE
by Kay Boyle
New preface by the author

When the American girl Bridget marries the Frenchman
Nicolas, she goes to live with his wealthy family in their
Breton village. This close-knit family love each other to the
exclusion of the outside world. But it is a love that festers,
for the family is tainted with an inherited bone disease and
Bridget discovers, as she faces the Old World with the
courage of the New, that plague can also infect the soul...

Kay Boyle was born in Minnesota in 1902. The first of her
three marriages was to a Frenchman and she moved to
Paris in the 1920s where, as one of that legendary group of
American expatriates and contributor to *transition*, she
knew Joyce, Pound, Hemingway, the Fitzgeralds, Djuna
Barnes and Gertrude Stein: a world she recorded in *Being
Geniuses Together*. After a spell living in the bizarre
commune run by Isadora Duncan's brother, she returned
to America in 1941 where she still lives. A distinguished
novelist, poet and short-story writer, she was acclaimed by
Katherine Anne Porter for her "fighting spirit, freshness of
feeling." *Plagued by the Nightingale* was first published in
1931. In subtle, rich and varied prose Kay Boyle echoes
Henry James in a novel at once lyrical, delicate and
shocking.

"A series of brilliant, light-laden pictures, lucid, delightful;
highly original" — *Observer*

"In delicate, satirical vignettes Miss Boyle has enshrined a
French middle-class family...The lines of the picture have
an incisiveness and a bloom which suggest silverpoint"—
Guardian

Other VIRAGO MODERN CLASSICS

ELIZABETH von ARNIM
Fräulein Schmidt & Mr Anstruther
Vera

EMILY EDEN
The Semi-Attached Couple &
   The Semi-Detached House

MILES FRANKLIN
My Brilliant Career
My Career Goes Bung

GEORGE GISSING
The Odd Women

ELLEN GLASGOW
The Sheltered Life
Virginia

SARAH GRAND
The Beth Book

RADCLYFFE HALL
The Well of Loneliness
The Unlit Lamp

WINIFRED HOLTBY
Anderby Wold
The Crowded Street
The Land of Green Ginger
Mandoa, Mandoa!

MARGARET KENNEDY
The Constant Nymph
The Ladies of Lyndon
Together and Apart

ROSAMOND LEHMANN
The Ballad and the Source
The Gipsy's Baby
Invitation to the Waltz
A Note in Music
A Sea-Grape Tree
The Weather in the Streets

F. M. MAYOR
The Third Miss Symons

GEORGE MEREDITH
Diana of the Crossways

EDITH OLIVIER
The Love Child

CHARLOTTE PERKINS
   GILMAN
The Yellow Wallpaper

DOROTHY RICHARDSON
Pilgrimage (4 volumes)

HENRY HANDEL
   RICHARDSON
The Getting of Wisdom
Maurice Guest

BERNARD SHAW
An Unsocial Socialist

MAY SINCLAIR
Life and Death of Harriett Frean
Mary Olivier
The Three Sisters

F. TENNYSON JESSE
A Pin to See The Peepshow
The Lacquer Lady
Moonraker

VIOLET TREFUSIS
Hunt the Slipper

MARY WEBB
The Golden Arrow
Gone to Earth
The House in Dormer Forest
Precious Bane
Seven for a Secret

H. G. WELLS
Ann Veronica

Other VIRAGO MODERN CLASSICS